# Finding Her Heart

By

## Tracey M. Borge

D1519191

# DEDICATION

To my mother, Judy, first and foremost, for always showing me by example how to be independent and not afraid of change. In my adulthood, I have come to appreciate the struggles she went through. She raised three daughters, each who have college degrees.

To my best friend, Samantha, for being my first reader, but more important, for her encouragement and wise advice.

To my inspiration, Christine, for her guidance, advice and support in putting my story to paper. I never would have been able to do this without her as a role model.

To my fiancee, Brett, for his contributions to the book and love and support. His patience with my ideas is remarkable.

To my friends and family, Tonya, who I met when I moved to Albuquerque; Leslie, my sister, and the one who backed me when I needed it most; Sarah and Cindy, who gave me a chance to start a new career and their trust means the world to me.

And most important, to my daughter, Lindsay, whose self-motivation has kept me centered and moving forward, even in the hard times. She makes me proud every day.

# PART ONE

# CHAPTER ONE

Kaci stared in horror as a huge passenger plane flew into the World Trade center, where she worked. Her feet were frozen in place as she watched the black smoke billow out of the middle of the building. This morning she was late, which was unusual for her. She had called the office manager to let her know, that was at 8:25 a.m.; she was usually at her desk by then. There was no warning that the next few minutes would change their lives forever.

Smoke and screams filled the air. The sky was raining paper from every open window. Before she could walk another step, police officers were walking toward her, and the other witnesses, yelling at them to 'Move back!" She saw people running out of the building, who were either wet from the sprinklers in their offices, or dusty from coming through the debris, or both. Firemen were racing by in their trucks, sirens and horns blaring.

As she turned, she heard a loud ROAR and the people on the street looked up for the source. Seconds later another jet plane crashed into the other tower. Until that moment, she had assumed it was a terrible accident that the first plane struck the building. Now it seemed clear it was an act of terrorism. Her heart raced as she tried to make sense of it all. As she ran cautiously in the opposite direction, she had to be careful of the glass and debris around her.

She willed herself to slow down after a block. Panting, finding it hard to breath, she looked closer at some of the debris and saw articles of clothing, shoes, purses and even a few mangled body parts. Windows were shattered, concrete benches were crushed, every car she passed had major damage.

Her mind was screaming in fear as she ran away from the scene. She found a bench outside an office building and sat down to process what had happened. She was still carrying her work bag, which held a bottle of water and her lunch. Suddenly, she felt like she was dying of thirst; she grabbed the water and emptied it in seconds.

The street in front of her was filled with fire trucks, police cars, rescue trucks and ambulances. These men and women were heading toward the towers. She didn't know what they would find at the base of the buildings. There had to be hundreds of injured people inside, and probably dozens of deceased.

Kaci looked down at her hands. They were shaking uncontrollably. Putting her palms on her legs, she tried to steady her nerves. Her anxiety was increasing as she worried about everyone she knew in the building. Her office looked out onto the other tower. She never met any of them, but she saw them every day, hard at work in their workstations.

She sat, not wanting to move, afraid of what she might see next. After a few minutes, people who were covered in water, and dirt staggered by, in a daze. They were most likely in the buildings when the planes hit. A few were bleeding from their hands, head, even lower legs. The horror of it all made her very emotional as the swelling in the lungs began and tears were falling from her eyes.

People were coming out from every building around her. Nobody wanted to take the risk that more kamikaze planes were on their way. She knew she should start walking home, but she was glued to the scene in front of the towers. As both buildings were burning from the impact and diesel fuel that ignited, a huge cloud of ashes fell on everything around the crash site. Her eyes were burning from the acrid air. She coughed, trying to clear her lungs from the particles she inhaled.

Kaci was still grasping for answers when the Earth under her feet began to rumble, similar to an earthquake, she imagined. She turned her head just in time to see the South tower crumble. She couldn't seem to wake herself from this nightmare in front of her eyes.

As she took in what used to be, a rolling cloud of dirt or smoke, at least 300 feet high, came barreling down the street toward her. Not having time to get out of the way, she crawled under a truck parked on the street. She inhaled a deep breath and held it for the fifteen seconds it took for the cloud to go over her. Immediately she sprung up and, holding the edge of her cardigan over her mouth, tried to make her way down the ash-covered street. The air was so thick, she couldn't make out buildings, cars, sidewalk. It felt like she was walking through a dark tunnel. She found the side of a brick building and carefully used her hands to make her way to what felt like a door.

Someone from the inside opened the door for her to enter, and quickly shut it behind her to keep more dust out. For the first time she was able to take a deep breathe, coughing and choking although. There were at least 50 other people inside the deli. There were a dozen tables throughout and several counter stools. Everyone made sure all were able to sit for a few minutes, even if it meant sitting on tabletops.

She saw her reflection in one of the mirrors. It looked like ash from a fireplace had covered her hair and clothing. It was everywhere, her fingernails, nose and lips. They were dry with the taste of ash. She had to make an effort to not lick her lips to moisten them. She was grateful to have the time to gather her thoughts.

It was then that she thought of those she knew in those buildings. What about her co-workers? Theo? Heidi? They all should have been there; they were always early, like her, until today. And what of Mrs. King, who operated the coffee cart in the lobby; and Mr. Everett who had his newspaper stand on the ground floor. Did they have time to get out?

Anxiously, with shaky hands, she pulled out her phone and called the office receptionist, Emily. There was no ringing, no recording to leave a message. She hung up and tried again, only getting a strange beeping sound, like a busy signal, but not quite. Not willing to accept the truth, she tried one more time. Now, the recording came on saying "All circuits are busy, please try your call again."

The owner of the deli and his family were busy handing out bottles of water to the refugees. Everyone was craving water or anything to drink to wash away the soot and ash out of their mouths. With no light except for the emergency exit lights, the deli was dark and getting hot from body heat. After another several minutes of sitting, she felt she had to get out of there. With no idea of where she was going, Kaci got up and moved through the people to the door to whatever awaited her outside.

She heard people crying for help but couldn't see where they were. The smell of burnt flesh permeated the air around her. She knew it was a smell she would never be able to forget. It was then that she looked up at the remaining tower. Kaci watched in horror as she spotted things falling out of the windows. People, there were people jumping to their death below; their choice to end it quickly rather than being burned or buried alive.

She passed a public telephone with a line of people down the block. No doubt, they were trying to reach loved ones to tell them they were alive. Should she get in line with them?

Her breathe was increasing as was her heart rate at the thought of contacting her husband. She wrestled with the idea of leaving him, just leaving, without warning, without giving him the opportunity to beg her to stay or worse, punish her for even considering the thought. Kaci had often thought of leaving him. His drinking and abuse had been getting worse every day it seemed. The scariest thought of all was what would Landon do when he found out she was gone? She was sure he wouldn't just let her walk away. He would contact everyone she knew to get answers.

Did Landon know what was happening? His office was almost a mile away. She started walking that way. That's what she should do, she told herself. But was it? Her pace slowed as her mind raced. Would her husband, Landon, be looking for her? Did she want him to? She knew he didn't love her anymore, or at least he didn't act like he did. Their relationship was far from perfect, but, she reasoned, as she had done hundreds of times before, what were her options? She didn't have any money to start over.

She dismissed the thought and began her walk home. People were out in the streets to get a better view of what was happening. There were dozens on the rooftops, looking up in disbelief. They had no idea what it was like at the heart of the attack. They were all safe. Some families most likely had friends or relatives who worked in the World Trade Center.

When she walked into their apartment, her cat, Lola, immediately ran to her. The purring and meowing were much louder than normal. As soon as she sat in a dining chair, Lola was up on the table, which was abnormal for her. She was craving attention. Did she know what was going on outside her world?

She hadn't yet tried to reach Landon. Not knowing where he would be, she called his office first. The phone rang several times before his voice mail picked up. She then tried his cell phone but got the same 'circuits are busy' recording that she heard earlier.

Coffee or wine? That was the decision she had to make first. It wasn't noon yet, but under these circumstances, she felt wine would be ok. The first swallow was a big one and felt like velvet going down her throat. Whether in her mind, or actual physical changes, a calm started coming her.

She had forgotten what a mess she was in her filthy clothing. A shower was her next priority. The hot water stung her skin as she scrubbed the dirt and ash off and washed her hair twice. The dirty water pooled at her feet. What was she going to do next? Was Landon wondering where she was? If he was, he should have tried calling the apartment. That would be just like him, she thought. Not concerned about anyone but himself.

With her bathrobe on, she went to the fridge to find something to eat. Nothing looked appetizing. But, to prevent the wine from hitting her hard, she grabbed a yogurt and some cheese. She sat on the sofa now that she had washed all the dirt off, with her feet up, and Lola on her lap.

Did she really want to stay here? With Landon? In New York City? After today, she just realized, she didn't have a job. Without a job, what's the point? Her job was the best thing about her life at the moment. Landon would never want to have children, and she always knew she wanted to be a mother. She didn't love him anymore.

Suddenly, her mind was tugging her to hurry and pack a bag. If she left before he got home, would he know she left, or assume she was at her desk when the plane hit? There was no one left to verify her whereabouts.

# PART TWO

# CHAPTER TWO

Looking back, she wasn't sure exactly when things turned bad. They had met freshman year in college. It was a small university that was a center point of a small Western Kentucky town.

She saw Landon at the first freshman mixer at the Student Union Building. Her roommates had convinced her to go with them. It was the first Friday of the first week of classes. She recognized him from her English 101 class. He was cute and seemed smart enough to answer a few of the instructor's questions. And, he wasn't shy, not at all like she felt. He caught her staring at him and waved.

A little later he came up beside her, "Hey, I'm Landon. Aren't you in my English class?" He waited a moment before asking, "Do you want to dance?"

The music was so loud, she couldn't hear him, so she just nodded. He smiled again and grabbed her hand gently. He led her to the dance floor. They tried talking but ended up shouting in each other's ears. "I'm Kaci by the way." Her nerves took over and her voice came out in a mumbled hush.

After another dance, they walked outside for a quieter seat. They covered the basic topics. Where were they from? Major? Music? Classes?

"My parents sent me to school to study business. Don't get me wrong, I want to go to college, but this small town wasn't what I had in mind." Coming from Clarksville, Tennessee, he saw Murray as a small sleepy town. "I really wanted to go to University of Tennessee in Knoxville, but my parents decided it was too expensive and too far away. They want to keep an eye on me, they said." His body language showed his annoyance of their decision.

Before they said goodnight, he leaned over and gave her a soft kiss. Electricity surged through her body. She wanted more, but he pulled back.

"So, what do you think?" Landon asked. He waited for her answer, but it was a rhetorical question. "Do you want to go out? On a date?"

The words stuck in her throat as her heart quickened. Butterflies exploded in her stomach. She never wanted anything so much. "Yes," she finally said, as her nodded in agreement. "I'd love too."

When he picked her up in his Mustang, he held the door open for her and held her hand in the car. He was a perfect gentleman. The restaurant and movie were great. As they shared popcorn, she leaned into his shoulder, resting her head. She inhaled deeply the aroma of his cologne. She felt tingly all over. He draped his arm over her shoulders and caressed her arm.

His hand was on her thigh as he drove her back to the dorm. She tried to be cool. "Don't act so desperate," she told herself. "You'll scare him off. Mama always said to play hard to get to keep a boy interested." She was sure she believed all that, but she wanted to be realistic. "He may not even want a girlfriend, probably just a one-night stand."

Landon parked at the back of the parking lot. He opened her door and walked her to the hood of his car. He leaned back on the car and drew her to him, wrapping his arms around her waist. The first kiss was soft and playful, the next several were more passionate. She couldn't think clearly, all she wanted at that moment was more. Her heart raced as her desire increased. She knew she had to wait to see if even called her again.

He walked her to the dorm lobby and gave her a quick kiss on the cheek, whispering in her ear. "I had a great time. I'll call you soon."

She had no appetite the next couple of days. Kaci realized that she was already falling for Landon. Her stomach was full of nerves. He was so cute, and she felt honored that he picked her. She even found herself doodling his name in her notebook in class. The night before their next class together, he called.

"Hey Kaci," he started. "It's Landon. What are you doing tonight? I was hoping we could study for the English test together." It wasn't what she expected, but that was fine. She was thrilled he called.

"Sure, do you want to meet me in the library?" She offered. She didn't want him to think she was expecting the girlfriend treatment.

"No way, I'll come pick you up, you shouldn't walk alone at night."

Did that mean he really liked her? It was a great feeling that he wanted her to be safe. She felt protected and important to him. She ran downstairs to meet him a few minutes later. He drove to a local pizza restaurant that stayed open to 11 p.m. Books were table, open to the chapters they needed. It didn't take long before the books were closed, and he was sitting next to her in the booth.

If she had any doubt of his feelings for her, he cleared it up quickly. He kissed her, and kissed her, and kissed her more. She could feel the roughness of his stubble against her mouth. When the waitress came over, he ordered them drinks and after that, they had a standing date for lunch after every English class. Most days they ended up at the Burger Shack next to campus.

"He really is the best boyfriend, Mama. He holds the door open, always pays, a nice guy." The words gushed out of her mouth and her cheeks were warm. She called her parents weekly, always excited to talk about Landon.

Kaci went back to visit her parents for Thanksgiving and Christmas that year. She drove her small car, packed full of dirty laundry and schoolbooks. Her parents showered her with hugs and kisses each time. She and Landon kept the phone company in business by talking almost every day, sometimes for hours.

She brought half the kitchen cupboard's food with her on the way back to college. Her mother insisted, "You have to take the cereal, we won't eat it, and the soup, I can get more. I've got spaghetti and noodles to last several months, take that too."

"I've brought out the extra cooler, filled it with ice so you can take the cheese, ham, hot dogs, juice, and whatever else your mother finds in the freezer." She was sure they thought she was going to starve.

She got back into town the Friday before the new semester started. She was so happy to see Landon, she almost jumped into his arms. "I missed you so much!" Kaci wanted him to know how she felt about him. She didn't know why some girls played hard-to-get?

"I missed you too," he said, giving her a long passionate kiss. He didn't care that it was in front of the other students moving back into her dorm.

Kaci felt the desire burning in her body. All she could think about was being with him. She knew better than to rush things. "We better back off, I'm getting too hot."

"Why stop? We're both adults, we can do whatever we want," his grin was contagious. She couldn't help but smile. "Don't worry, I'll use protection," he said smoothly.

"It's not that," she answered. "We just don't have any privacy, anywhere."

"You let me take care of that," excited to get a green light. "Next week, I am going to wine and dine you." She didn't know if she was being smart, but for once, she didn't care.

Landon left a note on her door that Friday afternoon. She took the envelope and felt her heart thumping as she opened it. Could it be a 'Dear Jane' letter? Tiny teardrops formed in the corners of her eyes. She was really falling for him, she though he felt the same. Was she wrong all along?

Inhaling deeply, she pulled out the note.

**Meet me at 7 in the parking lot. Pack for a sleepover. XOXO**
**Landon**

Relief washed over her as she wiped the wetness from her eyes. As she walked into her room, she paused at the bathroom mirror. Yikes! She knew a quick shower was needed and then, what to pack. This was the night she had wanted so badly. If he knew she liked sex, then he wouldn't want to stray with other girls.

Kaci watched for him from the vestibule, the temperature had dropped that week to a chilly 40 degrees. She struggled trying to dress sexy and warm at the same time. In the end, she chose an off the shoulder sweater and tight jeans.

He drove her to a small hotel on away from campus. Walking around to her door, he chivalrously opened it and took her hand to escort her out. As soon as they were inside the room, her nerves started. She had to consciously breathe slowly to clear her mind. Kaci knew she wanted to have sex with him, she'd known for months. He stepped out to get her small pink bag and a grocery bag.

As she sat on the edge of the bed, she had no idea what she should be doing, or saying. He turned the television on, presumably for noise. It was an old episode of *The Waltons*. "Just great! John Boy sure wouldn't approve," she laughed to herself.

"What are you laughing about?" Landon said.

She hadn't realized he could see her amusement. "Oh, it's nothing. Did you bring anything to drink? My mouth is dry."

"The lady wants a beverage, and I am happy to oblige," he answered as he bowed in front of her. She burst out laughing that time. He was such a card.

Handing her wine cooler, and himself a beer, he sat down next to her. The small dining table was within arm's reach and the bottles were set down carefully.

Landon didn't wait for permission, he started kissing her on the neck, licking her ear. "I have been waiting for this since I met you."

The statement startled her, "Since that first night? You're kidding? You didn't even know me then."

"Of course not, but I knew we'd be together Kaci," Landon softly whispered in her ear.

She shivered with the surge of feelings rushing through her body. In one second, she was jelly. Her senses were on fire. His hand touched her breast and she let out a moan. She felt she could orgasm at that moment.

He pulled her sweater off in seconds and unhooked her bra with his left hand. His right hand was moving between her legs. His heavy breath on her nipples caused her to squirm in anticipation.

This is their first time to have sex on a bed. Her past encounters had been in cars or truck beds, or on a blanket in the woods. She felt alive, like a volcano ready to erupt. Never feeling confident enough to be the aggressor, she waited for Landon to guide her hands.

As she laid back, he crawled on top and entered her immediately. The shock made her gasp, and the pain of his forcefulness had her biting her lip to avoid crying. After a minute, his thrusting opened her up and was smooth. She felt him growing inside her, his breath quickened as he came inside her with a final thrust. He collapsed next to her on the pillow and tried to catch his breath.

"Damn, you are amazing!" he complimented her, patting her arm. He rolled to face her, put his head on her chest and fell asleep.

Kaci didn't know what to think about the experience. She was unsatisfied in the orgasm department. It didn't seem like he knew or cared how it was for her. "Everybody's first time is awkward," she reasoned with herself. "Next time will be better."

She got up quietly from the bed and grabbed her overnight bag. Her face was flush with embarrassment at standing naked in the room. She hurried into the bathroom. Sitting on the edge of the bathtub, her head in her hands, she started crying softly. This wasn't how she imagined their first time. Pulling out soft sweatpants and a tee, she got dressed. She stopped at the sink to splash cold water on her face and pull herself together.

When she crawled back in bed beside Landon, his arm naturally found her waist and he pulled her close. He was half-asleep and muttered, "Love you", in her hair.

"Did I hear that right?" she thought. Careful to not let her emotions get carried away, she started examining her own feelings for him. Kaci knew she liked him, a lot; but 'love'? Maybe? If he said it again, she would have to decide what to say. For the time being, she closed her eyes and fell asleep listening to his breathing.

The next morning Landon woke up before her but crawled back beside her. When she opened her eyes, he was smiling at her, playing with her hair. "Good morning, starshine," he said giving her a small kiss.

Within minutes, his hands were taking her panties off. He was slow and patient, but ready for more sex. It took her time to make sure her body was awake enough to feel anything. He worked his magic and this time, she climaxed. It was the most wonderful feeling she had ever felt. She laid her head back on her pillow and closed her eyes.

They both found every opportunity to be alone and have sex. She knew how to please him, and she did. Landon was getting better at making sure she finished.

One night after their Sunday night date, and making out in his backseat, he surprised her, "Don't make any plans in February."

"Why is that?" she replied, batting her eyelashes and smiling sweetly. "She was dying to know what he as planning.

"It's a surprise. You'll find out soon enough."

"You are terrible!" she smiled, squeezing his arm as he drove her home.

# CHAPTER THREE

A knock at her door Saturday revealed a Floral delivery man with a bouquet of roses. 'Happy Birthday Starshine! Meet me downstairs at 3'. She held the note in her hand for several minutes, questioning what he had planned.

She rushed into the shower, grabbed clothes and waited. She spent time on her hair, makeup and making sure she wore the perfect outfit. Still, she had almost an hour before he was to arrive. "Calm down Kaci, he will be here soon. You look like you're going to jump out of your skin." Her roommate was right, she needed breathe deeply and relax.

As soon as his car pulled off the main street, she casually walked out to meet him "How long have you been waiting?" Landon teased.

"Maybe a couple minutes. Where are we going?" She asked, giving him a peck on the cheek when he opened the car door for her.

"If you will be patient, it will be worth the wait, I promise."

Kaci sat back, "Fine. You are killing me, you know?" He seemed to be enjoying torturing her this way.

Landon pulled up to the nicest restaurant in tn. "Mademoiselle, we hope you are pleased with your experience tonight." Bowing, Landon took her hand and escorted her to the entrance. She closed her eyes and inhaled the wonderful scent of steaks being grilled.

The cozy corner booth made it easy for him to sit close to her. She smiled as her kissed her hand. He ordered for them both, the house special, dinner for two. It was Valentine's Weekend, as well as her birthday and a school holiday weekend. All restaurants were booked solid.

The night ended with a drive out to the lake, to watch the sunset. They sat on the cold concrete benches at the water's edge. "Wait just one second," he said as he put his jacket on her shoulders. He ran to the car and brought back a bag.

"More? The fancy dinner and flowers were more than I ever expected." At that moment, she felt so lucky.

"Open it up," he encouraged. "I didn't really know what to get, to be honest. I never was a good gift giver."

She took the bag, apprehensively. Inside was a scented candle and a Murray State scarf. "How thoughtful. You must know how cold I've been." She tried to give him a compliment on the lame gifts. She thought it was something you'd give as a Pollyanna gift at Christmas, not to your girlfriend.

At Spring Break, they were separated again. "One day I want to leave this town and go to a big city. I love the excitement of a city." He confessed to her one day on the phone.

Another day they talked late into the night about their childhoods. "My parents took care of everything for me. I kind of wished they hadn't stepped in so often," he said. "They were more worried about me embarrassing them than what I needed."

She was left to wonder what kind of things he meant. Kaci knew she shouldn't pry; he'd explain when he was comfortable. On Saturday night she tried calling him several times with no answer. Despite her efforts, she tried to not think the worst. *What if he met another girl? What if was an old girlfriend?'* She tried to be patient, and not worry so much about what he was doing She was over 400 miles away from him, and she had heard his frat brothers joke with him by saying, "Over 200 miles, all rules can be broken."

Kaci woke up to a loud ringing close to midnight. Groggily she answered, "mmm hello, who's this?"

"Hey Starshine, sorry it's so late. I just wanted to hear your voice before I went to bed." It was Landon, obviously drunk.

"Hey, I'm sorry, I couldn't wait up." She yawned and kept on talking, "Where were you tonight?"

"My friends, uh, took me out to a club, on the other side of town," He answered with a slight slur. "Hey, Kaci? You're really good to me, you know? I love you."

"That's sweet, but I don't think you'll remember this in the morning." Her heart rate had shot up when she heard those words. "I'll see you tomorrow. Goodnight, sleep tight."

Turns out she was right. When they saw each other Sunday night, he made no mention of those three little words. Every time she was with him, she felt proud and special. His mannerisms were a little blunt and could appear arrogant to strangers, but not with her.

The rest of the semester was perfect in Kaci's eyes. She knew she loved him but still waited for the right time to tell him, preferably when he was sober.

The week before they left for summer break, Landon took her to their spot at the lake. The water lapped against the edge of the boat dock, while the birds sang and perched on the posts. There was a sweet smell of Honeysuckle in the breeze.

As she sat in a trance, listening to every noise around her, Landon came up behind her and covered her eyes with his hands. "Guess who?" he whispered in her ear.

Chills went up and down her spine and gave him a soft kiss on the lips. Before it turned into something heavier, she pulled away.

"I got you a little something, so you won't forget me," she said. "I want those Clarksville girls to keep away." She laughed softly, waiting for him to say something to assure her that he wouldn't stray. But he didn't say a word.

She pulled a small box from her purse and put it in his hand. He stared at the gift for a minute. Kaci immediately regretted making such a bold move and making a big deal of their summer separation Maybe he wasn't wanting to continue their relationship? Every bad scenario filled her head.

He finally opened the box and pulled out a chain, with the Aquarius symbol pendant on it. "I don't get it, is this a zodiac sign? I'm a Gemini. What's this?"

"Aquarius! It MY zodiac sign, remember?" She really wished she hadn't bought the necklace. He was probably going to dump her now. She was really pushing too hard.

"Ahh, ok, got it" he said, putting it over his head. "Nice. Oh, I have something for you too."

Now she really was surprised. "It's not as nice as this, but I didn't know what to get." He grabbed a small bag out of the car. Inside was a Beanie Baby Bear with two hearts on his chest. "Do you like it? The lady told me it's a limited edition, True Love bear."

"That's so sweet. I love it, and you." There, she said it.
"I love you too, Kaci."

# CHAPTER FOUR

The summer was spent running up their phone bills and both being lazy at home. He often said he would jump in his car and come visit her. But he never did. After the longest summer in history, according to Landon, they were both back in August, ready for their sophomore year.

Everything picked up where they left off. Classes, lunches, studying, dates and the sex. They went to the library at least twice a week to study together, at lunch on campus a few times, and spent time laying on a blanket, soaking in the sun in the Quad until the weather turned chilly.

Landon asked her to come to his parent's house for Thanksgiving that year since she couldn't get home to see her family. She excitedly accepted his offer, but only after she cleared it with her parents. The impressive new brick home sat back off the road about 200 yards. The long driveway was sheltered by huge trees still full of leaves of every color. The house itself had to have at least six bedrooms she thought as they pulled up.

As soon as they opened the car doors, the front door opened and out raced two golden retrievers, coming to her instantly. She noticed they stood back from Landon, not paying him much attention. She thought, *'That's weird.'*

"I see they like you," he said, "They don't care for me. I guess it's the alpha male thing." He shrugged off their behavior and the dogs and walked on by.

His mother spoke up, "You must be Kaci, so nice to meet you. This is Baxter and Millie, and I'm Louise and this is Jerry," she said as she pointed to her husband. "We're so happy you could join us. Did your parents mind that you weren't coming home?"

"Thank you for having me," Kaci said, always polite and courteous. "My parents were disappointed but since it's only a few days, they thought it would be better if I stayed here this year. The weather over there is calling for snow and ice this weekend. I didn't want to take the risk of missing classes on Monday."

"You see Landon," said Louise, "Spoken like a young woman determined to succeed. You'd better hold on to her."

Louise turned to pretend to whisper to Kaci, "I'm sure you know that homework and schoolwork aren't Landon's favorite things."

"Now Louise," said Jerry. "No need to tease him now, he gets good grades. Give the boy some credit. Let's go inside."

That weekend she met his brother and some friends who stopped by. Landon divided his time between hanging out with his buddies and shopping with Kaci. When he wasn't with her, she spent time reading, studying or playing with Baxter and Millie.

Saturday night they both wanted to go out. He had invited his friends to meet them at their favorite bar. After the DJ started playing dance music, most of his friends were out on the floor with their dates. Those that didn't bring a date, asked a girl from another table.

"Please dance with me," Kaci begged him. He used to love to dance, she remembered, but now he just wanted to sit and drink. The laughter at their table was louder than the music playing.

One of the 'dates' overheard her begging him and jumped in, "Shit! Landon, loosen up. You aren't a bad dancer, you danced with me all the time this summer."

Kaci couldn't believe her ears. She was in shock, couldn't seem to focus. *'Why wouldn't he dance with her? If it wasn't the dancing, maybe it was her'.* She was really confused.

The same girl asked all the girls at the table to go out on the floor together when the DJ played 'U Got the Look' by Prince with Sheena Easton. Kaci loved the song, was a favorite of hers about six years ago. She eagerly joined the girls and danced through two more songs. They finally came back to the table for another beer.

Landon was visibly irritated by something. "What's wrong?" Kaci asked him.

"Wrong?" he said defensively, "Why would anything be wrong? I just watched you trying to fuck one of my friends sitting at this table, right in front of me."

"What?! Are you serious?" Kaci felt tears welling up in her eyes as she tried to talk to Landon. "Damn you, Landon! I'm YOUR girlfriend. I never even thought of another guy this summer. What about you?" she said with all the courage she could manage.

"Are you accusing me of cheating on you?" Landon laughed. "You are losing it, Kaci. Not all guys think with their dick." He would sooner break up with her than be under this scrutiny. He decided they had better go before this got out of hand. This is one time he was glad his parents didn't allow them to sleep in the same room. He hoped her mood would change in the morning.

Kaci was relieved when he suggested they go home. She felt like she was punched in the gut. Her emotions were rising, threatening to spill out in tears any minute. She sniffled, coughed a little and stood up quickly. She would be embarrassed to be known as the overly emotional girlfriend.

When they walked into his parent's house, they separated to their different rooms. Kaci heard whimpering outside her door in a few minutes. She opened the door and let Millie and Baxter in. They proceeded to climb onto the bed as soon as she sat down. They covered her with sloppy dog kisses. Almost instantly, she was feeling better. She wasn't going to forget what happened, but she can't do anything at the moment, so she fell asleep, snuggled in dog fur.

The ride back to school was a little chilly, more like freezing. Landon didn't say much to her that morning except that he'd rather leave before lunch. He had things to do. Kaci was sure they didn't include her, and she was fine with that for the moment.

"Can you stop at Taco Bell so I can get something to eat, please?" She was trying to break the tension, which was a monumental task looking at his face. "I'll even buy your lunch too." She thought it was a fare offer.

"I guess. Way to a man's heart, is his stomach." He recited. "Isn't that what they say?"

When they got back to school, he kissed her when he dropped her off. The weather had turned cold almost overnight, and wet icy sprinkles fell on her face. "Thanks for taking me home with you. I had a good time." However, her abrupt tone implied otherwise.

"Yeah okay. I was a little drunk last night, I'm sorry I was so grouchy," Landon wasn't very good at apologizing. He hugged her close and kissed her on the top of her head. "I promise, I'll do better."

They exchanged Christmas gifts the day the semester ended; she was already packed up and ready to go home. He pulled into the dorm parking lot just minutes before she was planning on leaving. She had been waiting for over an hour.

"I'm sorry I'm late," were the first words out of his mouth. "My parents called and wouldn't stop telling me what to pack, and what to buy for my brother. You can imagine."

'*No, I can't*', she thought to herself. She opened her car and brought out a big box wrapped in Mickey Mouse Christmas paper. The package was tied up with the biggest red bow the store sold.

"Really, Kaci? Mickey Mouse?" he didn't seem to think it was cute at all. "Aren't we a little old for that?" He didn't waste another second before he ripped the paper and tore the box open. He pulled out a thick Ralph Lauren Polo burgundy sweater.

"I hope you like it. I saved every dime I made babysitting to be able to get you something nice," she explained with wide eyes. He sweater had cost her over $50. It was more money than she spent on her parents´ gifts combined.

"Very nice Kaci," he said as he held it up. "I see you do know good quality clothes after all."

'*Was that an insult to the clothes she owned and wore*'? Her mind was working overtime trying to decipher what he meant. "Of course. Just because I can't afford to buy them, doesn't mean I don't appreciate nice things." Maybe that would settle it.

Kaci waited and waited for him to say something about her present. He strolled to his car, tossed the sweater in the back, and brought out a sack from Wal-Mart. "Here, Merry Christmas, sorry I didn't have time to wrap it."

"That seems to be your pattern," she chuckled lightly. Inside the bag she pulled out a gift package of lotions, bubble bath and creams, with a loofah sponge. She looked inside to see if she missed something. A small box was in the corner. It appeared to be a box that jewelry came in. She opened it, expecting to have something nice to show her parents and friends. Inside was a pair of earrings, red and white candy cane earrings. She tried to hide her disappointment. "I don't have any holiday jewelry, thanks."

"What about the lotions? The lady in the beauty department said it would be a great gift for a young woman." He was obviously proud of himself for getting help to pick her gift.

"It's very useful, thank you so much. I love you." She stood tall to kiss him before she got in her car to drive the eight hours home.

"I love you too," Landon said, squeezing her in a big hug. "Call me when you get there."

# CHAPTER FIVE

When they returned four weeks later to start the Spring Semester, there was a little awkwardness. She had wondered every day if he was faithful. One the phone, he never acted like anything was different. She convinced herself it was all in her head.

They were still a couple, but only were able to see each other two or three days a week. While she was in her books, he was at the frat parties. He never worried about his grades. *'He must have a photographic memory. I've never seen him open a book,'* she thought.

This year for spring break, Landon was going to Daytona Beach with the guys. Her plans were still up in the air. She didn't really want to drive all the way home to just sit at home. Most of her high school friends had either married or moved away.

A few days before the beginning of the break, they were eating dinner at the Italian restaurant. The spaghetti special night always drew lots of college students who were on a tight budget. The aroma of the garlic bread reached out into the parking lot. It was intoxicating.

As soon as they sat down, Landon said, "I have something to ask you." He saw the surprise on her face and quickly added, "But it's not THAT." He laughed at his little joke. "It turns out all the other guys are bringing their girlfriends, so do you want to go with us?"

Kaci was stunned at his offer. She had never been to Florida but had always wanted to see the ocean, walk on the beach, smell the crisp ocean air. Without thinking of the details, she squealed, "Yes! I'm so excited."

"Okay, great," he said, leaning over giving her a kiss. "This is going to be a great vacation for us. Without having my parents in our hair. You just need to put in $150 for your share of the condo we rented."

"What?" She was embarrassed to even have to say it, "I don't have that kind of money laying around Landon." Her happy mood just took a sudden 180.

She felt like the poor kid at school who couldn't afford the name brand jeans and shoes that the other girls had. Back then, she would babysit to earn enough money to buy herself one Izod shirt and one pair of Levi's. Her heart pounded as she started to sweat a little. How was she going to afford to go? She couldn't ask her parents. Could she? That was out of the question, they already were paying for everything at college. They didn't want her to have to get a job. They expected her to put all her time into studying. Maybe she could ask them for a loan. She would get a job when she returned from Florida and pay them back.

Another deep breath and she was already starting to feel a little better. She closed her eyes to stop the frantic feelings she had. Slowly, she was able to relax somewhat.

Landon noticed her eyes darting around and her breathing getting quicker. He didn't understand what the big deal was. Surely, she didn't expect him to pay her way. It wasn't just a night out. He loved her and she loved him, but his parents wouldn't pay for her to go too.

"What's the matter? You look awful." He asked her.

"Gee thanks Sweetheart," she answered sarcastically. "I don't know how I can pay that, plus food and other things. I said yes before I thought it through."

"Okay, we can work this out," he said. "Let's think about our options. I guess technically the condo was already paid for in January by my parents, so I get to say who can stay there. I choose you." His smile made her feel somewhat better. "But you'd still have to bring money for food and stuff." The look on her face told him he said the right thing.

"That would be great." Kaci was grateful that he would stand up for her. She wasn't used to that kind of treatment. She had always been independent, especially since she was an only child. She learned how to entertain herself. She had a little money she had in cash from babysitting a few times for other classmates. She reasoned she could buy snacks at Wal -Mart and cut the high prices at the convenience stores.

"I can help by buying you dinner a few times too," Landon suggested.

"What if I bake some snacks for the trip? Maybe then the rest of the group won't think I'm a moocher," Kaci volunteered. She was going to do everything she could to make this a great vacation for them.

After she got to her dorm, she filled her roommates in on her new plans. "I can't believe he thought you'd have that money to put in. You had no notice!"

Claire joined in, "Sometimes I don't think men think like we do. In fact, I know they don't. They don't worry about details and that's all us girls do is worry about the details."

Kaci knew she had to call her parents and let them know about her trip, and maybe, humbly ask if they could loan her some money. She hated asking for things from anyone. She liked being more self-sufficient than that. How can you be an adult if you are always running to Mommy and Daddy when you need money?

The next morning, before her first class, she made the call. They were up at the crack of dawn, every day, so she knew they'd be wide awake by now.

The conversation started out with all the basic questions. "Yes, I'm doing fine." "Classes are going good." "Landon is great."

"That brings me to the reason I called," she bravely started to tell them. "Landon has invited me to go to Florida with the gang over Spring Break. I know it's expensive, but he said I didn't have to pay for my share of the condo because it's already been paid for. And all I need is money for food and other expenses. Landon said he'd pay for dinner some nights. I already have $50 I saved up from babysitting." She had to stop and catch her breath. She had been rattling on, not giving them a chance to respond.

"Ok baby girl," her Daddy said calmly, "Just slow down a little. I am getting a little hard of hearing."

"I'm sorry Daddy, I just feel bad to have to ask, but can you and Momma loan me some money." There, she spit it out, finally. Now, she just waited. But, when he didn't answer right away, she got nervous and kept on talking. "I hate to go somewhere and not have any money with me, in case something happens."

"Okay, okay, you do have a good point," her daddy agreed, "you ever consider being a lawyer? You can argue with the best of them. Would $200 be enough? And you don't have to pay us back, we are happy to help you. You never have asked for much, so I know this must be important to you."

"Daddy! That would be wonderful," she almost screamed into the phone. If he had been next to her, she would smother them both with hugs and kisses. They really are the best parents. "And I am going to pay you back. I'm going to start looking for job."

# CHAPTER SIX

They were all packed up Friday night, so they could leave early. It would take them over ten hours to get to Daytona Beach. Instead of taking four cars, they took two.

The morning started off with everyone talking and singing along to the radio. Kaci had brought a couple boxes of granola bars for their breakfast. By lunchtime, everyone was ready to pull over just outside of Chattanooga at a rest area. Kaci and one of the other girls, Leslie, had made sandwiches and brought chips. They had plenty of soda, and beer, of course.

Leslie had volunteered to drive next, and they were back on the road in 30 minutes. Because of the elevation of the mountain highway, the next leg of the trip took a little longer. They rolled their windows down and felt the clean mountain air blow across their faces. Leslie pulled over when they got about an hour north of Atlanta. Landon took his turn behind the wheel and did remarkably well at driving in Atlanta, which was a nightmare. At the next stop they ate more sandwiches and chips for dinner. The guys also started drinking the beer they brought along.

Kaci took the wheel about 5 p.m. for the final leg. She had only about one hour before it was dark, and five hours left to drive. As she drove through Southern Georgia, she was amazed at how flat the landscape was, but it did provide an excellent view of the sunset. The smell of the ocean and sand was in the wind. She was picturing romantic nights walking on the beach, laying out in the midday sun. This trip was going to be amazing.

She came out of her daydream when she heard Landon and Keith were singing loudly with the radio. She would have preferred they kept it down so she wouldn't be distracted, but she would manage. It didn't take long before Landon started annoying her, on purpose. He was trying to tickle her from the passenger's seat. Then he was whispering naughty things in her ear. Kaci was about to tell them she was done driving.

Thankfully, Leslie noticed the strained look on Kaci's face and came to her rescue. "Hey, Kaci, could I drive for a while? I'm getting bored in the back seat." Neither of them wanted the boys to drive, considering how many beers they had already drank.

Kaci looked in the rearview mirror and caught Leslie's eye, she nodded, and Leslie gave her subtle salute with her two fingers on her forehead.

"Sure Leslie, that would be great. My eyes were getting a little tired." She was so relieved. She found the closest stop, for a quick bathroom break, and hot coffee, and they switched drivers. The other two couples pulled in behind them and asked why they stopped.

Landon promptly told them, "Kaci is obviously a shitty driver, so Leslie is going to drive for a while." He turned his attention back to their car, "Let's go, piss or get off the pot."

Kaci felt her blood pressure rise as her mood darkened. '*Why would he say something like that?*' It was him who caused the problem in the first place. She took a deep breath and chose to ignore it this time. She didn't want to cause a scene here, in the middle of nowhere.

With Leslie behind the wheel, they made it to Daytona in another three hours. Everyone jumped out as soon as they pulled into their designated parking spaces. Each grabbed something, suitcases, coolers and bags of food. Evan checked in with the property manager and got four room keys, one for each couple. They all packed in the elevator. Landon went first into the condo and stood like a good doorman while everyone walked in, bowing and extending his arm into the large room.

A large sliding glass door overlooked the street below. The bright lights from the street could be seen from the hallway door of the condo. Even though they couldn't see the ocean, they enjoyed the lights from the restaurants and cars rushing back and forth. The atmosphere was electric. Everyone had a sudden burst of energy and started freshening up so they could go to an oyster bar they noticed from the balcony. Since they didn't bring all their bags upstairs, the girls borrowed clothes from Jessica and Rachel, who had brought their suitcases up.

The guys, on the other hand, just splashed cold water on their faces and were ready to go. "If you princesses don't hurry up, we are going to leave you behind," Landon said as he paced the room. "Let's go soldiers!" the other guys laughed and joined in. But Kaci didn't think it was funny. He was so impatient. *'Had he always been like this, and I never noticed',* she wondered.

It really didn't matter at that moment, she fixed her makeup and finger combed her hair and she was ready to go, wearing one of Jessica's summer tops with a plunging neckline. Landon's eyes opened wide when he saw her. "Now that's a great shirt for you, very sexy, unlike the mousy clothes you usually wear," he said.

Leslie saw what was happening and came to her rescue, again. "Hey Kaci, do you mind if I borrow that blue shirt, the one you wore the other night," she said, loud enough to let Landon hear, "I just love it."

Kaci's bad mood dissipated when she said that. She knew it was just to calm them down, but it worked. "Anytime, Leslie. Thanks."

The oyster bar had a good size crowd, which made it difficult to find a table to seat eight. They settled for two tables of four. As soon as the people at the table in between them got up, they planned on moving the two together. For the time being, Leslie and Keith sat at their table. She and Leslie talked for the next 30 minutes, until the other couple left. Then they played a little Do-Si-Do, and everyone sat in a different seat, but they were all together.

The waitress had already brought their drinks and food, so everyone grabbed their plates and moved over. In all the moving around, Landon bumped into Kaci, making her spill her dinner. "Shit Kaci, watch where you're going."

She knew what really happened and she didn't want to scene in public, so she helped the waitress pick up the mess and sat back down quietly. She was breathing heavy and feeling flushed in the face. She struggled with her emotions, trying to hide them from the group and forget the incident. Her margarita was still almost full. She took a long drink of the strong cocktail. By the time she was done, she had only a little left. "Whoa there, missy, pace yourself," Landon said to her, teasing her.

An hour later, the girls were huddled at one end of their table, chatting about anything. There was a DJ playing some good dance music, and since the guys didn't ask them to dance, they all decided to get on the floor. As she walked past Landon, Kaci couldn't resist giving him a little taste of his own medicine, "We girls are going to go dance, if that's okay with you, Sir."

Landon was a little stunned by her sarcastic and brave tone. He didn't want to dance anyway, so he and the guys just ordered another round. They were all exhausted from the drive, and the drinks weren't helping.

"Who's ready to go back to the condo?" Landon asked the table. "I'm really getting tired. And don't you dare call me a wuss."

Twenty minutes later, with more of their bags in their arms, they were upstairs in the condo. Everyone retreated to their rooms and shut their door. Landon followed Kaci into theirs and started undressing her from behind. Whirling around in surprise, she almost knocked him over.

"Can't you wait a minute?" she laughed as she playfully pushed him away. She opened her suitcase to get a tee shirt out to sleep in.

When she came out of the bathroom, he was already on the bed, naked. He definitely wasn't bashful, she thought. She slid under the covers he was holding down with his weight. He reached over to pull her close. His hands were hot against her skin. The stale smell of old beer from his breathe almost choked her. He was trying to get an erection, but nothing was working. Seconds later, he was snoring on her shoulder. Gently pushing him off so as not to wake him, Kaci rolled over and said a silent 'thank you', to whoever was listening.

She wasn't feeling great anyway. The room started moving back and forth with the sound of the tide outside their open window. She fell onto the pillow and closed her eyes. Asleep in minutes, she knew she never wanted to drink that much again.

The sun was up and shining in only a little over six hours later. The bright rays made her head scream in protest. '*Why did it feel like she had only slept three hours?*', she whined to herself. She reminded herself to not drink so much, so quickly, without eating. Landon must already be awake as he wasn't next to her. She eased out of bed, taking it slow, trying to not throw up. She needed Tylenol for sure. Almost everyone was already up, drinking coffee and laughing.

"Look who's finally awake. Sleeping Beauty," Landon teased her. He followed the comment up with a quick tap on her butt.

"Ha Ha,' she replied. "Does anyone have Tylenol? I feel awful."

"What you need," said Evan, "Is an old frat brother hangover remedy." She just looked at him, wondering what in the world was in it. "It's a large coffee with a shot of Jim Beam."

"No more alcohol, please," she whimpered as she held her hands to her mouth and stomach simultaneously.

"Trust us, it works." They were so persistent she thought she could give it a shot. At least the caffeine would help her feel alive she hoped. She couldn't argue with them, they obviously had way more experience drinking than she did.

She took a quick sip, trying to let it cool off. A few minutes later, she had drunk almost half, and miraculously was feeling better. "Are you sure you didn't put some magic potion in that?" she kidded Evan, "Because it really did work." By her second cup she was ready to hit the beach.

It took everyone over an hour to get ready for fun in the sun and sand. Kaci had never seen the ocean and stood frozen when they made it to the beach. "It's so beautiful," she said, smiling from ear to ear. Landon was standing next to her, with his arm around her shoulder. He gave her a gentle squeeze then turned to face her.

"I think I owe you an apology, Kaci," he said. "I was being a real pain in the ass yesterday. I guess my anxiety was working overtime and being cooped up in a car didn't help." She started to speak, but he stopped her. "Let me finish please. You are really bad about that, you know? What I wanted to say is I'm sorry I was picking on you. I never thought it would make you upset."

Kaci was surprised. He had never apologized for anything. If you wanted to call that an apology. But she could be understanding too. "Thanks, it's fine, we were all tired. Now let's hit the water." She took off running, slowly in the sand, to find the perfect spot for their blankets.

The girls spent most of the day tanning in the warm sun, while the guys were walking around doing God-knows-what. They came back after noon and decided to go back up to the room in a little bit to clean up and eat something. After that, they had plans to go down to the wharf and do a little shopping.

Once out of the shower, Landon pulled Kaci into their bedroom. She was only wearing a bathrobe, which he quickly took off her. Kaci was caught off guard and started to protest. But he just put his hand over her mouth, softly and walked her to the bed. He took his time with foreplay and within a minute, she was yearning for him. If he kept it up, she would have an orgasm even before he entered her. She moaned when he got on top of her. He put his finger to his lips and said "Shhh."

Another few minutes of lovemaking and they both climaxed. She rolled over, panting and started fanning her face with her hand. After a couple of minutes, she softly nudged Landon. "Hey, wake up. We'd better get dressed before they leave without us."

For the rest of the trip, she felt so much closer to Landon. He had apologized and they had makeup sex, which was great. She could only guess why he decided to apologize, but she bet one of the guys told him if he didn't, he wasn't getting any all week. *'That would do it'* she laughed.

The dorms wouldn't open until the next morning so they all divided up and slept at the ones who had off-campus apartments. Kaci and Jessica stayed at the guy's apartment off campus. After being around seven people for a week, Kaci was ready to get back to her room, and hibernate. She didn't realize how much she liked being alone.

She was also thankful she took advantage of the washer and dryer in the condo before they left. The guys teased her about playing the housewife, but she didn't listen to them. She didn't want to have to wash clothes when they got back.

"You are something else, you know that?" Landon had grabbed her from behind and nuzzled his head in her hair. "You are really turning me on with your domestic side."

She burst out laughing as she turned to face him, "You're kidding, right? That has to be the weirdest pick-up line I've ever heard."

"No, I'm not kidding," he had a twinkle in his eye, "So sue me for thinking about our future."

She was stunned. *What should she say now? Should she tell him she had already thought of their future together? Was naming their babies?* It was all very schoolgirl, so she decided not to say anything. Kaci smiled and hugged him closely.

# CHAPTER SEVEN

It was right before finals when Kaci's dad called her. She hadn't spoken to them since the day she was back from Florida and in her room. Kaci was stunned when he told her that they couldn't afford to pay for college next semester. Their savings had been cleaned out when they had to get a new heating and air system for the house. They had set aside money every month in savings for her tuition, but they had to deplete it for this.

Kaci didn't want to drop out, especially since she and Landon were doing so well. She talked to her dad about taking one or two classes. She was going to have to move out of the dorm she knew, but she was willing to get a full-time job. If she did that through the summer semesters also, she could still graduate on time.

That didn't happen as planned. She ended up working at the local pizza place on the dinner shift. She moved into a studio apartment, in an old house that was converted into smaller units, close to the city park. It was maybe 200 square feet and had a musty smell, but she was proud of it. It was all hers. She was able to get a futon at the local thrift shop to start. She added more furniture as time went by.

She started to feel like Landon was distancing himself from her. Since they didn't share any on-campus activities or classes, she could only see him on her nights off. One night she remembered cooking Landon a nice meal, a pot roast with the potatoes and carrots on the side.

Kaci had planned it as a romantic evening at home. When he finally arrived 20 minutes late, he gave a brief apology, said he lost track of time talking to his frat brothers. After they ate, the only thing he said was, "You should ask my mom for her recipe."

Her expression immediately changed to reflect the harsh criticism. He quickly added, "It was good, don't get me wrong. I'm sorry, I didn't mean to hurt your feelings." He gave her a big hug and kiss. "It's ok," he said laughing, "I love you anyway."

Through all her changes, Landon stood by her, helping when he could. They saw each other at least three days a week, if only for lunch. He talked about graduating in another year and then they would move off to somewhere big, Nashville, Chicago or New York City. She wasn't sure she was a big city girl, but she couldn't let Landon go off by himself. In her heart, she knew that if he left without her, he wouldn't be coming back.

That year, at Christmas, she made a quick trip home in her beat-up old VW. There was more rust on it than metal. The cold air blew in under her feet. Once home for the holiday, she asked her mom to show her how to cook a turkey and stuffing too. She had missed coming home on Thanksgiving, so they had a repeat dinner.

After they ate leftovers the next day, she and her parents were sitting around the table, playing rummy. Walter said, "Baby girl, I know it's been tough for you not being in school what you wanted. And I know that car of yours has too many miles on it. So, your Uncle Bob got a new car for Aunt Jean. She wants you to take her little Toyota. It also has high miles, but those Toyotas run forever."

Her mother, Evelyn, looked so excited to be able to do something nice for her only child. "Jean has always adored you, and she wants you to get all the help you need."

"Thank you, Momma, I'll go call them right away and thank them myself." She spent the next 20 minutes on the phone with Aunt Jean. She was so grateful to them.

Sunday morning, she was on the road at sunrise, wearing sunglasses and a heavy jacket. Walter had already done all the paperwork and had the new tags on the car. Saturday afternoon she told Landon about the car. All he said was, "That's great." Why did she feel like he was never really paying attention to her?

She got back to her apartment two weeks before school started. Her boss had told her she could work every day if she wanted to, and she jumped at the chance. Now she had a better car and was thinking about getting another job.

The winter that year was pretty harsh. Almost every week, it snowed. Kaci was able to get to work with little difficulty for the first snowstorm. It was the pizza parlor's busiest time, when people are snowed in, they don't mind calling for a delivery. She wasn't busy in the dining area, but she pitched to help in the kitchen when they asked.

The second big storm came at the end of January. The college called off classes, which they rarely did. Kaci was barely able to get out of her driveway, but she dd. The next two blocks made her wish she had stayed at home. Her car was sliding all over the road, and finally came to a stop in the ditch on the other side of the road. She tried to back out, but it was stuck. She walked back home to call her boss and tell her she couldn't make it.

Her second call was to Landon. Even though it was after noon, he sounded like he just woke up. Typical, she thought. No school meant he could sleep all day, but not her. "Landon, it's me! I need your help."

"What?" he slurred, trying to wake up. "What's wrong?"

"My car is stuck in the ditch across the street," she was almost in tears, "I can't move it."

"Well, what do you want me to do?" he said obviously annoyed at the phone call. "I can't pull it out."

"Landon! Please! Are you kidding?" she was full-blown hysterical, "You can't get out of bed to help your girlfriend?' She screamed at him. Her breathing quickened and she started to panic. Within seconds tears were streaming down her face. How could he be so insensitive?

He was trying to 'shush' her on the phone. "Calm down. Shit Kaci," he replied, "What am I supposed to do? I'm not very mechanically inclined, you know that. Nobody will bother it, and I bet the snow will melt by tomorrow. Call me later and we'll see what I can do,"

Despite how furious she was with him at that moment, he had a point, she thought, he couldn't drag it out by force. So, she might as well leave it there. She still was irritated at his lack of caring about her situation. But his advice made sense, even though she didn't like it. For now, she curled up with a hot aromatic cup of coffee and a book. One channel was showing classic movies, she loved Jimmy Stewart and Henry Fonda and tried to see every one of their movies.

# CHAPTER EIGHT

Landon came over around lunchtime with a snow shovel, to help get her car out. He brought Evan with him for the muscle. It only took twenty minutes of digging and gently rocking the car back and forth for it get back on the road.

"Hey," Landon said when they were alone, "I need to apologize about yesterday. I guess I had too much to drink the night before, and I wasn't thinking straight."

"You were right," she agreed, "We couldn't have pulled it out yesterday. We would have needed four more guys to lift it out."

That night, he stayed at her apartment. "I'm going to buy you dinner," he promised. "Then we'll see what happens." He gave her a quick kiss on the cheek and a sly grin.

The next few weeks he stayed with her if there was snow in the forecast. She felt safe and secure with him next to her, his arms around her as they slept. She had gotten into a routine of waking up early and making him a fried egg sandwich before he left for class. The smell of coffee and eggs dragged him out of bed.

Occasionally, he would have something planned for dinner. And, if she was lucky, he would have it ready. His cooking skills were minimal, so it usually involved a frozen pizza or sandwiches. If she got home first, she would have dinner ready.

They celebrated Valentine's Day on her birthday, since that was her first night off. Landon picked her up and took her to a nice dinner downtown. "You look beautiful tonight." His attention surprised her.

After dinner, they walked outside to fresh snow that had fallen in the last hour. Flurries were still coming down and gently landing on their faces. She looked up to the sky and twirled in as the snowflakes fell around her. Landon took her hand and guided her across the street, to a gazebo. It was a beautiful evening, Kaci thought. Things couldn't get much better than this.

In an instant, Landon was on one knee. He pulled a small box out of his jacket pocket and opened it in front of her. As she gasped in delight, Landon said, "Will you marry me? I can't imagine my life without you."

Kaci squealed, "What? Really? YES! Of course, I'll marry you. Oh my God!" She was almost in tears. She knew she would say yes if he asked her, but she wasn't expecting it today.

As soon as she got home, she called her parents, hoping it wasn't too late. "Guess what?!" she sang as her mother answered the phone. "Landon asked me to marry him!"

"Oh honey, that's wonderful," Evelyn replied. "I'm guessing you said 'yes'?" She knew her daughter did by the joy in her voice.

Kaci could hear her mother telling her dad the news. Walter picked up the phone then, "Congratulations, sweetheart. Are you sure you want to be married so young?" Leave it to her dad to be the practical one.

"Of course, Daddy," she remarked. "Why not? I love him. I know we can be happy together." As she said it, her voice betrayed the tiny hint of doubt that came from the back of her mind.

"Now, Kaci, you don't sound so sure," he added.

"I'm positive, just got a little overwhelmed for a minute," she answered with a smile in her voice. She was willing to do whatever she needed to make it work.

Landon and Kaci talked about the wedding often. Actually, she talked and he semi-listened. He said whatever she wanted was fine with him. They set a date for the end of May the following year. He would graduate one weekend and get married the next. To be sure he didn't get distracted from his studies, Kaci took on all the responsibility of planning the wedding.

That year, they skipped their vacation during spring break. Kaci did go with Landon to his parents' home for two days that week. His mother was happy to sit and talk to Kaci about the wedding. She didn't have a daughter, so she was more than willing to help.

During that summer, they took a few weekend trips to his parents. It was a vacation to be able to sit around the pool and soak up the sun. Louise had several ideas she came up with for the wedding and reception. Some were great, others weren't. But Kaci was very polite and told her, "That's a great idea Mrs. Jamison, but we had our heart set on…" She was always so welcoming and kind. She was lucky to have such a nice future mother-in-law.

One hot July day, they decided to wash his car by hand. She wore an old tank top and shorts so as not to ruin any of her good clothes. Landon met her in his driveway, carrying small towels and a water bucket and dish soap.

As soon as he turned on the hose, he filled the bucket and sprayed the car. They finished soaping up the car in a few minutes when he asked her to pick up the hose and spray the car again. The cool water was so refreshing on the muggy July day.

When she picked up the hose, a light went off in her head. Her eyes were bright with mischief. She concluded Landon needed to loosen up little and this just might do it. At least that's what she hoped. She started spraying and then 'accidentally' sprayed Landon with water. He stood with his mouth open, staring at her. She sprayed him again.

"What in the hell is wrong with you?" he yelled, clearly not amused. "We aren't children Kaci, for God's sake, grow up!"

"Why can't you loosen up a little," she tried to laugh off his rude remarks. "Doesn't the water feel good on this hot day?"

"NO," he fumed, "it does not. Don't ever do that again!" He turned and stomped into the house, not looking back. She was left there, holding the hose.

She felt awful, just like when a teacher would scold her in class, or her dad would punish her. What is wrong with him? How can he be so stiff? She began to wonder about their upcoming wedding, and marriage.

She waited until the next afternoon to call him to apologize, even though she didn't think she had to. "Hey, are you still mad at me?" she asked quietly. "I had no idea you felt that way, I'm sorry."

"It's ok," he answered, "I'm fine now. You just startled me."

They made plans to go to dinner the next night, after she got off work. He was always complaining that she was working too much and didn't have time to spend with him. So, every night off, she spent with him.

# CHAPTER NINE

By the start of Landon's last semester at Murray State, he had already been on dozens of interviews. He took any interview he could, with a degree in business, he was able to fit into any mold. Kaci was also ready for a change.

He accepted a great offer to work in New York City for a national insurance company. He would start off as a sales manager and work his way up to CEO if things went the way he planned. He had bragged to his new bosses that he was about to be married after graduation that year.

Knowing that her parents were struggling financially, Kaci never asked them for money for her wedding. Quite honestly, she thought Landon's parents would come through with something to help them out. But they never offered anything except the rehearsal dinner.

She was able to secure a small local church with more character than seating. They did, however, have a meeting area where the reception could be held at no extra cost. By agreeing to clean up after themselves, she didn't have to pay a cleaning deposit.

Kaci used her connections at the bakery, located next to the pizza parlor, to get a beautiful cake at a discount. Hiring a professional caterer was out of the question, that alone would use over half their budget. At the risk of looking cheap, she asked her boss if he would let her use his ovens to make an Italian feast consisting of Baked Ziti, Alfredo Noodles, Italian Wedding Soup (of course), garlic bread and salad. If they don't like something they like, they can go somewhere else.

She was taken aback when the manager called her into his office before her shift one night. After he told her how much he valued her as an employee, and would be sorry to see her go, Steve told her to not worry about the food, he would provide everything at no charge.

"Consider it my wedding present to you," he said. "I expect to hear of your travels to the Big Apple."

Things just continued to fall into place for their wedding. She knew she could do her own flowers, hair and makeup. The only thing left was to pick out bridesmaid dresses and the tuxes. They had decided on a small wedding party, and Kaci was able to find the perfect dress at JCPenney in a flattering color and style for both of her bridesmaids.

At least Landon took care of ordering the tuxes. That was one thing she didn't have to do. He wanted gray jacket and pants, with charcoal gray loafers and a simple necktie to match the ladies' blue dresses.

One month before graduation, Kaci noticed a change in his behavior. It wasn't obvious to anyone but her, she knew, but she noticed the subtleties that others would miss. He made the effort to be friendly with their friends, but it was a strain, she could see it in his eyes.

She was caught off guard when she came home after working an 8-hour shift and he was waiting at her little apartment. He hadn't mentioned he would be over. At that time, they didn't have cell phones, so they always called after she got home. His first question was where had she been, she was 'supposed' to be home hours ago. That part was true, she agreed to work a double, to earn extra money for their wedding and move. The more she explained, the madder he seemed to get. The neighbors were already looking through their curtains to see what the ruckus was all about. Kaci apologized just to keep him quiet.

Her parents called a couple weeks later to get an update on the wedding plans. She was shocked when her mother said, "We have a bit of a surprise for you and Landon." Kaci became anxious. "Your father and I set aside a little each month for the past few years just for this purpose. We would like to pay for your honeymoon." She almost dropped the phone. Her parents didn't have any money, they had always told her that. The most she expected was a few hundred for a couple nights in a Nashville hotel.

Kaci asked her mother, "Momma, what are you talking about? You guys can't afford it." She wanted to say, "I had to drop out of college because you couldn't help me. Now that wasn't really true?" But, being the obedient daughter, she didn't. After all, she thought, her tuition was over $3,000 per semester.

"We have enough for you and Landon to book a cruise in the Caribbean or a week at a nice hotel in the mountains or at the beach.

Talk to Landon and let us know where you'd like to go." Kaci agreed and hung up, still in shock.

She called Landon to tell him the good news, except he seemed more annoyed than excited. "Why don't they just give us the money and we'll make our own plans," he asked. "I or we might want to do something completely different."

She was frozen in place, not understanding why this was a bad thing. She grasped for the right words. "I don't know! Maybe, they are just trying to take the pressure off us by making the arrangements? Why are you being so argumentative?" she said defensively.

"I am not being argumentative Kaci," he yelled. He was tired of everyone trying to tell him what they thought he should be doing. That was when she knew, he needed to be in control of his life. "If you think I am going to let your parents dictate our marriage, you are dead wrong." Landon was getting angrier, "I'm not going to stand for it. We can call this thing off right now."

Kaci felt warm tears running down her face. What had just happened, she wondered. One minute, she was elated to be able to have a honeymoon, something she and Landon had never considered. The next minute, he was threatening to call off the wedding. He hung up on her, leaving her standing with the phone in her hand.

A few days later, Kaci called her parents and asked if it would be ok if they booked their own vacation. She remarked that Landon's dad had an old buddy who had a condo in NYC and they wanted to go look for a place to live up there. "This money would really help us get started and we would still be able to have a honeymoon up there." She was relieved her dad didn't fight it, in fact, she thought, he was happy to just sign the check and put it in the mail.

Landon's parents came into town for his graduation. They all went out to dinner, and she noticed the way his mother looked at him for the first time. It wasn't really an adoring gaze, or one of disappointment, but somewhere in between. She expected his parents to be gushing with pride over his accomplishment and the new job in NYC. The only way she could describe it was relief.

He was being the polite son they expected him to be, but inside he was barely tolerating their attention. He knew better than to talk back to his father, so he was silent for most of the night. He did thank them for coming to his graduation, however.

His father commented, "Now you can move on to the next chapter and leave all your past issues behind you." Landon looked irritated but offered a small smile. He just won't let it go, Landon thought. He can't just let me move on without that little reminder that he hasn't forgotten my past mistakes.

Kaci again felt like she was left out of the loop. She had no idea what they meant unless it had to do with his temper? She just wasn't sure. It made the rest of the evening uncomfortable. One day, she thought, she might sit down with Louise and ask her about Landon's childhood.

# CHAPTER TEN

As her wedding day approached, Kaci worked overtime often. She was sure to call Landon from the restaurant to let him know what time she should be home. Each time he seemed annoyed but never said anything. He knew she was saving money for the both of them.

The weekend before the big day, Landon's buddies were throwing him a bachelor party. Since there weren't any hot spots in town, the guys went back to Landon's hometown of Clarksville for the weekend. Clarksville was a great place to barhop and even see some more adult entertainment. It was home to the Fort Campbell Army Base, and the business owners knew what young men liked.

Kaci kissed Landon goodbye after lunch on Saturday and told him to behave. He pulled away slightly, looked her in the eye and said, "I can't make any promises, but I'll try." The small laugh he added hit a nerve with her, it felt like a lie.

She thought he would be good, maybe not an angel, but he wouldn't embarrass her. At least, she really hoped he wouldn't. Doubts swirled in her head all night. Could he resist a stripper sitting on his lap? Was that really cheating? They had a suite booked at the Ramada Inn. Would they invite girls back to the suite? It was the first time she really worried about him being faithful to her since before they were serious. She hated the feeling of doubt that crept in.

When Landon got back to his apartment Sunday evening, Kaci was there waiting for him. She welcomed him with a hug and kiss. He looked at her, obviously annoyed with her attention. He brushed her off, "How long have you been here? I'm going to bed. I'm exhausted." He couldn't deal with her now. He knew she would talk all night if given the chance. He eventually explained that his head was killing him, and he was going to bed.

Kaci just stood in the driveway and stared at the front door, and her car. How could he just brush her off? That might have been the rudest thing he could have done, she thought. Even if he did have a headache, he could have given her a hug and been more thoughtful. And whose fault was the headache anyway? Maybe he shouldn't have gotten drunk the night before?

She held in her tears as best she could while driving home. As soon as she opened her front door, she plopped down on her futon, picked up a pillow and screamed into it, while tears poured out. That was the worst feeling in the world. They were getting married in six days and he left her standing alone. She spent the rest of the night crying, finally falling asleep after midnight.

Landon showed up at her work after lunch with a big smile on his face and a big hug for his future wife. He acted as if nothing was wrong but did offer a small apology. "I know I shouldn't have been so abrupt last night," he begged, "Please forgive me." He made a sad face and batted his eyes. She couldn't resist his cute little face.

The next three days flew by. Both their families arrived in town Friday for the rehearsal dinner. Kaci had asked two of the waitresses from work to be her bridesmaids, she wasn't about to ask anyone from home to drive all the way to Kentucky to be in her wedding. Landon's parents chose a nice steakhouse for their rehearsal dinner. They were able to get a private back room. It started out as a great night. Even though Kaci was worried about their families and friends clashing, it all seemed to go smoothly, that is until the toasts started. She would never forget the look on her family's faces when Landon's Best Man started telling tales from their high school days.

He raised a glass, "I would like to make a toast to the bride and groom. I have known Landon for over ten years, and I never thought the same guy who had a different girlfriend every week in high school would be getting married. Ever." Landon's parents had looked down at their plates as he went on. "I remember on more than one night, Landon brought a date to our Friday night parties, and left with another girl." Jason wouldn't stop there, "I wouldn't be surprised if there are half dozen little Landon's running around Clarksville now." At that last statement, the silence was deafening. His parents audibly choking and coughing, her parents gasped.

Landon then sprang into action, "Thanks a lot old 'buddy', remind me to repay the favor at your wedding, if can ever find anyone who will support you like your parents do." The guys laughed while the rest of the room nervously snickered. He didn't need Kaci or anyone asking a bunch of questions about his past. It was exactly what it was, his past, not his present or future.

Landon's older brother, Garrett, then stood up for another toast. "To my baby brother and the poor, poor girl who had the misfortune to say 'yes', I wish you many years of happiness." Thank God, he made it short and sweet Kaci thought. But that wasn't the end, "Through all your past indiscretions, it takes guts to start over in a new town, in college and now going to the Big Apple." Once again, Landon's closest friends and family painted a not-so-flattering picture of the younger Landon.

The sound of the family's deliberately loud clapping drowned out the rest of his speech. Everyone then took big gulps of champagne and moved on. Kaci's maid of honor, Deedra, then rose for her turn. Thankfully, her toast was very sweet. "I just wanted to wish them the best. I've known Kaci for 3 years now, she's even babysat my daughter Lindsay. She has the biggest heart, and Landon is lucky to have her."

Kaci chose to spend her last night as a single woman in her tiny apartment. She was comfortable there. That's what she needed at that moment, comfort. Her nerves were working overtime. It's just cold feet, she told herself repeatedly.

The next morning was a blur to her. The wedding was scheduled for 5 p.m. It seemed like an impossible amount of time to wait, and yet, too soon at the same time. The girls had appointments at the day spa for the works. It was her first experience being pampered and she felt like she deserved it, and needed it

When getting dressed, her friends helped in every way. Her dress fit perfectly. Her beautiful golden strawberry hair was piled loosely on her head. She had chosen a tiara with attached veil that landed halfway down her back. Kaci had found soft and sparkly low heel sandals to complete the look. As she looked in the mirror, she took a deep breath and exhaled. Who was this pretty girl in the mirror? She couldn't believe how she looked. Kaci was never one to be conceited, but this was an exception.

As she looked at the clock, she realized she had just an hour to get to the church for pre-ceremony pictures. More than time she thought. But rather than take a chance, they left in the limousine

Landon had insisted on renting. For once, she was glad he did. She sat in the back and her dress pouffed up around her.

Landon had called her before the men left the hotel. He said he loved her and couldn't wait to marry her. They were staying the night at the nicest hotel in town that night, before driving to Nashville for their trip to New York. Kaci was excited to see a big city like New York. She had never been anyplace larger than Nashville. She could never have gone alone she knew, but with her new husband by her side, she had felt invincible.

Kaci waited in a small office with her dad, until they heard the processional music start, a recording of 'When You Say Nothing at All', by Keith Whitley. Her heart pounded so loudly she almost didn't hear the wedding march begin. As Walter opened the door for his only child to pass through, he whispered in her ear, "I hope you know, you can always change your mind and come home. We will never turn our backs on you."

The sentiment was very touching, but Kaci wondered what prompted that kind of a message? Did he know more than he had shared with her? Regardless of the reason, she felt relieved to know her parents would be there for her, always.

As she stood at the back of the aisle, she watched her attendants walk slowly up to the front. They looked so pretty in their matching periwinkle blue dresses. Lindsay was next in her role as flower girl. She was the perfect age, five, for the task. She knew it was important and loved being dressed in a princess gown, as she called it.

She doesn't remember much about the actual ceremony because it was over so quickly. She did remember Landon giving her a sly wink when the pastor said, "for better, for worse". What does that mean? She thought it was an odd thing to do. She dismissed it as jitters and almost danced down the aisle beside her husband. She was now Mrs. Landon Jamison.

The reception was wonderful. Great food from her boss, great cake, and great friends. They danced a little and laughed a lot. Garrett stepped in as DJ and surprised her by bringing out a karaoke machine. Deedra and Lindsay were first to jump up and sang "Friends in Low Places". Lindsay had the crowd eating out of the palm of her hand. After several others took their turn, Landon dragged her up and started singing "Islands in the Stream". She turned bright red but stuck it out. She didn't like being the center of attention like that, not the way Landon did.

Landon looked at her and laughed when they sat down. "You didn't see that coming, did you?" He knew she didn't like to get up in front of people, but he did it anyway. He had to try to get her to loosen up and be more outgoing. He would need her to help him in New York with his new bosses and clients he thought.

They got to their hotel suite after 10 o'clock. He was looking forward to sex with his wife. They had been having sex since their sophomore year, but this was different. He opened the bottle of champagne his dad's friend Michael had sent to the room. What a great guy, he thought. I'll be sure to have Kaci send him a Thank You card.

She had changed out of her wedding dress and into a sexy white lace negligee she received from Deedra. It wasn't something she would have felt comfortable buying for herself, but she was glad she had it for tonight. It was a good choice according to the look on Landon's face.

"Now THAT is sexy," he proclaimed as he stood up to meet her in the middle of the room. He handed her a glass of champagne and walked her over to the chair he was sitting in. He pulled her down gently to sit on his lap. As she was drinking, he was kissing her breasts and running his hands under the nightie in the back. His touch was so soft and arousing, she was barely able to finish the drink.

The champagne hit her within minutes. Kaci drank way too much wine earlier at the reception, and now she was paying the price. Landon tried to be considerate, but he still expected her to satisfy him that night. For the first time ever, Kaci didn't feel like having sex,, but she did anyway. She was so worried she'd throw up she was almost motionless. After they were done, she was feeling much more nauseous and barely made it to the bathroom before vomiting. The fact that he was sound asleep while she felt so awful made her wonder if she made question what the rest of their life would be like.

They headed to the airport before lunch and landed safely at LaGuardia Airport about 6 p.m. eastern time. They gathered their bags and found their way to the taxi line. The ride into the city was beautiful. The sun was just setting so it provided gorgeous lighting for the New

York skyline. How lucky were they? Starting their married life as yuppies in the city.

# CHAPTER ELEVEN

The building they were driven to was only a few blocks from the World Trade Center. When they finally were inside and looked out onto the lights of the city, she sighed with joy. It was everything she hoped it would be. But she didn't know if she would ever fall asleep with all the lights streaming through the windows. The constant murmur of traffic below could be heard 25 stories up.

The next morning, Landon had a meeting with his new employer, so he was out the door before she fully woke up. Kaci found a newspaper slipped under their door. She made herself a cup of coffee and opened the Classifieds. First, they needed an apartment, then she needed a job.

She was shocked to find that most one-bedroom apartments in the Manhattan area were over $3,000 a month. They had hoped to get a two bedroom, so Landon could have an office. That may not be practical Kaci thought. As she continued to read, she saw that if they moved to Brooklyn, they could get a two-bedroom place for around $2500 a month.

There were companies that specialized in finding their customers the best rental they could afford, for a small fee. It was after lunch, Landon wasn't back yet, so she made a few calls to agents in the neighborhood. She was able to get an appointment with Carol of Sanders' Rentals and made an appointment for 3 p.m. Hopefully, Landon would be back by then.

When he wasn't, Kaci left a note on the counter telling him where she went, and when she would be home. She was eager to walk down the city sidewalks and investigate the neighborhood in the daylight.

The bellman opened the lobby door and she walked out into the huge new world. She caught herself jumping at the sound of car horns and police sirens. An aroma of filth, pizza, cigarette smoke and car fumes assaulted her sinuses. While the street was shaded by the skyscrapers, she was blinded by the gleam off the mirrored sides. Everywhere she looked she saw people. She saw businessmen in nice suits, younger adults in ripped jeans and flannel shirts, and the homeless people, hiding in the alleys.

She walked into the agent's office and introduced herself as 'Mrs. Kaci Jamison', with a proud smile on her face. Carol had an inviting smile that reminded her of her Aunt Jean. She had spoiled Kaci, but it was more than that, she took the time to listen to her and treat her like a person, not a child.

After making a short list of wants and needs for their new place, she and Carol went out on their journey. The first apartment was only three blocks away in a beautiful brownstone, with stone steps and ironwork. When Kaci walked in, she fell in love with the high ceilings and wood floors. The kitchen was compact but had enough room for a small dining table. The bathroom had a claw foot bathtub that almost made Kaci cry. It was perfect.

"Don't you just love this place?" Carol asked. "I had a feeling this one was for you and your husband."

Kaci was afraid to ask but did anyway, "How much is it?"

"$3,400 a month, with a $2000 security deposit, and a one-year lease. If you'd be willing to sign a two-year lease, he would lower the rent to $3,200 and the deposit to $1700." She knew that was over what Landon said they could afford.

Carol reminded her how fast properties were rented and she needed to snatch this one up by the end of the day tomorrow. She had a deal with the landlord to let her show it for 24 hours first. She had two more to see that day. Carol hailed a cab and took them about 15 minutes uptown.

Kaci looked around at the street lined with small stores, bodegas, groceries, barber, florist, even a coffee shop. Carol pointed to the window over the florist, two stories up. The apartment was on the third floor of a walk up, which meant no elevator.

She was gasping for air by the time she opened the door. She didn't think she was out of shape, but the stairs were more than she was used to. The living area had 4 large windows, two facing each street. It did provide a lot of daylight, which she liked. The kitchen was galley style with a tiny window over the fire escape. It had a stacked washer and dryer in the corner. "That's great," Kaci thought. She had forgot about laundry in the other apartment.

Carol didn't play guessing games that time, "This one is $2,900 a month. $1900 security." "Okay," she thought, getting closer. Maybe the next one would be the one.

The next address was in Harlem. Kaci wasn't sure how she felt about that. She had heard it wasn't safe. The apartment was in another old brownstone, but one that hadn't been in as good of condition as the first one she saw. As they walked up to the fourth floor, she heard voices from the other tenants. Nothing to make her turn around and run, and maybe they would welcome them into the building and be friends. The door knocker was missing a screw, so it hung lopsided on the door of 4B. Opening the door, she went down a short hallway to the first door on the right. It was a small bedroom, very small, but certainly big enough for his office. It even had built in shelves. The living area was nice with commercial tile floors and room for a dining table. The master bedroom was a good size, with the master bath attached. The appliances were older but were still in good shape. It would need a little TLC but she knew she had time to clean it up while she looked for a job.

"How much?" she asked. "A mere $2400 with a deposit of $1900, but, if you are willing to rent it as-is, he will take $500 off the deposit. She thought this was the one that made the most sense. She needed to talk to Landon. She hoped he was at the condo by now.

# CHAPTER TWELVE

Landon lunged at her as soon as she walked in. The smell of whiskey on his breath made her back further away from him. "Where in the hell have you been?" he demanded. He wouldn't tell her he was scared that something happened to her on the streets of New York.

"What do you mean? You're scaring me, Landon." She was unsure why he was so angry. "Didn't you get my note?"

"What note? I didn't see a note. I expected you to be here." He looked like he could kill her. "I was worried you'd be murdered or worse! Fuck Kaci! Think!"

She was still standing in the same spot. She didn't know what to say or what to do. A million thoughts ran through her head. "Is he going to drink all the time now that he's away from his parents?" Of course, she never said any of these things. She just waited for him to speak. She wouldn't be the one talking first, that's for sure.

Finally, Landon broke the silence and ordered, "Come over here and tell me about the apartments." It was as if he flipped a switch and was now being 'the nice Landon' she fell in love with. When she started moving slowly in his direction he said, "You don't actually think I'm going to hurt you, do you? Don't be crazy Kaci, I love you and I was just worried sick."

She would let that one go, she said to herself. She smiled as she sat next to him with a pad of paper, all ready to describe and draw each of the places she had seen. Landon immediately thought the first brownstone apartment was out of the question.

The Grove Street apartment had a washer and dryer, which would save them at least $20 a week. It was also close the bus line that would go within two blocks of his office. The Harlem apartment, while being on the 4th floor, had the cheapest price. This landlord was willing to negotiate Carol had told her.

Landon decided he would call Carol first thing in the morning to see if they could possibly get it for $2300 since he knew he could do any small repairs himself. He really didn't like the idea of the superintendent in their apartment.

They made that decision easily enough. After talking to Carol, they signed the lease on the Harlem apartment. They were able to get some sight-seeing in later that day. Landon took Kaci by his office on West 41st Street. She was introduced to his bosses. They all smiled and patted Landon on the back. It was apparent they really liked him. She got the same feeling she had when she went with him to the frat parties in college. These 'good ole boys' groups were intimidating. She would never be seen as more than his wife, his anchor.

Their last full day they spent checking out a few help-wanted ads. Kaci noticed that Landon was very opinionated on what kind of job she should get. There was a small pub only three blocks from their new apartment that displayed a help wanted sign in the window. They walked in about lunchtime, and Landon took one look and the dark bar, 'regulars' sitting in chairs and few customers eating in the booths and just said, "No." He wouldn't let her be in that environment to be man-handled. "The only man who will be handling you, is me," he laughed.

She had circled a few other jobs. One was at a coffee shop close to the river. While, the clientele was better, she was sure the tips weren't. She talked to managers at a few other shops, before she tried the Design Museum, as a receptionist. She loved the idea of being close to culture. She was dressed nicely thank goodness since the manager was able to meet with her immediately. While Landon wandered through the halls, she talked with Mr. Wilder about the position.

It really was a good job. They offered a benefits package anyone would be envious to have. She couldn't contain her excitement; she would love to work there. He let her know he had other candidates, but things looked good for her. The following night, after they had returned to Kentucky, she had a message on her machine. She got the job! He would wait for her to move in two weeks.

# CHAPTER THIRTEEN

Over the next few days, Kaci and Landon lived at his apartment, which was easy because she already had several things there. The big task in front of them was packing. They had to decide what to take and what to sell. He left most of those decisions to Kaci.

Kaci had given her landlord notice weeks before the wedding and had started packing up what she wanted most. She called the newspaper and ran a garage sale ad for that upcoming Friday and Saturday. She knew some college kids who could use her futon and other small appliances.

Landon had decided to use his dad's SUV and move everything they could that way. Unfortunately, that meant they would have to buy several things when they got to New York. They agreed they could get by with just a sofa and a bed until they had money coming in.

She brought several of Landon's things over to sell that he didn't want. He had a large collection of cassette tapes and some vinyl LP's that he no longer listened to. There were also several boxes of books, lots and lots of books.

By the end of the day on Friday, she had sold almost half of her stuff, and several of Landon's gadgets. She hoped that on Saturday, the rest would go too. She had already contacted a local charity to come pick up the remainder as a donation. She always believed in the Golden Rule. 'Do unto others...'

"Landon, can you believe we made almost $300?" She was excited at the idea of having money to buy new things in New York.

"For that old junk? Wow." He said in shock. Most of the things had been secondhand to them, so that made the hassle worth it. "I guess it's true what they say, 'One man's trash is another man's treasure'."

By Monday, they had almost everything packed and ready to put into the SUV except Landon's bed and two old recliners from his apartment. One of his school buddies was coming to get those Tuesday, when they were pulling out of town.

Kaci spent Monday evening at the pizza place, saying goodbye to her friends and coworkers. She had tears in her eyes thinking she may never see them again since they wouldn't really have any reason to come back once they were settled. Landon's parents had talked about coming up to see them once or twice a year. Her parents, who didn't like to fly, had said they would buy her a plane ticket to come visit them in Arkansas whenever she wanted.

By lunch on Tuesday, Landon and Kaci had left town. They would be in Clarksville, at his parents, in a little over an hour, to say their last goodbyes. As they drove up the driveway, the dogs came from behind the house to greet them. They covered Kaci with dog hair and kisses.

Landon was trying to tear her away from them and make their way to the back of the house. The dogs led the way to where his family had gathered on the back patio. The smell of something on a grill made them both hungry. They hadn't really eaten anything that morning.

Louise had decorated for a small family party. She had burgers and grilled vegetables on platters ready to be eaten. They all sat down and filled their plates. "Whatever is not eaten, Kaci and Landon will take with them for the trip," she announced.

"It smells wonderful, Mrs. Jamison, thank you," Kaci said graciously. "You don't need to pack this up to go, we can get food on the road, it's ok."

Landon jumped in, "Yeah mom, we'll be okay, but I am going to stuff myself now, so I won't be hungry for at least six hours." He laughed as she took another helping of potato salad and baked beans.

As they got up to leave, Jerry gave Kaci a big hug and whispered in her ear, "You better keep an eye on him." Even though his tone was playful, she wondered if there was more meaning behind it. A quick peck on the cheek and he turned to shake his son's hand and gave him a hearty pat the back.

"You take care of this young lady," as he handed him a small bank envelope. "Use this to get a bed and sofa. Your mother and I wanted you to have something in that new apartment."

Landon took the envelope, and he looked speechless. Jerry added, "After all, we will need somewhere to sleep when we visit."

Kaci gave Louise a warm hug, "Thank you both so much. Isn't that wonderful Landon?" They all turned to Landon, waiting for him to say something.

"Of course, it is," he said, finally speaking, "Thanks Dad, and Mom." Again, he felt as if his parents were stepping in to fix things. He liked money, who didn't, but it's just the way they did it that annoyed him so much.

They stopped for the night close to Alexandria, Virginia. Landon had picked up a six-pack of beer at the convenience store across the street. She knew it had been a stressful day, driving through Nashville and Knoxville. He deserved a beer or two to unwind, she reasoned.

Kaci went to the Waffle House in the parking lot and order two big cheeseburgers with fries for their dinner. When she got back, Landon had already drunk two beers. They sat at the tiny table to eat. Landon took one bite of his burger and almost spit it out. "What in the hell is this? It's bloody in the middle. You know I like my burgers well-done."

"I'm sorry, I had no idea," she answered him. "Mine is well or medium-well. Do you want mine instead?" She certainly didn't want to start a fight before they even got up to the city.

"It's the least you could do," he quipped, "since you're the one who screwed up the order."

"I don't mind at all, but I didn't screw this up," she said firmly, "the restaurant did." He seemed pacified as he ate her burger. "In fact, I'm going to call them in a minute and tell them what you thought," she offered. She hoped that would calm him down.

# CHAPTER FOURTEEN

The next morning, they took time to eat a real breakfast. They were back on the road by 8 o'clock. Landon had mentioned he didn't want to stop until they were in Maryland, which would be five hours, at least, with the traffic around Washington, D.C. Just over 24 hours after leaving home, they saw the NYC skyline. Their new home was spread out before them.

Kaci's nerves had been on edge all day, and now they were finally there. A tear formed in her eye as she took in how beautiful it looked with the sun shining off all the glass.

Landon's boss had arranged for them to park in a nearby garage for a few weeks. They picked up the key from the building superintendent, Mr. Griego, and eagerly unlocked the door. Landon would have to get access to the freight elevator he was told when they had signed the lease.

Kaci was excited and nervous at the same time to be a real New Yorker, living and breathing the same air as a million other people. She was to be at work in just five days. Landon was starting his job the next morning. It didn't give them a lot of time to unload the boxes and find his garment bags. Luckily, she remembered there was a dry cleaner on the corner that offered two-hour pressing. If she got his suits out in the next hour, she could pick them up before they closed.

Landon parked the SUV on the street and grabbed a few things before heading up the four flights of stairs to their new home. When he got to the landing, in front of their door, he saw Kaci, lost in thought he assumed. "Here we are, New York," he said. She jumped when he spoke. He must have startled her. She had better toughen up he thought.

She had stayed up late that first night cleaning the bathroom from top to bottom so he could get a shower in the morning. She was going to make their first home together someplace they would both feel comfortable.

The next morning, Landon was slow to get up. The drive had been hard on both of them. Not to mention, they had to sleep on the air mattress they brought. It wasn't great, but it was better than the sleeping on the floor. The smell of bleach and 409 was still lingered where she had cleaned. She knew she would need to wipe everything down again due to the amount of dirt that had accumulated.

Landon was in a hurry to be on time, which meant early in his book, to his first day. He would try the coffee house down the street he told Kaci. No big fuss needed today. He left the house before 8 a.m. He had planned on it taking 30 minutes by bus to go the 2 miles it was to work. He took his time at the coffee shop, he even talked to the barista girl who served his coffee. She was cute, he thought, in a New York, tough girl way.

Left alone in the empty apartment, Kaci was still in disbelief that she was living in New York, the biggest city in the country. She found her radio and found a great classic rock station and turned up the volume while she cleaned. It wasn't util she felt the rumbling in her stomach that she realized she had skipped lunch.

The grocery was on her to do list also today. She cleaned up and left to check out the local store. Before she got any hungrier, she grabbed a hotdog from a street vendor at the corner. Another block over was a small grocery store. It was nothing like the supermarkets she was used to. This one seemed to be about the size of a college classroom. She had $50 to get the basics. The money Landon gave her didn't stretch like it did back home.

Once she carried the heavy bags home, she started unpacking and mentally preparing a meal plan. Kaci had tried to guess what time Landon would be home. Their home phone was not going to be installed until the next week. She really wanted to have a hot dinner waiting for him.

She knew the office closed at 5 but, he had said, that doesn't mean he gets to leave at that time. "I'm the new kid, so I'm sure I'll be stuck there doing the grunt work for a while," he had told her. Even so, she expected him before it turned dark.

He got home about 7. When he gave her a quick kiss and she noticed the familiar smell of whiskey. He wasn't drunk she knew, but he obviously had time to go have a drink.

"How was your first day? Smells like you had fun," she chided him. "Is this going to be a regular thing?"

He stepped back and walked to the bathroom, slamming the door. When he came out, he said, "I guess you don't think I deserve to have a drink with the guys? Don't you want us to make friends up here?" Why did she have to be so prissy? he thought. We aren't living in Kentucky anymore, time to live like the yuppies they were.

Kaci felt awful. He had just started his new career in a new place, of course he could use a stiff drink. "I'm sorry. I was just missing you, I guess. I know it's been a long day for both of us." He walked over and gave her a loving hug. He kissed her on the forehead as he walked toward the kitchen.

"So, what's on the menu?" he asked. "I'm starving." He was sure he could eat anything at that moment. Even if Kaci's cooking wasn't the greatest, he thought, I can eat it.

She pulled out the chicken from the oven where it had been warming for over an hour. It still looked good she was relieved to see. She put water on to boil for pasta and put the frozen broccoli in the microwave. Fifteen minutes later, dinner was served. Landon ate everything on his plate without commenting. She assumed he liked the meal, but he never said.

They spent the night listening to the radio and talking about what they wanted to do that weekend. The first thing they said, "Buy a bed!". Until then, they slept on a blow-up mattress they borrowed from his brother. Landon put her in charge of checking on the best place to buy a new mattress, and which ones delivered. He hoped she would be able to handle that task.

Friday morning, she made sure to take the rest of Landon's shirts and pants to the dry cleaners. They had access to a laundry room on the 2nd floor, but she didn't have an iron yet, so his clothes would be taken to Mr. Winkler at the corner. He was a kind older man who had welcomed her to the neighborhood on Wednesday. "If you promise not to go to Lucky's down the street, I'll give you a 10% discount." She gladly took him up on his offer.

Before she walked out, she turned and asked, "Mr. Winkler, do you know a good place to buy furniture that won't cost us a fortune?"

He thought a minute, then she saw the light bulb turn on. He told her about a local guy who offered free delivery in their zip code.

She ended up at Buddy's Best Furniture. Kaci looked around for 30 minutes before she stopped a salesman to help her. She told him she was looking for Full mattress set and a sofa that was on sale. The mattress set was only $400, and she did find two sofas she liked, one a flowery print the other a more masculine plaid.

"I will be back on Saturday with my husband," she vowed. But, on the way out of the store, she saw a clearance room. As soon as she walked in, she saw two small used bar stools that they could use for their counter, and two end tables, coffee table and a lamp she liked.

"What kind of deal will you give me on all this?" She nervously awaited his answer. He looked as if he was calculating in his head.

She was happy when he said, "for you, young lady, $100."

"SOLD," Kaci said. She handed him a $100 bill and told him to hold them until they came back tomorrow.

Kaci stopped and picked up hamburger and spaghetti sauce on the way home. It was a simple, comforting dinner tonight. The man who owned the vegetable stand next door had some nice tomatoes and lettuce for a small salad. She was starting to feel more comfortable in the neighborhood. Making friends or friendly acquaintances with the store owners on their street.

That night, even though it was a Friday and she expected him much later, Landon got home before 6 o'clock. "Surprise," he half-shouted when he unlocked the door and opened it quickly. She jumped but quickly smiled and ran over to give him a big hug.

"I'll start dinner as soon as I'm done washing the windows in the bedroom," she said.

"You mean it's not ready now?" he said. She turned and saw a little grin on his face. "WHEW", she thought, that could have been a bad night. He couldn't help but make fun of the fight they had the night before. "Kaci, I'm kidding," he said, "don't look so nervous. I'm not that kind of person. You know that."

# CHAPTER FIFTEEN

Kaci spent the evening describing her walk. She was talking so fast, Landon had to tell her more than once to "slow down, please. You sound like a New Yorker for sure." Laughing she continued, she told him about Mr. Winkler, the vegetable stand, and finally Harry and the deals she found. He seemed impressed with all she got accomplished that day, and yet, Kaci felt like he expected more.

After grabbing bagels and coffee the next morning, they walked over to Buddy's. Harry greeted them and took over by showing Landon the furniture Kaci found. The bed was good, but he'd prefer a firmer mattress. "Not a problem," Harry said. "Don't forget you'll need a bedframe also."

Next came the sofas she liked. She was kind of surprised that Landon didn't like either one. "Can we get away from the country bumpkin style? We are in the coolest city ever." She felt the insult as very personal. They both came from the same area, after all. He was obviously more concerned with appearances than comfort.
They spend another hour and sat on every sofa in the building she thought. He finally narrowed it down to two completely different styles. The first was a Chesterfield, with a tufted back, in a light blueprint. The price was double what they agreed to spend. The second was a stylish, comfortable sofa, with big, rolled arms. It was bright red and had wood accents. Kaci had to agree, both were gorgeous. Hoping the price of the blue one was negotiable, they asked Harry for a deal.

"I like you guys, and I understand you just moved here, with no furniture." It was more of a statement than a question. "I can give you 25% off the sofa since it's been discontinued."

He can't be serious, Landon thought. It's the oldest pitch line in the book. But it was either take it or don't at that point. "You've got a deal," Landon said. "Is there any way they can deliver everything this afternoon?" Kaci waited anxiously for his response.

After Harry checked with the delivery department, he promised that they could be at the apartment in three hours. The guys would bring it up in the service elevator if they could get permission.

The happy couple almost skipped back home in anticipation of the delivery. Just as promised, the delivery arrived on time. They were able to find Mr. Griego, in the lobby and asked if he could unlock the freight elevator.

The delivery went smoother than she could have hoped. Landon gave the men a tip, which they appreciated. He had no idea what a good tip was, but he had a $20 bill in his pocket and nothing smaller. The guys thanked him and said they would split it.

They sat on their new sofa, and relaxed, really breathed. "It's just beautiful," she finally said, "You have excellent taste, sir." "Why thank you, ma'am." "Oh no, don't start with the ma'am," she laughed.

There was a nice Italian restaurant a few blocks over that Mr. Winker had recommended. They decided to make it date night every Saturday night. A stroll through the city, in the early evening, the temperature was a pleasant 78 degrees with a slight breeze. "This is heaven," Kaci thought.

Kaci spent Sunday getting her clothes ready for her first day of work. Mr. Wright had explained that while the museum itself was a more casual environment, she was expected to dress in business attire. That meant she would be wearing a skirt or dress pants and heels all week. She owned two pencil skirts and one pair of black dress pants. She did have a tailored dress that would look nice with her one suit jacket. She knew she would have to go shopping soon to have more options for work.

While she cleaned, Landon set off to look for an electronics store where he could get a decent television. It was the one thing she had asked for. She almost regretted the request when he complained, "What do we need a damn tv for? Read a book or something." He grumbled, "I'll be working late a lot and won't even have time to watch it." It didn't help that even the smallest televisions weighed over 30 lbs. He was not looking forward to carrying it home.

"Well, while you're working late, I'll be at home," she sighed. "I would like to watch the news and other programs I like." He finally agreed when she mentioned all the sports he could watch.

He was clearly out of breath and not in a good mood when he finally got the television into the apartment. Landon had been gone almost two hours, but he did have a 13" color tv. It would have to do he thought. She had better not complain, he thought to himself, she could go carry a bigger one home if that's what she needed. Luckily, she really looked grateful for the little box. After plugging it in and fooling with the rabbit ears, she found three stations that came in clearly. That was something you couldn't use in Kentucky, rabbit ears.

Monday morning was a rush. They both needed to shower, get dressed, coffee and get out the door. Landon had his routine to leave the apartment at 7:30 A.M. He found he beat a lot of traffic on the bus that way, and he got to work almost an hour early, which the bosses loved. Anything to get a promotion.

Kaci had to squeeze in her shower after his. Her job was closer than his and she wasn't expected until 9:30. Still, she would have preferred to be early on her first day. By the time he left the bathroom, she barely had time to get her hair wet. "You took so long, now I'll be late," she complained. He really could be self-centered she thought.

He snapped back, "Really Kaci? It's not as if your job is that important, you answer phones." Why did she have to start complaining so early? He didn't want to start his day off with an argument, so he let it go for now.

Kaci stared, again, at her husband. She knew he was far from perfect, but she loved him. All she said was, "I'm not exactly sure what my job duties are yet, or how strict they are on their tardiness policy. I guess I'll find our today."

He grunted and put his suitcoat on. "If you hurry, I'll buy you breakfast for your first day," he said with a smile. It was his way of keeping the peace. Landon was tired of always being the one to compromise.

It took some quick work with her makeup, but she was ready at 7:45. I need to shower in the evening, she realized, that would make it easier on both of them. At least his mood lightened up. She didn't' want to worry about his feelings all day. She needed to focus on her new job.

# CHAPTER SIXTEEN

As soon as Kaci walked into the museum, she fell in love with the architecture and exhibits. Mr. Wilder had given her a quick tour when she applied for the job. Today, however, she took her time to really take in its beauty. Her receptionist's desk area was very classy she thought. Granite countertops, dark mahogany wood, and a leather chair would be her home.

Mr. Wilder gave her a brief idea of what to say when answering the phone and showed her where to find most of the information she would need. He assured her most calls would be about their hours, the cost of admission and calls for other staff. The phone system was intimidating, but she was confident she'd get the hang of it quickly.

She would be in charge of scheduling school tours. The museum was a popular field trip destination. Mr. Wilder explained that they had an average of two group tours per day. It wasn't a hard job to schedule them, but she needed to be sure there was a guide available and they finished in the allotted 90-minute time frame.

Clarissa, her immediate supervisor, came up to her later to relieve her for her lunch break. She said she always took the noon lunch, but she would switch with Kaci whenever she wanted.

Kaci took her first lunchbreak in the neighboring park. There was a soft breeze with the smell of freshly cut grass. She had brought an apple and banana she grabbed at the fruit stand for lunch. She had heard about people getting mugged in broad daylight but that seemed like impossible in the city she looked at now. She had also brought a book but never opened it those first few days. She went back to the park every day for lunch on her bench.

On Thursday, she got up to walk back and bumped into someone jogging past her. Her arm was being jerked away from her body as the man had his hand on her purse. A loud scream came from her throat and several people turned around. The thief ran off before he was surrounded. "I can't believe that just happened," she thought as she sat back down.

A minute later a small white dog dragging an older black man, about 60, came over to her. "You're not from around here, are you?"

"Is it that obvious?" she asked him. "I don't have anything really in my purse. I was just startled."

"I'm afraid so, you did the right thing though, that scream drew attention, and muggers hate attention." He continued, "My name is Oliver. Nice to meet you. And this is Jack," he said introducing his white terrier. "He's a ladies' man, so be careful." He chuckled to lighten the mood.

"I'm Kaci, my husband and I just moved here from Kentucky," she confessed. "We are trying our best to not stand out, but neither of us have lived in a metropolitan city before."

"Well, I'm sorry to say, our fine city has its flaws, crime being the biggest one I think," he said. "That and traffic. Oh, and pollution." He laughed. "You better take this," he said as he offered her a small whistle. "I think they call it a rape whistle, but any kind of whistle would work. This one happens to have pepper spray at the other end."

Kaci excused herself with a gracious thank you to Oliver for the whistle and for calming her down. She hurried back to the museum to relieve Clarissa for her lunch.

She called Landon as soon as she got back to her desk to tell him what happened. He didn't answer and she ended up leaving a message on his voice mail. She tried to sound okay but ended up sniffling and blotting her eyes. The reality of the incident suddenly hit her.

He returned her call right before she was about to leave for the day. "What the fuck happened Kaci?" She spent a few minutes trying to calm him down. He almost sounded angry. Either because she bothered him at work, or that she was almost a victim to a common thief. The shock had worn off by now and she was actually okay now. Kaci made sure he knew it, "Landon, calm down please, I'll be fine. I was just startled."

He offered to pick up dinner on his way home from the famous from Ray's Pizza. He reminded her to go straight home and to not make any stops. He really sounded worried about her safety. It was nice feeling loved and protected for a change.

"That was the best pizza I think I've ever had," Kaci told him. "And I worked in a pizza parlor!" New York pizza had a taste all its own. Made up of a thin crust, hand-tossed of course, with homemade sauce and lots of cheese and pepperoni. The standard size was about double of the ones back home. It was so large, the customary way to eat a slice was to fold it lengthwise and eat it with your hands, no utensils.

After a couple of weeks, Landon started coming home later and later. At first, he said he was working at the office. She had called his desk a few times and only reached his voice mail, so she started asking questions. He was quick with a response, "no, I didn't mean working at the office, I meant working for clients at their businesses."

That was his story but sometimes he changed it to 'a bunch of the guys went for a drink'. The drinks turned into 'grabbing a bite to eat'. She was still making dinner for him every night even though she didn't see him before 8 o'clock most nights. And most of the time, he didn't eat what she cooked, so the refrigerator was full of leftovers.

His father had called the week before to say that his friend with the condo from their honeymoon was back in the city and it would be a good idea if they invited him out to dinner. Landon knew that Mr. Bottino would be a great client for him to pull in.

Michael showed up at the Mexican restaurant a few minutes after six but that was still early by New York dinner times. He easily spotted them sitting by the front window. Kaci always liked to look out and watch the people going by.

Landon stood up and introduced them, "Mr. Bottino, so happy to meet the man who gave us two a great wedding presents, a head start in the city and a great bottle of champagne. I'm Landon of course, and this is Kaci." He shook hands and Michael took Kaci's hand and bent over to give it a quick regal kiss.

It didn't take long before Landon and Michael were deep in discussion about business. She tried to pay attention, but they weren't speaking to her directly, so she stared out the window. The margaritas were wonderful. She stood up to go to the ladies' room, grabbed onto Landon's shoulder and steadied herself. He looked up with one raised eyebrow. "I'm fine, really," she answered the unasked question

They took a taxi home and Landon immediately wanted to have sex. He grabbed her hand and led her to the bedroom. Kaci could barely stay awake as he undressed her and got on top of her. She didn't want to him to get upset so she never said 'no.' It will be over in a minute she told herself. And it was, every time.

Not long after that, Landon started staying out until almost midnight. She had tried to ask him about where he was. He had mentioned Michael's name a few times. Kaci didn't like feeling that she was being kept in the dark. He wouldn't be secretive if he didn't have anything to hide, right? All kinds of scenarios went around in her mind.

One night, when she couldn't take the tension any longer, she blurted out, "Are you having an affair?" She thought the not knowing would be the worst part.

"What?" he seemed overly surprised. "Why would you say that? I've been working, I told you. You really think I have a girl on the side? How about you trust in me for a change?"

"Surely your boss can't expect you to work 18 hours a day," her voice had a nervous, strained tone.

"Kaci, you're being dramatic," he said trying to calm her down. "And jealousy isn't very attractive. Not to mention you are exaggerating. I do not work 18 hours a day."

"Jealous?" she said. "Well, maybe I am jealous. I guess I'm jealous that you are out having fun and I am stuck at home alone. Maybe I will go out after work one night."

"Poor baby," he said, mocking her feelings. "You just don't understand the world of finance in business in New York, do you?" he answered. "This isn't like back home. What I do here matters, to a lot of people. Even if you can't see that."

She saw his expression turning from slight amusement to annoyance and was on the verge of angry. She really hated fighting, and eventually one of them would have to back down. It was usually her. "I'm sorry. Can you blame me for being lonely?"

"If it will stop this inquisition, I'll try to get home a little earlier," he agreed. "Are you satisfied?"

The next time Landon was going to be really late, she got a phone call from Michael, explaining that he was needed to help him with some contracts. What could she say? She didn't want Landon complaining that his wife was a nag. Michael was a friend of family, she hoped he would be hard at work. But she wasn't sure if she really wanted to know the truth.

Kaci and Landon fell into a rhythm of work, date night and weekend walks around the neighborhood. When Autumn finally arrived, they spent most of their weekends outside in the parks. A couple of times, Kaci had seen Oliver and Jack. The little dog always tugged the lead in her direction. Oliver held him back, and she gave him a little nod. However, he surprised Oliver one day and jerked so hard, he ran over to Kaci and Landon.

Landon jumped back, as if he was being attacked by a German Shepherd. "Keep your dog on a leash man." Oliver rushed over and apologized. "Yeah, well, I don't need dog hair and muddy paws all over me." Kaci looked at her husband, how did she not know of his dislike for animals? She didn't dare tell him that she knew Oliver.

One day in October, she ventured out for a walk at lunch, after telling Clarissa where she was going, just in case something happened. She had only been back to the park where she met Oliver a few times since the day she was almost mugged. She sat on a bench with her back to the stone wall, to give her a full view of the pedestrians. She realized she had been holding her breath after a few minutes. After she slowly exhaled, she felt better. She enjoyed just people watching, wondering where they were going.

After that day, she made a point to go to the park at least three times a week. There wouldn't be many days left with good weather she knew. On the last Friday of the month, Oliver strolled along with Jack. The dog immediately pulled him over to where she sat. "I can't believe he remembers you," he said. "Now, Jack, behave yourself. Don't get Miss Kaci all dirty with those paws."

"Hello, Jack," she said as she leaned down to pet the frisky guy. "Do you remember me?" He panted and wagged his tail. Looking up at Oliver, "I have to apologize for my husband. I had no idea he felt that way about dogs," she said.

"Don't worry about it, it takes all kinds," he said. "Now how have you been young lady?"

"I'm great, I finally started coming back here a few weeks ago. And I'm glad I did," she answered. "I don't like being the kind of person who is scared of her own shadow."

"Well, I for one, am glad you gave our park another tries," said Oliver with a smile. "It makes my day a little better also." They agreed to meet a couple times a week and sit and talk. Kaci had found someone to confide in and she was glad. She needed a friend.

# CHAPTER SEVENTEEN

One of her weekly chores, or errands, was to pick up their dry cleaning at Mr. Winkler's. She was there just before closing one evening after work. He was such a nice old man, she really enjoyed talking with him.

"Hello Mona Lisa, and how are you doing this evening?" he greeted her. He had started calling her Mona Lisa when she got the job at the museum. She didn't bother to tell him that where she worked was a completely different type of museum.

"I'm doing great," she replied, "How have you been doing? You haven't been here as much." He explained about his wife's continuing problems with her COPD and how he may have to retire soon.

"Oh, I'm so sorry," she said sympathetically, "I hope that she can feel better soon. I know I'm being selfish, but what would I do without you?"

He disappeared to the rear of the store to retrieve her cleaning. When he came out with several hangers covered in plastic, she noticed several things in his other hand. After hanging the clothes up, he gave her the items. "These were left in your husband's pockets."

There were a few business cards including one for Bottoms Up! Gentlemen's Club with the name Paul DiMaio written on the back and a phone number. The others were what looked like other client's cards, or prospective clients.

That night, Kaci handed the cards to Landon and said, "Gentlemen's Club? Really Landon?" She turned and started walking away when she was jerked by the arm.

"I'm a big boy Kaci, I don't need your permission," he said, clearly upset with her. "I will continue to work with my clients with whatever they need. It's called loyalty. You should try it some time."

She saw the determination in his eyes and decided he would win this one. She muttered an apology and he let go of her arm. There would be a mark left where his fingers had been.

Thanksgiving was spent with her cooking a small but traditional meal and Landon watching football. She had her mother's recipe for stuffing and whipped sweet potatoes. Everything smelled wonderful. She was just getting ready to call him to grab a plate when he came up behind her.

"Where's the dressing and giblet gravy?" Landon asked.

She was stunned. She hadn't made either, she had no idea he expected it. "We always have dressing," he said in a demanding tone. "And you know I hate sweet potatoes."

"I made stuffing, my mother's recipe, it's almost the same thing," she apologized.

"No, it's not the same thing," he argued. "Damn it, Kaci, can't you get anything right!" she knew that was the alcohol talking, but it still hurt her feelings. She walked to the bathroom to wash her face when she was struck in the back with an orange that was on the counter.

He threw it like it was a baseball. If it had hit her head, she might have been really hurt. She was crying now, "Why did you do that? What is wrong with you?" She spent 15 minutes in the bathroom. Cold water on her face made her feel much better, but it didn't take away the sting of his words to her.

"Kaci, come one out, I'm sorry," he said, "the food will be fine whatever way you cooked it, it'll be okay." His attitude told her it wasn't okay though. She was careful to not say anything that would set him off again that night. After cleaning up the kitchen, by herself, she went to the bedroom. She just wanted a quiet place to take a much-needed nap.

He spent the afternoon in front of the tv that 'SHE' made him buy. The football games kept him occupied for hours. After a few hours, as the sun set, he bellowed through the apartment. "Kaci! What's for dinner? I'm starving."

She couldn't believe what she was hearing. Did he really expect her to cook another meal? "I'm coming, you don't have to shout." Kaci walked into the living room to see him sprawled out on the sofa, with four or five beer cans on the floor around him. Added to the ones she saw him put in the trash, that made about nine. He was definitely drunk. All she knew to do at the time, was get him some food. "What do you want? I can make turkey sandwiches, or turkey and noodles?"

"Does it have to be turkey? We just ate turkey. Don't we have anything else?" he answered belligerently.

"We always have turkey sandwiches in the evening, but let me take a look," she mumbled as she opened the cupboards. "Looks like we have chili I can make nachos. Or just a bowl of chili with a couple of hot dogs. How's that?"

"Do I have another choice?" he almost whined this time, like a spoiled little boy.

"Tuna sandwiches? Soup? Or there's some spaghetti here," she offered. She was about done being nice to him.

"Yeah, whatever, spaghetti sounds good," he grunted. "Thanks Kaci, you're the best. What would I do without you?"

Kaci thought, "Yeah I wonder.

”

# CHAPTER EIGHTEEN

Kaci had been talking to her parents about two or three times a month. Landon's parents called less than that, and he was never the one to call them. Her mom had asked if she and Landon would fly home for Christmas. Between both of their jobs, they wouldn't be able to travel that year. Evelyn said she understood, but Kaci could tell, she was disappointed. She promised she would come home in the Spring if she could.

If they were staying in New York for the holidays, Kaci intended to make their apartment festive. She loved decorating for Christmas. If she could leave a tree up all year, she would.

Luckily, they were able to find a live tree at the produce stand. It was only four feet tall, but it was cute. She had a few special ornaments she had brought from home. Her favorite was the manger ornament her grandmother had given her when she was only five. Kaci's mother had always bought her one each year. A few had fallen apart over the years, but she still had several.

Kaci hung the manger in the front most prominent branch. It didn't take long to decorate the small tree. She only had a few other personal heirloom pieces to put in the apartment.

They both had company Christmas parties to attend. Kaci's was first on the calendar. The museum was open late one night during the week. The required attire was semi-formal, because several of the museum's donors were going to be in attendance.

It was a beautiful party, just like they show on television, Kaci thought. Landon spent the night handing out his business cards to the crowd. While it seemed a bit opportunistic, but they didn't seem to mind. Mr. Wilder even spoke to Landon for several minutes about coverages and deductibles.

Kaci only had two glasses of Pinot Grigio that night. Landon, however, made himself a regular at the bar. She had counted at least five double whiskeys on the rocks. She mentally hoped he wouldn't make a fool of himself.

That night, after getting home, Landon was visibly irritated. "Why didn't you tell me about the donors coming to this party?"

"I don't know, I didn't really know who was invited, other than their names." she answered. "It didn't seem important at the time."

"Not important? That's money out there, just waiting for me. I ran out of business cards. I am expected to bring in a certain amount of new business every quarter." His words were slurred. He plopped down on the sofa and started undressing.

"I'm sorry," she said, "You never mentioned it."

"Do you think they just pay me to sit at my desk all day?" He kept on. "Hell, Kaci! Are you trying to ruin me?"

With that last remark, he got up and shoved her, and knocked her into the Christmas tree. The ornaments scattered everywhere. Landon then took his foot and stomped down hard on the manger. The tears and anger were building up inside her. She wouldn't let him have the satisfaction of seeing her cry, not anymore. She knew at that point things had changed. She didn't recognize the man in front of her. How long would he continue to berate her?

His company's party was two weeks later. Landon had told her to go by a new dress. He wanted his wife to look high-class. He described something a little sexy, but not too much. She didn't even know what that meant.

She ended up at a department store in the Upper West Side. There were racks and racks of gorgeous dresses. She went straight to the little black dress section. After she looked for almost an hour, and spent another 40 minutes in the dressing room, she purchased a sleeveless black dress with a plunging neckline and rhinestone trim. With the money he had given her, she was able to get a necklace and earrings to match.

As soon as she got home, she modeled the dress for Landon. He stared at her, with a raised eyebrow. He finally said, "Very nice, not too plain, not too fancy. I approve." He laughed at his own joke.

His party was boring for her. He tried to introduce her to his colleagues and their wives, but after an hour, he quit. Kaci was left to walk around on her own. A few of the men had stopped to talk to her, but they were only asking where her husband was. Landon eventually introduced her to Mr. Robinson, his boss.

In the posh ladies' room, she found a tray of hair styling products, perfumes and makeup to suit any need. A few of the wives were touching up their makeup. Kaci tried to make small talk, but they didn't seem interested. She was younger, and from a different class.

The dinner provided was excellent, probably the best dinner she had ever eaten. The waiter kept filling up her glass of chardonnay. After the fifth glass, she felt woozy. She excused herself and went to the ladies' room. A little cold water on her neck helped some with the hot flashes.

She was purposely shoved against the wall outside the door. It was a man she recognized as Landon's office manager. He looked at her with an evil grin. She tried to back away but ended up in the corner. Before she knew it, his hands were all over her. He grabbed at her breasts and found skin. She tried to yell, but his other hand clamped down on her mouth. Panic was surging through her body. Why wasn't anyone in that area?

"Your husband thinks he is such a stud with all the women he meets after work, did you know that?" He whispered in her ear while breathing his hot beer breath. "Turn around as fair play. He left with my date last month, so now I can have you."

As tears streamed down her face, she wiggled and finally got enough room to raise her knee. With great determination, she kneed him in his groin. As soon as his hand released her, she ran back to the table. She was glad that Landon wasn't there at that moment. She had too much information to process. She pulled a tissue from her purse and dabbed at her face, careful not to smear her makeup. Out of the corner of her eye she saw the man, Doug she thought his name was, sit down at his table across the room. He looked worse than her, she was sure.

By the time Landon had returned, she was sober enough to tell him she was ready to leave. He looked at his watch, "It's only 10 o'clock, and it's in poor taste to leave before your boss." Kaci forced a smile, sighed and took another sip of her wine. If that's what she had to do, she would be staying in her seat.

Around midnight, she grew tired of waiting for him and found Landon talking to a man in a very expensive looking suit, it appeared to shine and glisten in the light. She knew he wasn't his boss, but they seemed very chummy. She walked over and quietly took her husband's elbow and held it.

The other man turned his attention towards her, "Is this young woman the wife you were telling me about?" She stuck her hand out and he bent to kiss it, "Paul DiMaio, a pleasure to meet you."

A light bulb went off in Kaci's head. "This is the guy from the 'club' whose name was on the back of the card," she remembered. She noticed Landon had stopped talking business and was giving her a small silent nod to 'get lost.' She left him for now, but she wouldn't be staying at this party much longer.

Kaci was sitting at their table, chatting with another young wife. Her husband had worked for the company for three years. She stated that he was usually home by seven, so it wasn't as bad as it could be with some bosses. In fact, she said, Mr. Robinson made sure the office was closed by 7 o'clock Monday-Thursday and 6 o'clock on Friday.

She couldn't believe what she was hearing. Not only was Landon not expected to put in late hours; he was encouraged to take time off. That wasn't how Landon portrayed his boss. She turned around to see Landon and Mr. Robinson walking towards the table.

She tried being the cute and proper loyal wife he expected. "Would you mind getting me a taxi? I'm not feeling well, and I can get home by myself". He glared at her and turned back to apologize to his boss.

Mr. Robinson spoke up, "Landon, you'd better get her home. You should not let her leave alone. This is still a dangerous city, especially after dark."

They spent a few more minutes saying goodbye to his colleagues before walking outside to the street. "You didn't have to leave on my account," Kaci said.

"Oh, I didn't?" he sarcastically replied, "Thank you, Mom, for your approval. Shit, what was I supposed to do when my BOSS tells me to take my wife home? I had more to discuss with Mr. DiMaio. I hope he will still talk to me Monday."

"How was I supposed to know that?" she asked. "What does he do anyway?" Kaci really wanted to know but was afraid to show too much interest.

"He is a business owner with connections is all you need to know," he said. She noticed that Landon clearly had something else on his mind, which was causing his terrible mood.

They hailed a taxi and were delivered home 20 minutes later. The walk up the stairs had to have been the longest climb she ever had made she thought. Landon helped her up the last flight. As soon as they got in the door, she sank into the sofa.

Landon didn't seem to notice her and went straight to the bedroom. Not much later, Kaci joined him. She assumed he had passed out. She was wrong. He rolled over on top of her stared at her with hatred in his eyes. "Did you think I wouldn't find out about you and Doug?"

She sobbed, "What? You can't be serious?" The anger in his eyes told her that he was dead serious. She tried to move but he held her tight.

"I should have known you wouldn't be happy here," he said. "I have worked and worked to afford our lifestyle, but you want more, don't you?"

"Lifestyle?" she thought. Was he kidding? Her salary helped to pay for this apartment, furniture, food. He is out of him mind, she thought.

"I think you need to show me some of what you were showing Doug," he demanded.

"He assaulted ME Landon!" She screamed back. "I never even knew who he was until he attacked me in the hallway." She took a breath. "he said you stole his girlfriend at an after-work party, he also said you were always with another girl. What about that Landon?"

His eyes were on fire. "Do you think I would do that? Really? I thought you trusted me?" In an instant his eyes went from fury to pleading. "You know I love you" he cried into her hair. "You are the first girl I have ever loved." At that moment she was crying also. He was more drunk than she had ever seen him. He wasn't rational and his moods shifted from second to second. She had no choice but to pat his head, to tell him she was sorry, and it would all be okay. She wasn't sure how much longer she could be the one to apologize, especially when she knew she was in the right. It was like living with a time bomb. She never knew when he would explode.

His habits didn't change, however. He was still home late, smelling like a brewery, as her mother would say. Some nights he called her from what sounded like a loud bar with music blaring in the back, but most night he didn't. The stench of whiskey and smoke was impossible to ignore when he walked in.

"If you keep this up, Mr. Winkler is going to charge us extra to get the smell out of your good suits," she complained one night in fun.

"Really Kaci? Is he going to charge me 'extra'," he mocked her. "What do you care? It's my money anyway."

Kaci's mind raced with a dozen smart ass comebacks she could say, "I thought we shared everything?" "Then you can start picking up your own dry cleaning" or "Then I guess I don't need to work" but she decided it would be better to drop it.

# CHAPTER NINETEEN

The next week before Christmas they were getting along much better. She thought the holiday season had lightened his mood and he was the Landon she met in college. They decided to go to Rockefeller Center and gave ice skating a try. She was always good with balance, and it didn't take her long to go around like a real New Yorker. Landon never stayed on his feet for more than a minute. He spent most of their rink time on the bench watching Kaci. She didn't think he would want to wait for her, but he did.

Instead of buying presents that year, Kaci and Landon had agreed to spend most of their Christmas money on a summer vacation at the beach. That didn't stop Kaci from getting Landon a few things for under the tree. On Christmas Eve, they unwrapped the presents their parents had sent them.

Evelyn and Walter sent them a couples' gift, a new DVD player with a couple of Kaci's old favorite movies, Miracle on 34th Street and Annie Hall.

"I guess 'New York' was the theme," Kaci said. Her mom even sent a new ornament, a big apple. His parents sent gift cards to a nice restaurant, one that Michael probably recommended.

The next morning, Kaci jumped out of bed like a nine-year old. She wondered what 'Santa' brought her. She was busy cooking a big breakfast for Landon when he finally woke up.

"What got into you?" he asked. "Why aren't you sleeping in? We don't have to go to work today. Come back to bed."

"It's Christmas, Landon," she answered. "Aren't you excited?" His expression told her he wasn't. "Well, I am. It's the most wonderful time of the year, remember?" She felt like singing carols but refrained.

After they ate, she led him by the hand to sit in his recliner and started handing him the small gifts. She could see he didn't put anything under the tree, it was hard not to notice. She had just assumed he bought it last minute and didn't have time to wrap it.

He opened a new wallet, printed socks with a matching tie and a bottle of the cologne Kaci loved so much. He looked at her expecting face, "I thought we weren't doing presents Kaci? I'm sorry I'm just confused. Thank you for these, they're great."

"Well yeah, but I wanted to get you a few things I knew you'd like," she said. The look on his face told her he wasn't prepared. "So, are you saying you didn't get me anything," she asked.

Landon hopped up and walked towards the bedroom. "No, I did too, but I, uh, forgot to put it under the tree, give me a minute." He spent about ten minutes before coming out with 2 small packages. The first one was the size of a small shoebox, in fact it was a small shoebox, to one of her recently purchased pair of heels. She opened it to find a plaid scarf. It still had the tags on from an upscale store on Madison Avenue. She remembered the store sold mainly menswear, but maybe they had unisex gifts also.

"This is pretty Landon," she said, slightly disappointed, "thank you." The second small box was smaller than the first, inside was a nice ink pen, like someone would receive at graduation or at work. Would it kill him to be a little more thoughtful or romantic when picking out a gift? Kaci was starting to see a pattern in his gifts.

"We can't have you catching a cold," he said as he leaned over and gave her a peck on the forehead. "I have one more thing, but I didn't get a card for it."

He pulled out a Starbucks gift card from his pocket. She rarely got their coffee because it was so overpriced. Landon loved it of course, he felt like one of the big executives when he brought a cup into work, not a man who struggled to pay his bills.

She thought these gifts were ones he received at work from his co-workers. They could have even been a Pollyanna gift because they were all generic, unsentimental. She realized that at her birthday, she'd better start hinting weeks prior.

New Year's Eve was another traditional New York City holiday. The crowds started gathering in Times Square as early as 1 p.m. Since the weather was mild by New York standards, a 'balmy' 40 degrees, they expected crowds doubled in size from the previous year. Even though it was their first New Year's Eve in New York, they had decided to stay home and ring in the new year in front of the tv, watching Dick Clark.

At midnight, they clinked their champagne glasses and kissed. "Here's to a more prosperous year," Landon said.

Kaci gave a small laugh, "Oh ok, very romantic. How about here's to our health and happiness?"

"Yeah, that too," he added with a wink.

January was cold with more snow. It seemed like every weekend the latest blizzard came through, dumping over four inches. Even though most people didn't venture out, that didn't stop Landon. He still went to work every morning and came home late from work.

The next time she took his suits and shirts to Mr. Winkler's she saw cream-colored smudges on the front of more than one of his shirts. She smelled the shirt. It was definitely a perfume smell, probably a girl's makeup on the shirt, looked like foundation that had rubbed off.

Wonderful, Kaci thought to herself. She was embarrassed to even bring the shirt into Mr. Winkler, but they had to be cleaned. She put the shirts in the bottom of the bag she used to carry the dirty clothes.

"Well good morning, Mona Lisa," he sang as she entered the dry cleaners. His tune changed when he saw her face. "What's bothering you?"

She had grown fond of Mr. Winkler, and he was always easy to talk to. He reminded her a little of her dad. He never spoke a harsh word to anyone that she knew of. And he was always a great listener. Sometimes that's all she needed was someone to listen to her. When they moved up there, she lost contact with almost all her friends, and she found it hard to make new ones.

"Is it that obvious Mr. Winkler?" she sighed. "I've been trying to not think about it, but it's not easy when your husband flaunts his late-night fun in your face. It's apparent that he doesn't care about hurting my feelings. He acts better for a short time, then back to the same old thing".

The look in the older man's eyes told her he had seen this before. "Young couples go through hard times at the beginning," he explained, trying to be gentle. "Not everyone is meant to be together. It's something you would need to think about. What is it worth to you to stay married?"

# CHAPTER TWENTY

The winter months were very cold in the city. The only thing that made it bearable to her was the site of fresh fallen snow blanketing the streets. Kaci felt like things were getting better between them, he even made plans for them to go out of town for Valentine's Day. Landon told her he had saved for a couple months and received a holiday bonus that he hadn't mentioned before now. She had a feeling that after seeing her disappointment at Christmas, he decided to make up for it now.

He walked in from work one night with travel brochures to Scribner's Lodge in the Catskills. He had booked a room at the lodge for the long weekend. He made sure she knew that because it was President's Day weekend and Valentine's Day, the rates were at the top of the scale. This was their prime tourist season. He also mentioned that one of his clients helped him get the reservation.

It was supposed to be a gorgeous weekend with snow, fireplaces, and great food. Once they were away from the distractions of home, she and Landon really enjoyed being together. She was sure to be attentive. She didn't want to appear ungrateful, but she didn't know how they could afford this vacation, especially when they were going to the beach that summer.

She walked in on him on a phone call the day before they were leaving. He rarely got phone calls at home, so this one made her curious.

"You don't know how much I appreciate this opportunity Mr. Bottino," he said, "I look forward to seeing you at the Lodge."

Now it made sense, Kaci thought. This wasn't a vacation; it was a business trip paid for by Michael Bottino. Kaci guessed that Landon invited her so she would think he paid for all this for her birthday. She quietly went back to the bedroom to finish packing. She concluded that at least she would get to see the mountains, even if he was busy.

When they got to their room, candies were laid out on the bed and fresh flowers were in the vase. It really was a beautiful place. She decided she was going to make the best of it. Landon encouraged her to book a spa appointment for the next morning. She was happy to do so.

There was a cocktail party before the 7 p.m. dinner seating. Just as they were about to look for their table for two, Michael walked over.

"Well, look who it is, Landon!" he greeted them, "Nice to see you again. And your lovely wife, Katie, right?"

"Kaci, what a surprise Mr. Bottino," Kaci answered him. She was annoyed that this wonderful friend or client of Landon's, that she has seen almost several times couldn't remember her name.

"You two need to join me at my table," he said. It wasn't really a question as much as a statement. "I insist." They all sat down as Michael ordered an expensive bottle of wine for the table to share. She sipped slowly and tried to pay attention to their conversation. As usual, it sounded like stock market stuff, which she had no interest in.

When they got back to the room Landon said, "Wasn't that a surprise? I had no idea he would be up here." He went into the bathroom as Kaci started undressing for the night.

She spoke to him through the door, 'Really? It looks like you planned it that way. I thought this was our vacation?"

Landon tried to look shocked and offended when he opened the door. Instead of arguing with her, he started talking about business opportunities and making more money. She knew there was no talking to him now.

On the ride home in the rental car they had picked up, Landon pointed out the little suburbs along their way. "One day, we'll be able to afford a nice little house out here. If I keep doing as well as I have been, Mr. Robinson has been talking to me about a promotion.

"That's exciting for you, Landon," she mumbled. She wasn't sure a promotion was as exciting for her.

"Hell yeah," he replied, "it's more than exciting. It's a great opportunity to make some real money for a change. Surely, you're not mad about that?"

"No, I'm not mad," she sighed. "I just have a feeling we will see even less of each other, that's all."

Landon shrugged his shoulders and gave her hand a gentle squeeze. "It'll be fine, I promise." Her feelings didn't ever enter his mind when he was thinking about money.

They got back into town and back into the routine of work. Date nights were still a thing they strived to have each week. Sometimes though, Landon's work got in the way. Kaci had gotten used to being home alone in the evenings. She started doing cross-stitch needlework as a hobby. Her first one was a family tree diagram made for her parents.

Landon did start working later, but when he did get home, he didn't smell of alcohol most of the time. She saw this as a step in the right direction. Maybe he was finally settling down. He would come home exhausted. He would just eat dinner and go to bed most nights.

As they laid in bed one snowy morning after their mini vacation, she asked him what had been on her mind for over a year, "When can we start talking about starting a family?" He stopped reading the financial pages and started laughing.

"What? Are you serious?" he said. "Oh, I guess you are," he added when he saw her face.

"I thought you wanted to start a family as much as I did," she said.

"I don't know," he answered, "I haven't really thought that much about it. Now isn't a good time, that's for sure." He didn't know if he would ever be ready to have a family.

"Landon," she said, "I didn't mean this minute but I would like to have an idea. I just meant talking about it, in the future.'

He got up and went to the bathroom, "We'll see I guess, depends on work and how things go." He knew he was not the father type.

Kaci was visibly disappointed. She spent the day trying to find a way to convince Landon that a baby is a wonderful addition to their family.

# CHAPTER TWENTY-ONE

By late Spring, her parents were begging to see her. She flew back home for Easter weekend. Kaci really noticed the quietness of her small town for the first time. It was a nice break from the noise of New York. During her flight, she began to think about her future. How happy was she in her marriage? No relationship was perfect she knew. Everybody said it would take work, she just never expected it to be this much work. Every day, she was asking 'herself how would Landon react' to this or that. It just wasn't normal or healthy.

She called her husband as soon as she got to her parents' house. Kaci made a point of calling him almost daily. Truth be known, she was making a note of how often he was home and when he wasn't. He had said he'd been busy at work, talking to clients and trying to earn his way up to another raise.

She tried calling one evening but didn't get an answer. It was pretty late in New York so she wondered if he was already asleep. But, in her heart she knew he wasn't sitting at home. He never was very good at being alone, she knew.

Her flight was scheduled to come in at 5 p.m. Monday. She asked Landon before she left for the airport if he could meet her when her flight arrived. His first reaction told her he wouldn't be very helpful. "You know I'm working Kaci. I can't just take off whenever you want me to."

She didn't want to fight about it so she agreed and said she would just get a taxi home. Her flight had a layover in Chicago. The next flight was delayed over an hour, waiting on maintenance crew. By the time she landed in La Guardia it was after 7 o'clock. She called Landon from the pay phone as soon as she could.

"Where are you?" he barked at her. "You were supposed to be home hours ago."

"You know I couldn't call you from the plane, but we were delayed," she explained. "We spent almost an hour on the tarmac. I thought maybe you could come pick me up?"

"You're kidding right?" he scoffed, "that's just a waste of money. Just take a taxi like we planned. I'll be here when you get home."

She was grateful to the cab driver who carried her suitcases into the foyer of the building. By the time she dragged them upstairs, she was exhausted. Landon was waiting for her on their sofa. She gave him a big kiss. She really did miss her husband. An hour ago, her answer might have been different. But, seeing him, brought a smile to her face. She accepted his warm hug, and they went to bed.

# CHAPTER TWENTY-TWO

Summer came, along with their anniversary. They spent that weekend at the Jersey Shore, this was the trip they had planned for months. Landon had rented a car for the trip. They were both allowed to leave work early Friday, in order to make it to Cape May before midnight. He had booked a room at a Victorian Bed & Breakfast, just one block from the beach. They awoke to the sound of seagulls and waves on the beach outside their window.

It was only 7 o'clock but they could smell wonderful fragrances from the kitchen, coffee, bacon and who knew what else awaited them. They weren't disappointed. Kaci ate quickly, she wanted to see the beach. They walked hand in hand to the sand where a small walking trail took them to the water.

"I could listen to this all day," Kaci said as she smiled and drank in the beach around her. "It's so relaxing, not like the city for sure."

"Wouldn't you get bored?" he asked. "You've seen one beach; you've seen them all. And the ocean water is just gross."

"I really don't think so." She sat down on a towel they brought and dug her toes in the cool sand. Seagulls were floating all around on the search for food.

They had reservations at the famous Lobster House for dinner, but before that they strolled down Washington Mall, looking in the shops. The outdoor mall was very quaint and picturesque. Something right out of a Thomas Kincaid painting, she thought.

It was a wonderful weekend. They drove back to the city in the late afternoon on Sunday. They were too tired to check the answering machine when they got home.

The next morning, she noticed it was flashing and hit the button. "Landon, please pick up. I need your help. Garrett told me how to reach you. Your son is in the hospital."

Kaci was frozen in place. What did the woman just say? Son? Who was on the machine? She immediately called Landon's office and left a message for him to call her, immediately. She had no idea what was going on and she didn't like that feeling.

It was lunchtime before she heard from Landon. "What's so urgent Kaci?" he was clearly annoyed.

"One question, and be honest with me," she started. "Do you have a son?"

The other end was silent, she only heard his breathing. "Why do you ask? What's going on?" His tone was turning from nervous to defensive.

"That's what I want to know Landon. DO YOU have a SON?" She made sure he knew she wasn't playing around.

"Well, since you asked so nicely,' he said sarcastically. "Yes, I do."

"Why didn't you tell me about him?" She could not believe what she was hearing. How could he have not told her? What else is he hiding?

"You never asked if I had kids," he unemotionally confessed, although it wasn't meant as an apology.

She couldn't believe what she was hearing. Why didn't he think that was important? She waited for an explanation. "Is that why you don't want to start a family with me? Because you already have one?"

"Geez Kaci, calm down," he said. "This has nothing to do with you and everything to do with an ex-girlfriend who was trying to trap me." Why couldn't she just leave him alone, he thought.

"Surely you told her you wanted a paternity test," she asked. Somehow, she knew it wasn't all the girl's fault. He is the type to have denied it to his grave. She was certain his parents were paying his child support.

"Of course, I did," he answered. "He's mine. In DNA only. His name is Kyle, and he's six, I guess. It was a mistake, that's for sure. But she wouldn't get an abortion so here we are."

She had to brush her anger at his last statement aside and get to what was going on now. "When was the last time you saw him?" This was getting worse and worse. How would they get through this?

"I haven't really 'seen' him. I saw pictures my mother sent me that first year." he said. "In the last one, he was about two maybe."

What irritated her the most, besides the fact that he had lied to her, was that he didn't care. Not one birthday card or phone call that she was aware he made. The comment about an abortion made it clear he never wanted a child. "Why? Why haven't you called him?"

"His mother and I didn't exactly part on good terms," he explained. "She said she didn't need me in his life, so I gave her what she wanted." He wouldn't admit to her that he had no desire to be a dad to this boy, maybe not ever. "She wasn't a very good person, Kaci. You know what I mean, wrong side of the tracks. She was cute but not in your class at all."

Kaci could rationalize his feelings. If this girl was as he said, a gold digger and low-class, she knew why he didn't keep in touch. She thought if the tables were turned and she was in her shoes, she might have felt the same. However, that shouldn't mean his son would have to wonder why he didn't have a father.

He needed to get back to work. He abruptly informed her they would discuss it when he got home. She knew he was right, no need to keep talking about it now. That gave her time to think about what she wanted to say. Her mind was racing about their talk about having kids. She was jealous that he shut down their talk about it, but she didn't know he already had a child with another woman.

He got home the usual time, around 7 o'clock. And he did smell like whiskey. If anyone needed a stiff drink, it was him. She just hoped he could and would call the mother. The only sounds in the room were the tv of the family next door and the cars honking in the street below. He finally said, "I guess I'll take a walk and call her and find out what's so important."

When he returned, he explained that Kyle has acute leukemia and needed a bone marrow transplant. His parents insisted he needed to get tested to see if he was a match. Landon knew deep down it was the right thing to do, but he was the King of Avoidance.

Natalie had said they were lucky that St. Jude's Hospital in Memphis provided free cancer treatment. Almost all their costs would be covered. They just couldn't find donors for every patient. Money wouldn't solve this problem as it had in the past.

Getting tested meant Landon had to take off several days from work. He wasn't happy to have to ask for time off for something that wasn't a vacation day. Thankfully, Mr. Walker didn't ask questions. He had the days off to use, it was nobody's business what he did with them.

Kaci accompanied him to the hospital the next week. They couldn't waste any time. Cancer wasn't going to wait to fit into his schedule. The technicians who administered the test made sure Landon understood he was the best possible donor. A blood relative was more likely to match than a stranger, and that was even a long shot.

"Why don't I just tell her I'm not a match? It's unlikely I will match anyway, then I won't have to go through this procedure."

"Landon! You can't be serious?" she exclaimed. Could he really be that callous and selfish? She gave his hand a tight squeeze. "I'll be right here through everything."

Within a few days, Landon found out he was a match, booked his flight and was back in Clarksville. He would drive to Memphis the next day and hotel room where he would comfortable, not in some awful hospital room. He was going to make sure Kyle's mother never contacted him again by having her sign a legal document, absolving Landon of any future financial claims against him. It would probably require a one-time payment of several thousands, but he knew his parents would pay it. They had been trying to make this problem go away since the beginning.

# CHAPTER TWENTY-THREE

Being alone in New York turned out being very exciting for her. She had thought she would be nervous to go anywhere except work and to the corner store, but that wasn't the case at all. Every day she took a different route to work and discovered several new stores and restaurants she made a note to tell Landon about when he got back. For the first time in years, she slept alone. She had never realized how on edge she was until she wasn't. And, for the first time in months she felt like she could really breathe.

Life with Landon had not been easy. His mood swings changed every week, sometimes daily. Most days she spent too much time wondering what state he would be in when he got home. The verbal abuse had been almost a daily event by the time he left for Memphis. She attributed a lot of it to the stress surrounding the surgery. At least she hoped that was the reason.

One evening, on her way home from work, she noticed a small black and white kitten following her. She decided she needed a companion, so she scooped up the little ball of fur. When she got home, she found a small bowl to hold milk. The kitten eagerly lapped it up in a few minutes and she had a new roommate.

"I guess I'm going to need to get you a name," she said out loud. "Are you a boy or a girl? I guess it won't matter for now. How do you feel about 'Scrappy'? The kitten turned and walked away, obviously he didn't like it. "Max?" "Tiffany?" She tried several names, but none seemed to fit, or catch the kitten's attention. "Lola"? As soon as she said it, she knew it was right. Lola came back to her and climbed into her lap.

That night she improvised with torn up newspaper for a litter box and a can of tuna for her food. The next morning, she would need to find a pet store. She thought she remembered passing one on one of her alternate routes yesterday.

When she walked into Mr. Winkler's dry cleaner to pick up their weekly order, he commented, "You look very happy today, Mona Lisa."

She never imagined other people had noticed any difference. She spent a few extra minutes telling him all about Lola. "A pet is a good thing for you," he agreed.

She had made plans to meet with Oliver every day while Landon was away. They talked about the city, local favorite spots, where he grew up, and where she grew up. The conversation inevitably ended up at how unhappy she was in her marriage. Oliver was like a father to her, she respected him and trusted him.

"One day," he told her, "When you can't stay any longer, come find me and I'll make sure you are safe. At the very least I can offer you friendship and a place to sleep."

Kaci got choked up. She couldn't believe what she heard. Was she really strong enough to walk away? She had no idea how she could and yet, she knew she couldn't stay forever. She kept telling herself that other women probably had it much worse than she did. He didn't really beat her, he just intimidated her and pushed her around a little.

Landon was flying home in a few days. The surgery went well. Even though he never told Kyle who he was, Kyle got what he needed, his bone marrow. She told him about Lola, and he didn't have a reaction. He just said, "Whatever". In her mind, saying 'Whatever", when someone was speaking to you, was one of the rudest things you could do. It basically told the other person that their opinion or feelings didn't matter.

Their lease on the apartment ended the month before. They gave their notice that they would be moving asap. Staying in that neighborhood didn't fit with Landon's plans. He told her about a nice apartment Paul owned and had offered to him at a great price. He was excited to tell her the good news.

"What's the catch?" Kaci asked first. "It can't be that easy."

"Shit, you really don't trust me, do you? No catch, I have helped him make a lot of money and he is repaying the favor." It was just like her to be ungrateful and suspicious, he thought.

The new place was beautiful and had several advantages, including washer and dryer, dishwasher, central heat and air, a second bedroom and half bath. She agreed he found the perfect place; even if there were strings attached. It only took her a week to pack up the few things they had. She was doing it alone because Landon couldn't be bothered. He claimed he did his job getting the place. Luckily, Mr. DiMaio offered them help in the form of muscle to make the move in a couple of hours.

Now, she thought, things will be better. She can provide the home Landon expected. All thoughts of leaving had gone away. The only sad part of moving, was leaving Mr. Winkler and Oliver. She had told both men she was going to try to come by every few weeks to check on them.

Kaci started looking for a new job that offered better pay and a shorter commute. She interviewed at several offices, medical, lawyers, accounting. When she went to the advertising firm of Branch and Glenn in the World Trade Center, she got a great vibe. She loved the energy behind the doors. The interview went great, and she was offered the job before she left.

That winter, Landon got promoted to Senior Account Executive, which led to more late nights. As hard as she tried, their relationship got worse, not better. When he wasn't home, she knew he was almost always with Paul at the club. A strip club has a certain smell about it, booze, smoke and sex.

She couldn't ignore his disregard for her feelings and the general way he treated her any longer. He was routinely belittling her and making her feel even more alone than she was. In her mind, she dreamt of being a single woman in New York City. There were so many things she wanted to do that she knew she would never get the chance if she stayed married to Landon. But she also knew she couldn't afford living alone.

Kaci made notes of the times he got home and anything he would tell her about his day. She had a sneaky suspicion that not everything he was involved in was legal. If it was, why didn't he invite her to come along? Or even mention what he was really doing?

One day she left work early to run some errands. She was going to the local market, when a limousine pulled up beside her. The rear window rolled down, and she saw Paul DiMaio in the back seat. "Mrs. Jamison, please come with me for a short ride around the block."

Kaci didn't know what she should do. Her heart pounded as she quickly looked around to yell for help if needed. She didn't want to offend him or make Landon angry if he heard about it. All she could do, she decided, was to get in and see what he wanted. Kaci was very aware of her surroundings at that moment, as if she was tacking a mental photograph. Maybe she had watched too many movies about the Mafia. But she wasn't taking any chances.

The inside of the new vehicle already smelled of whiskey and cigars. He politely offered her a seat across from him. "I hope I didn't scare you Mrs. Jamison. But I thought we needed to have a conversation." He took out a glass from the bar and offered her a glass of wine.

"No, thank you, Mr. DiMaio." she was very curious about his intent. "I'm confused, what did you want to talk to me about?" She played the small-town girl role and acted like she had no idea about anything.

"Let's just say your husband has been very helpful and his loyalty is appreciated." He calmly told her in a soft voice. "He has gone above and beyond for me. I have asked him numerous times to talk to you about his role in my organization, but he insisted it wasn't necessary. That you would do as you were told." The chauffeur drove past the apartment again. "But, as you can see," he continued, "I wasn't born yesterday. If I address every potential problem early on, then I can't be surprised. And I hate surprises."

"I'm not sure I understand," she asked again. "Landon hasn't said anything to me about work." In her mind, this was sounding exactly like what she feared. Landon was involved with the Mafia.

"I also am smart enough to know that you, as a bright young woman, have your own mind and can think for yourself. I would just ask if there was ever some personal information you came across in your apartment, or on his person," he said, "I expect that information to be private and to not be discussed."

He looked at her with a raised eyebrow. "I don't think that's asking too much. Do you? Are we understanding each other?" He patted her on the knee and grinned. "Let's say someone calls for Landon and he isn't home. Don't ask any questions, no messages, just a quick 'he's not home', will suffice."

"Yes Mr. DiMaio," she was scared to say anything at that point. "I can assure you I haven't seen anything personal. And Landon certainly doesn't discuss his business with me."

"That's a good thing, Mrs. Jamison," he went on, "you see, this city can be very dangerous, even in these nicest neighborhoods. Accidents happen all around us."

Kaci shuddered visibly at his warning. She didn't like him at all. He let her out in the same spot he picked her up. She watched as the limo turned at the corner. Only then did she exhale. She didn't know if she needed to tell Landon, or just keep this incident to herself.

She ended up calling Oliver and asked him to meet her in Central Park. She had to talk to someone she trusted. Jack ran up to her, so happy to see his friend. Kaci gave Oliver a big hug. She missed their talks. They walked through the paths, lightly covered with a dusting of snow. She held onto his elbow, and he listened to her.

# CHAPTER TWENTY-FOUR

By the time she got home it was almost 7 o'clock. Landon was sitting in his recliner, a glass of scotch in his hand. By the look on his face, it wasn't his first glass that evening.

"Where have you been?" he barked. "You complain that I'm not home at a decent hour, so I get home early and you're not even here!"

"I just went for a walk to see the park with the snow," she answered, trying hard not to look guilty. He wasn't born yesterday, he thought there had to be another reason she wasn't home at this hour.

"Is that so? Do you have a boyfriend you're seeing behind my back?" he demanded to know. Did she do this every night and he just never found out?

"You're kidding right?" she answered. "I have been here every single night. You can ask the Super. I don't leave after I get home, except a once or twice a month maybe."

"You obviously didn't care that I would be here, waiting for dinner." At that moment he jumped up out of the chair and lunged at her. Within a second, he had grabbed her hair and pulled her into the kitchen. "I think you'd better start cooking."

Kaci backed away as much as possible, into a corner, her heart was racing. Was he going to hit her? She couldn't be sure. He was in her face, spitting, "Before you go thinking you are irreplaceable, you aren't. But you can't survive here without me. So, it looks like I hold the cards." He grabbed her elbow, squeezing so hard she thought it might break, and shoved her into the stove.

She quickly threw together a meal of hamburger patties with mashed potatoes and gravy and vegetables. As she suspected, he had plenty to say about it.

"What's this garbage," he shouted, "You know I ate a cheeseburger for lunch." He took a bite and continued to eat it, grumbling the whole time.

She felt the tension increasing as she waited for his next outburst of cruelty. How much longer could she take his mood swings? Landon wasn't the man she met in college. He had turned into a callous workaholic.

Thankfully for Kaci, he went to the sofa, and drifted off to sleep. How many more nights of this could she endure? Was there anything Mr. DiMaio had said that could give her any safety from Landon? It appeared she was all alone.

She took a chance the next evening and told him about DiMaio's visit and warning. "I'm not sure what he was talking about Landon? What do I know? OR should I say, what do you know?" His face grew tight, and he held his breathe. Kaci waited nervously for his reply.

"What do you mean? What are you talking about?" he asked, clearly flustered. She knew he was trying to act innocent and unaware of DiMaio's business.

"That's what I'm asking you Landon. Why would he threaten me?" She was getting worried by the minute.

"Ok. I really think you misunderstood what he was saying. He wouldn't come out and threaten you, or anyone else for that matter. But I would say, if he wanted to scare you, then I would be very careful. He has done things or arranged things to ensure loyalty from his colleagues." Landon started to calm down. After finally letting the secret out he actually looked almost relieved. He was arrogant enough to think he was invincible.

The very thought that Landon was involved with a gangster made her shiver in fear. She rubbed her upper arms as if to warm up the chilly feeling. She knew her life in New York was in danger, how could she live this way? But she also knew that those types of people have ways of tracking you down. She couldn't just move back home.

For the time being, she made sure his dinner was waiting for him at 7 o'clock. A few times he got home before it was ready, but it was cooking. In the evenings, she would either read in bed, or watch tv if he was in the bedroom. She was grateful Lola was with her, always ready for a snuggle.

The days turned into weeks, and months. Spring passed and they were into the hot summer months too quickly it seemed to her. Her parents noticed the change in her voice when they talked but she never opened up to them about her problems.

Every day she thought of what she really wanted in life. She just knew she wasn't happy.

And that's the way it went until September 11, 2001.

# PART THREE

# CHAPTER TWENTY-FIVE

She knew this was her chance to escape, to disappear. She didn't have much money on her and knew she couldn't pull money out of the ATM undetected. She did have her wedding ring set that she could sell or pawn if she needed. Other than that, she had a hundred dollars she had saved for surprise Christmas present.

The phone began ringing and she hesitated to answer it. As soon as she heard her mother's voice, she hurriedly picked up the phone. "Kaci, honey," her mother's voice cried out in relief when she answered. "Yes, Momma it's me. I'm here. I'm okay. I have to hurry and get off the phone, but I will call you back tonight. Just don't say anything about talking to me to anyone, especially not Landon."

"Why? What's wrong honey? Why can't I talk to Landon?" her mother sounded very confused. As far as her parents knew, their marriage was fine.

"I'll explain later, just don't say a word, please."

She grabbed an old backpack from the back of the hall closet and threw in only the basics, underwear, some tees and shorts, leggings, and toiletries. She made sure to throw any wet towels, robe in the hamper. She took one last look at the apartment, she grabbed her address book, with her personal contacts, off the counter, put a hoodie on, pulled the hood to cover her face, and left. She had been sure to grab her dirty clothes and shoes and threw them in a dumpster down the street. As she turned to look back at the Brownstone, she was surprised to see Landon walking up the front steps. She couldn't believe how close he had been to catching her.

Oliver answered his door and ushered her inside. "Thank the Lord, you are a sight for sore eyes," he said, giving her a quick hug and welcoming her inside. She had called him as soon as she left. It had taken her over an hour to get through on her cell phone. Time had stood still in the city, but at the same time seemed to be moving too quickly for her.

"You need to throw that phone away," he advised. "Do not take it out of the city. I've heard they can track people that way." She wasn't taking any chances now, so she threw it on his concrete patio and stomped on it. No one would be tracking that phone.

Kaci borrowed his house phone and dialed her parents' number. She didn't know how to explain what was going on, they were an hour behind Eastern Time Zone, so it was just now getting to be 11 a.m. They picked up on the first ring.

"Hello? Kaci? Is that you?" her mother cried into the phone. She was sure thousands of family members and friends were getting the same phone calls, if they were the lucky ones to have walked away.

"Yes, Momma, it's me," she whispered, getting choked up. "I need you to listen carefully, I am okay. I wasn't at work when this happened. But I am leaving Landon, right now. I can't live this way any longer. You can't tell him anything when he calls. Please just say you haven't heard from me. And whatever you do, don't tell him that I have contacted you. Let him think I died in the terror attack."

"Honey," she interjected, "what are you talking about? Where are you going?"

"I don't honestly know at the moment, but you will be the first to know," she assured her mother. "I promise." She spoke to her dad also and they said their goodbyes, for now.

She met Oliver outside on his small courtyard, playing with Jack, and grilling some burgers. The sirens and traffic were still ringing in the air. Later that evening, Kaci was glued to the television coverage of the day's tragic events. All her bottled-up emotions flooded out and she cried without regret. All her co-workers, dead. Her old life gone too.

Lola had made herself comfortable in Jack's dog bed. Oddly enough, Jack didn't seem to mind the company. She knew the cat had found her new home.

She was so nervous at the journey she had ahead of her. Kaci was also sad that she would never see Oliver again, or Mr. Winkler. Without them, she would never have had the courage or the means to leave.

The next morning, Oliver had tried to buy her a bus ticket out of town, but no buses were running yet. His next attempt with Amtrak was the same. They both told him that perhaps the next day or two. She spent the next three days hiding in his apartment. She wasn't going to risk anyone seeing her, not even a neighbor.

He came back the next afternoon from Jack's walk with an interesting story. Oliver told her that he ran into Landon in the little park. He appeared frantic and was asking questions about her. He assured Kaci that he didn't say anything to indicate he had seen her that week, let alone that she was living in his spare bedroom.

"I wonder why he's looking for me. Was I being followed by one of his 'associates'?" Kaci wondered out loud. "I thought everyone would assume I was in my office when the plane hit." It was something that would weigh on her mind, she was sure. Was there evidence to the contrary? She couldn't worry about that now, she just needed to get out of the city.

By Saturday, she was sitting on a Greyhound bus, headed west. She remembered something from philosophy class, a Phoenix will rise from the ashes and start anew. That is what she felt like now as she left the city. The bus was eerily quiet, filled with all types of passengers, desperate to leave.

She sat next to a woman who looked to be about 50. Shelly was on her way to stay with her daughter in Cincinnati. "Who knows what will happen tomorrow or next month," she explained, "all I know is I'm going to be with my family. I'm not sticking around here to find out when and where the next attack will happen."

"Sorry, my mind wandered off," she said. She had been lost in thoughts of what-ifs. "This week has been very emotional for me too. My name is, uh," she suddenly realized she needed a new name, "Nina, nice to meet you." She chose the name of one of the girls in her office, who she was sure perished in the attack, just in case.

After the sun went down the cabin of the bus was almost pitch dark, she and Shelly softly talked about their lives and family. The older woman told of her family being from the eastern hills of Kentucky. Her childhood was a little rough, not much money in her house.

"We were all expected to get a job as soon as we turned 14," she said. "My parents didn't really think high school was of any value. So, I started at the shirt factory, operating the button machine."

Nina could see the far-away look in her eyes. "I had worked there for six years when my mother passed away. As soon as I could, I moved to Richmond. It's a college town and I easily found a job and a cheap room until I got my own apartment. That's when I met Hank. The rest is history as they say."

Shelly had a sweet, loving smile on her face as she was lost in her fond memories. "Now, it's your turn."

# CHAPTER TWENTY-SIX

While Kaci was still in the neighborhood, at Oliver's, Landon was calling everyone he could remember. He had come home that afternoon to find their door wide open. No sign of her being there, or the cat. He was sure the car ran off in the chaos.

Nobody from the museum had heard from her, neither had Mr. Wilder. He was supposed to think she perished in the office building however, her cat was missing. He knew Kaci would not leave Lola. She adored that cat. Sure, the car probably ran off, but don't they come home to whoever feeds them. She should saunter back in any minute, he thought.

Landon had returned Mr. DiMaio's call as soon as he heard the message. "Hello, sir, yes, I just got to my apartment. You don't happen to know anything about my wife, do you?" He was starting to feel the hair stand up on the back of his neck. Something was going on he was sure of it.

"Now, now, calm down," he started off, the tone was very condescending, and made Landon even more nervous. "We are a family, and we take care of our own." As if that was the only explanation he needed to provide, he was in the midst of hanging up when Landon shouted back.

"Now wait a minute! Sir, please! I'm sorry to have yelled," he apologized.

"You'll need to watch that," DiMaio answered, "I don't appreciate it. And weren't you the one who complained that he didn't want to be married anymore. It was a nuisance, you said."

"Again, I'm sorry, Mr. DiMaio," he pleaded. "Yes, I said that, but I didn't really mean it. Can you please tell me if my wife is out there? Do you know of anything that might have kept her from being home?"

"All I can tell you, Landon, is that things happen for a reason," he said. "You may not like what you find out if you keep looking for her."

The phone was dead. He stood there for a minute, trying to figure out what DiMaio meant by his statement. Would he really have arranged for Kaci to go missing? Even kill her. Why? She wasn't smart enough to be any threat to them. It just didn't make any sense to him.

That week, Landon spent every evening after work going to all the places Kaci visited regularly. Mr. Winkler hadn't seen her. Landon had to describe her since the man didn't recognize him. "Ahh, you mean Mona Lisa," he answered Landon.

"Who? Her name is Kaci Jamison. Surely you know her, she brings our dry cleaning in every week," he said.

"Oh yes I know her," he said with hesitation. "I call her Mona Lisa because of her job in the museum. And she always had such a pleasant smile."

Landon thanked him and left a business card in case he saw her. He also stopped at the grocery, produce stand, coffee shop. Nobody in their old neighborhood had seen her. He was really getting worried.

His office was still closed the next day so he spent that time trying to find anyone who would know his wife. He was at the museum when they opened. He asked for Mr. Wilder first. Landon had to remind him who he was, but he remembered Kaci fondly.

"She was such a sweet woman, always very attentive to the visitors, especially the children." He added, "I can't believe she's gone."

"Wait a minute," Landon interjected, "nobody said she was gone. Do you know something you're not telling me?"

"Of course not, but this past week has caused heartache all over the city," Wilder finished, "Even the country."

Clarissa came up to their conversation. "I'm sorry to eavesdrop, but are you Kaci's husband?" She gave him a thorough inspection. He certainly didn't look like the monster Kaci had told her about a few times. She attributed it to newlywed squabbles. "I do know Kaci used to go to the park several times a week, maybe someone there will recognize her."

Landon excitedly got up and made his way to the exit. This was more information than he had heard in days. He knew she went to the park, why didn't he think of that? And what was that man's name with the little dog? Was it Jack? No, that's the dog, he remembered. It will come to him later he hoped. If he was lucky, the master and dog would be there today.

He ran across the busy street to the benches where Kaci had told him she took her lunches. For a brief minute, he really thought he missed her. It didn't last long. She was just an obstacle in his plan to advance in DiMaio's organization. However much he didn't want to be married to her, he never thought she would be dead.

Landon was surprised to see how many people were in the park, walking, talking and just sitting. It appeared they were taking in the beauty of nature. After the terrifying events of that week, people just wanted the calm of the outdoors. He thought the best way to look was to not look.

He found an empty bench and sat down. He intended to try and look relaxed. It wasn't easy. His nerves were fried. All he wanted was to know is if she died in the attack or was, he going to be charged with murder? He knew the FBI was always watching DiMaio and the nightclub.

When his current location didn't yield any results in finding the man with the dog, he moved about a block down the street. It was only a few minutes later that he recognized the dog. He started barking as soon as he saw Landon. "Stupid dog", he thought.

The man seemed like he was trying to avoid Landon, but maybe he was just imagining it. He called out to him, which made the dog growl and bark even more. He jogged over to the path where Oliver was holding Jack back with a tight leash.

"Hey, man," Landon started, "Don't you know my wife, Kaci? It seems like you're the one we met in the park that day."

Oliver didn't know what he should say. He never thought he'd be talking to Kaci's husband. He bent over to pet Jack and tried to calm him down. Dogs know bad people, he knew. And Jack was right this time for sure. "Yes, I know Kaci," he answered. "What's the matter? She worked in Twin Towers, didn't she? Oh No! I thought I probably knew someone who died there but had no idea it would be her. My name is Oliver by the way. I didn't catch your name."

"I didn't give it," Landon answered, visibly annoyed. He hated giving his name to strangers. What did they need it for anyway? "You can call me Mr. Jamison." He said in a condescending way. He had already dismissed Oliver's comments in his mind as useless. "Well thanks anyway," he murmured.

The next week, he started looking in their new neighborhood. They hadn't lived there very long, so many of the shop owners didn't know Kaci by name. One woman who worked at the new coffee shop they frequented did know her and told Landon about the limousine pulling up and her getting in months ago. Other than that, nothing unusual was reported.

Would he ever know the truth? More importantly, if she wasn't found soon, would he be charged with her disappearance or murder? Lucky for him, the terror attack was a perfect alibi. Nobody would ever know if she perished in the rubble or not. He had every reason to believe she did, except the cat. Where did the cat go?

If DiMaio orchestrated her disappearance, he was very quick to action, and sensed that day would be the perfect day. Landon still couldn't believe she was gone. He was tired of her nagging, and questioning him, that's for sure. But he never considered she would disappear or die.

# CHAPTER TWENTY-SEVEN

Nina wasn't sure how much she should tell Shelly. She thought of this as her dry run at her new life story. Shelly would never know if what she told her was the truth or not.

"I grew up in Scranton and moved to New York about ten years ago with girlfriends." She hoped that would be enough.

"Obviously you're married?" Shelly pointed to her ring. "Or no? The ring that has a tale to tell."

Nina looked down at her hand. Dang, she forgot to take it off. "Yes, recently divorced. I guess I'm not used to being without it yet. And my friends said it will keep guys from hitting on me."

"That's a good point," Shelly agreed, "at least until you get where you're going. Where are you going?"

"St. Louis," she pulled out of the air, "I have family there, a few cousins." They talked a little more about what happened in New York. After that, they both settled in to get some rest on the overnight trip.

They got to Cincinnati about 4 a.m. Shelly gave Nina her phone number and address to keep in touch. Nina knew she wouldn't, but she didn't want to be rude. Her mother taught her better than that.

She was able to fall back asleep for a couple more hours, until the sun was rising. The bus stopped in Louisville to allow passengers to grab some breakfast at a small roadside gas station and restaurant. She knew she had to be very careful in the area because anyone from Murray could have moved in this area. She put sunglasses on and walked with her head down.

The rest of her trip was very quiet. She was grateful that no one sat next to her in all the additional stops they made. She really didn't feel like sharing anymore.

As soon as they crossed into Arkansas, she made the decision to see her parents, one last time. She never told her mother about her visit, so they both would be surprised to see her. The bus stopped for lunch about 40 miles from her hometown. It was there that she used the pay phone to call collect.

"Mom, hey, it's Kaci," she started. "I know you've been worried, and it's a long story. Can Dad come pick me up at the bus station in Little Rock?"

Evelyn was silent. "Is that really you Kaci?" she finally asked. "I've been waiting since your last phone call to find out what's going on?"

"Mom! It's a long story, I will explain when I see you," she assured her. "Tell him I will be on the Carter Street entrance, watching from inside."

Walter arrived almost an hour later. His blue Dodge truck pulled up to the door. Kaci almost ran to see her dad. She jumped in the passenger seat, scooted over and gave her dad a big hug. "Hi Daddy, it's really good to see you" Kaci squeezed him one more time before she buckled up.

"You too Little Girl," he said. Walter never was the chatty type; Evelyn took care of the conversation in their house.

On the ride home Kaci told him how bad her marriage was. The fights, mood swings, accusations, she told him almost all of it. When he asked if Landon had hurt her, she couldn't lie. "A few times I had bruises. But thankfully I never had to go to the Emergency Room." Walter's mood turned serious, and he was firm when he spoke, "You are never going back to New York, let's make that clear right now."

"I don't want to be anywhere near New York, that's the truth," she was relieved he was on her side.

As they pulled into the driveway, her mother almost leapt out of the kitchen side door. She ran to the truck before Kaci could even get the door opened. Evelyn gave her the biggest hug, just like when she was little, and afraid of something.

They went inside and sat down with coffee and cookies. Evelyn was already jumping up to fix her something else to eat. She had missed her cooking. Her stomach started rumbling just thinking about it.

"I sure have missed your cookies, Mama," she said. "No matter how I've tried, I can never make them taste the same way."

"Now, Kaci Lianne, you need to stop stalling and tell us what is going on!" Her mother insisted. "You're not getting one more cookie until you start talking."

"Daddy, do you want to tell her?" she asked with big hopeful eyes.

"No ma'am," he said, "This is your story." Walter gave her a smile and put his hands up in the air as if to say, "not it."

Over the next hour, Kaci told her parents about everything. On top of what Walter had already heard, she told them about Kyle, and Landon's job, his fondness for Scotch, and the other factors that led her to the decision she made. She left out his ties to the mob. It was safer that way.

"When the Twin Towers were attacked, and I was late for work." She continued, "the perfect opportunity was in front of me. I knew there had to have been hundreds, if not thousands, who were going to be dead and/or missing."

"The last I heard there were over 2,500 presumed dead, is that right Dad?"

"That's the last I heard honey," Walter said. They all held hands and bowed their heads in a silent prayer.

"Anyway, I won't be missed by many in New York," Kaci went on, "Oliver was such a good friend to help me get here. He reminds me a lot of you," she said looking at her dad. He smiled back at her.

After dinner they relaxed in the den and made a plan. Kaci gave them her new name, Nina and birthdate. "I need to come up with an easy last name."

Evelyn said, "You could always use my maiden name, Smith. There's no way anyone could find all the Smiths across the country."

Nina Smith, from Scranton, Pennsylvania, rode with them back to the bus station in Little Rock the next morning. Her dad paid for her ticket to Santa Fe, New Mexico. She knew she could get a job in one of the art galleries and maybe a gift shop. As the bus pulled in and she got up to board, she gave them one last hug. Walter handed her a bank envelope with over $700 in it.

"What's this Daddy?" she asked, a few tears on her cheeks.

"I don't want to worry about where you're staying or if you're safe. I also bought you a trac phone and a 300-minute phone card. You need to call us once a week." He made her promise and let her board with a new bag filled with some of her old clothes from school.

As the bus drove west, Kaci finally felt calm. She knew she would face hurdles in this new journey, but she was confident she made the right choice. She could do this. She fell asleep, dreaming of her future. She pictured herself in a small apartment, cooking in her own kitchen and relaxing in a comfortable chair.

# CHAPTER TWENTY-EIGHT

The bus pulled into Santa Fe just about 6 a.m. The sun was rising in the mountains. She looked up and was surprised to see several hot-air balloons, gliding across the clear sky. It was one of the coolest things she had ever seen. It was as if she had a sign, that her future was bright, and the sky was the limit.

Even though it was still September, the air was cool and dry. She shivered with the chill that ran down her back. She had always loved Fall in New York, this was completely different, and yet just as pretty. She took in a deep breath and started off on her way to her future.

The aroma from a coffee shop floated onto the sidewalk and lured her inside. As she sat with a large cup of house blend, she picked up a copy of the local newspaper that was left on the table next to her. She was happy to see that there were several help-wanted ads and, more important, rooms for rent.

She pulled out her cell phone to start calling the listings, and realized she forgot to tell her parents she made it safely. Evelyn answered on the second ring. "We were beginning to wonder if you stayed on the bus?"

"No Momma," she answered, "I just now got somewhere I could use my phone."

She scanned the rooms to rent section while a server was cleaning off the tables for the night. Nina kept to herself; she wasn't sure yet how much she wanted to meet new people. She knew she wanted to make friends, but she didn't trust her judgement since she had picked Landon. There wasn't as much at stake, but it was still a gamble.

The server or barista, whatever they were called, spoke first. "Are you here on vacation?" Nina looked around her to be sure she was speaking to her.

"Me? Uh, I don't know yet I guess," she stammered.

"I just noticed your backpack," she continued, "and it looks like you've been traveling."

"Well, yeah, I just came from my parents," that wasn't a lie, she was trying to be truthful as much as possible. There was less of a chance she would be caught in a lie if what she said was close to the truth. The one thing she knew she could never mention was her husband and the mafia.

The girl went back to work, leaving Nina alone to peruse the classifieds. When she was finished, she went for a stroll around the plaza area. It was full of tourists' shops and art galleries. She went ahead and picked up applications in the places with a help-wanted sign in the window. She suddenly realized she would have a small problem getting a job; she had no social security number for Nina.

She was looking forward to sleeping in a bed tonight, any bed. There was a small hotel about five blocks off the plaza. It was in a less expensive neighborhood she could tell just by the condition of the buildings and the vehicles parked in the yards. The Hacienda Herrera advertised rooms for only $39. She knew she couldn't expect much but as long as it was relatively clean, it would work.

She entered the front office and found a young man at the desk. His nametag read "Tony". He looked up and slid open the office window. "Can I help you ma'am?"

Again, with the 'ma'am'. "Do I really look that old" she thought. "Hi, can I get a room for the night, just for me?" She was pleased to smell the faint scent of disinfectant cleaner and thought they must clean regularly.

"Of course," Tony answered. "I just need your driver's license and you can fill out the card please."

"Crap! Driver's license! Another obstacle." She thought to herself. "I just arrived in town, and I have misplaced my I.D. but I do have cash. Can you just take my name and number?"

"I suppose my parents won't mind, you seem like a nice lady," he replied. "You're not a serial killer, are you?" He chuckled at his own joke.

"Uh, what?" Did she hear him right? "No, I'm not." She answered his silly question with a smile. "Does your family own this hotel?" she was curious.

"Sure do. It's been in our family for generations. They opened it back in the 50s. Tourism started taking off back in the day of the

Cowboy movies. In fact, several of John Wayne's movies, and others, were filmed in our area."

"You are just a wealth of information," she kidded him. "Maybe you could help me on where to find a job and a place to live? I don't know anything about Santa Fe." Somehow because Tony was younger, and only an acquaintance, she felt at ease with him. She really needed to try to start trusting people again.

Tony showed her to an upstairs room on the street side. They weren't busy that weekend, so he thought she'd like to take in the view, he had said. "I wish I could say we have breakfast in the morning, but we are a small hotel. But my family also owns a local restaurant a couple of blocks over. If you want a great Mexican breakfast, I can give you a coupon."

"That would be helpful," she smiled. "Thank you."

The first thing Nina did was take a long hot shower. The room had a tiny bathroom, but it was functional, and the water was hot, which was a plus in her book. After the shower, she plopped down on the bed, and covered up with the blankets. She awoke startled and unfamiliar with her surroundings. Her heart was beating so fast that she started having trouble breathing.

She was in Santa Fe, in a hotel, she finally recalled. The sky outside was dark. She hadn't meant to fall asleep, but according to her watch, she must have slept for almost three hours. Her stomach was making a lot of noise and was probably the reason she woke up. She hadn't eaten since the pastry at the coffee shop much earlier.

She got dressed quickly, noting she would need to buy other clothes soon. It had only been a week since she left but she had washed her few pieces of clothing twice already.

Downstairs, Tony was still at his post. "Good evening to you." He was watching the small television on his desk but jumped up when she walked into the room.

"Hi, I must have fallen asleep," Nina responded. "And now I'm starving. I'd love to try that restaurant. Can you give me directions?"

Thirty minutes later she was sitting at a small table in the outdoor patio area. He had called ahead and told his mother, Julia, that she would be coming, and that Nina was a guest at the hotel. Julia had greeted her at the front door. Nina had a hard time believing how laid back and friendly everyone was. It was definitely not like New York. Yes, she had met some very nice people, but for the most part New Yorkers were more focused on themselves and didn't engage in small talk.

After the server bought fresh-made tortilla chips and salsa, she ordered the enchiladas with green chile. Nina wasn't disappointed. It was delicious, and a little spicy, but worth every penny.

Nina had noticed a small sign on the hostess podium for help needed. When Tony's mother walked by her table, she politely asked what kind of job they had open. She was interested, in anything that paid money. Working in a restaurant was best for quick cash.

Julia sat down and began telling her what she needed, cooks, dishwasher and a server. "Do you have any experience?" she asked Nina. She told her about the pizza parlor. She gave a fake city however, just to be safe. She didn't think anyone checked references for a waitressing job.

"We serve breakfast, so we are open 7 a.m. to 10 p.m., is that a problem for you?" she asked first.

"No, I can work any shift you need." Nina glanced around at the servers and their uniforms. They all had on black pants with red polo shirts or button-down shirts and black bandanas at the neck.

After a tour of the restaurant, including the kitchen, storage areas, break room and bar area, Nina hoped it was a good sign. Julia sat down with her after the tour to talk a little more. "I like you Nina, I'm willing to take a chance on you. When can you start?"

"YES!" Nina shouted in her head. "Right away, anytime." She was excited to start working as soon as possible. She was told to arrive at 10 a.m. the next morning.

She almost ran back to the hotel feeling elated at her great news. She promptly called her parents and told them she had a job, this way they wouldn't worry so much about her struggling in another town. She unpacked her backpack, shaking out the clothes she had. The clothes that had been worn, she promptly handwash in the bathroom sink.

At the bottom of her bag, she found the address book she grabbed as she was leaving the apartment. She suddenly realized it wasn't hers. Being in a hurry, she just snatched it up, not really looking at it. This was Landon's. As she opened it and started reading the entries, she knew it wasn't full of addresses, but personal information and numbers, lots of numbers. Is this what DiMaio was warning her about? It looked like Landon was creating his own insurance policy. Except that now, he would be frantic because it was missing. He had to know she was alive, who else could have taken it.

Several hours later she finally fell asleep. Her mind was racing with worrying about her safety again. She wasn't tired due to her long afternoon nap, and that didn't help. She was keeping the book if she ever needed a get-out-of-jail free card.

The next morning, she rose just after dawn. Old habits were hard to break, she thought, but she knew she couldn't go back to sleep. There were too many things on her to-do list. She had over two hours before she had t to be at the restaurant. What she really needed was work clothes. While in the lobby that morning, she saw that Julia was at the desk.

# CHAPTER TWENTY-NINE

"Good morning!" Nina beamed as she talked to her. "I can't thank you enough for the job. You won't be sorry. I do have to ask what I need to wear, and since I packed light, where could I find clothes at a bargain?"

"Buenos Dias," Julia answered her with a smile. "We wear black bottoms, pants or knee-length skirt, and a button-down shirt, preferably red or black. In a few weeks I will order uniform shirts for you. As for where to shop, you can usually find decent clothes at the Goodwill, about a mile down this road."

"That sounds perfect," she said. "Do you think I can walk there and get back before I need to come to work?"

"Normally I would say yes, but since you are still new in town, I will tell Antonio to drive you. That boy is always looking for a chance to drive my car." Julia laughed and called out for 'Antonio' behind her office.

Tony quickly appeared. When he found out what he needed to do, he went back to the apartment, Nina guessed. He came back out in ten minutes, clean shaven and dressed. Julia instructed him to take her to the coffee shop down the street first before the Goodwill.

Nina was grateful for the caffeine stop and paid for Tony's energy drink. "I see you have met Tony, our teenage tour guide," a voice said behind her. She turned around to see the same server she saw yesterday. It was a good feeling that everyone was so nice to her.

"I got a room at the hotel," Nina explained. "I'll be working at their restaurant and staying at the hotel I guess until I can find someplace to live."

"My name is Lauren, by the way," she introduced herself. "I can help you if you want." She must have noticed Nina's hesitancy because she quickly added, "I'm sorry, you don't even know me."

"No, it's ok, I need to loosen up a little," she replied. "Everything back home was always so tense. That's one reason I had to move." Nina thought that explanation would be enough.

"Well, my offer still stands," Lauren said and went back to work.

"I hope I didn't offend her," she told Tony. She had to learn to forget the New York attitude she had adapted while living there.

"Huh?" he said. "Who? Lauren? Not likely. She's nice, for being an older woman."

Nina had to laugh at his characterization of 'older'. She had guessed Lauren to be about her age, mid 20s. She knew she had to be more trusting but was still very nervous about it.

She was focused on getting something to wear to work primarily. They arrived at the store just minutes after it opened. Tony said he'd wait in the car for her, so she promised to be quick. She felt awkward imposing on him this way.

Nina walked out 20 minutes later with a bag full of clothes. She didn't bother trying anything on, she could tell by looking that they would fit. "All of this for only $20!" she told Tony. "Thanks again for bringing me, I now have time to get a shower and dressed for work."

Her shift began the next morning with another waitress, Tonya, being assigned as her coach. Tonya said she had been working for the Herreras for almost four years. In the restaurant business, you become more like family after the second year.

"Julia is pretty cool most of the time," Tonya explained, "But whatever you do, don't be late. That's a big pet peeve of hers." "Now, her husband, Gabe, is only worried about keeping the floors clean and countertops. You'll get the lecture about bacteria on surfaces. I just keep some Clorox wipes in my pocket."

Over the next four hours, Tonya gave her so much information, she wasn't sure she would remember it all. Nina had come prepared, with a notepad, to take notes. But some things couldn't be written down. Their shift ended at 2 o'clock on floor, with another 30 minutes to clean up and restock their station. Tonya was nice enough to split her tips with her that day, even though she didn't need to.

"But I really didn't do anything," she said. Nina couldn't believe how generous people were here. She felt very fortunate to have found nice people to befriend her already.

"You'll understand one day," Tonya answered. "You treat your co-workers good, and they will return the favor." She smiled at Nina.

"Got it," Nina replied, "do unto others."

"Exactly," Tonya said. "Now on to more important things, how did you end up here?"

Rather than go into a long-drawn-out story, which would be all false anyway, Nina said, "You know how it is. One day your stuck in a boring 9 to 5, the next day you move across country".

Tonya took that as a hint, no need to pry. So, Nina wasn't the type to chat about her life, no big deal, she thought. Some people just liked to keep to themselves. Tonya hoped her quietness wouldn't get in the way of her doing her job.

Julia stopped her before she left and had a stack of papers to fill out. "Nina don't forget your paperwork. If it's not filled out by Friday, you won't get paid."

"Do you think I could pay up front for the week at the hotel, maybe half?" she shyly asked Julia. "You can hold my paycheck if I don't pay the rest by the time I get my first check."
"I think I can do that," she answered. "Since I know your where you'll be and where you work." She patted Nina on the shoulder as she went back to her office.

After work Tonya tried to make sure she got a safe ride home. Pat, the bartender, had offered to take her but Nina had politely refused the ride. Tonya took that as a sign that she didn't trust men easily, so she offered to take her. She accepted and Nina was back in her room before dinner.

Nina took a little walk to familiarize herself with the area. She fell loved the somewhat primitive adobe architecture. It made even the small homes looked warm and inviting. Almost every home was decorated with potted flowers and brightly painted doors and window trim.

She was scheduled to work the same lunch shift, with Tonya, all week. Nina tried to avoid Julia, for fear that she'd find out about her not having a social security number and fire her. She kept busy and made sure she was on the opposite side of the building.

When she did see her on Friday, Nina explained that she forgot and left the paperwork at home. She promised she would return them on Saturday. It was either, confess or quit at that point.

Saturday came and she was so nervous about talking to Julia, she felt nauseous. Thankfully, the restaurant was busy when she clocked in, and stayed busy all through lunch. She made almost $40 that day alone, and that was splitting with Tonya. She really needed this job, she knew. "Julia, I have to be honest with you," she said, trying to hold back her tears. "I was in a bad situation and had to leave my previous identity behind. I don't have a new social security number."

"Sweetie, come now, don't start that," Julia said, patting her hand across the table. "Everyone has their own story. I think I know enough about you to see that you are kind, considerate and genuine. I can't imagine anyone being able to fake that."

Nina was so relieved. She found a confidant. "I can't tell too many people, in case he shows up here, but I feel I can trust you." She proceeded to tell her the abbreviated version of her departure from New York on September 11th.

"You were very brave to make your way out here alone. Your secret is safe with me." Julia said. "Now, what to do about your ID?" They both sat for a few minutes and thought. "Can I just pay you cash, under the table, until we can find a better solution?"

She quickly agreed. Anything is better than nothing. "Can you make it look like I'm getting paid in a check, like everyone else?" She didn't want to give the others a reason to think she was special.

# CHAPTER THIRTY

Nina made a habit of stopping at the coffee shop each morning on her way to work. She talked to Lauren a little more each time. She had a hint that Lauren was a truly nice person. Nina had told her she was looking to rent a room or small apartment immediately. She also knew that most landlords would insist on a credit history or at least her social security number.

One morning Lauren greeted her at her table, one by the window, with her large coffee. She told Nina she had an idea. "Why don't you live with me? My place isn't huge, but I do have a spare bedroom I'm not using."

"Are you sure?" Nina asked her. Could it be this easy? She felt she had made a real friend and would love the chance to get to know her better. It had been so long since she'd had a real girlfriend.

"If you don't mind cats, I have two by the way. Lila and Jewel," she explained, "They love people."

"Well then, looks like we have the start of a beautiful friendship," Lauren added. "It's going to be nice to have someone to talk to finally. Living alone isn't all it's cracked up to be."

"Living in a bad marriage isn't any better," Nina thought to herself.

Nina stopped back at the coffee shop after her shift ended and waited until Lauren was ready to leave. It was only a 10-minute drive by car. By New York standards, that meant a 30-minute walk, but she was used to walking longer.

The apartment was on a somewhat busy street, full of restaurants and small stores. Lauren unlocked the door, and Jewel and Lila rushed to weave in and out of her legs, making it almost impossible to walk inside. They really were friendly little animals, she thought.

Nina looked around and fell in love with everything about it. Even though it wasn't large, it had character. There were arched doorways and wrought iron accents outside. It reminded her of a

Mexican villa. The spare bedroom wasn't much bigger than a walk-in closet, but, Nina reasoned, she didn't have much.

Lauren fixed them a frozen pizza for dinner. She called Tony earlier to tell him she was going to be leaving that night. But for the moment, she sat at the breakfast bar and enjoyed a cold soda and pizza. Every day, this is getting easier, she thought.

Over the next few weeks, business got busier and busier. Tourists from all over the world were arriving for the Albuquerque International Balloon Fiesta set to begin the next Saturday. Most of the hotels had been booked up for months in advance, so many who made the last-minute decision to attend had to stay in Santa Fe or other towns.

Tonya told her that balloonists came in from Germany, Sweden, Canada and probably every state in the U.S. Her husband, Chris, was a pilot of his own balloon, 'American Beauty'. Tonya invited her to come with them on opening day.

Nina was excited to see what all the fuss was about. On the weekend she had seen several balloons flying in the sky in the mornings. She couldn't imagine it being much different. She had to get up at 3 a.m. to leave Santa Fe by 4 and get to the field by 5 o'clock. They picked her up in the big Jeep they used to tow the balloon trailer.

By the time they saw Albuquerque from the I-25, the traffic was backed up for miles. Red taillights were ahead for as far as she could see. As they pulled up to the gates with their badges displayed, they were waved through and given a map and directions to their spot. Nina didn't remember ever seeing this kind of traffic, even in New York.

The temperature was barely above freezing that morning, about 40 degrees with very little wind, thankfully. For the first time that season, she could see her own breath in front of her. Chris explained on the ride down there that wind was a pilot's worst enemy and best friend at the same time. It could blow the balloon way off course or give you the sweetest ride.

They were met by another truck full of Chris' friends that were there to help get the balloon in the air. The guys started by unloading the basket from the trailer and taking it to their launch spot. American Beauty was then rolled out, stretching nearly 50 feet in front of them.

Nina was amazed at how that same balloon rolled out in front of her would soon be up in the air. A big fan was brought out to start filling the balloon with air. There were already dozens of balloons standing up, the flames from the burners lit up the pre-dawn sky and warmed up the immediate surroundings. The cold air hung low on the grass fields, making her feet wet in the tennis shoes she had worn. Within minutes, she was wishing she had thicker socks, boots, anything to warm her toes.

"So, what do you think of your first morning glow?" Tonya asked her. "Pretty cool, right?"

"Is that what this is called?" Nina replied. "That's the perfect name for it. Kinda sounds magical." She just stood in place, turning her head to take in everything around her. Everywhere she looked she saw trucks, balloons rolled out and burners being lit.

"If you want hot coffee, there are several food trucks over there," Tonya said as she pointed to a street full of booths and trucks. "A little later the souvenir booths will be open. It's a great place to find some authentic Indian jewelry and art."

"Is that where the wonderful smells are coming from?" she asked. "Do you think it's safe for me to head over that way alone?" She didn't like this new scared person she was becoming. It will take time, she reassured herself.

"Of course, there are police all over this place. This is a pretty friendly crowd." Tonya wondered why she was so nervous suddenly. "I'll go with you if you can wait a few minutes," she offered.

"No, I'm being silly," Nina tried to cover for her weird behavior. "I'm a big girl, I'll be back in a few minutes."

As she made her way through the other balloon sites, she noticed the trailers and license plates from all over the country. She saw North Carolina, Florida, Michigan, Illinois and even Maine. Everyone was so friendly and greeted her with a smile and a wave. There were trailers with state flags and even other countries' flags. She made out France, Germany and United Kingdom.

The smell of roasting chiles, chorizo sausage, and fried dough filled the air. Her stomach began rumbling for food, so she ordered a breakfast burrito and fresh sopapillas along with the 2 hot drinks. She had everything packed in a small cardboard box as she carefully made her way back across the grassy field.

At daylight the first group of balloons lifted off and up into the clear blue sky. In the next hour, the sky was filled with over a hundred, if not two hundred, balloons already. Each one was unique. There were the bright colored ones, some were sponsored by major companies like Kodak, AOL, Pepsi, and Buick. The coolest ones she thought were the special shapes. She saw a duck, a pig, a cow, a stagecoach, an airplane, a cactus, Smokey the Bear, Tweetie and even The Flying Purple People Eater.

Chris offered to take her up in the balloon, but she declined. This first time she would prefer to keep her feet on the ground. The balloon went up several minutes later when the field master gave them the okay. She was amazed at the amount of organization they had on the field. She was in awe of the number of balloons in the air at one time. It was unlike anything she could have imagined.

After that, they all piled in the Jeep and took off with the trailer, to be the chase crew. She assumed the citizens of Albuquerque were used to people driving through town looking up at the sky, but it was all new to her. Trying to guess where the balloon would land was difficult. They had pulled over at a small park, with a huge open field where Chris has thought he could land. He was wrong, the wind took the balloon up again. Tonya jumped back in the Jeep and followed him to a high school. The soccer field would be perfect, if they could avoid the power lines, and if they could drive onto the school grounds.

Tonya needed to be able to drive to exactly where Chris landed so they could load it into the trailer easily. She had to call Chris on the walkie talkies and tell him to go up again, she couldn't get past the security gates. Within minutes, Chris had found an open mesa to land. It was made of mostly dirt and sagebrush, so there were no worries of trespassing. Tonya put the Jeep into 4-wheel drive and drove up the embankment to meet Chris.

They pulled They quickly realized just over the small hill was a neighborhood park. Kids of all ages were standing in a circle, watching them disassemble the balloon. Tonya called the kids over and started handing out trading cards. Each balloon team had their own trading card, with some basic information about the team on the cards.

Nina had never had so much fun as she did that morning. Once they were back on the field, Tonya pulled out everything to make breakfast burritos. It was the Albuquerque version of tailgating. "It's a tradition, you have to fee your crew," she explained. They had enough food to feed three or four crews.

They got back in the early afternoon. She was in much need of a nap, and yet, she was still pumping with adrenaline. Tonya dropped her off on their way home. First thing she did was turn on the television and watch the news coverage of the Fiesta. The pictures she was seeing were amazing but didn't compare to seeing it live. Her eyes were fighting to stay open. The pillow on the sofa was so fluffy, she was asleep in minutes. Just in case she was sleeping, a note was left on the counter for Lauren, telling her to not let her sleep too long.

# CHAPTER THIRTY-ONE

Nina awoke to the small of food cooking and Lauren talking on the phone. "Sure, we could probably make it, let me just ask my roommate. I'll call you back in a few minutes."

She was still on a natural high from the morning, so it wasn't hard to get out of bed. "Hey, what did you have to ask me?"

"One of my girlfriends wants me, and you, to come see her boyfriend's band play," Lauren explained. "I've heard them before. I think they're good, but they play old rock n roll."

"That's cool," Nina agreed. "I love the old stuff, and new stuff, and in between, I guess you could say I like all kinds of music."

After eating, the girls spent some time getting dressed up. Luckily, Lauren had several pretty things that Nina could wear. She ended up wearing a white lace blouse over a red tank top with jeans. After fixing her hair and makeup, and adding jewelry, she was ready to hit the club.

In another hour, they were sitting with Renee at a table towards the back of the room. Lauren ordered Long Island Iced Teas for the table. Nina hadn't had a real cocktail in months, she hoped she wouldn't make a fool out of herself. She never did like drawing attention to herself.

The band, Chain Reaction, came on stage about an hour later. Renee pointed to the drummer. "That's my boyfriend there. Hands off!" She made sure they knew she was joking. "His name is Tomas, isn't he adorable?" She laughed again, "I know he's a sweaty mess, but he's my sweaty mess."

They started off with "Let's Dance," by David Bowie, and some brave souls actually got up to dance. Next was some Talking Heads and Rolling Stones. The playlist appealed to the crowd, and they continued to cheer. Every couple of minutes someone, usually a girl, was walking up to the lead guitarist and handing him a piece of paper.

"What are they doing?" Nina asked Renee. The guitarist was only able to open a few of them between song breaks. The others he left on a pile on his amplifier.

"I'd say about 50% are song requests," she answered. "The rest are probably their phone numbers." Renee rolled her eyes when she said it.

"They're awfully forward, don't you think?" Nina questioned. "I don't think I could ever just hand my phone number to a stranger." Of course, Nina had other reasons. It would take a long time before she trusted another man, or herself to make a good choice. She still partially blamed herself for the trouble in their marriage. She should never have married Landon. The signs were all there, but she was blinded by love.

At the first intermission, Tomas made his way through the crowd to give Renee a quick kiss. He sat down and gulped down a glass of ice water. "Tomas, this is my friend Lauren, and her roommate, Nina."

"So, what did you ladies think about the first set?" he asked them. Tomas was always looking for input from the audience. If they wanted to keep working, they needed to know what the people wanted.

Lauren spoke up, "We loved it, right Nina?" She nodded in agreement. "A little heavy on the old stuff. How about some Green Day, Nine Inch Nails, Foo Fighters?"

Nina spoke up then, "Now speak for yourself, I happened to love the music you chose. But I've always been told I'm an old soul."

"That sounds like our lead guitarist, Bennett." Tomas went on, "If it doesn't have a little age on it, he hates it."

"I never said hate," she replied. "But the classics are classics for a reason. They appeal to a large population."

After the next set, Tomas came back to the table, dragging the guitar player behind him. He took a chair and flipped it around backwards and sat. "Which one of you ladies likes classic rock?"

Nina saw three fingers pointed at her. She was so embarrassed. She just was commenting, she didn't mean to open up a big discussion, or even have to talk to the guitarist. "Yes!" she said in exasperation, "Me. I'm the one who likes classic rock. You guys act like I just came from Mars."

"Who cares what they think," he piped up. "You are apparently the only one with taste." He smiled at her with a twinkle in his eyes. "My name's Bennett by the way, since these cavemen didn't introduce us."

Was he flirting with her? She was so out of touch she really couldn't tell. All she knew is she couldn't do this now. She couldn't jump in and date anyone. Not for a long time. "Excuse me," Nina told the table, "I'm going to the little girls' room." Lauren noticed her face getting red and her smile had faded.

"Hold on," said Lauren, "I'll go with you." She had to weave through the bar to catch up with Nina.

As they both entered, Lauren asked, "Are you ok? You looked like someone slapped you in the face. What happened back there?" Nina was already in a stall. Lauren waited patiently without talking.

"I'm okay," Nina said. She didn't want to make a scene. "I'm sorry I worried you. It's no big deal really; just some personal things I need to work through I guess." The thought of dating never entered her mind. She would have to think long and hard about that.

"Well, if you're sure," Lauren asked. Nina nodded and they both made their way back to the table. The guys had gone back to the stage. Renee had already ordered another round of drinks for them. Nina hadn't finished her first one yet, but quickly drank the rest. If there was ever a night, she needed to calm her nerves, this was it, she thought.

Tomas and Bennett came back to the table at every break. Nina tried to be friendly, even though she didn't really want to say too much. She brought up some of her favorite bands and they discussed them. That was a safe subject. Nothing too personal.

"I could pick one band from each decade who are my favorites," she started the conversation. "In the 70s, I'd say Queen, 60s Beach Boys, 80s I think Rolling Stones, and of course, 90s is Peral Jam."

Bennett's mouth was wide open. "You can't be serious!" He said in obvious shock. "The right answer is … 60s the BEATLES, ever heard of them? 70s Led Zeppelin and The Who, but I'm sure that's too hard rock for you." The twinkle in his eye told Nina he was teasing her. "Now the 80s I would have to say you made a good choice, but don't count out KISS. And finally, the 90s is Nirvana of course."

He really knew his music, Nina thought. To make his point, in their next set they played "Start Me Up', 'Come Together' and 'Black

Dog'. She had to admit, the band did a great job on anything they played. And, after she got over her anxiety, she had a good time.

# CHAPTER THIRTY-TWO

By the end of October Nina had saved up enough tips to get her own apartment. She loved living with Lauren, but they both needed their privacy. Luckily, she had met a woman at the restaurant who owned several rentals in town. Mrs. Elliott had told her about a partially furnished one that would be available on November 1st. "It's nothing fancy but it does have a patio and a full bathroom. A sofa and dining table comes furnished. You really just need a bed and you're set.," she explained.

Nina had one week to find a good used bed. She only really needed a mattress, foundation and bed frame. She went to the Goodwill first to see if they had anything. She was able to find a couple lamps, end tables, a small chest, quilt and curtains. An employee suggested she try Angel's Attic, another thrift store, for a mattress. She saved time by calling first and found out they didn't have any for sale.

She only had a few small things to move into the apartment. Starting with nothing certainly made moving easier, but at the same time, made it kind of sad. She missed her personal keepsakes she left behind in New York.

A light bulb went off in Nina's head. She could ask her parents to contact Landon and ask him to send them her things. The clothes and books weren't important, but this would cement the fact that 'Kaci' was gone for good. She was fairly certain Landon had already moved on. She could see him now, drinking in a bar after work and crying to some unsuspecting woman about how his wife was killed in the attack. Sympathy is a great pick-up line.

The next day at work one of the bartenders she knew only as Pat, approached her. "I heard you need a mattress," he said.

"How did you find out?" He seemed too eager to help her, which threw up red flags. "I do, desperately," she replied. She would be sure to ask Tonya about him later. If he was trustworthy.

"Well today is your lucky day," he said with a wink. "I happen to have one I need to move out of my spare bedroom so I can make it my home gym."

"I'll take it," Nina agreed. "How much? When can I get it?"

"Hold on," he said, "you haven't even seen it. It's a full size, is that ok?"

"I don't care, it's fine. I don't have any way to pick it up, so could you bring it over on Wednesday?" She asked again, "How much do you want for it?"

"How about $30? And I will gladly deliver," he said. "Then you can buy me a beer."

Not sure about the beer proposition, she agreed for the moment. It was a small price to pay she knew for something to sleep on. They exchanged phone numbers so she could call him when she was at the apartment.

On Wednesday, she got up early so she could take Lauren to work and borrow her car to get stuff moved. She had a couple hours until when Lauren got off work. First thing she did was take her tables, lamps and a few boxes over. She met Mrs. Elliott who gave her the key, in exchange for her first month's rent and deposit.

Nina was so excited to have her own place. She made it, she thought, "I'm free!" She is really living here and left her abusive husband behind. There was a part of her that was always afraid something terrible was going to happen.

Walking in, she smelled the clean smell of Lysol mixed with a yummy pumpkin spice scented candle and a Christmas Cactus. "That's a little house-warming present for you," said Mrs. Elliott, "to make it homier."

"I love it, thank you so much." Nina said, giving her a quick hug. She started unpacking the car, which only took about 15 minutes. She spent another 30 minutes putting away what she brought in the first trip. She had a few kitchen items and food items like cereal, tea bags, pasta, sauce, tuna and other staples.

On her way back to Lauren's, she called Pat and asked if he could meet her and Lauren in a couple of hours. She felt better having another person there when he came over. That would give her time to pack up the rest. She had just finished taking in the last lamp when he showed up, 20 minutes early. Lauren wasn't there yet, so she had to trust him. She was a little annoyed, she had a long list of to-dos left to go. She would never say anything, she was grateful he showed up at all.

They were able to get it in the bedroom and set up quickly. "This is awesome," she beamed. "Thank you so much." Pat had brought the bedframe and foundation too, which Nina had forgotten about again.

"I had ulterior motives," Pat grinned. "I've been wanting to talk to you for a while now."

"What? You're kidding right?" she said, noticeably shocked. He wasn't her type, but he was good-looking. He stood about 6'3" and had plenty of muscles. She guessed he was a ladies' man.

"I'm totally serious," he said. "You are nicer than most of the girls who work there, and prettier."

"Uh thanks," she had no idea what to say to that. He was making her nervous suddenly. She never was good at accepting compliments. Was he going to put the moves on her?

"Come on," he teased her, "Surely you know you're a knock-out."

"No, not really," his tone made her uncomfortable, as if he were picking out a steak at the butcher's. How could she get rid of him politely? She still had to see him at work.

Her phone rang at that moment, saving her from going further in that conversation. She apologized to Pat and took the call outside. It was Lauren, just checking to see if she needed anything before she came over. When she hung up, she walked back in to find him sitting on the small sofa. "Now where's my beer?" he said jokingly.

She laughed, "Hold on there, cowboy. I haven't been to the store yet. I've still got things to do today. Lauren is on her way over. Maybe all of us can meet up later tonight. You pick the place." They made a 'date' for that night at the Jackalope Inn. Before Pat left, Lauren had pulled up, thankfully. She had never been so happy to see someone.

She and Lauren spent the rest of the day, shopping for the basics. Another trip to the Goodwill and Albertson's supermarket and she was set for a while.

Nina told Lauren about Pat's flirting, "There is no way on this Earth that anything would happen there. He is much too aggressive, reminds me of an old boyfriend I had. It did not end well. Tonya said he flirts with everyone anyway."

Just to be safe, Nina talked Lauren into coming with her to The Jackalope. They pulled in to see the band unloading their equipment from a van that read "Chain Reaction". The girls looked at each other and laughed. At least they knew they would enjoy the music. They saw Pat immediately because he was waving at them over to the bar. Once there, Pat told the bartender, "This is Nina, and her friend, I'm sorry, we haven't met."

Nina stepped in, "This is my best friend, Lauren. I thought you met her at the restaurant?" Pat shook his head and offered to buy them a drink, since he already had one.

The band was just setting up on stage, tuning their guitars. She was ready to hear some rock 'n' roll. Landon never took her anywhere to hear live music. There was never anywhere to go in Murray and once they got to New York they were too busy.

The lead singer was at the microphone, introducing the band, and their first song, 'Sweet Emotion', by Aerosmith. It was an easy way to get the crowd involved from the beginning.

Pat found them a table. He started almost immediately with the heavy pick-up lines. "I love your hair" and "Do you like this music?"

"Yeah," she said, "we saw them a few weeks ago, they were great."

"If you like ancient stuff," he answered. "I can live without it. You're much too hot to listen to this junk."

She laughed, "Does that stuff ever work for you?"

"Not really," he laughed. "I'm sorry. I guess I can be a little overpowering at times. I blame it on the bartender in me. Always there to strike up a conversation."

"It's ok, I'm just not dating anyone for a while," she replied. While Lauren and Pat talked, Nina watched the band. When their set was over, Bennett came over to their table. If she thought it was to see her, she was wrong.

"Hey dude," he addressed Pat, "How you been?" They shook hands like good old buddies do, very macho. Bennett turned to them and looked surprised. "Wait! How do you classy ladies know this scumbag?" Bennett asked Nina.

She politely answered, "He works with me, or I work with him." She watched as he took a seat next to Pat.

Pat looked at everyone, "We go way back. All the way back to Clovis High School marching band, Class of '86."

Lauren added that they had seen them play a few weeks earlier with Renee, the drummer's girlfriend. "Where is Renee by the way? and marching band? Are you kidding?"

"Guilty," Bennett answered. "I think I saw Renee over on the other side of the bar. She'd be happy to see you ladies, I'm sure."

"Now back to the marching band part. I can believe Bennett was, but YOU?" asked Lauren. "You are not the type I knew in high school. I was also in band., Las Vegas High, class of '89, first chair flute."

Pat puffed up his chest, "Trumpet," he pointed to Bennett. "You'll never guess what Mr. 'Guitarman' played."

Nina looked at his height, long arms, "Trombone! Right?" Pat and Bennett were both amazed.

"How in the world did you know that?" Pat asked.

"I'm a little psychic," she laughed. "Well, plus you have long arms, that would be an asset for any trombone player, or is it trombonist?"

He laughed, "Buy the lady a drink on me."

"Whatever you say," said Pat. "How about a Colorado Bulldog? It's a local favorite."

She asked, "Never heard of it. What's in it?"

"Vodka, Kahlua, Pepsi, trust me, you'll love it." He answered. The cocktail arrived just as Bennett went back to the stage.

Nina took a long sip trough the tiny stir-straw provided. Her eyes grew big as she savored the chocolatey-coffee flavored drink. "This is amazing. I've never had anything like it."

The band opened the next set by introducing the members. Tomas was on drums, Antonio was on bass guitar, Leo played keyboard and a little percussion, George on vocals. Together they made a great sounding band.

As the night went on, she and Lauren were ready to leave before the last set, but Pat begged them to stick around a little longer.

Bennett stopped by just in time to say goodbye. The guys did a manly handshake/pat on the back. "See you around," he said to the table.

# CHAPTER THIRTY-THREE

As promised, 'Kaci' talked to her parents every week. They rotated days to fit her schedule. When her father called her two days before their next call, she was instantly worried. He asked her to sit down, he had something important to tell her.

"Oh my God, what's wrong Daddy?" She pleaded into the phone. Her mind was racing with possibilities, all bad ones.

"Honey, your mama was taken to the Emergency Room last night," he explained. "The doctors think it was a stroke. We're still waiting to hear more."

She sobbed, "How? Why? She's only 61 years old."

"I don't know honey, all I know now is she is in the best hands," he sniffled as he told her. "If anyone can help her, these doctors can. They considered sending her to Little Rock, but the same doctor works here and there, so there wasn't a need."

Lauren came over right away when she called. She needed a friend right now. When she walked in, Nina's face was red and splotchy from crying. "Oh no, what's wrong, Sis?" 'Sis' was a nickname they had given each other after a stranger had commented that they must be sisters because they looked and acted alike. The girls never saw the resemblance, so they just blew it off, but thought it was a cute name, ironically, since neither one had a sister.

She told her about her mother. "I don't know what to do, what if she doesn't make it?"

"Now don't think that way," Lauren assured her, "you really don't know that will happen, do you?" She threw an arm around Nina's shoulder and gave her a quick squeeze.

"You're right," she sniffled and got up to go wash her face. The cold water felt good and helped ease her mood some.

"I know what we should do," Lauren offered, "Let's go get a drink. I always said if you're drinking at home, it's a problem. If you're at a bar, it's being social."

"I don't know, Sis," she answered, "I'm a mess. Nobody wants to see me like this." She wasn't sure what kind of company she would be in the mood she was in.

"You are crazy, you know that? You look fine. Maybe a little tired," she said enthusiastically. "Let me help you get ready, who knows what might happen tonight." Lauren was hard to ignore. She helped Nina fix her hair and get makeup done. She pulled out a cute pair of jeans and a modest sweater.

They had picked out a club with live music at random and headed out. Nina was sure to pet both Lila and Jewel before walking out. She loved the cats; they were great therapy for her.

When they pulled into the dusty gravel parking lot, Nina had to wonder what kind of a place they had chosen. It had the look of an old horse barn, with cheap lights strung around the door. It could be considered a watering hole, she thought to herself.

The sat quietly for a few minutes, watching the crowd. She saw all types inside. There were couples, dressed nicely, a date night she guessed; young adults in their grunge look; single men from 21 to 71 and a few older single women on the prowl.

As soon as the band started playing 'Ring of Fire,' the crowd cheered. They followed that song with 'The Chair', one of George Strait's first hits, and one of her mom's favorites. She wasn't a huge fan of country music but some of it was ok, she decided.

Suddenly, Lauren's eyes grew wide. At the same time, Nina heard, "Are you cheating on me with this band?" She turned quickly to see Bennett standing beside her. She was speechless. What should she say?

"You are obviously stunned by my sharp wit, and blue eyes," he said grinning. He knew how to break the ice, that's for sure. His sandy blonde hair was tied back in a ponytail. It was an old look, but it worked for him. She caught a glimpse of his face. The last time it was so dark, she would never have recognized him in a line-up. His crystal-clear blue eyes and long eyelashes were the prettiest she had ever seen. Standing next to Pat, she guessed him to be about 6'1".

"Imagine seeing you girls in this dive. Why are you here anyway? I'm sorry to be so blunt, but this isn't a place for ladies like yourselves to hang out. I'm sorry, that was rude." he said. "Can I sit here? I feel stupid standing here."

"Uh, sure, I guess. What are you doing here?" Nina asked, suddenly feeling uncomfortable. "You said before that you didn't like watching other musicians perform."

"No," he corrected, "I think what I said was that I can't enjoy watching other musicians. Almost anyone who plays would tell you the same thing. I don't hear the song like you hear it. I just hear chord changes. It's a blessing and a curse." He laughed as he pulled up a chair.

"So, you never did say what you're doing here," she asked again.

"Well, if you must know, I was asked to fill in for someone," he said teasing her, "but at the last minute the guy showed up." They ended up talking most of the evening as Lauren was being asked to dance by half the men in the bar.

"I have to tell you in advance that musicians are terrible dancers," he said. "But would you dance with me?" The band had just started playing 'You Look Wonderful Tonight'. He took her hand in his and led her to the corner of the dancefloor. She was grateful he did, she didn't like being in the middle with everyone staring at them.

Lauren had decided she wanted to leave around 11 o'clock. Nina agreed. She had to work the next day and needed sleep. This day had been a mess but being out with her friend and seeing Bennett made up for it. She liked talking to him. He seemed like a real nice guy, but she was not ready to trust someone like that yet.

# CHAPTER THIRTY-FOUR

Her dad called her the next day with an update. She was doing as good as could be expected he said. The stroke had affected some of her motor skills on her left side. Her speech was also affected, and she was having trouble with her speech, all typical, he said.

"The doctors keep telling me she's lucky, it could have been much worse," he sniffled. "If she keeps improving, she will go into rehab next week. They say she could be home in three or four weeks."

"That's good news, right Daddy?" she asked. "When can I call and talk to her? I don't care what time; you call me right away."

"You know I will. It's just so hard since she isn't home," he said. "I haven't slept alone since you were four and I was out of town with work. After that trip, I promised her I would never leave her side again. I knew what she was going through, and I didn't help matters."

"Daddy, what are you talking about?" Nina asked, very confused.

"We had never told you, because it was just too painful," he said. "But your mother was pregnant when you were four. We had just found out after your birthday in February. Her due date was to be in October." Nina was in shock. How come her mother never talked about it? She would have had a younger sister or brother.

"As you probably guessed," he continued, "she lost the baby when I was out of town, in April. They rushed her to the hospital, but it was too late, and they told her she could never have kids again. It crushed her. For weeks after, she wouldn't get out of bed. I didn't know how to help her." She didn't know if she had ever seen or heard her daddy cry. It broke her heart to not be there with him.

"I called her sister, your Aunt Jean, and asked for her help," he said. "She came and stayed for a few weeks."

"Wait, I think I remember that. Auntie Jean took me to preschool a few times, and then out to lunch," Nina said. "I had forgotten all about that."

"She was a big help with you, and your mother," Walter said. "When your 'death' was made public, your Auntie Jean took it very hard. She always thought of you as her closest niece."

"Yeah," Nina agreed, "I remember Momma used to call me Jean by mistake. She said it was because I reminded her of Aunt Jean's mannerisms. This whole mess I caused over the past couple of months just added to the pain, I'm sure. I feel horrible."

Maybe one day," her dad said, "you can set the record straight." They talked for a few more minutes. Nina decided she had to make a trip home as soon as possible. She didn't care how much she had to save. Her dad needed her, probably more than her mother did at this point.

Nina called back the next afternoon for an update. She hoped asking for the time off wouldn't be a big problem. Tonya said late autumn was their slow season. She got a bus ticket that had her traveling overnight.

That morning, she got off the bus to see her dad waiting for her. A big hug and a kiss on the cheek later, they were in the truck going home. "Now, Sugar, remember," he warned her. "She has trouble with motor skills on her left side. And her speech is a little hard to understand. We're all getting older," he solemnly said. "It was bound to happen to one of us eventually."

Their first stop that day was the hospital. Evelyn was still in recovery but not in ICU any longer. She started getting emotional as she walked down the hallway to her room. One day, she thought, she and her dad would be gone, and she would be alone. She knew she wasn't ready for that yet, maybe not ever.

The door was open, and Nina poked her head in and saw her mother, hooked up to several machines. She was napping peacefully and didn't want to disturb her, but a nurse came up behind her, "It's okay honey, go on in. I have to get her vitals anyway."

Evelyn opened her eyes and smiled widely. A tear started trickling down Nina's face. "Oh Mama, I have missed you terribly," Kaci cried on her mother's shoulder.

"Honey girl, now why you crying?" Evelyn said. "I didn't go anywhere. I'm here."

Nina noticed her R's were giving her trouble. She now knew what her dad had meant, her speech was a little slower and more deliberate, but she still looked good. A sight for sore eyes they say.

Over that week, Kaci took over in the kitchen and made dinner almost every night. That is, except once when they ordered pizza. It was one thing Evelyn didn't like so, whenever she was out with friends for dinner, they ordered pizza

She was happy to be home, to be able to see her mother. They went to the hospital every day, at least twice a day. Not seeing her was the worst part about what she did just weeks before. They had just read the week before the list of presumed dead from the Terror Attack. "Kaci Lianne Jamison" was listed. Her name had jumped off the page when she read it.

Saturday afternoon she was about to call the bus station to get a ticket back to New Mexico, when her dad knocked on her bedroom door. "Honey, I want to talk to you for a minute."

Nine looked at him, noticeably worried, "What is it Daddy?"

"It's nothing bad, don't you worry," he said. "We want you to take your mom's car. It's yours now. She will never be able to drive alone and it's just going to sit here."

She was stunned, "Are you sure?"

"Of course, I'm sure," he answered, "What am I going to do with a Nissan? You know I'm a Dodge man." They both laughed, it was a laugh of relief she thought.

"We'll work out the paperwork later," he explained. "For now, I'll write a letter giving 'Nina' permission to drive it."

She left that Sunday morning, promising to return as soon as she could. It was hard to leave her mother in that condition, but she was still improving, that was good news. She had forgotten how liberating it was to be able to get in your own car and go somewhere, anywhere. Nina felt a new sense of independence. This was just what she needed.

# CHAPTER THIRTY-FIVE

When she got back to work Pat made it a point to pull her aside to talk. "Do you remember my friend, Bennett? The guitar player?"

Of course, I do, she thought. She wasn't sure where this was going, so she just said, "Yes. Why?"

"Well, he has been in here a couple times this week," Pat said. "He was trying to make it appear coincidental, but I think he was looking for you." Pat gave her a wink and a grin.

Nina was caught off guard. She thought he was nice, and a great guitar player, but the fact that he was hunting her down made her uncomfortable. "If you talk to him and he asks about me, just tell him I'm not looking for a boyfriend or anything."

Whatever you say," Pat blew it off and went back to the bar to get ready for the lunch shift.

The next week she was sitting in the break room after the dinner rush, when Pat poked his head around the corner and mouthed, "He's here."

"This is getting ridiculous," Nina said. "Doesn't he have to work or something?" How many times was he going to 'casually' drop in? Men were so unpredictable. She saw the transformation in Landon when he started drinking. Would this Bennett guy be the same? Nina wasn't eager to find out right now. "Tell him I went home already," she begged Pat.

By the time Thanksgiving rolled around, the tourists had started trickling back in. Most it seemed were in town visiting family. A few of the souvenir shops remained open in the Plaza and most of those had changed their hours. The restaurant also started getting a little busier, but still, she was only making about half of what she made in the summer.

Nina had always saved money for a rainy day, and this was it, she thought. If she was careful, she could live through the winter without having to look for a second job. Because of cost to travel, and loss of wager, and the impending bad weather, she had told her parents that she couldn't make it home for Thanksgiving that year.

She and Lauren celebrated Thanksgiving with the crew at the restaurant. It was a 'Friendsgiving.' The restaurant was closed for the holiday, and Julia allowed them to use the restaurant kitchen and dining room. She even contributed by buying the turkeys. The smell from the kitchen was mouth-watering.

As people kept coming in, she noticed Pat and Bennett coming over to their side of the table. "Are these seats taken?" Bennett asked.

"Of course, they aren't," Pat answered. "We are all one big happy family. Sit anywhere you like." Nina made sure Pat noticed her reaction, she wasn't happy.

The food came out of the kitchen with a loud cheer from the diners. Lauren brought in a homemade pumpkin loaf; and she brought whipped sweet potatoes, from her mother's recipe and everyone raved about them. The Green Chile Dressing was the best thing she tried. It was going to be one of her new traditions.

Nina felt uncomfortable immediately. Her eyes darted from Lauren to Pat and back to Lauren. She didn't know how this was going to end up. She had been avoiding him for weeks. Nina counted 19 adults who didn't have other plans, and he had to sit by her?

Bennett was very polite and kept their conversation plain and simple. He made an effort to not pry into her personal life like she dreaded. In the end she had to admit she had a good time. She knew she was beginning to like him, as much as she tried not to. He was nice and interesting.

"I know this will sound a bit pushy," he said. "But since I've been trying to talk to you for weeks, I'm not letting you go without asking for your phone number."

Nina didn't know what to say. She wasn't sure she wanted him calling her multiple times a day and her having to tell him to stop. She finally decided that there was no harm in talking to him. If he brought up a date, she would just tell him she wasn't ready to date. She would make up some excuse.

Lauren had driven them that night, so she dropped Nina off in the early evening. They were both stuffed from the wonderful meal everyone put together. It was one of the best holidays she could remember in a long time. As soon as Nina walked in her front door, her cell phone was ringing. She automatically thought it was her dad, but it was a local phone number.

"Did you get home safely?" Bennett asked. His voice put a smile on her face. Damn! He was growing on her.

"Yes, I did. You didn't have to call," she said a little annoyed, "I'm a big girl from the big city."

"I'm sorry I didn't mean to imply anything," he said. "What city is that?"

Damn! There she goes, she already messed up. She wasn't going to tell him too much about her background, that way she wouldn't get tripped up in a lie. She hated lying, but she still didn't know who he was and how trustworthy. Nobody knew she had lived in New York. She had to think quick. "Actually several, I've lived in lots of places."

Bennett kept her on the phone for over two hours. By the time they hung up for the night, she had learned he was a twin, his sister, Rebecca, lived in Albuquerque with her husband, Don, and two girls and a boy. His younger brother, Beau, was married with a young daughter. He and his wife owned a small restaurant near Old Town in the city. Bennett also had attended a year of college at University of New Mexico but didn't like much about it at all. His parents lived in Albuquerque. His dad retired from the Air Force in Clovis almost 25 years ago. They had stayed since the kids were in school. After Beau graduated, they moved to the home they lived in now.

Nina was surprised he opened up so easily, especially when she didn't ask. He had tried to get anything out of her about her background, but she would change the subject. If she did answer it was only in vague comments. He thought she made an effort to hide something, but maybe just didn't like talking about herself.

"Where did you go to school?" he asked. Now, he saw it as a challenge to gather small bits of information. One day, she'll trust me enough to tell me her story, he thought.

"It was a small school in Indiana," was her answer. She heard all about his music. He had lived in Austin for a few years, trying to get his break into the business. He was able to make enough to live on, but just barely. He did make some good friends that he was still in contact with today. He came back and lived with his parents for a few months before one of his Austin friends called him from Santa Fe.

Bennett moved up there that week, taking Leo's offer to play guitar in his rock band. He had an extra room where he could crash until he could get his own place. That was over six years ago, and Bennett was still living with him. He explained that they each had their own space, so it just made sense.

He finally asked her out on a real date. They didn't make any other plans except he would pick her up Tuesday after work. Not knowing where they were going was both exciting and scary to Nina. She had to tell herself that he was a good guy. If he had a bad reputation, or was a bad guy, then surely Renee and Pat wouldn't have introduced them.

They agreed to meet on Sunday afternoon for coffee where Lauren worked. She was still going to have her safety net. Definitely not ready to be all alone with him. He pulled up in a small truck with NIN, AC/DC, BEATLES stickers in the back window. She noted that he did like some newer rock and roll after all. She was going to have to ask him about that.

# CHAPTER THIRTY-SIX

They ended up sitting in the café for over two hours. "I hate to rush you guys," the owner said as he walked over with a towel in his hands, "but I need to close up for the day." She couldn't believe it had been two hours. Bennett sure could talk, she found that out.

The first thing Nina did when she got home was call Lauren. She had left the café after they had only been there 30 minutes. Nina gave her the thumbs up sign that everything was ok.

"Tell me everything!" Lauren begged her immediately. "Did you really just get home?"

"Yes, I did. He can really talk, I found that out. And if you ask him about music, anything about music, he talks even longer," she said laughing. "I think I like him, or at least I think I could like him."

"Well, yeah," Lauren stated, "we all like him. He's a nice guy. But he like-likes you, I'm sure of it."

"We are going to talk a little more on the phone and then I'll consider a date," she promised.

Nina made herself something to eat and was just sitting down when her phone rang again. "Lauren, I said I would let you know if he called again."

A deep voice answered back, "I hope you're talking about me?" It was Bennett. He didn't miss a beat. "I mean, it's okay if you're not. Well, no, it's not ok. Geez just tell me already."

Nina was laughing so hard she almost choked on her sandwich. She was able to spit out, "Yes, it was you. I'm so embarrassed." She had recovered from her full mouth and could finally talk normal. She put her food down and got a drink of water just to be sure.

"Are you okay?" he asked her. She felt silly nodding when she realized he couldn't see her. This is a disaster she thought.

"Yes, I'm fine. I'm sorry I worried you," she apologized. "Just a little shocked that you called so quickly. It hasn't been an hour yet since we left."

"Did I mention one of my worst flaws?" he asked.

Her hands suddenly started to shake a little and her breathing sped up. Please let it be he can't tell time or something silly. She just couldn't do anything major right now. "No, you didn't."

"Patience. I'm terrible at waiting." Bennett felt he had to explain, "My mom says I get it honest; my dad is the same way. Which is somewhat funny considering he is retired from the Air Force. All they do is wait."

"Oh ok, that's not bad at all," she calmly stated.

"What did you think I was going to say? That I am a stalker on the side?" she knew he was teasing, but she had to admit, that idea had crossed her mind.

They seemed to find plenty more to talk about and stayed on the phone for another hour. He finally asked her out for a real date. She felt she knew more about him than she ever did with Landon, so she said yes. He was going to take her site-seeing he said.

Wednesday came and she was as nervous as she was when she went to prom with Jared Hughes back home. Jared was a football player, but also was in the top 5% of their class. He was a catch. But seeing as how they were both going to college out state, they agreed they would just be friends. She hadn't thought about Jared in years, she thought.

He was there promptly at four. "Are you ready for fun in the sun?"

She laughed, "Oh sure, what do you have planned? The sun will be going down soon."

"We still have an hour. Let's get a move on. And you'll see soon enough." He opened the door of the truck for her to get in.

She loved his chivalrous side. As soon as he started the engine she asked, "Now will you tell me where you're taking me?' She felt like she should have told Lauren where she was going, but how could she? She didn't know herself.

"It's a surprise, but I know you are going to love it," he reassured her. "And don't worry, I would never put you in any danger." Thirty minutes later, he pulled the truck over on the side of a mountain. When she turned to look at him, he leaned over and gave a gentle kiss on the lips. Nina felt a spark go through her body.

"I've been wanting to do that since the first night we met," he confessed.

"You have?" she seemed stunned. "I hope it was worth the wait." She could tell she was blushing by the warm feeling in her cheeks.

"Yes, it was! I was just nervous, didn't want to come on too strong and scare you off," he explained. "But I do have a confession to make. I begged Pat to let me come with him to Thanksgiving dinner."

Nina smiled, it was kind of sweet, the way he went to such lengths to see her. Just then, she heard a noise coming up behind them. She turned and couldn't believe her eyes. She saw a whole herd of horses, at least eight or nine. "Someone must be missing those guys."

Bennett chuckled softly, "No, those are wild horses. They roam wherever they like in these mountains. In fact, the landowners here will tell you they are as destructive as deer or raccoons to their vegetation."

She sat in amazement as they walked by the truck. Several of them had the spotted Palomino coat, a few others were a light buff color. They were just beautiful.

After they passed, Bennett got out and opened her door. Taking her hand in his, he walked to the back of the truck and opened the tailgate. He lifted her up and he sat down beside her.

"In about 15 minutes," he said glancing at his watch, "you will see something just as beautiful." They waited, holding hands, her head on his shoulder. He smelled wonderful, she thought as she inhaled again. She always loved the smell of men's cologne.

He took the opportunity and kissed her again, with a little more passion than the first one. They finally broke away, smiling at each other. "There, it's starting now," he said. The sun had begun to set over the horizon. It was as if a painter's palette was used to color the sky. Shades of lavender, peach, orange, and pink stretched as far as they could see.

"I've seen the sunset before, but up here, it's even more beautiful," she stared in amazement.

"So are you," he said quietly. She turned to look in his eyes. She laid her head on his shoulder and squeezed his hand. "I had something else I wanted to show you," he added, "but I think it will have to wait until another date. If you think we will be seeing each other again?" He was hoping she would say yes, again.

She smiled; his face told her he was nervously waiting for her answer. "Let me think about it, but your chances are looking good." They drove back to town, holding hands all the way.

"I'm ready to eat, how about you?" he asked her. "Do you like Mexican, Italian, Chinese or something off the wall?"

"I've had all kinds of food, we used to get take-out a lot," she let slip. "In college I mean." She hoped that he didn't notice her stumbling for words. "I will say, I have a soft spot for Italian. I worked at a great little Italian place in college." That part was true, thank goodness.

He had planned on taking her to a nice steakhouse for dinner, but when she said she loved Italian, he changed his mind. There was a locally owned Italian restaurant that was very romantic and delicious. He thought tonight was the perfect night to try it out.

He pulled into the parking lot of La Trattoria just before 7 o'clock. "I hope you're hungry, I've heard this place is fantastic."

The hostess led them to a small half circle booth in the corner. The dim lights and candles on the tables made the atmosphere very romantic. As she sat down, Bennett scooted in next to her. They sat elbow to elbow, nice and cozy.

The server recommended the fried provolone as an appetizer, and they agreed. He also brought out the carafe of Cabernet Bennett ordered. The menu was so large, Nina couldn't decide. Again, their waiter stepped in to suggest the Pasta Primo dinner for two. Four dishes on the plate to be shared. By the end of their meal, they weren't sure they would be able to walk to his truck.

This had to be the best first date she's ever had, she thought as he drove back to her apartment. He walked her to the door. Nina didn't want the night to end, so she invited him inside. Lauren would be home after her night class, about another hour or so. After giving him the two-minute tour, they sat down on the sofa. She didn't know if it was the food, wine, or long day, but she laid her head on his shoulder and fell asleep in minutes.

She was dreaming of running down a long highway, headlights behind her. Knowing she couldn't outrun it she dove into the grass beside the road. The car turned around and parked next to where she laid. She heard footsteps, the familiar gait of a man in loafers. At that moment, he spoke, "Kaci, Kaci, where are you? I know you're there." It was Landon, he had come for her. She woke up to Bennett softly shaking her shoulder.

"Nina, hey cutie, wake up, you're dreaming," he said. "You were breathing really heavily, are you ok?"

Nina took a minute to think about what had happened. It was a nightmare. She'd had it before. Landon was chasing her, wanting her back. "Uh, yeah, bad dream, I guess. You probably think I'm a psycho."

"Not at all," he told her, "We all have our demons." He drew her closer for a soft kiss and she felt instantly better. He knew what to do that's for sure, she thought.

# CHAPTER THIRTY-SEVEN

The next night Nina was expecting him to call but he didn't. She guessed he was rehearsing with the band and would call her when they took a break. She waited up until midnight, but he never called. The next day was the same, no word from him. She finally called him, against her mother's rule that a young lady doesn't call a boy. He finally answered. He grumbles, "Uh hello," his voice sounded really down. She could hear a Beatles CD playing in the background.

"What's wrong," she asked. "You sound like you lost your best friend. Never mind, I shouldn't have called. You changed your mind about going out, it's ok."

"No, that's not it. I mean I haven't changed my mind. I'm just in a bad place right now." he answered solemnly. "George Harrison died yesterday. He was an idol of mine. Brain cancer finally got him."

"I heard about that," she said. "That's awful. I am so sorry. I remember you telling me he was sick."

"Yeah, it's the end of an era. The worst part is that there isn't much coverage on the news about it, because of damned 9/11," he was clearly agitated. "Can't we just move on for God's sake! The world just feels empty to me right now," he said. "I'm going out for a walk. I'll call you back in a while." He hung up, leaving Nina to wonder what she should do now.

Later that afternoon, there was a soft knock at her door. It was Bennett. He looked tired, exhausted. He clearly didn't get much sleep.

"You better come in before you fall down," she told him. He sat down next to her and laid his head in her lap. He was asleep in minutes. She really needed to get up and put away her clean clothes she had just washed, but she didn't want to disturb him. The fact that he would show his vulnerable side she considered it a good thing. Not many men would.

He woke almost an hour later, not sure where he was in those first seconds. When he saw Nina, he smiled. He apologized and got up, put on a jacket and just walked out as she stood and stared at the door. He was really taking this hard, she thought. Nina was left alone to wonder how she could help, make it better. She knew nothing she did would change the fact that another one of the Beatles had died way too soon.

He finally called her later that night. "I'm sorry I just ran off earlier," he mumbled. "I'm just confused and didn't know what to do. I still don't. But I wasn't going to put you in a bad mood too. You are wonderful. I'll call or stop by soon."

Nina just stood with the phone in her hand. I guess he did have some issues to work out. At least he was polite enough to apologize and make sure she knew why he was in this mood.

The next day, he was knocking at her door in the early afternoon. She let him in. He didn't look much better. He just wanted to sit down for a minute. "I am lost, really lost. I don't know what all this means if someone like George can lose everything to brain cancer."

"Hey, would you please stay here while I go to work?" It's the least she could do, she thought. "I know I'd feel better if I knew you were here, and not roaming the streets or driving. He agreed.

Nina got home several hours later, after the dinner rush. She walked in to see him in the same spot, but he did find a blanket so maybe he got some sleep. Nina's heart ached to see him that way. "Tell me what I can do to help you through this," she offered.

"There's nothing to do really. Did you know that the Beatles broke up with they were all about 28-30 years old? They had so much success at such an early age, and so quickly, no group would ever be able to do that again," he told her. "Today there is MTV and VH1 to push the videos in front of fans. It seems like fame today doesn't have the longevity it did back in the 60's and even 70's. It really is the end of an era."

The rest of the night they spent, sitting together, listening to his George Harrison collection of CDs. She was amazed at how much he knew about every single song and CD he played. She always suspected Bennett had a more serious side, but she hadn't seen it until now.

He was quiet for days. Only talking for a few minutes each time she called. He spent a lot of time listening to his collection of CDs and watching the video tapes he had of concerts and interviews. Anytime a tribute came on tv, he was watching. She was beginning to wonder if he would ever recover. She didn't know him that well, but he seemed to be really depressed. If this was going to continue, she might have to just leave him alone, and not see him anymore. She had her own problems to deal with; she didn't think she was strong enough to take on more.

Instead of ignoring him, Nina vowed to give him another chance. She invited him over the next day for dinner. She thought he needed a home-cooked meal and something to take his mind off recent events.

He arrived ten minutes early and brought her flowers and a bottle of wine. He opened the bottle, poured them two glasses as he sat, and watched her finish up in the kitchen. It was nice to be able to cook for someone who really likes my food she thought. Landon wasn't always complimentary about her cooking. Bennett asked for seconds. She was going to be sure to send the leftovers home with him.

They had finished eating dinner and she was cleaning up her mess when he came up behind her, wrapped his arms around her waist and gently kissed her on the back of the neck. He found another ticklish spot of hers. She started to giggle, "Stop Bennett! I have to finish these dishes, or I'll never do it."

"Let me help you," he offered, stepping around her to the sink. He picked up a towel and started drying. They spent the next few minutes putting everything away. They went to the living room and sat down for the night. She picked up the remote and found an episode of *America's Funniest Home Videos*. It was sometimes corny but it didn't take a long attention-span to watch.

She sat down next to him to talk. "Hey, I know life sucks sometimes, everyone would agree with that. But you can't let this take over your life."

"You just don't understand," he said quietly.

"You're right, I don't," she replied, "but I do know how it feels to have lost someone close to you, but it was a family member, not someone I never met."

As soon as she said it, she regretted it. He wouldn't say anything in reply. "I'll leave you alone since you don't want to talk to me," she said as she got up to walk away. But before she could he grabbed her hand and pulled her onto his lap.

"I'm sorry, I know I'm being selfish," he said. "Your mom has been sick and I'm mourning someone I never met, albeit an awesome guy I never met, but nonetheless," he smiled.

They continued talking on the phone that week. Seeing each other for lunch or dinner some days. She had never felt this comfortable with anyone, even Landon when they first started dating. What was her favorite food? Movie? Musician? He was starting to notice that Nina wasn't very open about her past. He didn't really care, he always believed in living in the present, but it was a bit odd he thought.

# CHAPTER THIRTY-EIGHT

In between work and talking to Bennett, Nina had been in constant touch with her parents. Her mother was to be sent home from rehab that week. Walter asked her if she could be there, to help her transition easier. He knew Aunt Jean would make a big fuss, but he already told her she needed to wait a few days.

Nina was going to have to tell Bennett she was leaving town. After another one of her great meals, she blurted out, "I don't know how to tell you this," she started. She saw the sudden confused look on his face and changed her words. "I mean, unfortunately for us, I need to go home to see my mom." She had been telling him about her parents and the challenges they were going through.

Bennett looked relieved, "Oh God, Nina. I thought you were going to say we're done." He took a few breaths as he processed what she said.

She quickly apologized, "No! Never! That would never happen. But I am going home for a week or so. Julia gave me next week off, so I don't have to worry about work, except the money I won't be making."

"Don't worry about that, I'll help out if you need it." he said, "Is there anything I can do? Let me drive you."

"No, this one is all me," she answered. "I will call you every day. I just need one favor."

"Anything you want," he said. As he said it, he knew he meant every word. He would do anything for her.

"Anything?" she asked with a big grin.

He let a loud laugh, "Oh really? What did you have in mind?"

"I just need you to water my plants," she laughed.

"Just as long as you don't hold me responsible if they die," he joked. "If you won't let me do anything else, let me fill up your tank with gas before you leave."

"Okay, okay, I accept your offer." They sat down on the sofa and turned on the tv. Nina leaned over and put her head in his lap. She was so tired. Bennett began stroking her hair and she was asleep in minutes. She had a dream that they were both on a hike and met for the first time when she tripped and sprained her ankle. He, being a perfect gentleman, carried her to safety.

Nina left her apartment early the next day. It would take at least ten hours to get to her parents' house. She really wanted to get there before dinner, but she knew that was unlikely. Driving across the flat farmland along I-40 gave her lots of time to think. The wind picked up around Amarillo and was working to blow her off the road. She had to force herself to concentrate on the road, and not daydream.

Her visit wasn't going to be a long one, but she knew she could stay as long as she was needed thanks to Julia. She got to her parents' house just before bedtime. She fixed her and Walter a snack then they both tried to get some sleep. They were expected to the hospital before noon. She wanted to get there much earlier to be sure to get everything out of the room and packed into the truck.

Evelyn was making small improvements. Each one was a milestone. When Nina got to her room, Evelyn was waiting in a wheelchair at the door. The sight of seeing her in that wheelchair tore her heart into pieces. She knew she was going to do anything her mother needed her to do.

"There's my baby girl!" She was excited to see her, but she needed to keep it down. Everyone in town knew her daughter had died in the attack. Nina brought her finger to her lips, "Shhh. Remember? Let's say I'm a niece?"

Her mother would say anything to get to go home at that point. Walter came up behind them and bent to kiss his wife on the forehead. He picked up her two tote bags while Nina grabbed the hospital bag with all the extras in it. They had decided it would be easier for Evelyn to get in and out of the truck, so Walter went to get it and pull up to the main entrance.

On the way home, Evelyn asked to stop at McDonald's for a cheeseburger and large fires. She was craving any kind of fast food that had some flavor. Hospital food was always so bland and healthy.

They took their time helping Evelyn out of the truck and into the house. Thankfully there was only one step to get into the kitchen door. They sat and devoured the burgers and fries in a matter of minutes. "Every once in a while, you have to throw the diet out the window," Evelyn said.

That same night, Bennett called her, "Hey cutie, I sure do miss you. How's your mom?"

"Doing good I guess," she said, "She will never be the same but at least she is still here. I don't know what my dad would do if she died."

"We all do what we have to do," he said. "You'd be surprised at what some people can do when they have motivation and put their mind to it."

They talked every night. When he was playing at a bar, he called her during their first break, while he cooled off outside. Even though they wouldn't have seen each other because of work, the fact that she was 500 miles away made him miss her even more. If she was really serious about Bennett, she would have to tell her parents.

She left to come home after two more days. She got to see her mother, and that made everything ok. She wouldn't admit it, but she felt like she had been having an anxiety attack, because she had no idea how her mother was really doing.

As soon as she pulled into her parking apace, he was waiting in his car. He got out and picked her up. "Don't you ever leave me again," he said warmly as he hugged her tightly and kissed her.

The last time she heard those words, Landon was threatening her during a fight he started about their marriage. The words had a completely different meaning coming from Bennett. Of course, Landon had ended it with, "Or you'll be sorry. You are mine, period."

It was after 8 o'clock and she was exhausted from the long drive. But, as she laid next to him, feeling loved in his arms, she knew they wouldn't be going to sleep.

"I love you," he told her.

Nina, blinked, a little surprised that he said it first. She felt the same but didn't want to rush things. She whispered, softly, "I love you too."

His warm hand moved down her body, making her senses come alive. She felt a yearning stir inside her that she had never experienced with anyone else. As he removed her bra and touched her breasts, she was on fire. She frantically pulled his shirt off, so she could feel his bare skin against hers.

He kissed her neck, a weak spot for her, making her moan with pleasure. He worked his way down to her nipples, which he licked gently then sucked with more passion.

Nina began unbuckling his belt and using her hands to pull off his jeans. He was hard and she took it in her hand and gently squeezed, and stroked, making him groan. She felt like she was in charge of their lovemaking, which turned her on even more.

She pushed him onto his back and straddled him. His hands came up and squeezed her breasts and nipples, driving her crazy with desire. She began gently rubbing his crotch, moving up and down. They were both panting, wanting more. He took his hands and almost tore her pants and panties off. His fingers found their way inside her. She was wet and warm. She cried out with every touch.

He entered her while she sat on top of him. They both moaned with ecstasy as they moved up and down together in a perfect rhythm. It only took a minute before Bennett came inside her. It was the best feeling, pleasing him. He rolled her over onto her back in a second and started moving down her body with his tongue. When he reached her inner thighs, his tongue found the sport that made her cry out in passion. As he played, moving his tongue around, her body shook all over when she climaxed.

They laid in each other's arms for what seemed like an hour but was only a few minutes she realized. This is how love making is supposed to feel, she thought. She was too tired to move, and yet energized at the same time. She rolled over, putting a hand on his chest, looking into his eyes.

"What are we going to do about this?" she said playfully.

"About what?" he smiled.

"I am not going to be able to take my hands off you," she said. "It might be embarrassing for you, in public." She laughed.

"I guess I'm just going to have to keep you close at all times," he said.

# CHAPTER THIRTY-NINE

Christmas was coming soon and Nina thinking about all her keepsake ornaments she left behind in New York. She finally decided it couldn't hurt to have her parents call Landon and ask him to mail them. Nina told her mother she would give them her new address when they needed it. In fact, she may have it delivered to Lauren's just to be safe. She wasn't even sure if Landon would do it. He's just the type to have thrown everything away that had been hers.

Just over a week later a box arrived at her door. It was from her parents. She realized it had to be the things Landon sent them. This might be the last letter I get from my mom, she thought.

After work that night, she sat down to unpack it. There were a couple yearbooks, a few pieces of inexpensive jewelry he obviously didn't want or need and a box that was taped shut. She carefully opened it and found most of her Christmas ornaments. She sat down and cried a little as she unwrapped each one. Each had its own personal story and memory.

Christmas in Santa Fe was beautiful. The town was high enough in the mountains to get snow regularly. The trees with snow on their branches, coupled with the bright sun or glowing moon made a perfect painting. New Mexico snow was much different than that of Kentucky or New York. It had a powdery texture, not as icy and dangerous for drivers.

That year, Bennett took her into the Chimayo mountains to hunt for their own live tree. He had a friend whose parents had given them permission to come up and cut one down. Since her apartment wasn't very big, the tallest they needed was seven feet, if it wasn't too big around. After a couple hours, they found the right one. It took almost an hour more to get it cut and tied in the back of his truck.

As they came down the mountain the lights of the town came into view. "This has to be the most amazing place I've ever seen, and I was in New York City for Christmas." She suddenly stopped talking, realizing she had just told him about Kaci's past, not her own.

"I didn't know you had been to the Big Apple," he said. She is full of surprises he thought.

Nina played it off, "There are lots of things you don't know about me." She laughed so he would think she was teasing him. At the same time, her mind raced, thinking how close that was.

She knew she wanted to get him something special for Christmas and knew it was the right time to sell her wedding band set. There was a man in town who did custom leather work.

Bennett had invited her to his parents' house for Christmas Eve dinner. It was their family tradition and she felt obligated. She was extremely nervous about meeting his family, but she knew it would happen sooner or later. At least this way, the holiday would distract attention from the new girlfriend.

They drove to their home, in the foothills of Sandia Mountain. It was a gorgeous home with a wall of windows that looked out upon the Duke city, as Albuquerque was nicknamed. His father, James, took their coats, and laid them on the bench in the foyer.

"We're keeping them in your old room," he announced. "You remember where that is, don't you?" It was a sarcastic comment referring to the fact that they don't see him very often.

"Dad, please don't start," Bennett said, rolling his eyes.

"I'm just playing with you, take it easy young man," he said. "Bennett here has come a long way from overcoming his obstacles."

Nina looked at him, questioning the comment. "I'll tell you in a minute, it's no big deal," he promised her.

Bennett was clearly annoyed with his father's comments and quickly changed the subject, "where are my nieces and nephew?"

At that moment, squeals came from the other room. The sounds led their way to a great room the size of a small restaurant.

"Nina, what will you have to drink?" James asked politely.

"Red wine is fine, Sir" she answered. "Thank you."

James came back with her glass of wine and a cold beer for his son. "No 'Sirs' in this house, please." He turned to call after Bennett, "I see you finally found a woman with a little class, that's a nice change for you, isn't it?"

He gave his dad another annoyed look. Bennett didn't look like he thought it was funny. Apparently, the comment touched a nerve. What is it with fathers and sons, she thought.

Nina directed their attention to the small children running around. She counted one young boy, about four, and three girls, ranging in ages from three to eight. One of the women in the room stood up and walked over to them.

"Since my brother hasn't introduced us, I'm Becky, the prettier twin." She smiled as she gave her brother a big hug. "Where have you been the past couple of years? We've missed you." Nina looked her over casually, trying to see any similarities in their looks but found none. She did notice that they had a little of the twin ESP people talk about.

"I hardly think so with this mob to take care of," he joked. "By the way, don't listen to anything Becky says about me, it could all be true." Becky laughed at that and gave him a wink.

Becky pointed out the young boy, Jay, and two older girls as hers. Molly and Daphne were busy running circles around the youngest girl. "And that little cutie is our niece, Beau's daughter, Amy. Beau!" she said above the noisy bunch, "Get over here."

"This young woman," Becky said, introducing Nina to Beau, "is Nina. Hopefully, she can tame our wild brother." She said it with a smile and squeezing Bennett's forearm. His expression told her that he was used to the sibling teasing.

As Nina shook Beau's hand, she noticed a strong resemblance to Bennett. He was maybe two inches shorter, and a little thinner, and his hair was cut short; but you could still tell they were related.

Bennett and Nina made their way into the living room. As soon as they sat down, Daphne came over and started asking her questions. "What's your name? How old are you? Do you have any pets? Uncle Benny must like you. Did he kiss you yet?" She was like a miniature Barbara Walters.

"Uncle Benny? Very cute," Nina teased him. He actually was blushing she thought.

Within a few minutes, Amy brought over a book and handed it to her. She didn't say anything, but Nina knew what she wanted. She started reading to the younger ones while Bennett watched.

"You're really good with them," he said. "They never listen to me."

As soon as she was able to get up, Bennett stole her away to the deck. "You are such a trooper," he said. "My family can be a little intimidating." He pulled her into his arms and hugged her warmly. "Thank you," he whispered in her ear.

"For what?" she asked. "I didn't do anything."

"Just being here, with me, is enough." He paused then said, "I feel like I need to say something. I had a drinking problem, which led to some bad decisions. A lot of bad decisions. I will always be honest with you, so ask me anything you want. The last few years I spent most of the holidays feeling sorry for myself, or showing up here, drunk. I am embarrassed now when I think of how I acted."

"Oh honey, it's ok," she comforted him, "I don't care about that. We all have a past. But" she said with a smile, "you don't have a secret family hidden off somewhere in the mountains, do you? No children?" A tiny warning bell went off in her head. This is when Landon first screwed up in her book.

"Nope. Absolutely, no other family than what you see here," he answered. "And that's more than enough."

When they turned around, they saw two little noses and 20 fingers pressed against the window. "Looks like the peanut gallery found us," he joked.

Once inside, his mother walked out of the kitchen with a plate of hors d'ouevres for the hungry crowd. Her eyes lit up when she saw her son, "Benny honey, you made it."

"I told you I would," he said as she grabbed his face and kissed him on the cheek. "Mom, this is Nina. Nina this is my mom and Queen of this wild bunch, Gwen."

"You have a beautiful home," she said. It sounded like a rehearsed line, but it was true. "I mean that sincerely. I mean it is gorgeous." Nina was starting to look nervous, waiting for Gwen to reply.

"Nina, sweetie, don't look so scared," she finally said. "We won't bite. Well, most of us won't, I can't vouch for Jay or Amy."

Bennett laughed along with his mother. Nina smiled and started feeling a little more at ease. They all made their way back to the family room where the kids were corralled to the sofa area. James had set up a camera to a tripod to take a family photo.

"We need all the men behind the sofa, the ladies sitting and the munchkins on laps and standing," he instructed.

"Grampy, we are NOT munchkins," yelled Daphne, fists planted on her hips. "We are children!" It was clear no one should cross Daphne.

James looked through his camera lens before setting the timer. His head popped up, "Wait a minute, where's Nina?" he asked. "Nina! Go sit next to Becky, she won't bite."

Nina was surprised and froze in place. "Why? I'm not in your family."

"As far as I'm concerned you are," he replied. "If you are good enough for Benny to bring home for the holidays, that's good enough for me."

She smiled and sat down, as Becky grabbed her hand and gave her a squeeze. "Too late now," Becky said, "You're in the family Christmas photo. Can't escape."

After the delicious meal Gwen had prepared, with help from Beau and Charlotte, his wife, they went to the formal living area with their Irish coffees. The fireplace was lit so the room was nice and toasty. She had never felt so accepted by complete strangers. It gave her a warm fuzzy feeling all over.

On their way home, they listened to Christmas music in the truck. "Tonight, was wonderful," she told Bennett. "It gave me the warm fuzzies."

"What are the 'warm fuzzies'?" he asked.

"Just like it sounds, warm fuzzy feelings, the kind you get when you're in love with a great guy," she said, hugging his arm.

"Oh really?" he asked, raising one eyebrow. "Well, the feeling is mutual, warm fuzzies."

Christmas morning, she woke up, started the coffee pot and turned on the tv to watch the parades across the country. The smell of butter and cinnamon filled the house from the monkey bread that was baking in the oven.

Bennett walked in the kitchen and headed straight for the coffee pot. "Coffee, then presents." It wasn't a question it was a statement. He was not an early riser, or a morning person.

"I'm just happy you're awake before nine," she said smiling back at his disheveled hair and squinting eyes. Nina took the monkey bread out of the oven, being sure he got a big whiff of the delicious smell.

"What is that?!" he asked with wide eyes. "I don't care really, as long as I can have some of whatever you call it, now."

Laughing, she answered, "It's called Monkey Bread. My Momma made it every Christmas morning. I haven't made it in forever, I hope it turned out okay."

"If it's half as good as it smells, you will have to make this more often than once a year!" Bennett was salivating as he waited for the first piece.

They went to the other room to sit by their adorable little tree. She waited a few more minutes, until he was fully awake, before she unwrapped a nice jacket from her parents. She only had one other and it wasn't nearly as nice as this one, lined with faux fur. He opened a few small gifts his family sent home with them the night before.

Bennett picked up a small package with a big bow and gave it to her. "I don't know if you realize how much you mean to me," he said. "I love you. More every day."

She nervously took the bow off and opened the box. Her mouth was wide open, in disbelief at the diamond heart necklace. "I know how much you love hearts; you end up doodling them on every scrap of paper."

"Do I really?" she finally said. "That is so sweet. I can't believe you noticed that. It's beautiful, I love it." She knew she would wear it every day.

"Wait one minute," Nina said as she got up and went to the bedroom. She came back out with a large, wrapped present, almost as tall as she was. It was obviously a guitar case by the shape of it. "You want to guess?" she said as she laughed.

"Hmmm?" he said, "a BB Gun? Tennis Racket?'

"Just open it already," she urged. She was hoping he would like the custom guitar case, and guitar strap she bought.

He was very careful to undo the tape on the paper. He gently took the paper off. Then he started folding it. "Oh My God Bennett! Would you just go ahead and rip the paper? The suspense is killing me," Nina exclaimed.

"Oh, so you don't like suspense. I'll have to remember that" he laughed as he teased her by moving even slower.

"You are terrible!" she said as she tried to reach over and rip the paper for him.

He stopped her with his arm, "No ma'am, this is MY present and I will open it as I see fit. There is enough paper here to be used again next year." She rolled her eyes in an exaggerated gesture to make sure he knew she was joking.

Finally, the paper was removed to reveal a beautiful navy hardback guitar case with his initials on it. He took care admiring the "Open it," she said with anticipation.

Inside was a small box, about the size of a tie box. "You got me a tie," he joked. "You shouldn't have."

"Very funny, now please open it."

He pulled out a custom leather guitar strap, with a small section dedicated to George Harrison. Bennett was speechless.

"Do you like it?"

"It's awesome," he said, "where did you get it? How much did you have to pay? You shouldn't have spent that much, whatever it was."

"A guy in the plaza makes them, and yes, you deserve it." she assured.

"Well, it's great. It's the best gift I have ever got," he said. "Thank you, thank you."

"I have a question for you," Nina said. She wanted to ask his opinion on something, but she was nervous about what his answer would be. "Bennett, do you think you'd consider moving in here with me?"

He looked surprised at the question. "I don't know. What do you think? Is it too soon?" He posed some really good questions of his own.

"I don't know all that," Nina said. "I just know I am happiest when I am here with you. And, logically, we would save money. No need to pay for two apartments."

"Me too," he said. They didn't need to say anymore, they both needed to think about it.

She wanted to be sure she didn't make a mistake and wasn't rushing anything, so she didn't tell him a date, but just said, "We'll see what happens."

# CHAPTER FORTY

The band was still playing two or three nights a week in town. Nina went to every show when she wasn't working. She was proud to be his biggest fan. She usually sat at the back of the room, just so she wouldn't go deaf from the loud music.

One night, Bennett took the microphone and asked her to come up to the stage. "Ladies and Gentlemen, this is Nina. She saved me from myself." He was trying not to cry she could tell, "And, I can't imagine living without you." At that moment he got down on one knee, pulled out a ring from his pocket and said, "Nina Smith, will you marry me?"

The crowd cheered and clapped noisily. "Yes, yes, yes, yes," they chanted.

Nina was speechless. How could she marry him when she was already married? "I can't," she said as she cried, "not now."

"Of course, not now," he pleaded with her. "It's too soon, isn't it? I don't know what I was thinking."

"No, it's not that," she said. Her heart was breaking for him. He bared his soul in front of this crowd and his friends, and she crushed it. That's the last thing she wanted to do. "I'm not saying no," she assured the crowd, "It's just complicated."

"You are the only one that I have ever loved this way," she grabbed his face. She pulled him closer and whispered, "I want to, but be patient, please?"

"And that folks," he said as they turned to look at the crowd who were busy whispering to each other, "is why you always have a back-up plan." Bennett turned around and talked to the band, and they went into 'Love Stinks' by J. Geils Band.

Nina knew he was playing the victim, jokingly, so she rolled her eyes and laughed before making her way through the crowd. Several girls stopped her and asked why she didn't say yes. All she could say at that moment was, "I have my reasons, but don't get any ideas; he's not available."

Renee was waiting for her back at the table with a full beer. "What was that about? Why did you say 'no'?"

"It's complicated to say the least," Nina answered. "I'm just being careful. I can't say yes right now." She stayed through the rest of the night, trying to ignore the stares and whispers of the crowd.

At the end of the night, Bennett sat down next to her and said, "I'm not sure what happened before? I thought we were on the same page."

She just looked at his face, she had never seen him so sad. "I love you, with all my heart. Can we leave it at that for now?"

"I know you think I can't help you with whatever this is, but please let me try." He leaned in close and whispered, "I love you too much to let whatever it is get in the way."

He knew she had more to say but this was not the place. When they got home, maybe they would talk more. He wasn't going to let her go. They got back to her apartment after 2 a.m. He didn't let her go very far. He took her hand and they sat on the sofa. She knew this could end up with him walking out. How could she tell him that she was married?

"Now, can you please tell me what's going on?" he asked. "I hope you know you can trust me."

Nina took a deep breath and told him as much truth as she thought he could handle at the moment, "I do love you, and we are on the same page. All I can say now is that I've rushed past relationships and they didn't end well."

"Okay, I get that," he answered, "but that's not us. And it's not fair of you to judge me by your last boyfriends."

"No, you're right," she agreed. "It's not fair. And please believe me, I feel closer to you than I have to anyone before. I am comfortable with you. We think alike and have the same values."

He sighed. "So, what now? I'm not going anywhere." He stretched out on the sofa as if to stake his claim.

"Please don't," she asked, "I need you. You are the best part of my life. Can we talk about this later? Please?" She was insistent and hard to say no to.

"Ok," he agreed. "We'll wait a while and talk about it again. And I promise, next time, I won't be asking you in front of a crowd, on stage."

"You really are too good to be true, you know that?" she said as she covered his face with playful kisses.

# CHAPTER FORTY-ONE

Several weeks later, Nina's cell phone was ringing on the kitchen counter while she was in the shower, getting ready for her shift that afternoon. She yelled from the bathroom, "Honey, can you get that for me. It's probably Lauren."

Bennett picked it up. Before he could say anything, an old man started talking, "Hello? Kaci?".

"No, I'm sorry, you must have the wrong number," he told the caller.

When she came out, dressed for work, he said, "I guess it was a wrong number. An old man was asking for someone named Kaci."

Nina didn't know what to say. Her past was flooding through her mind. She calmly said, "That's weird." She knew it could only be her father. She would have to return the call as soon as she got to work. Bennett was driving her to work that night. He felt better picking her up late at night, instead of her driving home alone that late. She went inside, pausing at the door to turn around and blow him a kiss.

As soon as she got to her locker in the breakroom, she took out her phone and dialed her home. "Daddy, what's wrong?" she asked when he answered the phone.

"Honey girl, I'm sorry to bother you, are you at work?" He apologized again, "but your momma isn't doing too good. She went back into the hospital late last night. She was really weak, couldn't stand up by herself."

"Oh!" She cried. "Daddy, I'm coming home now. First thing in the morning."

"Now, now, don't cry," he tried to soothe her. "You still have a to work. Call me when you're leaving tomorrow. I'll be up early, as usual."

The rest of the night, she was just going through the motions. Her heart wasn't in it. Halfway through the dinner rush, Julia pulled her aside. "I don't know what happened, but you're a mess."

Nina choked back the tears and told her about her mother. "Now, you know what I'm going to say," Julia comforted her. "You have to go see her. Your family is top priority. Until then, tell Pat I said to fix you a shot of whiskey or something to calm your nerves."

"Julia, thank you," she said, "I don't know what I'd do without you." She hugged her with all her might.

Julia talked to a couple of the other servers, who had the next couple of days off, and asked them to cover Nina's shifts. She had off until Friday, five days.

All she had to do now, was to tell Bennett. She didn't know what she was going to say. He would insist on coming with her, that's the type of man he is. She didn't know how long she could keep avoiding the truth, but she had to go on a little while longer.

Bennett arrived about 30 minutes before closing. He had a drink at the bar while he waited. He caught up with Pat about the band's schedule and old friends they had seen. "I sure hope Nina feels better," Pat said.

"What do you mean?" he asked. "What happened? Is she ok?"

"I don't know exactly," Pat said, "but Julia told me to fix her a shot. She was obviously shaky about something."

Nina walked by and gave Bennett a kiss on the cheek. He grabbed her elbow as she was about to walk off, "Are you okay?" His tone said he knew something had happened since he dropped her off earlier. She didn't want to make eye contact, she thought. She would end up crying, and that's the last thing she wanted to do right now.

"Yeah, I'll be fine," she quickly answered, "I'll tell you later. Let me clean up here."

On the ride home, she talked about work, trying to avoid the fact that she was leaving in the morning. Finally, as they pulled into the driveway, she turned to him, "I talked to my dad and I have to go see my mom, tomorrow morning. She's at the hospital. Again."

"Ok. I hope she's ok." The wheels were turning in Bennett's mind, "Wait. Is that who called today? Why did he ask for Kaci?" he asked. He was more confused than ever and needed to find out what was going on. They had just walked into the apartment and sat down.

"I need to start by saying I never thought how this would affect my life in the end," she told him that night. "I did what I thought was best at the time." His look told her he was getting very impatient. "Do you want a beer? A glass of wine?" she asked, clearly stalling.

Bennett begged, "Just start please. Whatever it is."

Nina took a deep breath. "My real name is Kaci Jamison. I was in New York City, living with my husband in an abusive marriage, when the terror attack hit the World Trade Center. I was actually only blocks away, on my way to work in the first tower that was hit."

She paused and looked at Bennett, trying to read his thoughts. He was getting agitated, she could tell. "It's a long story, which, I know, you deserve to hear," she promised him. "It's just really hard for me to talk about."

"So, you were married? That's not a big deal," he said. "Why all the secrets?" He couldn't understand what was so secretive about her past. "I will say that just hearing how close you were to the site of the destruction makes the hair on my neck stand up."

"It's more than that. My marriage was horrible, but I didn't know any way I could leave," she explained. "I felt trapped. I had no money, nowhere to go. And, my husband, could talk sweet a little old lady out of her savings, so I knew I was stuck. I became really scared when he started hanging around with a bad group of people."

"I never dreamt the perfect opportunity would fall into my lap. On the morning of September 11th, I was late for work that day and I was never late. But, that day, I was outside on the street, walking to work when everything stopped. I woke up on the ground, covered in soot and dirt. People were screaming all around me, and at the same time, there was a muffled silence."

Nina paused, waiting for Bennett to react. When he didn't say anything, she continued. "I realized he would assume I was dead; it was the chance I needed. I had a friend who helped me buy a bus ticket and got me out of the city. I eventually made it here."

"That's quite a story," he said. "What you're saying is you are still married, right? I don't know why you couldn't have been honest

213

with me from the start?" His feelings were clearly hurt. He took a deep breath and sighed. "It's all starting to make sense now."

"Please try to understand how hard it was for me to start over. And then I met you, and you are the most wonderful awesome greatest human being I have ever known. I felt awful that you didn't know the truth but at the time, I didn't know what I was going to do next month or next week." She was crying as she tried to talk. "I mean, Kaci is married to Landon. Nina is not. I didn't mean it to be a lie, or to keep the lie going, but I had no choice once it started," she pleaded.

He stood up and went to the kitchen, turning his head to give he a quick smile. "I think I will take that beer now. I think you need one too."

"I had to keep it a secret or else I had to wonder if he would find me. He is that type of person, he would do it, just to prove a point."

"I'm trying. It is a lot of information to process Nina," he flashed her a smile when he said it. They spent the next several minutes not talking, just thinking. He finally broke the ice. "I trust you. I do. If you have to deal with this, then I'll be beside you every step."

She couldn't hold back the tears any longer. She felt grateful, relieved, calm, trusted and loved. All her emotions came flooding out in tears.

"Please don't cry," Bennett begged. "I told you I can't handle it." He leaned over and gave her a big hug, taking her head in his hands and started kissing her tears away.

She had almost forgotten why she confessed to him in the first place, she had to go home right away. They discussed him going with her, but knew the time wasn't right. Plus, he had to play the next two nights. She just looked at him and said, "warm fuzzies."

He quickly caressed her face, "warm fuzzies." He wasn't going to let her go, ever.

With that settled, he pulled her towards the bedroom. She knew what he wanted, but she had never seen this side of him, being very assertive. He wasn't forceful, or threatening, but it was a desire that showed on his face. That desire made him even more attractive and made her want him even more.

He quickly undressed her as he kissed her body. He picked her up and she wrapped her legs around his back. Gently he laid her on the bed. He went to the dresser and opened a drawer. She had no idea what he could be looking for in there.

He came back to the bed with two of his socks in his hand. "What are you up to?" she asked. "Shhh," he said as he put his finger then his lips to hers. "Do you trust me?" he asked her.

She nodded.

He took her right hand and tied one sock around it and did the same with the left. He held both socks firmly in his hand, making it almost impossible for Nina to escape.

What happened next, she could have never imagined. Being out of control made her senses heighten. Every time he touched her, she felt a jolt of electricity. She begged him to touch her in other places. But he just hushed her pleadings wants. He took his time, building up her desire and his own, until she thought she would reach orgasm without him ever nearing between her legs.

"Bennett, please," she panted, "I want you so badly, you're driving me crazy!"

"Good," he whispered in her ear, "that's how I planned it."

"Please, please baby," she begged, "Now! I need you now!"

At that moment, he released her hands and was inside her. The first thrust made her scream in ecstasy. He kept entering her harder and harder, as she begged for more. Moments later he made her body shake all over and he came when he felt it.

She was on the road before breakfast. Driving through Eastern New Mexico, she watched the sun rise, and was in awe. It still made her smile to see a beautiful sunrise. She had been listening to the classic rock station when 'Love Stinks' came on the radio. She started laughing, thinking of his awkward proposal. She didn't pull over until lunch time., and that was just to grab a bag of chips and use the ladies' room. By dinnertime, she was finally entering Arkansas on I-40. She was exhausted but adrenaline was making her anxious to see her mom.

The front door opened as soon as she pulled in. Her daddy came out to help her carry her one suitcase. "You sure do travel light," he said.

"I wasn't thinking clearly, I just threw in a few clean things." She asked, "How is she?"

"Today was a little better," he said, his voice wavering only slightly. "She knew me and knew you were coming to see her. I just hope it's the same tomorrow."

Nina sat down and stared at her mom's red paisley swivel chair. "What can I do, Daddy?" She would always picture her gliding as she watched 'The Tonight Show' and 'Magnum P.I.'"

"There isn't anything to do, honey," he said. "You being here is all we need now." He walked over and kissed the top of her head, just as he did when she was younger.

She fixed eggs and pancakes for them and then went to her room. She noticed that they had tried to change the room into a guest room, since the last time she had been home, only a few weeks ago. There was a new green comforter on the full-sized bed, and a pair of floral curtains on the window. Most of her stuffed animals were now packed away and replaced with accent pillows.

She had promised Bennett she would call as soon as she got there safely. He picked up the phone right away, "Nina, are you okay?" He sure sounded upset.

"Yes, I'm fine," she assured him. "I got here about an hour ago, ate with my dad, and am ready for bed."

He asked again, "Are you sure I can't come be with you? I want you to be able to lean on me."

"I really do love you, and your offer," she replied, "but no, I need to do this alone this time. I promise, next time, cross my heart."

The next morning, visiting hours started at 8 and they were right on time. She walked quietly into her mother's room, and saw her in the bed, helpless. She started crying, here we go again, she thought.

Her mother turned and looked at her, a little confused for a second, then she recognized her daughter. "Kaci, baby, don't cry."

"Momma," she whispered as she walked over to sit on the edge of her bed. She was careful not to touch any wires attached to her but gave her a big hug anyway.

"It's okay," she soothed her as she stroked her hair. "I'm just so happy to see you. How are you feeling today?"

"Now stop your crying, I'm still here." Evelyn said calmly. "Why don't you tell me all about who the man was who answered the phone when your daddy called you. You certainly surprised him."

Nina was happy to change the subject off her mother's health and started telling her about Bennett. She told her about their first real date, to see the sunset in the mountains. How his family had welcomed her and finally told them that he had moved in together. "He really is wonderful," she told her mother. "I know I said the same about Landon, but this really is different. I love him, but I know, and I can feel that he really loves me."

"I just want you to be happy with you," she said. "You've been through enough at such a young age. You are smart enough to know you don't need a man to be happy, but they sure are nice to have around." Her mom gave her a mischievous grin. Soon after that, her mother fell asleep, and the nurses came in to get her vitals and administer her afternoon meds.

While sitting in the waiting area, her dad told her about a phone call he received a month ago from the 9/11 victim's foundation. They told him there was money he was entitled to through the charity. He told them he didn't need anything, to give that money to a young family who lost their mother or father.

"You know that won't be the end of it," he said. "There have already been reporters here from People magazine and the New York Times, asking about you."

"What did you tell them?" she was nervous. It was what she had feared the most, someone would track her down and expose that she was still alive.

"I didn't want to talk to them I said, it was still too early." He explained. "But I'm sure there will be more."

"That brings up another thing, Daddy," she said as she told him about Bennett's proposal. "I'm stuck. I can't do anything, can't erase the past, or move forward."

"Yeah. Looks like to me, you have two options. One, contact Landon, and tell him the truth, file for divorce; or two, get an official new identity with a new social security number." Her dad always had the right answer, she thought.

"Ok, I am not calling Landon. So, how do I do get a new identity?" she asked. Nina didn't believe it would be easy to just change your name, legally. She certainly didn't think her dad would know anything about the specifics.

"It can't be too hard," he explained. "I hear about it all the time on 'Dateline'."

"OK Dad," she said, with a chuckle. "You know you can't believe everything you see on tv. It can't be that easy."

"Just something to think about," he answered. "I can get used to calling you Nina. It's a beautiful name. Let me see what I can find out." She shrugged her shoulders and squeezed his hand in agreement.

The next two days, they did the same thing, went to the hospital, then home for dinner. There wasn't much change in her mother's condition. She was still stable.

"I found someone; he's expecting us before lunch today." Her dad was calling to her from the hallways as she was getting dressed. "The man I talked to said he can get you a legitimate social security number. And from there, a driver's license should be easy."

She had been driving for months without a license on her at all, or any identification. Every time she got behind the wheel, she began rehearsing what she would tell the officer if she got pulled over. She knew she was lucky she hadn't been pulled over.

Bennett had called the night before. They talked about seeing each other again. The pain of being away from him was real, but she tried not to think about it. "You just be home Friday night," he told her.

# CHAPTER FORTY-TWO

Thursday morning, her dad took her to a light gray painted concrete building across town. It was a check cashing place, with a rusty metal sign for 'official ID's' on the side. It wasn't nearly as shady as she had pictured. There was an office, with chairs in the waiting room. The other person waiting was a younger man, maybe 20, who was visibly nervous. She wondered what his story was.

A young woman came out and asked the young man to come in. She looked at Nina and Walter, "We'll be with you in just a minute." She sounded very professional. She came back about 20 minutes later and showed them to an inner office. "This is Don, he will be happy to help you."

They spent the next few minutes explaining what they needed. The 'why' wasn't important he said, actually, he'd prefer NOT to know. She filled out a few pages of information about 'Nina' and was handed a new social security number. It was registered to Nina Joan Smith he told her.

The next stop was to the driver's license office. She thought if she could get a legal Arkansas license, she could easily transfer it in New Mexico. And then, the possibilities were limitless. She ended up having to wait over an hour, take the written test and a road test, but she passed, barely. "I know those weren't the same questions that were on it ten years ago," she told her dad.

When they got back to the house, she finished packing before heading back to the hospital to say goodbye to her mother. They spent hours talking about her childhood, college days and even her New York life. She stayed with her until they made her leave when visiting hours were over.

Bennett called her before she fell asleep. He told her how much he missed her, couldn't live without her. She laughed at his jokes and promised to be careful the next day.

The next morning, she woke up at dawn. She knew she had to get an early start on the drive home. She gave her Daddy a hug and made him swear to call if there was any change in her mom's condition. The next time she came, she said she would bring Bennett. She couldn't wait for them to meet him, but the timing had to be right.

The whole drive home she was energized, ready to see her wonderful boyfriend. She had thought about him every day. She couldn't live without him, she knew that. The radio kept her company, and she sang along at the top of her lungs, grateful that no one could hear her.

She was only three hours from home when her car swerved in the lane, making a loud thunking noise. She was able to pull over on the side of the road just in time, before a tractor trailer zoomed by at over 70 mph. It took her a minute to catch her breath. She was still in shock. The sun was setting behind her and she did not want to be out in the desert alone at night.

Nina walked around the front of the car to find a flat tire. What was she going to do now? She sat back in the car and just cried for a minute; she didn't know what she was going to do. "I am so tired of being tested," Nina said out loud, to no one. She wiped her tears away and called Bennett.

"When are you getting home?", he asked eagerly. "I miss you."

"Well, calm down soldier, I have a flat tire," she told him she was near Tucumcari. "Bennett, I don't know what to do? I've heard stories about the desert at night, even along the interstate."

"Don't worry honey, I'll get help to you," he said in a soothing voice. "I played once at the Coyote lounge at the Holiday Inn," he said. "Maybe the bartender is still there, he owes me a favor."

"Now, that sounds like an interesting story," Nina tried to calm her anxiety with a joke.

"Let me call the hotel and see what I can find out. I will call you right back. Do NOT get out of the car," he warned her.

She was relieved to let him handle this one. As she sat in the car, she thought about what she would tell Bennett about Landon and 9/11. Yes, she knew she lied, and had been lying about almost everything, but she has a good reason. Life is complicated. She dreaded it, but there was no choice. It would be talked about, probably for several days.

Her phone rang after a few more minutes. "Hey, the guy I know just got off work. His name is Jeff, and he's a good guy, I trust him," Bennett said. "He's married with two little girls."

"If you say he's ok, I trust you," she replied. More than you can trust me she thought.

"He will be there in 20 minutes or so, and take you back to the hotel," he explained. "I'm leaving town now, and I'll be there as soon as possible."

"Wait, what about my car?" Nina went into full panic mode again. She hated being out of control.

"We will worry about that tomorrow. It's not going anywhere," he assured her.

Jeff showed up shortly after and helped her take all her bags out of the car. "So, you're the girl who tied Bennett down?" he asked.

"What? I haven't tied him down?" she said defensively. What stories is he telling people, she wondered?

"I just mean he used to have women fighting over him, but he never was interested in them," he explained. "A couple of us even wondered if he was, you know, gay."

She laughed out loud at that, "Bennet? Hardly. So how long have you known him?"

"It has to be over 3 years now, maybe 4," he said. "He used to play up here at least once a month. When he got tired of hotel food, I started inviting him over for a home-cooked meal. My wife felt sorry for him. You know, the poor pitiful bachelor."

Nina laughed at his description of the Bennett she knew. "I can't picture that," she said, "however, I know he loves a good meal."

"Anyway, I'm glad he has you," Jeff continued, "A guy like him needs a woman who really cares about him, not just a one-night stand."

They pulled into the Holiday Inn parking lot and Jeff carried her bags to the registration desk. "Annie, get this girl a nice room, with my discount please." He turned and winked at her. "She's had a rough night." Annie was more than happy to help. Jeff explained that Bennett should be arriving that night, just in case he came looking for Nina, it was ok to tell him the room number.

"I know the guy who has the towing service in town," Jeff added. "I'll see if he can get your car off the highway. If it's just a flat tire, he can fix it in a few minutes tomorrow."

"Do you have your ID?" Annie asked as she started filling out her information on the forms.

Nina proudly pulled out her new license and presented it to Annie. "Arkansas huh? I have friends in Little Rock."

"Oh, I just lived there for a little while," she said, trying not to sound like she was rushing the conversation. She did not want to have to explain her past.

"You are in room 112. Take the hallway over there and turn right at the corner," she said as she handed Nina two room key cards.

As soon as she entered the room, she fell on the bed. She didn't realize how tired she was. After a few minutes, she got up and called her dad to tell him what happened.

"I haven't even met this man of yours and I already like him," Walter said. "He knows how to take care of you. That's important these days."

He reported her mom was doing a little better, and they hoped she would be out of the hospital the following week. "The doctors seem pleased with her progress, and there really is no reason for her to stay there."

"I know she would be much happier in her own bed," said Nina. "That's good news Daddy. I will call you tomorrow, when I get home."

All she could do now was wait. She laid down on the bed to close her eyes for just a minute. She must have fallen asleep; she had no idea for how long. She awoke when she heard Bennett knocking softly on her door. "Hey, Nina, are you still awake?" He knocked again, a little louder. "It's me, I'm here."

He heard her walking toward the door, and thought he saw her eye, peeping through the spy hole. She opened the door, still rubbing her eyes. "Hey honey, you made it," she said as she yawned.

"Of course, I made it," he said, "I wouldn't let my girl stay the night by herself in a strange city." He made his way to the bed and sat down before asking if she had eaten anything.

"No, I never did," she said, "I was too tired. I'm starving now though."

"Denny's it is then, they are open all night." She gladly changed clothes and brushed her hair, before grabbing her purse and leaving.

The sign read "Please seat yourself" and they did. There were only two other diners in the restaurant at that hour. It was almost 11 p.m., too late for date night, too early for bar crowd. Neither of them wanted coffee so they just ordered water.

Nina ordered the country fried steak platter. Bennett stared at the huge steak on her plate. "There is no way you can eat all of that," he said. "I might have to help you." He picked up his fork and made a move towards her plate.

"Uh watch it buster," she said. "This is mine... that is yours". Bennett ordered the Grand Slam, of course, he needed his protein. After eating for what seemed like an hour, they surrendered and put their forks down.

"I can't eat another bite," she said, and he agreed. "I need to get to bed," he added.

They had walked over to the restaurant in the parking lot, so they made their way back. "Let's go walk this off," she said.

As they crossed the parking lot, they saw several people coming out of the hotel lounge. Most of the women were either holding up their man, or too drunk to walk themselves. "I bet you see that all the time," she asked him.

"More than you could imagine," he answered. "It's even harder when I think about how I was one of those guys. If I started drinking, I couldn't stop. That became a big problem. I lost our band a few gigs because of it. But they helped me and picked me back up again. I'm really very lucky."

It was after midnight when they got back to the room. She had missed him so much, his warm hug, his smell. But, they were both too full and tired to do more take their jeans off. He put her in bed, pulled up the blanket to her shoulders, just the way she liked. He got in next to her, spooned her closely, and they fell asleep until daylight shone through the drapes.

"Rise and shine sleepyhead," she was singing as he opened his eyes. He was not a morning person, a life of playing music and staying up late had stopped that. She had made a mini pot of coffee, which helped him open his eyes. His motto was "no coffee? No talkie."

They spent the next few hours finding a tire to replace the blown one, and getting it put on. After that, she loaded her stuff back into the car, and began driving home with him following behind.

Nina had talked to Julia a few times to let her know what had happened. She was needed back at work today, for dinner. She barely had time to get a shower and get dressed. She had missed everyone at work and was ready to get life back to normal.

# CHAPTER FORTY-THREE

Bennett had to play a gig that night, so Nina went straight home after work. She made her apologies to the work crowd when they invited her out for a drink, telling them she was still exhausted from her trip.

She called Lauren as soon as she was in her pjs. "Do you think you can come over?"

"Sure, what's wrong? What happened?" Lauren was all about getting the information. "Never mind, I'm on my way."

As soon as she walked in and sat down, Nina handed her a glass of wine. "I guess I need to come clean with you too."

Lauren turned to her, "What are you talking about Sis? Why all the secrecy?"

She proceeded to tell her about Landon, NYC, Kaci and her escape on 9/11. Lauren had sat down on a dining chair. She seemed stunned. "That had to have been horrible for you," she finally said. "I know you are a good person. That's all I need to know."

They ended up drinking the whole bottle and talking for hours. Nina told her all about New York. Lauren had a hundred questions, or more. Most of the questions were about seeing famous people or the restaurants. "Did you ever go to the Central Perk coffee shop?" It was good to just sit back and laugh for a change. Lauren ended up falling asleep on the sofa, so Nina tucked her in with a blanket and went to bed.

Her head was throbbing when Nina opened her eyes. The bright sun coming in through the blinds didn't help matters. This is the price for drinking too much, she thought. She made her way to the kitchen and started a pot of extra-strong coffee.

Nina knew she would need all the help she could get to get through the lunch shift today. She went in a little early, as soon as Lauren left, so she could present her license and social security card to

Julia and be official. Her shift went smoothly, and her headache went away with more caffeine and Tylenol.

When she got home that afternoon, Bennett's truck was parked in front. She almost ran inside to see him. It was less than 24 hours since she last saw him, but for some reason, it seemed like weeks. So much had happened in the past couple of days.

He met her at the door with a bouquet of flowers. She could smell the wonderful smell of pizza drifting in from the kitchen. "You sure know how to get to my heart," she gushed.

They took a few minutes to eat and get comfortable for a night in. When the pizza was put away, Bennett grabbed the hem of her red shirt and pulled it over her head as she walked back to the sofa. She was unfastening his belt as fast as she could. "Oh God! I need you so bad," he said in a heavy panting breath on her neck. In minutes, they went from talking to making love on the sofa.

They laid in each other's arms for several minutes before Bennett got up and led her to their bedroom. Once in bed, they started again, his hands touching, caressing, stroking her back, making her moan with delight. He kissed her breasts, suckled her nipples and slipped his hand between her legs. Her breathing was heavy and wanting. Just as quickly, he turned her over, pulling her up onto her knees, and entered her from behind. She gasped with pleasure as he repeated the motion, going deeper and deeper, until he came with an explosion that made him shudder. The rest of the night was spent holding each other.

The next morning when Bennet woke up there was a small, gift-wrapped box on the nightstand. "What's this?" he asked her as he gave it a little shake.

"I hope this tells you that I am committed to us," she said as he opened the box to find a key on a red ribbon. "You've been just wonderful throughout all this mess I've dumped in your lap. It's a key to the apartment." She answered. "More correctly, your key to our apartment. I want you to move in with me." She held her breath as she waited for him to answer.

"Are you sure?" he asked, "I'm not all sunshine and rainbows. I haven't lived with anyone for years, and years. I think I forgot how."

"Yes, I'm sure," she said. "Just two rules, no leaving the seat up and no dirty dishes on the counter."

"Man, you are slave driver!" He laughed as he pulled her back in to bed.

The next few weeks were busy with moving in his furniture and moving out Mrs. Elliott's furniture to her storage building. In addition to furniture, Bennett had several guitars and a couple amps to move. He put them in a corner until they could find a way to keep them out of the way. They would need to start looking for a bigger place he thought.

Her father called her the following week to tell her that her mother was coming home from the hospital. She had improved enough that she could be semi-independent.

"That's wonderful Daddy," she said. "I'll call her tonight. I can't believe it. Be sure and give her hugs and kisses from me."

Bennett insisted they go back to her hometown to see her mother that next week. "I don't know if I can get off work again," she said. "It was only two weeks ago."

"I'm sure if anyone will understand it will be Julia," he said. He was very convincing. And, she was eager for her parents to meet him. She didn't want to wait much longer.

"You have to remember," she warned him, "Back home, everyone thinks I died on September 11th, so I can't be out in public very much. With my luck, I'd run into old friends. I've really been pushing my luck these last visits."

"Got it," Bennett said. "Operation undercover in progress." He laughed and raised his hand in a pseudo salute.

She loved his laugh, it was from deep inside, and she knew it was genuine. Another quick peck on the cheek and she got up to get ready for her night shift.

Bennett had only been playing the local gigs with Chain Reaction, so most of his weekends he was working, but had the weeknights free. They were booked into O'Brien's Cantina the following weekend. He was sure they could get back before then.

Julia let her off for three days. That was plenty of time, she confirmed, to get there and back. "So, you're taking Mr. Wonderful home? It's about time."

This time, they took his truck just for the inside comfort. He made sure it had a recent tune up, and they checked all the tires. With the two of them driving, they were able to make it faster than if she drove alone. She had also saved time by packing drinks and snacks. By only stopping for bathroom breaks and gas they got into town by 7 p.m.

Her mother was still awake, barely, when they walked into the house. She was gliding in her favorite swivel chair. Nina dropped her purse at the door and ran to give her mama a big hug and squeeze.

Bennett stood patiently at the front door, waiting for the dust to settle. Her father walked over and invited him to step all the way into the living room. "You must be Bennett," he asked.

"Yes, sir, Bennett Moore …. Nice to meet you." He extended his hand for a courteous handshake.

"Oh Daddy, don't be so formal, come and sit down, Bennett, my mama wants to meet you too," Nina said as she patted the sofa next to where she sat.

They spent about an hour talking about her childhood, the jobs her father had after he retired from the Post Office, and her aunts and uncles who missed her terribly. She didn't know of any way to let them know she was alive, without jeopardizing her safety. She still wasn't sure what Landon, and his associates were capable of.

Her parents let them stay in her bedroom together, which seemed very strange to Nina. She still remembered dating in high school, and her parents not even letting a boy in her room for a minute. They were exhausted from the drive, so she didn't have to worry about anything besides sleep.

The next morning, she got up and fixed a full breakfast. She knew her mother wouldn't be able to, and she always loved bacon and eggs. Nina was taking orders like a short-order cook, "Over Easy" "Lightly Scrambled". She made two pots of coffee and made sure everyone's cups were full.

"You must be a great waitress," her momma complimented. "Or is it just for us?" She smiled and gave Nina's hand a loving squeeze.

After breakfast, her father asked her to sit down with him. He showed her a manilla envelope that had been delivered days earlier. It was addressed to 'The Parents of Kaci Robbins Jamison."

"What's this?" she said as she stared at the envelope with her former name on it. A soft pain grabbed her heart as the feeling of having lost so much filled her head.

"I think you had better read it," he said as she pulled out several very legal looking documents. Attached to the front was a paper clip with a note *'Sign where indicated and mail back.'*

As she read, her face became pale. Her mouth fell open, she didn't know what to say. "They are going to pay you $500,000 for a life insurance policy on me? That's crazy! Who started the policy?" she asked.

"It appears that Landon did, or I should say, his parents did." Walter explained. "I'm still not clear why? But there it is. They listed themselves and him as beneficiaries." That made sense she thought. His parents were always being overprotective, even though he hated it. He was ready to collect his payout on her accidental death policy. As far as she knew, he couldn't collect anyway. She would have to be missing for seven years, then he could have her declared legally dead.

"If you sign these, wouldn't you be committing insurance fraud?" She now wondered what his parents had suspected but never told her about their abusive son. Maybe they realized there was a chance she would be killed 'accidentally'. The whole thing made a shiver go up her back, making her shudder. Not to mention the fact that his dad was friends with the gangster who got Landon into the business.

"Of course, I have no intention of signing it," he assured her, "all we need is right here. The house is paid for as is the truck."

Nina had only considered briefly the insurance angle of what she did. She didn't know enough about insurance to think it through. She could not let anyone know she was alive, and yet, she couldn't bring herself to commit a felony either.

The next day they spent in the house, it was raining anyway, not good weather for running errands. Her mother wanted to play Rummy, and they all sat down at the dinner table for an afternoon match. They had the old console record player opened and picked out a few Golden Oldies. They started off listening to Herb Alpert and the Tijuana Brass. It was an album that always reminded her of home whenever she heard it.

"Great music, by the way. One year our high school band actually played one of his songs, it's made for a good brass section," Bennett told them. "By the way, I've never been very good at games."

"You're kidding?! Who doesn't know how to play Rummy?" she teased him. The twinkle in his eye told her he might be fibbing, a little.

Thirty minutes later, they all realized he was bluffing. Bennett was leading on the score pad. "You are such a rat," Nina said playfully. "Too bad they don't offer Rummy at the casinos. We could make it big."

Later, Bennett brought his guitar out from the bedroom. Her parents had asked if he would play something. Evelyn had made her way to the piano in the living room. She explained she hadn't played since her stroke, but maybe she could manage. Her face lit up as she started playing some simple tunes. Together, they played some of the old church songs she knew by heart. Bennett then started playing 'My Sweet Lord', by George Harrison. He was surprised when her parents started humming along. They started requesting other Beatles' hits.

"Remember this one, Evie?" Walter asked his wife. He hadn't used her nickname in quite a while. Bennett was playing 'Something'. Walter stood and asked his wife for her hand and they began slow dancing.

As they laid in bed that night, Nina reflected on how much fun they had just by being home. They had to get back to reality in the morning. She turned to face Bennett who was sleeping quietly. "You give me warm fuzzies every day I'm with you. I don't want to live without you in my life."

With his eyes still closed, "You won't have to," he said, pulling her closer.

# CHAPTER FORTY-FOUR

In the morning, they got up early to get on the road. She found it easier to leave, now that her mother was comfortably recovering at home. After a quick breakfast, hugs, kisses and promises of a return visit, they were on their way.

They pulled into Santa Fe by early evening. Instead of going straight home, she suggested they go get a nice meal, just the two of them. It had been a while since they had gone out for dinner. They both worked so many evenings. He pulled into the parking lot of the same Italian restaurant where they went for their first date. As luck would have it, their booth was available. He ordered a bottle of wine to share, and they started with the bread and olive oil on the table.

After he finished eating, Bennett excused himself to go to the bathroom. While he was gone, the server came and removed their dirty plates. A minute or two later, she was looking around to see where he was. She spotted a cake being delivered with a sparkler in it. She assumed it was someone's birthday.

As it came closer, she realized Bennett was following behind the two girls. He had purposely hidden from her view. The cake was placed in front of her as he got down on one knee. He had drawn the attention of the other diners with the delivery of the cake. Once he was on his knees, a hush fell over the room. The servers backed away to allow a better view for their customers.

"I was going to wait, but I can't keep a secret, here goes nothing," he said. "I love you more than anything. I don't care about anything in your past. Will you please marry me?" He pulled out a ring box from his jacket pocket.

"But you know we can't," she said in a hushed voice. "I want to more than anything, I promise you."

"We don't have to do anything right away. I don't mind being engaged forever if that's what it takes," he was on his knees, wobbling slightly, trying to keep his balance. "It's not easy for a tall man to get down on his knees. Please say yes."

Her hands covered her mouth as she let out a cry of happiness. "Yes, YES." The other diners and servers burst into cheers and clapping. They had waited patiently for her answer.

It wouldn't happen right away, but one day they would. They would work out the details later, but as of right now, they were engaged. That was enough for her. She was so distracted by the beautiful ring he had held on to for months.

She had thought of this moment for months, ever since she said 'No' earlier that year. Deep down she was scared he would never ask again.

"We have to call my parents! They will be so happy." Nina couldn't stop smiling, she had never felt so happy. "And your parents! And Lauren, Julia, your brother and sister."

"Slow down Andretti," he teased her, "of course, we will be calling everyone! But let's wait until tomorrow morning. I'm exhausted and we have our own celebrating to do tonight."

As they drove home, the leftover cake in her lap, she continued to gaze at her beautiful engagement ring. "Where did you get it? It's absolutely gorgeous."

"Well, it's not new." He paused to wait for her reaction. "Before you start thinking the worst, I have not given, or attempted to give it to anyone else."

"Ohhhkaaay," Nina's mind was trying to fill in the blanks. She had never considered it might have been from an ex-girlfriend. "You have my full attention now."

Bennett kissed her hand, "I got it from my mom. It was her mother's, my Grandma Ivy. She saved it for me, for the right person. And you, My Sweet Nina, are the right person."

Nina was speechless. Her emotions would not be contained one second more as tears fell on her face. She sniffled as she wiped her eyes. Barely able to speak, she finally said, "I love you so much."

As soon as they pulled into the driveway, they quickly walked inside, leaving all their bags in the truck to retrieve later. She closed the door behind them, turned to face her fiancée, stood on her tiptoes and pulled his lips to hers.

Her passion for him bubbled up as they aggressively explored each other's mouths with their tongues. She couldn't get close enough to him. She needed him so deeply, her whole body ached. He responded by picking her up, her legs wrapping around his waist. She had never known desire quite like this.

Bennett carried her to towards their bedroom, stopping to sit her bottom on the breakfast bar. His head was buried between her breasts as she grabbed his hair, jerking his face upward. She was not going to let him go. She drew him into another long kiss.

He unbuttoned her blouse, tearing it off as quickly as possible. Her bra was removed in seconds. She moaned when his lips found her nipples. He slowed his pace, taking his time to play with her breasts with his tongue and mouth. Each time he back away, she pulled him back.

She tugged at his shirt, pulling it over his head. Feeling his chest hair on her skin sent jolts of electricity through her body. Her pleasure spot was hot and wet. Her breathe was heavy. "You have to fuck me. Now. I need you

He undid his belt buckle, unzipped his jeans and kicked them to the side. He then picked her up off the counter and carried her into their bedroom, all while kissing the cleavage between her breasts, rubbing his razor-stubble chin gently across her erect nipples.

This time, their love-making was on the wild side. It was as if any inhibitions she had in all her years were washed away and she was a new woman now. Forever gone was Kaci, Nina was a woman who was in control and would never be the victim again

The heat generated by their bodies kept them both gasping for air. When she climaxed first, she made sure he experienced the same pleasure as he laid back and she teased his throbbing cock with her breasts, stroking it and finally taking him into her mouth. His groan told her he was ready to explode. A couple more deep-throat motions and he came.

Sometime later, Nina woke up to find Bennett staring at her. "What are you doing might I ask?"

"Just watching my future wife, the most beautiful woman in the world, sleep like an angel." He smiled, touched her nose gently and kissed her.

"Ok, Romeo, off to the shower I go. I have too many things to do in the morning." He held her hand for a moment, caressing the new ring on her finger.

"Mind if I join you?"

They ended up having a lengthy shower, full of touching, playing and more sex. Bennett ran out to his truck in his robe to grab a few of their bags before they went back to bed. He noticed it was a clear night with several bright stars lighting up the sky. A chilly breeze traveled through their street, bringing with it leftover smells of roasted chiles and corn tortillas.

# CHAPTER FORTY-FIVE

The next weekend was Valentine's Day, and 'Kaci's' birthday weekend. Bennett surprised her by taking her out for the day. He wanted to take her someplace special in the Jemez Mountains. She had always liked nature but wasn't sure how much she wanted to be in nature at one time.

"Are you ready for an adventure?" he asked her. He was pretty sure she'd follow him anywhere, but this wasn't just a little walk or stroll.

She nervously answered, "I guess so?" The question made her a little nervous, but she trusted him.

"Ok good," he said, "Better grab a couple towels. And bundle up, it'll be colder up there." He knew by the look on her face she was confused and had no idea what his plans were.

Now, she really was curious. Why the towels? How long would they be outside that they needed to 'bundle up.' It was only 45 degrees now, if it was much colder there would be snow.

The drive into the mountains took almost an hour. Bennett pulled over onto a clearing on the side of the road and turned the engine off. There were already two vehicles there, but nobody was in them. A trail leading into the forest laid before them, down the side of the mountain.

Nina turned to look at him. "Where exactly are we?" she asked.

"Welcome to the Jemez Hot Springs, at least the footpath that will take you to the hot springs," he explained. "It's one of the few places in the country that has a natural hot spring."

The path was narrow, barely wide enough to get one person down the side of the steep rocky hill. Bennett went first, holding one hand behind him to hold onto her hand. She was holding onto his jacket with her other hand, trying not to trip on the uneven ground. At one point, the path was so steep, she was almost holding on around his neck, piggyback style. Soon, the it widened and flattened out.

Bennett asked her if she wanted to take a break. She eagerly agreed, "I just need a minute to settle my nerves, that walk was no picnic."

"Don't worry," he replied, "I would never take you anywhere dangerous. This is a well-used path."

"It may be well-used, but not by me," she laughed. She didn't add, "Well-used by whom? Squirrels and wolves?"

"OK, I'll take it easy on you," he promised. "I promise."

They walked for another 15 minutes before she heard running water. Around the next row of trees, was a stream about eight feet wide. The question in her mind was, how would they get to the other side? The sign posted pointed across the water to the hot springs.

He took her hand and led her down to a huge tree that had fallen or been placed across the stream. It didn't look that sturdy, she thought. She was afraid of falling, and there was over 20 feet until she would hit the ground if she fell off. "I don't think I can do this," she told him.

Bennett said, "it's perfectly safe, there's a rope guideline for balance. Do you want me to show you?" He went ahead of her and walked across in a couple minutes. He made it look like a stroll in the park. "It's that easy."

"If you promise to save me," she said. She took a few steps and stopped. She was frozen. He thought she was joking, but she really wasn't. "I can't do it."

"How about if I come back over and walk with you. I'll make sure you don't fall." She agreed and within seconds he was standing in front of her. "You know I'll save you anytime you need it," Bennett said softly. "I'm your knight in shining armor." Anytime, anywhere, I'll be there, he thought. He wasn't about to screw this one up.

She took a deep breath and carefully walked across, holding tightly to the guide rope with one hand and his arm with the other. She wanted to look down at her feet, but he convinced her not to. When they finally made it, she was so relieved, she fell into his arms.

"Are we there yet, Dad?" she joked. Please let this be the end, she thought.

"Almost," he answered, "now we have to go up a little bit."

Another sign was posted on a nearby tree pointed an arrow to Hot Springs, 1000 feet. 'Clothing Optional'. She stood and stared at the sign. "Clothing optional huh?" she asked him.

"Oh yeah," he grinned, "Did I not mention that part?"

"Bennett! You are awful!" she teased.

"It's okay," he replied, "you don't have to do it, but it will be hard to test the water fully clothed. I told you it would be an adventure."

They heard voices getting louder as they got closer to the springs. She wasn't expecting there to be a crowd. How embarrassing, she thought. She couldn't do this. No way.

Bennett already had his shirt off when they walked up. Through the steam she could see a young couple, maybe early twenties, and a much older couple, late sixties she guessed.

"Hey everyone, how's the water?" Bennett asked. He always was able to talk to strangers.

The older man answered, "Just wonderful, makes my old bones happy. I'm Luis and this here is Maggie." After the young couple introduced themselves as Finn and Chelsea, Bennett was in the water.

"C'mon babe, it's no big deal." Bennett said, trying to be calm about it, but also trying not to push her either. "Do you trust me?"

"You know I do," she answered, "but this is completely different."

Maggie helped out, "Your first time, I'm guessing. Don't worry so much. Anyone who comes up here isn't thinking about getting a quick peek at your naked body." As she nodded, Maggie said, "It's no big deal, we're old hippies, been there, done that." They both laughed. "Really sunshine, don't give us another thought."

Nina turned to look at the younger couple, and they were too busy with each other. She summoned up her courage and started by taking off her socks, shoes and jeans. Sitting on the rock on the edge by Bennett, she dangled her legs into the water. It was so warm and inviting. Within minutes, she decided 'what the hell' and went in, everything off except her panties.

The water bubbled like a jacuzzi, but better. The water was so relaxing, she felt like she could stay there for hours. She had forgotten how cold the air was until she touched her hair and found it was frozen in icy pieces.

Bennett looked at her, "Well, what do you think? I wouldn't mislead you or put you in danger, I hope you know that."

"I have to admit," she said, "you really surprised me. I never would have guessed this is what you had in mind. And I like it. It's very refreshing. If only the journey to get up here was a bit easier, I'd do this every weekend."

Luis said, "We've been coming up here for years, almost ten, I guess. It has changed in popularity for sure. We used to be the only ones, and the path was barely passable."

Nina laughed, "USED to be, I barely made it up here. It gave me a whole new respect for hikers."

The group of six decided to walk down together as it was getting dark, and nobody wanted to be left behind. Neither of them had much hiking experience so they were taking it slow. Climbing down a mountain side was a lot harder than climbing up they agreed.

At that moment, Nina stepped on a rock that wasn't firmly planted, and gave way. She couldn't help but slide down. She landed 20 feet from where Chelsea was still standing. Bennett raced back up to pick her up. "Told you I'd rescue you."

"A little late," she laughed quietly, "Are you going to carry me now?" He didn't offer, but he did lean over and whisper in her ear, "I love you so much." She blushed a little and smiled widely.

Bennett stuck by Nina's side the rest of the way out of the mountain. When they reached the log across the stream, Nina didn't hesitate. She wanted to be home so bad, nothing would stand in her way. She crossed in minutes and was up the path to where they parked before Bennett could catch up.

"Wait for me," he yelled up at her. "You may end up rescuing me."

It was pitch black when they reached his truck. She was never so happy to see anything before in her life. The towels were used to dry off their cold frozen hair. Nina had dirt down the side of her jeans, but she didn't care.

"I need coffee, food, anything," Nina said. He agreed and they drove to find the closest store. The small gravel roads down the mountain were very dark due to the moonlight being obstructed by the forest of trees.

There was a gas station they had passed a few miles back. If it was still open, they would stop there he said. It took them twice as long to come down the mountain road in the dark for fear of wildlife surprising them. Nina was scared they would some upon a deer, raccoon or coyote in the road and made Bennett slow down to a snail's pace. They pulled into the small store's parking space and watched as the sign was turned from 'Open' to "Closed'. Luckily, the owners heard their car and opened the door for them to come inside.

Nina begged them to let her use the restroom. (Another thing she had forgotten about.) When she returned, Bennett held two fresh large cups of coffee and a bag full of snacks. They thanked the owners and went back to the truck. "I thought I'd find something you'd eat," he said, offering her the bag.

"Thanks," she smiled, "But what will you eat?" They both laughed.

They got back late that night, too tired to do more than fall into bed. Bennett wrapped his arms around her and pulled her close, into a spoon position. "Oh, and I love you too" she yawned as she fell asleep.

# CHAPTER FORTY-SIX

The next morning, she paid the price for their adventure the night before. Every muscle in her body was sore. "You did this to me," she said as she punched Bennett in the arm.

"Ow! Don't be so mean," he teased her. "I didn't mean it."

Getting out of bed was a struggle. Making her way to the bathroom, she saw herself in the mirror and almost screamed at the face looking back at her. They had fallen into bed almost immediately after they got home. Neither one had taken a shower.

"Oh my God!" she said.

"What's wrong?" Bennett said as he got up in a hurry.

"I look horrible, a total mess," she told him. "Why didn't you say anything?"

He shrugged his shoulders, "You look fine to me. I didn't really notice."

"Men!" she said as she turned on the hot shower. "You really must be blinded by love."

"Guilty," he smiled. He loved the way she didn't fuss over her makeup or hair. She was usually not worried about her appearance. But he laughed to himself, she did look a mess.

Bennett got dressed and went to the coffee shop to grab them breakfast. On the way home, he saw two young boys, maybe 8 or 9, sitting at the corner with a box and a sign that read, "Free Kittens". He couldn't resist. He knew Nina would love a kitten. She had such a big heart.

He pulled over and asked the boys how old the kittens were. "They were weened last weekend and mom said we had to find them good homes," the older one said.

"Well, my girlfriend, oops, fiancée, would love to be a mom to one of these cuties," Bennett told them. "Which one do you think is the cutest?"

He ended up taking a black and white female. When he walked in, he called out for Nina to help him with the bags.

Nina walked out of the bedroom and stopped in her tracks. "What did you do?"

"This young lady needed a home and I thought ours would be perfect," he told her. Nina took the fluffy girl out of his arms and snuggled her close.

"Oh Bennett, she is perfect," she gushed. "What should we name her?"

They thought for a few minutes and spat out a few names, 'Georgia' 'Janis' 'Jimi'. "What about Kashmir?" he suggested. "With a K like the album, not the sweater."

Nina laughed and decided Kashmir was the right name. Kashmir was already curled up on her lap. She didn't have the heart to wake her, so they both sat, relaxed.

Later that afternoon, she called Lauren to see if she wanted to bring her new boyfriend over for dinner one night that week. "Where were you last night?" she asked. "I tried calling you for hours."

"Bennett took me up to Jemez Hot Springs," she said. "Not my idea, but we had a good time in the end."

"Look at you," Lauren teased her, "Ms. Adventure. A new hiking guru as I live and breathe."

"Very funny," she replied. "Why were you calling? Is something wrong?" Nina knew it wasn't serious if Lauren was in this good of a mood.

"I don't know," Lauren answered. "Sam hasn't called me in four days. Do you think he's married?"

Nina rolled her eyes. She did tend to attract married men. She didn't know how, but she did. "I wouldn't think so. He told you where he worked, right?"

"Yes," she conceded, "he said he worked for his dad as a mechanic. I never asked for more details, I didn't want to seem nosy." Maybe she was overreacting.

"Well," Nina said, "when he does call you, tell him you are both invited over here. You just tell me what night. You have to remember that men think differently. They don't see the need in touching base with women every day. That's a girl thing, I'm sure of it."

"Well, what about Bennett?" she asked, "He sure seems to keep you up to date on where he is and what he's doing."

"Yeah, he's great," she agreed, "but he's not average." They both laughed and knew that was true. Nina had hit the lottery when she met Bennett.

That seemed to calm her down a little bit. She knew Lauren was quick to fall for men who were not the best people. She really hoped this one was different. Most of the men she dated she met through her new job near the college. There was a small burger bar that most of the faculty and some students frequented. Since she was taking a few night classes, it was easy to get to class, and work without looking for a new parking spot.

Lauren had wanted to be a fashion designer since she was a little girl. The community college offered an introductory textiles class that she was taking now. She was doing well but it was awkward being ten years older than most of the other students. That had to be a factor in the professors hitting on her. There were also several men that kept asking her out at the coffee shop. She often talked of finding an office job, where she wouldn't be in the public eye so much.

# CHAPTER FORTY-SEVEN

Lauren called Nina the next morning to say that Sam had finally called the night before. He apologized and told her his dad had several cars they had to get done before Monday. They had worked late every night. He only had time to shower and sleep, before he went back to the garage.

Lauren was relieved when he accepted Nina's invitation to dinner on Wednesday night. He had promised Lauren that he would get off work in time to take a shower and clean up before he picked her up.

Nina was looking forward to meeting Sam. Hopefully Bennett would be able to talk to him and see if he was as good as Lauren described. She had never had couple friends or a dinner party. Even when she was in New York, Landon had never brought anyone from work over to their apartment. Landon didn't want her getting into his business.

Bennett was rehearsing with the band for hours every day. They had a long booking coming up next week. The band was going to be playing at the Blue Iguana for two weeks, five nights a week. The money was good, but Nina knew they wouldn't see much of each other. It was the life of a musician's family, late nights and lost days.

He got home from rehearsal and jumped in the shower to get ready for their company. All clean shaven and dressed in a nice button-down shirt and dark jeans, he walked into the kitchen to see what was on the menu. "I don't know what it is, but it smells wonderful," he said.

"You're not hard to please," she laughed. "I wanted to try a new recipe but changed my mind. I thought comfort food was best." She pulled off the lid to a big pot containing chicken and vegetables. "I present to you, Chicken Cacciatore." She said with a little bit of an Italian accent.

"Hmmm, smells delicious," he said. "What do you want me to do?" One thing Bennett didn't mind is helping in the kitchen, especially if she was cooking a meal.

"Can you open a bottle of wine? A cabernet I think, and bring out the cheese tray from the fridge," she asked him. She was expecting the couple to arrive in a few minutes. He snuck up behind her and gave her a quick peck on the cheek.

He grabbed the tray, took a few bites of cheese from the board. "Never met a cheese I didn't like," he said with a smile. He proceeded to turn on the stereo and put in one of his favorite CDs, The Beatles' 'White Album'.

Soon they heard a car pulling into the empty space outside. Bennett opened the door promptly and reached for what Lauren was holding. He carried it the kitchen and set on the counter. "Dessert I hope?" he asked her.

"Of course," she said, "Ask and you shall receive. I brought a homemade cheesecake. Who is this?" Kashmir had heard the door and came out of hiding. She loved attention. New people meant more scratches for her.

"This is Kashmir," Nina said. "Bennett got her for me last week. He said he's mine, but she is clearly in love with him."

Nina had set the small table with her new set of dishes and napkins. "Thank you for inviting me over," said Sam. "Lauren says you've been friends forever." He stepped closer and gave Nina a kiss on the cheek before she even knew what was happening. She jumped back so quickly she almost fell down. Nina rushed to the bathroom as her heart pounded and her face was getting hot.

Bennett was right behind her, worried about what was going on and trying to help any way he could. "Honey, are you ok? What's wrong?" He kept knocking on the door. "Please let me in."

The door opened and she hid behind it as Bennett walked in. He shut the door and turned to see her breathing heavy with tears in her eyes. "Please say something. Did I do something?" she shook her head 'no'. "That's a relief," he continued. "Was it the kiss from Sam?" She slowly nodded as she looked up at Bennett. "I don't get it, Nina. It was just a little kiss on the cheek."

"I didn't think you would. But, In New York, all of Landon's acquaintances would kiss me like that. All innocent right?" He was happy to see her calming down as she explained. "And more than one lingered too long or gave me a squeeze. Once, it went too far." She stopped. This wasn't the time or the place.

"I want to know Nina," he begged. "Tell me what happened."

"No Bennett, not now. I promise I will tell you later tonight, okay?" She looked at him with pleading eyes and stood to wash her face and pull herself together. "I'm going out there and apologize and hope they don't think I'm crazy."

And she did. She made her way to the table and sat next to Lauren. "I'm sorry you guys, I just had a strange flashback I guess you could say. I didn't mean to react like that. Honestly, I had no idea I would." Lauren was squeezing her hand as she spoke. "Can you forgive me?"

"Of course, we can. Don't think about it." Lauren hugged her. "What are friends for?"

"In case you didn't know," Nina was now addressing Sam, "We've been through a lot together. Technically we've known each other for only a few months, but it feels like years. I guess you could say she gave me shelter when I needed it most."

Sam made sure he put her at ease, "It's my fault, I'm just one of those people who hugs and kisses, but totally platonically. I know others don't do that. I really am sorry."

Bennett followed her into the kitchen and brought out the wine and cheese tray. "Dinner will be ready in just a few minutes," she called from the kitchen.

They sat down and enjoyed the meal with their friends. Bennett told them stories about playing in a band. He always had some funny tales of drunk groupies and bad managers. "This one time, a couple of older women, about 40 I'd say, came out onto the dance floor. They had been drinking for a while and before we knew it, one of them started undressing!"

"You have got to be kidding me man," Sam said, laughing out loud. "What did you do?"

"Looked straight ahead and kept on playing," Bennett said. It was nice to relax with other people they liked for a change, instead of work friends.

The stories about what happens behind the scenes of the bands always made her laugh. "Tell them about the tip jar," she asked Bennett.

"OK, if you insist," he said. "One night we were playing at a bar for the first time and we had our tip jar on the stage, like we always do. You may not realize that the tips we get often are more important than the money we get from the manager, especially if we're only playing one night that week. Anyway, one of the waitresses came up and took the jar!"

"No way!" Sam and Lauren said in unison. "Why?" They were clearly in disbelief.

"She told me that the band always splits the tips with the waitresses," he answered. "I am not kidding! Well, I calmly explained to her that this is the only job we have all week, and we don't ask for a piece of their tips. It just wasn't fair to expect us to share ours. From that point on, I was put in charge of negotiations." He shrugged his shoulders and laughed softly.

Sam said, "Better you than me, I would have blown a fuse. You are much more diplomatic I guess."

The couples spent the evening eating and talking. Bennett invited them both out to see the band the next weekend if they wanted. Nina and Lauren tried to get together every week from then on. It was nice to have close friends when her family couldn't be here, she thought.

# CHAPTER FORTY-EIGHT

The winter seemed to stick around in Northern New Mexico, longer than it did in Albuquerque. They still saw snow until the end of April. Nina thought she would never get tired of seeing the snow-covered trees. It was just like a magazine.

The next time they went out to dinner with Sam and Lauren, it was at their favorite Italian restaurant. Of course, Lauren knew it was where Landon proposed, but Sam hadn't heard the story. The waiter was the same one and was able to contribute a little behind-the-scenes action about that night.

While waiting for their meals, Sam announced, "I have something to ask you." He was looking directly at Lauren. Everyone stopped what they were doing and gave Sam their full attention. Lauren eyes grew and her hands flew up to cover her mouth.

"Oh my God! No," Sam said. "I mean, maybe one day, but No. Not today." Lauren's expression went from excitement to sadness in a flash. "I am so sorry, honey, I didn't mean to do that to you." He leaned over to give her a kiss. He really felt like a heel. "What I meant to say is, I would like to invite everyone to a long weekend in Taos. One of my dad's customers has a cabin and offered it to us for the middle of April."

"Wow, that's so awesome!" Bennett said. "Oh wait, when are we talking?" Nina had the same question. She would have to move some shifts around she knew.

"I believe it's in three weeks. He said we could go anytime that week if that helps," Sam explained. "I've seen pictures, the cabin is cool, and Taos will still have lots of tourists and skiers hitting the slopes." Lauren had perked up and was clapping from the news.

Bennett took Nina's small calendar book she was holding out for him and turned to the week in question. "Looks like I will be done with the band booking that Saturday night. So, I could leave as early as Sunday. What about you girls?"

animals. New Mexico was gorgeous but there were still some parts that were home to wildlife.

After striking a deal with Jared they stopped by Nina's to make it ready for Kashmir's guests. Since it would be vacant, she would move the litter box into the kitchen.

Tony stopped by the next evening, just before Bennett was about to leave. Nina had her key off the ring to give to him. Bennett shook his hand, "Now young man, no parties and no girls. Don't make me call your mother." Tony started sweating a little, until Bennett smiled big. "I'm just kidding with you. But seriously, you can't have anyone here, the landlord will kill us."

"Yes sir, I understand," he answered nervously.

"It's ok. I'm harmless," Bennett assured him. If Tony was anything like Bennett at that age, the cops would be here in minutes. He hated being THAT guy, the old stodgy man who tells kids to 'keep it down.'

Lauren brought her two cats over the next day, and Kashmir looked very confused for a while. The three of them spent a while just circling the room and staring at each other. As soon as Nina put their food in the three dishes, in different corners of the room, the tension was gone. After liking their paws, she found them all in one chair, huddled together.

Two days later, Tony met Nina and Bennett around noon and got the last-minute instructions on the feline care. It appeared that they would all get along. Nina knew that was not set in stone. Cats could be very unpredictable. As long as they were all alive when they returned, it would be a win.

The drive to Taos was beautiful. Nina was getting used to the scenery around Santa Fe, but Taos was further up the mountain. The snow was still a couple of feet deep on the sides of the road. Most of the way up there, the snow was still pristine, except for a few small animal tracks.

# CHAPTER FORTY-NINE

When they arrived at the cabin, Sam came out to help them with their bags. There was a wide wood staircase that led up to a deck that was home to a hot tub. Nina never considered bringing a swimsuit on the winter vacation. Hopefully, Lauren brought an extra one for her. She was not about to skinny dip like they did at the Hot Springs.

In the corner of the main room was a fireplace that was keeping the room toasty. The big leather furniture made the room very comfortable. At the same time, it looked like a great vacation place, with a pool table in the upstairs loft, a large island/bar with stools around and just the right amount of wilderness décor. Sam showed them to their room on the first floor, behind the fireplace. Nina grinned when she saw the oversized king bed. It was really like a dream. The cherry on top of the cake was the jacuzzi tub in the bathroom.

The guys decided to go pick up dinner and make sure the bar was stocked for their stay. They were staying in that night and relaxing. Tomorrow they would get up and walk around the town and see what they could find.

After a dinner of pizza and beer, they settled in front of the fire. Bennett had brought his guitar and picked it up to play after Lauren and Sam begged. While Nina listened and watched the fire, she grew sleepy. The next thing she knew, Bennett was whispering in her ear, "Bedtime for you, sleepyhead."

They climbed up into the huge bed and snuggled under the thick comforters. Nina felt like she was sleeping on clouds. She dreamed of being married to Bennett, with small kids all around. This was what she always wanted, to feel safe and loved.

A scent of strong coffee wafted into the bedroom the next morning. Bennett and Nina would have preferred to stay in bed all morning, but at the same time, they were eager to explore. Making their way to the kitchen area, they stopped at the deck, gazing out at the snow-covered mountain and the bright sun bouncing of it.

Lauren was already dressed and ready to take them to the small diner just down the street for breakfast. The sidewalks were cleared of snow which made it easy to walk the couple of blocks. After they finished their huge meals, the group started with their tourist shopping. The guys were good sports and followed along behind Nina and Lauren until they begged for them to stop and get a drink.

Nina had already picked up tees and a sweatshirt and found several pieces of Indian-made jewelry. She knew she could find them cheaper if she looked, but she didn't mind paying for quality. They returned to the cabin in the late afternoon and made plans to go out to a nice restaurant, then maybe hit the hot tub after.

They emptied two bottles of wine with their dinner of steak, potatoes and vegetables, which made the walk home much harder than the walk there. Upon entering the cabin, the coats were shed in the foyer, and they ran to turn the fireplace on. The temperature had dipped to below 30 degrees so far. She didn't know now if she really could live up there year-round.

As expected, the hot tub was the end to a perfect day, steaming bubbling water made every muscle in her body relax. Bennett brought out another bottle of wine and the four enjoyed the scenery in the warmth of the water. After an hour, she knew she needed to get out. Her head was spinning a little and she didn't want to get sick near the hot tub.

She dried off quickly and fell into the bed to get warm again. She didn't even bother getting her pjs on, just panties and a tee shirt. As hard as she tried, she couldn't keep her eyes open. Bennett had said he was coming in right after her, but he wasn't there yet. She felt embarrassed to admit it to herself, but damn, she wanted him.

"Hey, you awake?" she heard whispered in her ear. She rolled over to see Bennett's face just inches away from hers. The smile on her face made him smile even bigger. "Hey there beautiful."

"Hey there yourself," she whispered, with a flirting tone. "You better get in here, now."

He did as he was told. All he was wearing was a towel around his waist, which he quickly dropped to the floor. He reached out to draw her closer to his body.

"Your hands are freezing!" she quietly squealed playfully. Nina soon found that the contrast of his cold hands on her warm skin made her whole body writhe in anticipation. She tried to lay still and let him trace her body with his fingertips. The tingling sensation she felt just made her want him more.

"Oh my God Bennett!" She cried out, careful not to let the others hear their lovemaking. He got on top of her and brushed her nipples with his chest. She let out another gasp, grabbing his butt cheeks.

His hand flew up to her mouth as he whispered, "Shh, they'll hear us." Then, he started kissing her lips then her breasts, finally sucking on her nipples. She danced in bed with desire to have him. She couldn't take much more foreplay. They rolled over to where Bennett was on his back. Now, it was her turn to tease him.

Nina licked him down his torso, including his nipples. He was moaning in delight. As she made her way down to his groin, his breathing was getting louder and louder. His breath was heavy and rapid. He didn't want to make her stop, but if she didn't, he would finish before she did.

He finally entered her, causing her to dig into his arms with her fingernails. He thrusted in and out, each time getting deeper. Nina gasped at one point, and almost achieved her orgasm. He finished only a minute later. He fell to the bed on top of her, both out of breath. It would take him a minute to recover. Nina was still panting, and he knew she didn't climax with him. She was still on fire, wanting to orgasm so badly, she felt like she would explode when he touched her again.

He rolled onto his side and used his fingers to hit the right spot for her to climax. It only took a few seconds until she stopped breathing and her body began shaking with her erotic release.

Neither one could move or wanted to move after that. They slept for a few hours before even stirring. When he woke up, she did too. "Hey, come with me," he asked her.

"Where? What are you doing?" Nina felt wide awake and was curious as to what he was thinking. He looked out the window to where the hot tub sat. Pointing at the tub, he gently tugged her out of bed. "I have a better idea, definitely more private," she said as she walked into their bathroom and took his arm to follow her. She filled the bathtub with hot water, and slid in, waiting for him to join her.

He knew he could never walk away from her. She was the most beautiful girl he had ever seen. In that moment, in the bathtub, looking up at him, he knew they needed to be together forever.

"Damn, woman. You need to stop putting that spell on me," he laughed. She smiled flirtatiously and took his hand to allow him to step into the tub, facing her. As they both caressed each other underwater, she was getting turned on again. She turned around and moved back into Bennett's open arms. She rested her head back onto his shoulder. He was kissing her ear, and down her arm. His hands wrapped around her from behind and found her breasts. He squeezed them very gently and was sure to give her nipples a little pinch too.

Minutes later they had just finished making love in a bathtub, a first for both of them. Nina didn't know she was going to function tomorrow, and she didn't care. Making love with Bennett was always better than anything else she could be doing.

The remainder of the vacation was spent eating and shopping in town. One night they found a bar with a live band. But it only took a few minutes for Bennett to know he didn't want to stay. "That guitar player missed a bunch of chords. They need to leave the playing to the professionals."

Nina noticed he was getting grumpy watching the band. She leaned over and whispered, "Before they come back for the next set we will leave. I promise." She squeezed his hand under the table and kissed his cheek.

"Thanks, I think you're getting me." The waitress had just brought another round to the table, and they all made a toast. "I'm trying," she answered him.

"To good friends, and a great cabin! May we get to do it again soon."

# CHAPTER FIFTY

When they arrived home, they saw several bags of trash sitting outside of their door. They appeared to be full of beer cans. They couldn't believe their eyes. Would Jared really throw a party at their home? Bennett got out of the truck first and walked to the front door briskly. He wasn't sure what he would find when he opened that door.

The bags contained beer cans, pizza boxes and cups and glass bottles. When he went inside, he was greeted by the three cats, all longing for his attention. He glanced around the room and stuck his arm out to wave Nina to come on in.

"What happened here?" she asked. "Tell me they didn't have a party, please!"

"Well, I can say that if they did, they did a good job cleaning up," Bennett reasoned. He went to the freezer and noticed a bag of ice, where none had been before. "It's all in the details, dude."

"What did you say?" she asked. She was looking in the bedroom and bathroom. Except for a missing roll of toilet paper, and paper towels, nothing was out of place.

"I was just saying they did a good job, except for some small details. I'm actually kind of impressed," he remarked. They both stood for a minute and started laughing. They had both either thrown a party or been to one in their school days. "I think I'm going to ask him to come over tomorrow. That way he can sweat it out tonight."

"You're awful," she said. "But I agree. He needs to know we caught him. In lieu of telling Julia, what should we do?"

"I'm sure we can come up with something before tomorrow," he said.

Bennett called Jared and told him he wanted to talk to him before lunch tomorrow. "This is just between you and me and Nina at the moment," he warned him. Jared sounded nervous but agreed.

He showed up by lunch and knocked on their door. It opened to Bennett and Nina standing there, checking him out. "Come on in young man." Bennett addressed him. "Have a seat."

Watching him pace back and forth, Nina thought of what a great father he would be one day. She started to smile, then quickly remembered she was supposed to be looking upset at Jared.

"First of all, we're not going to tell your parents," Bennett started. Jared looked marginally better after he heard that. "Second, if you are going to throw a party, watch the small details."

Jared finally spoke, "I am so sorry Mr. Bennett. I was over here, with my girlfriend. I know I shouldn't, but I wasn't thinking. Next thing I knew my best friend was here, with his girlfriend and two others. I swear it was only the six of us."

"That's a lot of beer cans for six young people," now it was Bennett's turn to be confused. Clearly there were more kids, right?

"You mean the trash bags?" Jared answered. "That was my fault. Ricky needed to clean out his truck bed, so I helped, and we just put it there. He was supposed to take the bags with him when they left but I guess he forgot. I'm so sorry, I'll make it up to you Mr. Moore. I can wash your cars. Do your shopping? You name it."

"I'll think about it," was al Bennett said. But he patted the boy on the back to let him know he wasn't furious with him.

Spring brought intense thunderstorms across the town. The difference between a desert thunderstorm and a big city thunderstorm is one minute you can be looking at a clear sunny sky, the next minute you'll be in the middle of a storm with high winds and pounding rain. The black clouds would blow in usually in the afternoon, but within an hour usually, the sun was out again.

On a warm weekday when both she and Bennett were off, he suggested they needed to wash their cars. "I don't like going to the drive-thru car washes. They always seem to bend my license plate and hardly ever get it totally clean."

"That's fine, I'm sure this car hasn't been washed for weeks before Dad gave it to me," she replied.

She was able to find some rags and a bucket. After quickly changing into 'old' clothes, she met Bennett outside. He was already hosing down the vehicles in preparation for the soapy suds.

They worked hard scrubbing off dirt as they listened to their favorite rock station. After washing the windshield, Nina picked up the hose and carefully sprayed off the suds. She hasn't seen where Bennett was at that moment until he stood up and looked at her, soaking wet, over the hood.

"OH, I am so sorry," she stammered. "Maybe you better do the hose, I'm obviously doing a terrible job. Don't hate me. I didn't mean it."

"Calm down," Bennett laughed. "It's actually pretty funny, and pretty stupid." Nina had no idea what he meant, but she didn't like what he just said. It didn't help that he kept laughing at her. She never liked it when she was the object of other people's laughter.

"What do you mean stupid? I apologized. What else do you want?" her temper was rising. She was never going to be in a relationship again where the man had no sense of humor and called her names.

"Hold on," he comforted her. "I'm not mad. All I meant was it was stupid of you to lay the hose down at my feet." At that moment he bent down, grabbed the nozzle and soaked Nina to the bone. They laughed so hard, they had to sit down.

# CHAPTER FIFTY-ONE

The warmer days brought thousands of tourists in buses, trains and airplanes. The temperature at night was still cool so sweaters and jackets were needed after sundown. Nina had been promoted in a way to a permanent schedule with two lunch shifts and three night shifts a week. Julia also gave her the first crack at picking up an extra shift when she was in need.

She had opened a savings account at her bank and tried to put back money every paycheck. Nina thought to herself how lucky she was, she was independent and financially secure. The summer ahead would be busy she guessed. More people meant more customers at the restaurant and bars where Bennett was still working three or four nights a week.

Nina was really enjoying the normal, some might say boring life they had now. No drama and no worries. However, she had a feeling deep down, that her disappearance wasn't the end of her New York trouble. She explained it away by saying she was just looking for something to go wrong. Nothing ever came to surface though. Feelings weren't facts, she knew that.

Summer in Santa Fe started by the first week of June. Due to the low humidity, the sun didn't have long to heat up the atmosphere from the still cool nights. It was a heat she had never experienced before, dry dusty heat.

Bennett's birthday was in late June, so they took a long weekend off and booked a room at the Black Hills Casino and Resort. It was run by Native Americans. There were several located in the state, but this one was the closest. As soon as the stepped through the door, she thought they had gone to Las Vegas. There were bright lights everywhere, and the loud noise of slot machines and customers hollering with big wins.

Bennett had mentioned that these places pay pretty good for a house band. It was much more than he was making now. "But is that what you want to do?" she asked. "Show up in a suit every night?"

"It's not that bad, I don't think they require suits," he explained. "There is a small theatre here that has live music. They bring in famous artist like Dwight Yoakum, Doobie Brothers, Bruce Hornsby, I think they even booked The Scorpions in here."

Anyway, they need an opening act, that would be us. We only need to play about 45 minutes of cover songs, twice a night." He was really wanting her opinion on the job, he was torn. He could stay with Chain Reaction and play different places every weekend, hopefully. Or, he could have a steady job, in one location and not have to move his equipment from bar to bar.

"That does sound like a great job," she said. "You would be home most nights before midnight I guess."

"If not before, very soon after. I think my last set would end by 1030 pm. I was going to go talk to the manager while we are here," he asked, "if you don't mind."

"Of course not," she agreed, "It can't hurt to ask a few questions."

They spent the next day having a fancy dinner in the most expensive restaurant in the casino to celebrate his birthday. Nina had arranged for a small chocolate lava cake to be delivered to their table after the meal. It had one lit candle on it.

"The staff told me," she said with a smile, "that they could only put one candle on. If they put the rest, it would be a fire hazard."

He laughed with her. "Very funny, ha ha," he grinned as she playfully teased him. "You do realize that I am just 14 months older than you? And my birthday isn't until tomorrow."

"Oh yes, I know," she said, "and women age so much better than men." He leaned over and blew out the candle. "What did you wish for?" she had to ask.

"Well, number one, I can't tell you or it won't come true," he laughed. "And another thing, I have everything I want right here."

The rest of their trip was spent eating at the huge buffet and losing money on the slot machines. At night, they got in the heart shaped jacuzzi in their room. It really felt like she was getting pampered in a spa. She didn't want to go home.

The drive home was quiet, but in a peaceful, relaxed way. As soon as they pulled in their driveway, they could see Kashmir waiting in the window. They had left her at home and Lauren had volunteered to come by and feed her. She was probably starving they joked. The cat ate more like a cougar.

"There's my girl," Bennett said to Kashmir as they walked in. He really did love animals, she thought. That's a good thing. "Excuse us, we want to be alone," he said to Nina with a laugh.

There was a message on their answering machine when they walked in. She was always nervous when she the blinking red light. But she had already confessed about her past to Bennett, so there wasn't any reason she should be nervous. She pushed play and waited.

"Hello? Benny? Nina? Benny, this is your mother." A sigh of relief washed over her as Gwen continued to talk. "Your father and I wanted to wish you a happy birthday and ask you and Nina to come by this Sunday for a small birthday party for you and your sister. Call me when you get this. We love you."

"Oh Benny!" Nina chuckled. "What do our weekend plans look like? I know I'll be working until four or five that day. What if we combine your 'party' with the Independence Day Fireworks? I bet the view from their house is amazing."

"That's not a bad idea," he said. "Let me call Becky and see if she's free next Tuesday, on the 4th. I bet the munchkins would love it. I guess I need to call my mom too."

He spent the rest of the evening talking to Becky and Gwen and Beau. They were all for a birthday cookout with the fireworks as the grand finale on the evening. Nina loved spending time with his big family. Growing up as an only child, she always gravitated towards friends with siblings.

"I hope you don't mind but I volunteered us to bring potato salad," he told Nina. "Are you sure you can get off work that night?" She hadn't seen him excited like this in a while.

"It shouldn't be a problem if I ask her tomorrow, before the schedule is made," she answered. "And, if we're bringing potato salad, then you are on peeling duty." She knew the night would be great. They had such a good time at Christmas. She couldn't remember the last time she made plans to watch the July 4$^{th}$ fireworks.

# CHAPTER FIFTY-TWO

As soon as they arrived at the Moore's home, Daphne came running out to give her a big hug. She bent down to her height to let her whisper in her ear. "Are you going to be my aunt?" The smile on Daphne's face was contagious. "I think so," Nina answered. Daphne giggles and squealed as she ran back into the house.

They didn't see Amy standing behind her cousin until she was gone. "Hello there, Miss Amy," Bennett addressed the young girl. "Do you have a hug for me?" She lifted her arms up and he bent over to pick her up. "Have you gained weight?"

"I don't know Uncle Benny, what does that mean?" Amy truly was confused at the comment.

Nina laughed and chided Bennett. "Don't you know you never ask a lady her weight? Shame on you." She wagged her finger in his face as if to scold him. "Amy, he just meant you sure are getting big, like Daphne and Molly."

"Oh yes, I am." Amy proudly stated. "I had my birthday and I'm free!" She was a pretty good talker for her age, Nina thought. Bennett took her hand that was holding up three fingers and pretended to gobble them up. Amy was giggling just like Daphne had been.

"When is your birthday?" Nina asked her, making a note to put it in her calendar for next year.

"I don't know," she was thinking, with her fingers under her chin and her eyes looking up as if looking for the magic answer.

"I bet I know," said Bennett. "Is it May 24th? Around the Memorial Day weekend usually."

"What's Memorial Day?" she was on a different line of questioning now. "Do we get presents on Memorial Day?"

As much as they tried, they couldn't keep from laughing at her adorable face, and questions. She was very curious, that was for sure.

"What's so funny?" she giggled along with her uncle.

"Oh nothing, Amy. You are too cute." Nina gave her a big smooch on the cheek and tickled her under her arm. Bennet put her down and she scampered away to playing with Jay, her younger cousin.

"I'll be right back. Don't go anywhere" she gave Bennett a quick peck as she walked off with the potato salad.

Nina delivered the dish to the kitchen island and grabbed two beers out of the fridge. She realized she must feel comfortable enough to help herself at the caught up to Bennett on the back deck. The sky was clear and was starting to cool off. "Every day, it just gets better and better," she thought.

James was in charge of the grilling that night. Until he started neglecting the burgers and chicken, and they got a little too done on one side. "You had better leave the cooking to the professionals," Beau said as he stripped him of the apron and utensils.

"Dad, come sit over here," Bennett motioned to the empty chair next to the loveseat he and Nina shared. "This is a great view, but you know that."

"How are you kids doing these days? How's the music biz?" Bennett pushed back his twinge of resentment. He was an adult; he knew his dad loved him and didn't want to shame him. That was the old Bennett, he thought.

"We, the band, are playing almost every week," he explained. "I love it, but it is tiring moving the gear around. I'm thinking of getting a job at Black Hills, in the band. If they ever call me."

"That would be a big change," James said. "You have to be careful with the casinos, they don't all keep the best company."

Bennett laughed, "Come on Dad, this isn't 'The Godfather' or the Sixties. It's a small local American Indian owned casino in the middle of the desert."

"Just where do you think Las Vegas is? How did it come to be?" James went on, "It too was just a casino in the middle of the desert. Now look at it."

"Ok Ok," he conceded. "I'll be careful. Now let's talk more about this photography hobby you've taken up. Have you taken any classes?"

"Not yet," James replied, "but I am considering it. I'm thinking about turning part of the utility room into a darkroom." They spent the next several minutes in deep discussion about how to get it done and what kind of photography he wanted to do.

"Rebecca Diane and Bennett James would you please join me over here?" Gwen was calling everyone to pay attention. The birthday kids walked slowly with a little embarrassment to their mother's side. "I was working at the PX 28 years ago when I started having bad back pains. My shift was over, and the pain was getting worse, so I went straight to my doctor's office. My due date was another four weeks away so naturally I began to panic. The doctor told the nurse to call an ambulance and I was taken to the hospital."

"This is where I join in," James started his side of the story. "I was with my troop, running drills about 15 miles outside of town. I got a call on my radio that my wife was taken to the hospital. You have never seen a man move so quickly. I was in that hospital waiting room in under 30 minutes."

"Now James, let me finish, they're all getting hungry," Gwen stepped in and took over. "I was in labor for over eight hours. First came Bennett, born at 9:52 p.m. and then Rebecca born at 10:23 p.m." She pulled out two big birthday hats for each to wear. The grandkids were laughing hysterically at their mom/aunt and uncle in the silly hats.

"To look at them now, you wouldn't know they each weighed less than five pounds. Thankfully, they only needed to stay in the hospital until they gained another pound, which was only two weeks. I love you both." Gwen had a tear in her eye as she kissed each twin.

Beau stood up announcing, "A toast to the most annoying older brother and sister, oh, I meant to say most awesome." The adults laughed along and raised their glasses. "Now, let's eat, we are starving."

Nina was quiet all through Gwen's story. She was daydreaming of what it will be like when they have their own children. Bennett seemed uncomfortable at the details of his birth, but she knew he had heard the story probably every year

"What are you thinking?" Bennett said as he walked over and saw the big grin on her face.

"Oh nothing. Just about our future," she replied, kissing him. The little girls were watching and giggling again. There is no way anyone could get mad at these kids, not even a little bit. Nina knew she would be the parent that wouldn't spank her kids.

After eating dinner, the adults pulled out Yahtzee and played a game before the fireworks started. As she expected, Bennett was a master at games. "How many hours of your childhood did you spend playing board games?" she asked. She rarely had the chance since she was an only child.

Becky answered for him, "All summer long, well, after sunset and when we on winter break. He was always begging me to play with him." She rolled her eyes and smiled. The best part was when Beau wanted to join us in playing Monopoly. She pointed at their younger brother. "Yes, you! You would always stomp off after 30 minutes if you weren't winning."

Gwen came up behind them holding a large birthday cake with sparklers standing up in it. The kids closed in quickly. James pulled out a lighter and lit the sparklers while everyone sang 'Happy Birthday'. They all carefully removed the lit sparkers and handed them to Molly and Daphne. Amy and Jay were too young to handle them.

"Mom this cake is delicious! Where did you get it?" asked Becky.

A somewhat quiet Charlotte humbly raised her hand. "You really like it? We've been thinking about opening a bakery next to the restaurant. That recipe is white chocolate strawberry."

"That would be awesome! I know where I would order all my cakes from now on," Becky answered. "One less thing on my busy schedule."

The fireworks display didn't disappoint any of the Moore clan except maybe Jay, who fell asleep before they began. He was peaceful in his mother's lap. Amy wasn't far behind. Nina was happy to volunteer to rock the young girl in her lap. Her body was limp in her lap. "This is what I want," she thought to herself. "It's all perfect."

# CHAPTER FIFTY-THREE

The restaurant had opened patio dining and the tables outside were almost always full. She didn't mind working outside in the heat, as long as she could see the sun. She still remembered the long days in New York where she went to work in the dark and came home in the dark. The sun always put her in a good mood and gave her a little tan to boost.

One day in August, she was taking the order at one of the tables of tourists on the patio when she heard a familiar voice behind her. She politely finished with her customers and took a minute to peak over her shoulder. The next table had four men, clearly not locals by the way they were dressed.

The one with his back to her was saying, "Now I'm paying you a lot of money to find me something to shoot up in the mountains."

"Don't worry Mr. Bottino, it's all being taken care of," said the young man sitting next to him. "We are all set to go up to the hunting cabin of my friend tomorrow afternoon. They already have the licenses needed for Pronghorn Antelope and Bighorn Sheep hunting."

As soon as she heard that name, she rushed inside the ladies' room to an empty stall and tried to not get physically sick. The last thing a patron wanted to hear in the restroom is someone losing their lunch. She was able to switch her table with Tonya and successfully hid from Michael for the length of their meal.

Tonya had said when she saw his table, "Did you catch a look at those guys out there? They look like central casting sent them in to play the mafia." Their table was full of plates and wine glasses. It looked like they ordered everything on the menu.

They heard a cell phone ringing and Michael's young friend answered it. "Yeah, he's right here, hold on," he said. "It's that Jamison guy for you, he is talking about coming out here to join us this weekend?"

"No, no, that's not possible tell him I need him in New York," Michael said. "We'll make plans for him to join us next time."

At that moment, Nina's whole past and future flashed before her eyes. Tonya noticed the strange look on her face. "What is going on Nina?" She wanted to laugh but she was too afraid to say anything. How was it possible that the one person who was the most dangerous to her would end up here?

She didn't know if she should let Bennett know what happened or not? She hadn't included the part about her husband being linked to the mafia. That would be one more hard fact to swallow she thought. It could not even be an issue. If she was able to stay out of sight for the next several days, Nina thought he would be occupied and out of touch for at least three days.

She decided to wait to talk to Bennett until after they were out of the state and going home. However, when she got home, he could tell something was bothering her? Why was he so observant?

"Honey, what's wrong?" he said taking her hand and making her sit down next to him. "Did something happen at work? Are you ok?"

She guessed her face told more than she wanted. She took a deep breath and told him about Michael Bottino and Paul DiMaio. She realized she sounded a little crazy. The look on his face was total confusion. She knew she wasn't making much sense at that moment.

Nina knew she should start over at the beginning. "There's more," she said as she got up to get more coffee. "Let's just say they are another reason I had to leave New York the way I did."

"Really? More?" he repeated. He had no idea what the mafia had to do with her. She had never mentioned anything like this before.

"Yes, more. Landon was involved with those mafia guys. In fact, it sounded like Landon had called one of them while they were there." She tried to finish quickly. "And I took his black book by mistake when I left. It has hundreds of names, numbers and dates."

Bennett looked at her, "You can't be serious? I didn't know that was a real thing. A mobster with a book of numbers?"

"Believe me," she said, "it's real. Some of the things you see on film are exaggerated, but the mafia is still real and dangerous. That book may save us one day; it put me on their most-wanted list. I thought by leaving I could escape danger, but it found me. I know any one of those men would kill to get their hands on that book."

"Where is the book now?" he was truly worried. She shouldn't be dealing with all this alone.

"It's in a small box under the bathroom sink. Totally safe until I need it," she answered.

"I think you need to stay home as much as possible this week," he suggested. "And, when you do go out, wear disguise. Have you ever thought about dyeing your hair? I've always been partial to redheads." He smiled and winked at her, hoping to lighten her mood.

"I am a redhead if you haven't noticed," she huffed, "more of a strawberry blonde, but it's still red. But yeah, I understand what you're saying. Maybe it is time for a change."

"A darker shade would look great on you," he encouraged. "Think of Molly Ringwald or Debra Messing. Something in those shades. It's very sexy," he said with a big grin.

"Oh really? So, I'm not sexy now?" she teased him.

"No, I mean yes, you are sexy now," Bennett was clearly struggling for words. "You will always be sexy to me, no matter what hair color."

"I'm just kidding, I know what you meant. I'm willing to try it," she agreed. "What's the worst that could happen, right? Never mind, don't answer that."

"Well at least we settled one problem," he laughed.

# CHAPTER FIFTY-FOUR

By the end of the week, she was back at work with dark auburn hair. She got several compliments on her look. When they asked what her reason was, she just said she was ready for a change. Her new look gave her confidence that she wouldn't be recognized that easily.

Nina spent the day, looking over her shoulder constantly. She hated feeling like she would turn the corner and run into someone who knew Kaci from New York. She had been very lucky so far. Santa Fe was a huge tourist destination after all.

The next week she felt more at ease. She was pretty sure the mob guys had gone back to where they came from. Business was picking up again once the temperatures started dropping a little. The winds were changing from hot and dusty to mild and dusty.

They were spending another lazy Sunday in bed reading the newspaper. It was a routine Nina loved. They split up the sections like they always did, Bennett took Sports and the Financial pages. Nina took Life and Metro section. She froze when she saw a picture of Landon on the page in front of her.

The headline read, 'The survivors of 9/11, One Year Later, How the Families are Coping with their Loss.'

She skimmed over the article to the paragraph about her. Landon was quoted as saying, "We were just starting our lives together when this tragedy happened. She had just told me she was pregnant. So, I didn't just lose my wife, I lost our unborn baby as well."

She was numb. How could he have lied like that? She had made sure she wasn't going to get pregnant by taking her birth control pills religiously. He clearly was looking for sympathy from anyone who would listen. The article went on to say that Landon had received a generous advance on her life insurance policy, which was still tied up in the court system. If he finds out I'm alive, he will have to pay that money back. She knew he didn't care about her as much as he cared about his money. He wouldn't give that up easily she was certain.

"Honey," Bennett asked, "What's wrong? Your face is white."

She showed him the page she was reading. "This is my husband." Her voice almost came out in a whisper.

"What? Are you serious?" he asked her. He took the paper and read the article. It was a lot of information to digest. He was trying to be understanding, but at the same time, he felt like he just got punched in the stomach. Bennett could feel Landon's insincere personality coming off the page.

She nodded her head. "By the way, I was never pregnant," she finally explained. "I certainly don't want to commit insurance fraud, but it looks like the only other option I have is to show up and file for divorce."

"Geez Nina," he said, "You don't make it easy, do you?" He gave her a wink. "Let's take a minute and think this through. Surely there is something we could do. Maybe make an anonymous tip?" He smiled and she knew he was going to stand beside her to see this through. It was a wonderful feeling.

All she could think about was Landon and the mafia. What if they found out where she was and thought she had his book of numbers? She was not only afraid for her safety, but for the safety of all her friends she made this past year.

"Nina, we have to do something," he said. "This is not going to end well." The last thing he wanted was for her to be in danger. He couldn't stand the thought of losing her.

She knew she had some big decisions to make. But, at that moment, she couldn't think any more about it. She got up and got dressed. Kashmir was waiting for breakfast, and she started cleaning the kitchen. Maybe if she kept busy, she could forget what was happening.

Her phone was ringing in the other room. As soon as she answered Lauren was talking so fast, she had to tell her to slow down. "That's your husband in the paper, isn't it? He looks like a total jerk. I can see why you had to leave."

"Thanks, and yes, that's him. I have to tell you too that I wasn't pregnant, was never pregnant," she clarified, "He made that up, just like everything else he has lied about."

"If you need anything, let me know," Lauren offered as she hung up.

Nina walked back into the kitchen where Bennett was making another pot of coffee. "I have a feeling this will be a two-pot day. I would bet you money this isn't over, you know," he continued.

"Yeah, I know, but I need to think." She had to get to work. "We'll talk after I get home."

"That's fine," he agreed, "I'll support you, whatever you need to do. As long as it won't cause you any harm. We could always run away to the mountains and live like hermits." He smiled, trying to inject a little humor into the stressful morning.

# CHAPTER FIFTY-FIVE

A few weeks later, Bennett got a call from the Black Hills Casino Entertainment Manager. He asked him to come over that week and bring his guitar for an audition. The manager gave him a free room for the night and was encouraged to bring his fiancée.

They both were glad to have the distraction of his work, instead of the Landon mess. Bennett picked Nina up from work Wednesday and they left. By dinner time they were already checked in and had changed into their dinner clothes. The delicious meal at the steakhouse was being paid for by the hotel.

Nina noted that they were getting the VIP treatment. She had never felt so important before. Bennett wasn't auditioning until the next morning, at a respectable 11 o'clock. Everyone knew musicians loved to sleep in late. They had been invited to attend that evening's show, with Blues Traveler as the headliner. It was his chance to see what the job he was auditioning for was like from the audience.

They were escorted to one of the better tables in the theatre. Since their tab was covered by the hotel, Bennett went ahead and ordered a moderately priced bottle of champagne. When the bottle arrived he poured them each a glass and raised his in a toast.

"Here's to the hope that this will be the first step in advancing our lives together, and a great job opportunity," he said.

Nina clinked glasses with him and added, "But if it doesn't happen, it's okay. We are doing good now. This would just be another leg up for you, and you deserve it."

Up in their room Bennett started talking about their future. His family loved her as much as her family loved him. They knew they would have to stay together for their sakes. It was funny, but mostly true too. Neither of them wanted to explain to their parents why they let a good one slip away.

Sam already knew Lauren's classes would be on break for the week, and she could the time off from her jobs also. That just left Nina to approve. "Do you think we could leave Monday morning? Sunday is one of our busiest days and I'd like to work if I can."

"Agreed," replied Sam. "I might talk Lauren into going up with me on Saturday, then you two can join us." He was looking forward to some alone time with his girlfriend.

The next three weeks flew by. Nina and Lauren kept busy shopping for cool warm clothes for the weather on the mountain. They lucked out by finding several once-expensive ski jackets at Goodwill. Of course, they also had to pick up clothes for the guys, if it was up to them, they'd pack jeans, tee shirts and a couple sweatshirts.

"What am I going to do with Kashmir?" Nina asked Bennett one day. "Maybe she could stay at Lauren's?' She just realized that Lila and Jewel would need to be taken care of also. What they needed was a responsible young person who would take care of them for a small fee.

"I know!" she startled Bennett when she said it. "What about Jared/ Julia's son? I bet he would like to earn a little cash. Lauren could bring her girls over here and they could keep each other company." She had it all worked out, now, if only Tony and Lauren would agree.

Lauren had been having the same worries and was relieved with Nina's plan. That afternoon, she went to the hotel in hopes of catching Jared. They found him in the parking lot, as small as it was, shooting basketball with his younger brother. He stopped as the girls walked up to him.

"Hey Senoritas," he sang. "Long time, no see. What can I help you lovely women with?"

"Damn Tony, you really make a girl feel old." Lauren laughed. He was also so respectful to them. "We need a favor, a paying job favor. We will both be gone for a few days on a small vacation. We need someone to feed and check on the cats."

Tony looked at them and smiled. "I'm sure we can work something out. Are they inside or outside cats?"

"Definitely inside," Nina answered. "I don't know anyone who would let their cats out at night with the coyotes everywhere." She shuddered at the thought of their babies being dragged off by wild

"I want to have kids with you Nina," he said. "I don't care what your real name is or was. I just know that I've never really thought about it much before I met you, but now it's all I can think about. When I saw you with Amy at my parents' I knew you'd be a great mom."

She was speechless for a minute; she couldn't believe he brought up kids. She purposely avoided the subject because of the reaction she had gotten from Landon. She did not want a repeat of the heartache she felt that day.

"I would love to have children with you," she said excitedly. "I can just see us with little Bennetts running around. Oh no, what if you impregnate me with twins? Since Becky didn't have any, I bet we will."

Bennett surprised her with his next idea. "Let's skip the formal wedding, and get married in the mountains, in front of our friends. It won't be official, but it will be to me. That way, we can get on with our lives."

She couldn't believe her ears. She loved him so much at that moment. Once she was 'married', she could just officially change her name whenever she chose to his. Their children would all have their father's name.

"Do you realize that we haven't even known each other a year?" she looked at him. "I've barely been Nina for a year. Are you sure I'm not rushing you?"

"Of course, you aren't rushing me, it was my idea. I don't care how long or short it's been," he assured her. "I know I can't be without you. I know this is right for us."

"OK, let's do it," she happily agreed. "How about in about four months, in February? Is that too soon?" she laughed. "I've always loved the look of a winter wedding, with the snow all around."

"Not too soon, but do we have to wait to practice getting you pregnant?' he teased her as her started undressing her.

# CHAPTER FIFTY-SIX

Bennett made his way to the theatre the next morning. Jim Longbranch was the manager who set up his audition. There were at least six other men in the theatre that Bennett could see from the stage. He was told to pick two or three of his favorite songs. One needs to be with the house band backing him up.

He had talked to the guys behind him and they started in by playing, 'Pretty Woman.' The men seemed to like it, he thought. Next, he started playing 'Little Sister' by Dwight and then the bridge to 'Stairway to Heaven'. At that point everyone of the onlookers were on their feet applauding.

"So, how did it go?" Nina asked him eagerly as he got back to the room. "They were blown away, right?"

The big smile on his face told her he had done great. Jim had called him over afterwards to introduce him to Chief American Horse, the manager of the casino. He was then offered a contract to play five nights a week for $1000 weekly.

"Are you kidding?" she screamed, "that's fantastic. That's more than I make in almost a month."

"They really want me Nina, what do you think the guys in the band will say?"

"I really don't know; you know them better than me." She hoped they wouldn't be jealous or envious, Bennett really wanted this job.

Bennett was quiet for a few minutes, deep in thought. "We had always said anyone could leave whenever they wanted. But nobody has left yet. I'll be the first."

"Then you should ask Mr. Longbranch for a day or two to think about it, and to talk to your bandmates about it," she suggested.

They left as soon as he talked to Jim and had packed up their bags. On the ride home, they held hands the whole way. It was a big step they were taking. First with their faux wedding, or commitment ceremony. Second, his new career. So many changes in such a short period of time.

The guys in the band were really nice when they heard of his offer. Of course, they were sad to see him go, but they knew he had to do what was best for him. Bennett had softened the blow by telling them if there was an opening up there, he would try to get them in the door to audition.

They decided to invite Sam and Lauren over to talk to them in person the next evening. She was going to make something simple for dinner. Nobody cared about impressing anyone anymore. They were just as happy ordering in pizza.

Bennett took their coats when they arrived. They all sat at the table with their glasses filled with wine. "I have an announcement to make," Bennett said as he stood up. "Nina has agreed to marry me."

Lauren looked confused, "Yeah, we know that. Is that why you asked us over? I'm confused."

"Well, we're not getting married in the legal sense, we are doing a commitment ceremony, in a few months, and we need your help to pull it off." Nina explained to them.

Lauren jumped up to hug Nina, then Bennett. "Oh my God! That's awesome. Of course, we'll help."

"Oh! and I have an announcement," Nina said as she stood up. "Bennett has been offered a permanent gig at Black Hills, in the house band."

Glasses clinked as they all were congratulating the couple on their big news. Nina and Bennett were lucky to have great friends, they knew that. The rest of the evening was spent talking about wedding preparations and the idea of moving into a bigger apartment. Bennett always knew he needed more space to set up his equipment so he could practice.

He had called his parents to let them know what they were planning, and how they wanted his family to attend. All he told them was that Nina's family couldn't make it, so it would be nice if his mom helped her with the plans. Of course, Gwen jumped at the chance. Ever since they moved to town, she'd been bored and looking for things to keep her busy.

"Benny honey," she said, "Why don't we just do it here? Out on the deck, overlooking the valley. It could be beautiful." He would run it by Nina but thought she'd like the idea.

He had almost forgotten to tell them about his new job. "I'll be working five nights a week at Black Hills. The pay is great, so we are currently looking for a larger place to live."

"That's fantastic sweetie," Gwen replied. "It looks like everything is coming together for you. I'm so happy you're happy. And, by the way, we love Nina. She's a wonderful girl."

"Yeah, I really am," he told his mom. "I finally feel like I can settle down now. I always felt restless, like I was supposed to be doing more, but I never knew what. I finally found my peace."

# CHAPTER FIFTY-SEVEN

They were happy, really, really happy Nina thought to herself. Finally, she felt at home. She could feel a new sense of calm wash over her. She and Bennett had driven back to see her parents again that month. Her mom's health was getting worse, and she wasn't able to travel or be alone. It was a tremendous strain on her dad. It looked as though he had aged five years in the last six months. Her doctors said she could live like this for years if nothing else changed.

Nina decided to plan on coming back once a month, if only to give his dad a break. It's possible they could come together and make it for when Bennett had his nights off at the casino. Bennett didn't like the idea of her driving alone, especially since the flat tire incident.

They were busy almost every day off they shared looking for a new place to live. Nina had given Mrs. Elliott her 30-day notice of plan to move out. She did make sure it was okay if she stayed longer, if needed. It wasn't easy finding a house or apartment that had everything they wanted. She wanted a big kitchen with an island, and he wanted a garage or basement where he could set up his equipment.

By the end of October, they had almost given up when they came across a small adobe bungalow on the south side of Santa Fe. It was clearly built as a 2 bedroom with a small eat-in kitchen. The surprise was that there was addition that went across the back of the house, hidden from the street. The addition was a family room and master suite.

"There is no way we can afford this place," she told Bennett. It was too late, they both knew it, they loved the place, they couldn't pass on it. They both agreed to make a few sacrifices until they got their budget worked out. No more stops at the coffee shop or buying drinks at the bar.

In no time at all they moved in and Nina worked hard making it their home. Kashmir loved the home too, especially the back yard where she could wander and chase the birds and lizards. Once they put their furniture in the big house, they knew they didn't have much. The next weekend, Nina took Bennett to the Goodwill and Angel's Attic to look for good quality used furniture. They wanted a couple of chairs or recliners, a cabinet for the television and stereo system, and a dresser for the bedroom. She was also going to need a few area rugs. The natural adobe terra cotta tile floors made every sound echo. A couple of area rugs would solve that problem she hoped.

As soon as they had moved in, Bennett was at the casino more, going in a little early to work with the band, and staying later to pack up. It definitely wasn't all wine and roses. The fall was the busiest season and the resort stayed booked almost every night. People couldn't do as many outdoor activities as they did in the summer. They got their first snow of the year during the first week of November.

Nina was able to come to see him play every now and then. He got a free room and they used it as often as they could. She usually stayed in the room, taking a long hot jacuzzi bath and watching a movie on a premium channel. It was relaxing to not have to rush anywhere, she knew she wouldn't have this luxury if and when they had a baby.

One night, while he was in the theatre, getting ready for the first show of the night, she decided to venture to the casino floor and try her luck at the slot machines. The penny and nickel slots are all she had the nerve to play. She never was lucky; she wasn't risking losing any big money. As she sat in front of one of her favorite machines, she felt the hair stand up on the back of her neck. She couldn't see anything unusual as she scanned the room, but she heard it, even above the din of the casino machines.

"Landon, over here!" a man was yelling from the bar area. Her head snapped around to see her husband walking towards Michael Bottino. Who was she more afraid of? She wasn't about to wait and find out. They were both equally as dangerous she thought. She left in a hurry with the money she had accumulated still on the machine.

As she was walking in a rush towards the ladies' room, she caught another look at him. It was definitely Landon. How in the hell did he end up here? She wondered. She was almost frozen with fear. She took a few minutes to collect herself and calm down before she went to find Bennett. What would Landon do if he saw her? What would

Bennett do when he saw Landon? Not to mention Michael he was the one with the most to lose.

Ten minutes later, she slowly peeked out of the bathroom door. The coast looked clear, but the bar was around the corner. She wouldn't have seen him anyway until she walked by the bar. Luckily, she found her sunglasses in her handbag and a rubber band for her hair. She kept her head down, trying to not be obvious. The second she was out of sight, she let out a huge sigh of relief. She didn't realize she had been holding her breathe the whole time.

Nina was hoping she made it undetected. She wasn't sure if Landon would be angry that she left or if Michael would see her as a lost thread that should be eliminated. She glanced over at where they had been sitting and the table was empty. That meant they were walking around somewhere in the casino. She didn't want to risk bumping into them again, so she headed straight for the theatre. She made her way backstage, to the band's green room. Bennett had just come offstage after their final set of the night.

"Baby, what's wrong?" Bennett asked immediately when he saw her. "What are you doing backstage?"

"It's my husband, Landon. He's here," she answered. The panic in her eyes told him whoever it was, scared her.

"That's impossible," he said, trying to calm her down, "Are you sure it isn't a lookalike? They say we all have one."

"No, I'm sure, it's him alright. I don't know how, but he ended up here." Nina sat down but was still very shaky. "One of his mob associates called out his name across the casino."

Bennett said quietly, "I'm going to talk to Jim and see if he can do anything. You just stay here."

"Please don't leave me here," she begged him. "I'm too scared to sit here alone."

He picked up a bottle of scotch and poured a tall shot. That should help, he thought as he handed it to her. He took a shot for himself also, they both needed to be calm for the moment. "I won't let anything happen to you," he reassured her. "I'll stay with you. I'll call his cell phone and ask him to meet us here when he's done."

They could hear Jim on stage, introducing their headliner for their last performance. Immediately following he knocked on the door.

Cautiously, Bennett let him in. The room wasn't big at all and having more than five people in there was a struggle to get comfortable. Thankfully the other band members had already left. Jim was able to sit on the desk and asked the couple what was going on.

Nina told him a little bit of her history. She didn't elaborate on details, just that she was in a bad marriage in New York City and escaped to where she was now. She met Bennett and everything was great. She had changed her name so her husband couldn't find her.

"Who are these men you saw at the bar?" Jim asked her.

"Michael Bottino is his friend, with mob connections, and Landon Jamison is my husband." She had to tell him that much.

The look on his face told them he knew the names. "We are going to have a problem here Bennett," Jim said. "Mr. Bottino is a frequent guest of this place. Let's say he's an 'advisor'."

They both sat, speechless, waiting for Jim to finish. "He and the people he works for back east have a small stake in what we do here. And, any friend of his…" He didn't finish the sentence; he didn't have to. They knew what he meant.

"I can and will tell you that I will not tell him about you or our conversation," he continued. "I doubt he would have any interest in the life of one of our musician's and his girlfriend." He stood up then, patted Bennett on the back and said, "If I were you, I'd be staying inside your room tonight and order room service."

# CHAPTER FIFTY-EIGHT

Nina waited until Bennett was ready to go to the room before she left the green room. They walked briskly towards the main lobby and the bank of elevators. She put the glasses back on and added a ballcap someone had left backstage. This was going to be the only place they could get caught. Their room was on the third floor, so they were able to get off the elevator quickly.

When they got in the room, they both let out a loud sigh. Bennett still had another set to do downstairs in about just over an hour. He didn't feel comfortable leaving Nina alone in the room, but what choice did he have? She'd be safer behind the locked door, than in the lobby walking around.

Nina took a shower and ordered room service to be sent up about the time Bennett would return. There was nothing wrong with spending a quiet night in a luxurious hotel room. She had slept in worse places, like a bus station, she thought.

Almost an hour later, there was a knock at the door. It was the waiter with their room service tray. She let him in and asked him to leave the cart. She explained she would be happy to set it up for him and return the cart with the dirty dishes to the hallway. As she was getting the tray to the window where the table was when there was another knock at the door. "Hello? Ma'am, I gave you the wrong cart," she heard the waiter say through the door. Nina looked through the peep hole to see the same young waiter who had delivered her tray a few minutes before.

She opened the door in time to hear the man yell down the hall, "Hey DUDE, what is taking so long?" In a matter of seconds, she was standing face to face to Landon Jamison.

She turned quickly and tried to shut the door, but his hand held it firm and shoved it open. "Kaci! What the hell! I always suspected you were still alive!"

His face told her nothing had changed. He still had the temper of a raging bull. His face was getting redder as he pushed his way into her room. Landon slammed the door behind him, leaving the waiter and the cart in the hallway. He grabbed her by the forearm and yanked her across the room to the window. "What did you do? How did you end up here? You better start talking! I know you took that book you bitch! You could get me killed!'"

She didn't know what to say or how to say it. Should she stand her ground and stand up to the bully that he was and finally tell him off? Should she be calm and try to pacify him with a little sweet talk and apologies? She knew Bennett would be coming in soon, she just hoped she could calm Landon down before then.

"I can't explain it Landon," she finally answered. "It happened so quickly. I just decided in that moment as I was watching the North Tower collapse. I didn't want to be married to you anymore,"

"Michael told me that Paul and his guys took care of my little problem," he said as he sat in a chair. "They thought you were getting too close to finding out about their offshore accounts and money laundering. And they knew I wouldn't let you go willingly, so they made a choice I couldn't make myself. They told me to blame it on 9/11 but they knew differently."

"They obviously didn't have a clue. You thought they murdered me?" she screamed at him. "And you did nothing, said nothing to my parents? Did you hate me that much?" Somehow, she gathered up enough rage and courage to really fight back, if only verbally.

"I am just not marriage material. I need a housekeeper and that's it. Maybe a woman every now and then," he explained. "I think hate is a strong word, don't' you?" Landon then smiled a little grin that made Nina cringe on the inside.

"Well Landon, for the record, I didn't take your book on purpose" she spoke, with a new toughness in her voice. "You were awful to me. You clearly didn't care one bit about me or my happiness. As far as I'm concerned, you might as well be dead to me too."

At that moment, the door flew open and there stood Bennett. She had never seen him that angry before, and she was scared of what he would do to Landon. Bennett stood a couple inches taller and had more upper body strength, she was sure. Those amps weren't easy to pack around every night.

"Are you ok honey?" Bennett asked as he pinned Landon's arms behind him. "I can't believe he has the balls to come in here and threaten you!"

"I did not threaten MY wife," he said. The words sounded foreign and stung. "We were just talking. Tell him Kaci."

"Number one, your being here is threatening enough. Number two, her name is now Nina. Number three, why are you here and how did you get in?" he asked. Bennett pulled his arm a little tighter and harder, making Landon wince in pain.

"Nina? Really? Nice, but not as melodic as Kaci, is it?" Landon smarted off. "It really doesn't matter what your name is now, when they find our you're here, they'll find you."

He wasn't winning any points with Bennett. Nina nodded and softly asked him to let him go. He loosened his grip and shoved him into a chair. "Talk Mr. Tough Guy," Bennett demanded. He wanted answers, and now.

"The only thing I know is I was told by Michael's boss that 'Kaci' had been taken care of" he said. "We all knew what that meant. I didn't ask any questions. If it hurt me, they didn't care, they were showing me what they could and did do."

"If that's true," Bennett asked, "and you knew about it, how could you go on with the story that she died in the 9/11 terror attack?"

"Good Luck?" he said with a small smile, "Or maybe I should say Bad Luck? Either way, after that day, nobody was looking for her, that was the most important thing. All her co-workers were in the building and perished. The people from the museum just assumed you had. I got a few calls the week following, from Mr. Wilder, Mr. Griego, a few ladies on the block who used to talk to you on your way to work. But they never pursued it, I'm sure they thought they were saving me the pain."

Nina laughed nervously at that point, 'Saving YOU the pain? That's a laugh." She still didn't know if she believed his story, but it really didn't matter. Hi smug mannerisms hadn't changed. Always playing the victim whenever he could.

Nina asked. "I think we need to open this bottle of wine before I have a panic attack." Bennett took it off the tray and poured two glasses in the stemware they provided, and Landon had a coffee cup of white wine. After Nina gulped her first glass, Bennett filled it up again. Her nerves were a little calmer after that.

"For one thing, I know Michael can't know you are still alive," Landon offered. "The only thing I can do is promise you I won't say a word. I would hardly think he would recognize you the way you look now. It wouldn't be good for me either."

What he said next Nina and Bennett could have never imagined. "I've been in touch with the FBI. Or I should say, they've contacted me. They are very interested in what I know, but I don't have any proof. I haven't committed to telling them exactly what I have, but I know that book is very valuable. My biggest concern is how much does my dad know about Michael's business?" It was the first time he sounded sincere. Landon explained what they already knew about witness relocation. He wouldn't be able to contact his family at all, unless the FBI could arrange something. But, Nina thought, Landon was never really close with his family. She could count on one hand the number of times he talked to them while they were in New York. He could easily pick up a trac phone anywhere just to call and tell them he is ok.

Nina and Bennett sat on the edge of the bed, staring at a possible Federal Witness. He said they already had enough information to send him to prison for over 20 years, just from my sloppy meetings. That is unless he cooperated and testified against Michael and Paul. "I have honestly become tired of the lifestyle. I don't like looking over my shoulder, waiting to find out if the 'boss' wants to see me." He could get a new identity and start over in a small town, with a small insurance business. He could even work in a bank with the new references the FBI would provide for him.

"I need to think about this tonight," he said. "Your being alive has changed everything. They might see you as another loose end or someone who would know my whereabouts. We need to make your death a permanent thing."

Bennett quickly jumped to her defense. Nina said, "It's okay Bennett." She turned to Landon and said, "You know that could sound like a threat."

Landon apologized, "No, that's not what I meant. Geez, how stupid do you think I am?"

"I will call your room in the morning. Maybe I will have an answer for you then." Landon knew he had to make a decision that would work best for him. He really wasn't concerned about anyone else. He got up and walked out the door. There was no phone call the next morning. They did get a note under the door though.

'Dear Kaci, you won't hear from me again, you can get married now,

legally without worry, L.'

Bennett just looked at her, thoroughly confused. She didn't have any idea what that meant.

The phone rang and they both jumped a little. Maybe Landon changed his mind and did call them to explain what his note meant.

# CHAPTER FIFTY-NINE

"Is this the room of Nina Smith?" the female voice asked.

"Yes, it is? Who's this?" Bennett said. He answered to be sure to screen her calls. He didn't trust Landon or anyone of his associates.

"This is Kelly Thomas, I'm a field agent with the FBI. Can you and Nina meet with me somewhere private?" The request made him feel like he was being drawn into a cloak and dagger scenario. He was going to do everything in his power to make sure Nina was safe from harm.

Bennett didn't know if this woman was really FBI or not. She could be just a hotel employee Michael paid to hunt Nina down. He asked for Ms. Thomas' supervisor's name and her badge number and local office of the FBI. He would call them independently and set up a meeting that way.

He hung up the phone and told Nina what the woman wanted. "This is out of control Bennett. I don't know if he's gone undercover or committed suicide. His note makes it sound so final," Nina said, in tears. "I'm just in shock."

Bennett held her and wiped away her tears, "I know, you have every right to be upset, sad, mad, whatever. He put you through hell."

"But I made it through, and I have you now," she said. "I guess we better find out what the FBI wants with me?"

Instead of using the phone number Ms. Thomas gave him, he called directory assistance for the number of the Albuquerque office. He wasn't taking any chances of being tricked. The consequences were too high. After asking for Ms. Thomas' supervisor, Mr. Blake, he was put on hold for several minutes. He was just about to hang up when he picked up the phone.

"I apologize for your wait. Is this Mr. Bennett Moore?" Mr. Blake inquired.

"Yes, it is. We received a phone call from one of your agents today and I am just calling to confirm her credentials," he explained.

"I believe it's Ms. Thomas you are speaking of," He answered. "I was just talking to her. She was getting me up to speed."

Bennett felt some relief when Blake talked about Agent Thomas. He went on to confirm her badge ID and her phone call to them. After he thanked him for the information, Bennett called Ms. Thomas back.

"Sorry about that Ms. Thomas," Bennett explained, "I'm not taking any chances. I don't know much about these things, but I've heard stories."

"Thankfully, most of the time the rumors are much worse than reality," she said, "But I still advise everyone to be on their toes in these situations. I need to speak to Ms. Smith if you don't mind."

He gladly handed Nina the phone. "Nina Smith, Mr. Jamison has unknowingly involved you in his relocation plans just by talking to you. So, we had to hustle to find out how we could protect you, away from him." She continued, "What we are proposing is issuing a death certificate for Kaci Jamison, effective September 11, 2001. And, also, creating you a new identity, using the new name and social security number you have already obtained."

"Seriously?" Nina asked. "Is it that easy? What about my parents?" She absolutely would not involve her parents in any lies.

"They really won't be in danger. You have told them the truth. Nobody will be checking on them. They are far removed from being in direct contact with Mr. Jamison. But they will have my phone number just in case."

Nina quickly told Bennett what the FBI proposed. They agreed that the idea seemed like a good one, an answer to so many loose ends. They really couldn't think of a better way to get on with their lives. She accepted the offer and made plans to meet at the Tumbleweed Shopping mall parking lot in Albuquerque the next afternoon.

They returned home as soon as they checked out of the room and Bennett talked to Jim. He told him to forget what they had told him earlier. There was no problem.

"I would appreciate a heads up if those clowns are booked into the casino. I will make sure Nina won't be here at that time." Jim agreed that was reasonable. The last thing he wanted was a big FBI raid on the property.

Kashmir was waiting for them when they walked in. "There's my little girl," Bennett said as he scooped her up in his arms. "We missed you too." The cat absorbed all the love he was giving her and began a soft deep purring sound.

"No, she's not spoiled," Nina laughed. "Why don't you two get a room?"

"You're just jealous she likes me more than you," Bennett teased her. "You have nothing to worry about, you are my one and only." As she unpacked, Bennett started talking about their wedding. "Should I tell mom to get us a real minister to perform the ceremony and make it all legit?"

"Bennett, it might take months to get the paperwork finalized so I can be Nina for real," she cautioned him.

"That's ok, I can wait," he said.

# CHAPTER SIXTY

"I want to look for a wedding dress. Or start looking, maybe make an appointment for the next few weeks and I want you ladies to come with me," she told both Tonya and Lauren over the phone that night.

Tonya was beyond excited. "It's been so long since I got married, but I can remember the feeling I had picking out my dress."

After Tonya's call, she dialed Lauren, and told her the same story. Lauren said excitedly, "Of course, I'll come, but, what if I offered to make you a dress?"

"Are you kidding me?" Nina said, clearly shocked by her generous offer. "I would love it! But we can still go look and try on different styles. I want to help me pick what I like, and I'll need your fashion expertise. Not that I don't have faith in you, I do. Totally."

Bennett drove her car to Albuquerque and parked in the pre-designated spot, waiting for Ms. Thomas. He was surprised to see a black Pontiac Grand Prix pull up next to them a few minutes later. He expected an SUV with tinted windows. This was hardly a government issue car, however, upon second thought, it was probably better that it didn't scream 'FBI'.

Thomas rolled down the window but made no effort to get out of the car. She handed Bennett a manilla envelope with no writing on it. He gave it to Nina to hold on to.

"She has something for you also," Bennett told Thomas. "This book was picked up by mistake, it belonged to Mr. Jamison. What else do you need from us?" he asked as he handed over a smaller envelope.

"That's great. It certainly will provide us more leverage with the case. I think you'll find everything you need in that envelope, including a generous payout on an insurance policy for Mrs. Jamison," she said.

"What? How is that possible?" Nina questioned. Her mind went through a million questions, but she was so in shock she couldn't say much at all.

"Let's just say a young man close to Mrs. Jamison felt like he owed it to her, with a dose of friendly persuasion, to give her a portion of the policy he had just cashed in," she explained. There was to be no further contact with Landon. All the agent would say is that he was working at a bank in a small city in the Northwest.

Bennett and Nina were speechless. They thanked Agent Thomas and then she was gone, as quickly as she arrived. Nina eagerly opened the envelope to see what exactly was inside. Several papers fell into her lap. There was a birth certificate for Nina Joan Smith, date of birth: August 4, 1977. Her parents were listed as Walter and Evelyn Smith of Tulsa Oklahoma.

The next piece of paper was a copy of a resume for Nina. It listed several waitressing jobs as well as curator of a small museum in Oklahoma City. She had always wanted to get back into working in art galleries and museums, and now maybe she would have the credentials to pull it off. There was a bank book from the Bank of America on Coors Blvd in Albuquerque. There was a $250,000 deposit entered on August 31, 2002. They both stared at it for a moment before busting into laughter.

"Do you know what this means?" Nina said. "We can afford to buy our dream house! No more rent payments. You can keep playing music, and maybe I can think about going to school. I've wanted to take art history classes for years now."

"What are we going to tell everyone when we plop down cash money for a house?" he asked. "They all know we couldn't pay for a house."

"Well, what if we say I had an uncle who passed away and he left it to me?" she answered. "And he didn't have any family other than his nieces and nephews. Which reminds me, I need to call my parents right away, they need to be kept up to date."

"Sounds plausible to me," Bennett said. "Do you feel like heading over to this bank and asking in person for some of that money? To make sure it's really there before we go house hunting?"

An hour later, Nina walked out of the bank with a cash envelope in her hands. When she got to the truck, she told Bennett she was able to withdraw $1,000 today. Nina and Bennett went to one of the nicest restaurants in town for a romantic dinner before they headed back to Santa Fe. The feeling of financial security was something foreign to her and she liked it. Living without money taught her she could be happy with very little. But this was much better.

Bennett surprised her by pulling into a jewelry store on the way out of town. She wondered what he had in mind. "Why are we stopping here?" she asked.

"I have an idea," he said. "I hope you like it. It's just an idea, if you don't want to, it's ok."

"I'm waiting. What are you thinking?" she asked.

He jumped out of the truck and came around to her side. He opened her door, "Right this way my darling." He held out his hand and escorted her into the store. A young woman approached them and asked if they needed help.

"We are looking for unique matching wedding bands," Bennett told her. Nina just smiled and squeezed his hand. He really was a prince.

"Congratulations, and I can show you several we have in the store, or you can talk to our jeweler about getting something custom made," she directed them to the back of the store where the more expensive rings were displayed.

"I can't believe you thought of this," she whispered in his ear. "I hadn't even thought about rings."

"I was worried that I couldn't afford, we couldn't afford to get you the ring you wanted," he said quietly.

"I honestly don't care about a fancy ring," she told him. "Whatever you pick out, I will love."

The woman showed them about a dozen matching sets, but nothing looked right. They were either too flashy or the man's band was too plain. Bennett finally asked if they could talk to the jeweler.

The man came out of the back with an eye piece on his right eye, used to magnify his work. They spoke for a few minutes about their engagement, their interests and courtship. He excused himself and headed back to his office. A few minutes later he walked out with a gorgeous wedding set, his and hers, on a black velvet board. They were made of 14K white gold, buffed down to get most of the shine off for a matte finish. He explained they were made to be engraved either on inside or outside. Bennett waited for Nina to speak first.

"I love that idea," she said, "how about you?" She waited nervously for Bennett's reply. She couldn't tell by his expression what he was thinking.

"I do too," he agreed. "What if I work with him on yours and you can design mine? That way they will be unique and a surprise for both of us?"

The jeweler was eager to help them get started. He took Nina to his office first. She sat down at a table and started going through a catalog of designs. She spotted a treble clef design, intertwined with a heart and vine around the whole ring. She asked Nick if he could add a guitar somewhere on the small space. He would also need to engrave the inside, "To my Knight, I will always love you". She was surprised that it was so easy to find the design and she was very curious to what Bennett would pick for her.

Twenty minutes later he came back with a huge grin on his face. The suspense was killing her. "What does it look like?" she prodded.

"You'll have to wait until you are my wife to find out," he laughed as she punched him in the arm playfully.

# CHAPTER SIXTY-ONE

The holidays were right around the corner, as was the wedding. They had decided to keep the money in the same savings account until they had time to look for their perfect home. Nina was more excited to plan her wedding to Bennett than she was a few years ago. This time, she didn't feel like she was alone, doing all the work. And, on top of that, Bennett was genuinely interested in helping her.

They wanted to get married in February and knew the date would depend on what was open. Since it was mid-winter, they planned most of their activities for the bridal party and guests around a snow theme. On one day, if the weather cooperated, they would all go up on Sandia Mountain to ski. Nina had never been skiing, but she was willing to try it. He had been up a few times in the past, mostly with his sister and her kids.

Nina and Bennett planned on a big wedding, with all the trimmings. His nieces would all be flower girls and his nephew the ring bearer. Beau and Charlotte were doing the catering and the wedding cake, and Lauren was making her wedding dress. That saved them thousands, so they were able to afford professional photographers, florists and a nice venue for ceremony and reception. Gwen understood that booking a venue, instead of her house, meant less trouble for her and a bigger guest list.

They were looking at more professional venues between Santa Fe and Albuquerque. Nina got several recommendations from the girls at work, including a couple of large estates that were designed just for weddings. She made appointments to view each one before Thanksgiving. She had already had to cross off half of the places on her list because they were booked for the next six months.

She and Bennett drove out to a secluded ranch in the foothills of Sandia Mountain. The entrance to the Sagebrush Ranch was lit up with tiny white lights that were strung overhead and along the fencing leading to the front of the venue.

Nina couldn't believe how beautiful it was. "This is the perfect place for a wedding. I just love it! What do you think?"

"It's pretty special," Bennett agreed. "If we plan the ceremony for around this time, twilight, it will be amazing. Of course, I'd marry you in the courthouse."

"That's sweet, honey," she said with a smile. "But, for our friends and family's sakes, I think we need to avoid that alternative."

They got out of the car and walked up to the patio, where they were met by an older couple. Nina looked at Bennett, at the same time he looked at her. They both laughed when they realized they were standing in front of the couple from the hot springs, Maggie and Luis.

"I can't believe we meet again," Bennett said to the couple. "Do you own this place?"

"Actually, Luis' family has owned it for years, since about 1965," Maggie explained. "We moved in and took over the day-to-day operations a few years ago, after his father wasn't able. Now what brings you two here?"

Nina quickly answered, "I made an appointment to talk to someone about a wedding. I guess I talked to you, Maggie."

"Yes, I was expecting a couple of young people. Let's go inside and we'll show you around," Maggie said as Luis opened the large, heavy solid wood door, and let them walk in first.

They took longer than they had planned walking over the grounds. Most of the talk centered around wedding plans, but often they found themselves talking about work, the casino job, and other hiking opportunities. By the end of the tour, they went back to Maggie and Luis' suite on the south wing.

"What date were you thinking of?" Maggie asked Nina.

"I was hoping for some time in January or February, a winter wedding," she answered. "I know this is short notice, but is there anything open?"

"It looks like we have two Fridays in January, one in February and one Saturday in February, the 20th and 21st." Maggie turned her booking calendar around so Nina and Bennett could see.

A February wedding in the mountains would be beautiful, she thought. Being born in February herself, she always thought of it as a magical and lucky month for her. "We'll take the one in February," Nina said. "That was the weekend we wanted. It's perfect."

Maggie happily wrote their names on the calendar. "I'm sorry, I never got your last names," she said.

"Mine is Smith, his is Moore. Speaking of, we don't know yours either." Nina asked her. She was a little surprised when she answered.

"Mine is Jacobs, and Luis's is Montoya. I bet you thought we were married," she asked them.

"Actually, yes we did. You seem so comfortable together," Bennett said.

"Well, back in our day, people didn't care very much about being 'legal'. They knew what was in their hearts and just skipped the expense." She explained. "But, when I see the weddings here, I sometimes wish we had done it for real. But I'm not complaining, so many people never find a real love like ours, and yours."

"I need to tell you that any wedding on a holiday weekend, is 10% more, due to the popularity and the fact that some of the vendors being used will add a fee for working on a holiday weekend." She was being very nice; Nina knew she wasn't lying. She had heard the same thing from other people she talked to.

"Having said that," Maggie continued, "Since we are friends from months back, I'll see if Luis is okay with not charging you the holiday rate." Maggie whispered to them, "Don't worry about it, He agrees to anything I ask."

Once they got home, Bennett called his brother to confirm the date with them for the catering. He already had it penciled in he said. Next step was to decide what they would serve. Everyone agreed they should do a semi-formal meal. It could be buffet style with some great main dishes like baked chicken and flank steak. Beau and Charlotte would get some recipes made in the next week, for them to sample. They agreed to take them to Thanksgiving at James and Gwen's and get their opinions also.

Nina called Lauren to ask her out on a wedding dress scouting day. Lauren was ready to start creating her original dress but needed some ideas of what she wanted. She brought along her sketch pad and some fabric swatches to start. One thing Nina knew she wanted was a lacy fabric. She was always looking to have a full gown, like Cinderella.

Of course, Bennett's band, Chain Reaction, would play, as their gift to them. On top of that, the casino band also volunteered to provide music, so the other guys could take a break.

# CHAPTER SIXTY-TWO

Thanksgiving at the Moore's was much like Christmas, but with more food. They had gone over in the morning to watch the Macy's parade with the little kids. Nina sat next to Bennett and squeezed his hand tight when she saw the shot of where the World Trade Center had been.

"You don't have to worry anymore," he whispered. "I'm here for you." Just him saying that made her feel calmer. He picked up her hand and gave it the gentlest of kisses.

After the parade, the kids ran outside with Uncle Benny and the guys to play a little flag football, a Moore family tradition. It was a mild day for the end of November, however by the time they were through, all the kids were begging for hot chocolate.

Beau and Charlotte presented several dishes, served on one large platter, just a bite or two of each for sampling some recipes. They didn't want to ruin their appetites for the turkey dinner Gwen had prepared, so they tasted the bites more than an hour before the scheduled dinner time. Everyone loved every dish they created except for the green beans, one of the things Nina won't eat, and Bennett didn't care for much either. They also asked them to substitute glazed carrots in their place and add either asparagus or broccoli.

As for the main course, the kids loved lasagna, but to Nina, that reminded her of her first wedding. The flank steak was a big hit with everyone so that was a must. Beau let the couple cleanse their palates before bringing out a second plate. The aroma reached the dining room way ahead of him. She couldn't put her finger on it though.

He placed the plate in front of Bennett and gave everyone forks. One toothpick size bite wouldn't be enough he hoped. "I present to you, Parmesan-Crusted Chicken Breast. We ordered it at a nice restaurant last summer while on vacation in San Francisco. I came home and started testing recipes to make something just as good. And, I think I have."

Nina sampled her bite first, and quickly took another one. "This is fabulous! Oh my God! I want to eat the whole thing." Bennett tried a bite immediately after hearing her praise of the dish.

"She's not kidding, little bro, this is wonderful!" he beamed. "Home run!"

Just like that, their dinner menu was set. The kids, as well as their dads, proceeded to clear the remaining food off the plates. The rest of the evening, after eating the huge dinner Gwen had prepared, was spent talking about the wedding.

They planned on doing a cake-tasting at Christmas. Charlotte was in charge of that. Daphne promised to leave plenty of room to help them taste all the cakes.

One expense they agreed on was a nice honeymoon. Nina suggested an island somewhere, sun and sand. Bennett thought a cabin in the mountains for a ski trip sounded like fun. Either one would be a great vacation.

A week before Christmas, Bennett was still trying to negotiate his cabin honeymoon idea whenever the topic came up. Nina was sure she would have to compromise and agree to the mountains. They could always do the island trip at another time.

Before they left to meet the family on Christmas Eve, Bennett gave her a small box with a huge bow. She had no idea what he was up to. They were going to do their presents the next morning. He nudged her to open his gift. Inside she found a pamphlet and two airline tickets. The look on her face told him she was really confused.

"I thought that I could be perfectly happy on a beach somewhere with you. I got us tickets to Hawaii." He was so excited to tell her, she couldn't get a word in. "We are leaving the day after the wedding and coming back in about two weeks. Well? Are you surprised?"

She couldn't resist laughing at the boyish look on his face. "Of course, I'm surprised! You are so cute when you're excited. I've always wanted to see Hawaii."

They were going to stay the night at Maggie and Luis's guest house, as did most couples on their first night. It enabled them to drink and have fun, without the worry of driving somewhere else.

Later that day, the Moore clan was all gathered again to eat and celebrate. When they sat around the tree to exchange presents, James got up and gave a large flat box to Nina. "What's this?" she asked. "You didn't need to get me anything, really." She continued, "It's pretty heavy for a small box."

"It's customary for the recipient to actually OPEN the gift she is given, instead of playing 20 questions." James grinned. She was glad he felt comfortable enough to joke with her.

After the ribbon, paper and box was torn apart, she found a large, framed picture of their last Christmas family picture. The first time she and Bennett had their picture taken together. It truly was a beautiful portrait. She jumped up and gave James a big hug, thanking him again for accepting her into his family.

"I don't think you need classes at all. This is wonderful," she exclaimed. She got an idea but thought she had better ask Bennett first. After all, it was his wedding also. As soon as she got him alone, she told him of her idea. "Would your dad be our wedding photographer?" She waited anxiously for his answer. "The other guy said he'd pencil us in, but he might have to cancel anyway."

"You think he's that good?" he replied. "I always thought he was the embarrassing parent, always trying to document our lives on film. I never really thought of him as a professional at anything except Master Sergeant."

"Trust me, he has a great eye," she assured him. "Remember I used to work in an art museum. And I think you should ask him. I think it would be a nice gesture," she explained. "It will be like giving him a compliment, which I don't think you'd ever do."

He smiled, "Anything for you." They walked back to where the family was still seated around the tree. The kids were restless and playing a version of Duck, Duck, Goose, around the cocktail table. Bennett and Nina stayed standing and tried to get everyone's attention. "Ok, little elves, find a seat, Nina has something to ask you." He smiled as he offered her a small bow to step forward.

"We have a big favor to ask you all," she said in ab excited voice, "How would each of you like to be IN our wedding?"

Jay was the only one looking confused. "I don't want to get married!" They all chuckled as Becky pulled him closer and gave him a hug. "No honey, they want you to bring the ring to Uncle Benny to give to your new Aunt Nina." He still looked a little confused, but since mommy said it was ok, he was ok.

And, as expected, the girls were squealing and clapping. Molly and Daphne had been to a couple weddings and knew they would be flower girls and get to wear fancy princess dresses. Amy was too young to remember, but her cousins filled her in. "Do we get tiaras?" asked Daphne. Nina agreed that they would find the three of them tiaras.

"Now, my turn, Beau, will you be my best man?" Bennett asked. "And Dad, we would like you to take the wedding photos. Just do what you do. You're great at capturing the sprit in your photos. We don't want them to look staged."

Gwen was thrilled and jumped up to hug Nina and Bennett first. "This is just fabulous," she gushed. "I am so happy right now." She turned to Bennett and smiled, "Now Benny, don't mess this up, we don't want to lose Nina."

"Very funny Mom," he replied, "I always suspected you liked her more than me."

James was right behind her, giving his son a strong side hug, and Nina a kiss on the cheek. "Are you sure you don't want a professional? It's just a hobby of mine."

"Dad, it took Nina to make me see how talented you are," he said seriously. "It would be the best gift you could give us."

Beau stepped in, "And you know I would be honored to be your best man." The mood in the room was getting very emotional and Nina knew it was time to change the subject, before everyone started crying. "Now before this gets too weepy in here, it's time to do the cake taste-testing."

Molly and Daphne were the first to get a chair at the table. Bennett and Nina sat at one end, in front of a platter with about five different flavors it looked like, several small slices of each. Charlotte took over from there. She described each flavor and icing flavor and paused for them to taste them and get a drink of water in between 'to cleanse the pallet', she told them.

They finally decided on a strawberry cake with vanilla buttercream icing. It had been one of Bennett's favorites growing up and Nina agreed. The decorations on it were another matter. Undecided on flowers, or ribbons, or a hundred other ideas, they finally decided to let Charlotte have the last word. "Surprise us," they told her. "We trust you."

"Now, who's ready to make a toast?" Nina asked, "I know I am." She led the toast to the wonderful future that laid before them.

# CHAPTER SIXTY-THREE

When they got home that evening, there was a huge box on her doorstep. Special delivery from her parents. They hadn't said a word about mailing a box, so Nina was curious as to its contents. It took both of them to bring it into the house. 'OPEN IMMEDIATELY' was written all over the package so they did as they were instructed. Underneath the layers of foam peanuts, which Kashmir quickly claimed as hers, were several heavy pieces wrapped tightly in more bubble wrap. Nina started to cry as she realized what her mother had sent them. It was the nativity scene and English Village set of ceramics buildings that Evelyn put on display every year.

Bennett quietly asked, "Why do you think she sent these now?" He was stroking her back trying to get her to stop crying, without any luck.

"I think she isn't able to decorate the way she once did, and she wanted us to have them to start our own tradition," she answered, wiping her eyes.

She immediately called her parents, thankful that they were one hour behind them in Arkansas. "Daddy, Merry Christmas!" She said trying to sound cheerful, but still sniffling.

"Now baby girl, what's the matter?" Walter answered. "I bet you got our box today, didn't you? I was hoping it would get there earlier, but you know how the mail is. Please stop crying and I'll gg get your mother."

A minute later Evelyn was on the line. "From now on, those decorations are yours for your new family to enjoy. They have brought us joy for almost 30 years."

"Are you sure? You still have many years left to use them, I'm sure." Nina asked again.

"I'm sure. Just send me pictures when you get it set up. I'd love to see it." Nina promised Evelyn she would get busy and set it up now, pictures to be mailed the next week. "Oh, we got your wedding invitation the other day. It was beautiful, just like you."

"I really wish you could be here," she said sadly, "but one of the groomsmen is going to videotape the ceremony, so you can watch it at home."

They spent the rest of the night setting up the manger and village on every flat surface they could find. After pictures were taken, they both went into different rooms to wrap presents to put under the tree. They had waited because they didn't want to give Kashmir any play toys. They also had been careful to not use any dangling ornaments this year. That night they both put their gifts to each other on the dining room table, with the other gifts they had to open from her parents and their friends.

Nina awoke to Bennett shaking her gently. "Nina, honey, wakey wakey." He then started kissing her cheeks and shoulder. "It's Christmas morning."

She was awake but kept her eyes closed and let him keep kissing her. For the first time, she wasn't the one begging someone to wake up on Christmas. It made her feel warm and happy just knowing he was as excited as she was. She wrapped her arms around him, gave him a kiss and hugged him tightly as she whispered in his ear, "Good Morning to you too."

He had already made coffee and fed Kashmir. All she had to do was sit and wait for the gifts to be delivered in front of her. When he was finished bringing all the presents to the coffee table, they started unwrapping.

She picked out on for him from her and let him start. The tiny box contained a black chain necklace with the guitar pick pendant inscribed with 'I'll always pick you'.

"I love it, babe," he gushed as he leaned over to kiss her. He then picked out a similar size present for her to unwrap. "I was going to wait until the last present to give you this, but I couldn't wait."

The bow on the box was larger than the box itself. She carefully opened the jewelry box to find a gorgeous diamond ring in white gold. "Oh my God! When did you? How did you? I don't understand." She stammered, surprised by the ring.

"I never got you an engagement ring, so when we were with Nick, I picked out an engagement ring too. He had your ring size and he set it aside. I went back to pick it up on day on my way to work." During his explanation, he took it our of the box and placed it on her finger.

The rest of the day was spent snuggling up on the sofa, watching 'It's a Wonderful Life' and 'Miracle on 34th Street'. She had bought egg nog and a small bottle of spiced rum when she found out Bennett had never tried egg nog. The next day they both had to work so they used their day off to make wedding plans.

Bennett picked out a simple suit to wear for the wedding. They thought is it was in black he would be able to wear it again, often. They decided to jazz it up with a dark royal blue shirt and patterned tie. He asked her if she would wear flowers in her hair. He had seen a picture in one of her bride magazines and knew it would look beautiful in her hair.

Next decision was what her bridesmaid, Lauren, and Maid of Honor, Tonya, would wear, as well as Beau and Sam. They went back to the magazines and she found some simple blue dresses that would go with Bennett's shirt. She tried really hard to pick a style that they could wear again. Everyone said that about their bridesmaid dresses, but it was rarely true. Too make it season appropriate, she picked a sundress with a long sleep bolero jacket. The jacket may not be worn again, or maybe it could go with another outfit they owned.

Flowers were going to be a struggle since it was in February and if they weren't out of season, they were going to a fortune, because of Valentine's Day. However, since the wedding was after the 14th, the flowers should be a little easier to get. She really wanted white daisies and red roses, so she was going to have to make some phone calls as soon as possible to get them ordered and set aside for them.

She made sure to get white princess dresses for the little girls and tiaras. Jay would wear black pants and a blue shirt like Uncle Benny and a black vest. Since her mother couldn't be there, she asked Julia to wear a blue dress and to sit in as her mother. Of course, Julia was all too happy to accept.

They didn't worry much about the invitations, since everyone already knew the date, and no one would be traveling in from out of town. Nina did order some, to send to her parents, so they could keep it in a scrapbook. She also put one for each couple at the reception dining tables for them to take home.

January came and went quickly, their days off were filled with more wedding preparations. They both worked an average of 30-40 hours a week. Bennett's nights weren't nearly eight hours, but when he added in his commute, it was over 40 hours a week.

She talked to her mom again when they received the invitation. Her mother sounded in better health, but considering the weather in February, her dad didn't want to risk traveling. Bennett had offered to go get them, but Walter politely refused. Nina knew her mom well enough to know if she felt comfortable coming down there, she would have.

# CHAPTER SIXTY-FOUR

Before they could have ever imagined, they were picking up flowers, dresses, suits and decorations. Maggie allowed them to start decorating on Thursday night before their Saturday wedding. Nina realized she wasn't one to sit around and pay someone else to be her coordinator, she was too much of a control freak. For once, that trait will do her good.

Thursday was also Valentine's Day. Nina overlooked the day due to all the items on her to-do list. At four o'clock the doorbell rang. She opened it to a large bouquet of white and red tulips. She was tongue-tied. "Who did this?' she wondered out loud.

"It had better be your future husband," she heard Bennett say from behind the flowers. "These are heavy, help me to the table."

She was happy to lend a hand. "Why aren't you at work?" He stood at the doorway until she came out of the shock and opened it to let him in. "They are absolutely gorgeous!" Her hand flew up to cover her mouth. "Oh my God honey! I completely forgot Valentine's Day!" She laughed because she knew he understood. He gave her a warm hug and let her know he didn't mind.

"I do hope you will allow me to take you out for one last meal as my girlfriend?" he asked on one knew. "Well, except the rehearsal dinner tomorrow night, that is."

"I accept." She hurried to the bedroom and bathroom to get ready for their special night out. She felt awful, regardless of what Bennett said, about forgetting the day. She would make it up to him later, somehow.  For now, she would enjoy the night with her soon-to-be husband.

He drove them to 'their' restaurant, La Trattoria. "We'll never get a table Bennett, I'm sure they are full, with a long wait." Bennett looked at her and grinned as he ignored her comments and walked around to open her door. "I guess you're going to prove a point?"

"Don't you worry about it, I've got tonight under control," he replied with a quick kiss. "You've been planning everything for the wedding, I thought you needed a break."

They walked into the lobby, where it looked like Cupid had attacked and sprinkled hearts and arrows everywhere. As he went to the podium, around the other waiting diners, she followed as the hostess picked up two menus and asked them to follow her.

They were led to their table and she saw Bennett tip the hostess. He had never done that before, she guessed he arranged for their table to be reserved. She was overwhelmed by how much effort he put into that evening. She couldn't believe how lucky she was. She made her feel warm and tingly inside. Everything was perfe4ct, she could never have dreamed life would be this good two years ago.

The next morning was a confusing mess. She was confirming deliveries and pick ups with three or four different people, as well as organizing shifts for family to help. In the middle of the day, she heard a car pull up in the gravel space outside the window. She guessed it was Lauren or Bennett returning from one of his errands. The soft knock told her it wasn't one of them.

She opened the door to see her Aunt Jean and Uncle Bob standing in front of her. Her mouth was wide open, and she stared in awe of her family. "How did you find me?"

"Baby, you know how?" Jean answered. "Your mother confessed finally. Of course, that was after I found your wedding invitation sitting on the coffee table the last time we visited. How could you keep this from me?"

Nina was afraid she would be angry or upset at least, but her tone and smile told her she wasn't. "Oh, Aunt Jean, I am so sorry. I never wanted to hurt you, but it was the only thing I could do at the time." She embraced her long and tight. "I have missed you so much!"

"Not half as much as we've missed you," she replied. Uncle Bob wiped away a tear from his eye and took his turn for a hug. They all sat down with coffee and a snack Nina threw together. As they talked about the past couple of years, Aunt Jean held her hand tightly to offer support. If her parents couldn't be here, then her aunt and uncle were the next best thing. She couldn't wait to introduce them to Bennett.

They didn't have to wait long. Before they finished their second cup of coffee Nina heard his truck pull up. She got up and ran outside, without her jacket, to meet him. "You'll never guess who just showed up?"

By her enthusiasm he knew it was someone very special to her. His mind was blank, mostly because she didn't talk much about her past. "I don't know. Cupid? Ed McMahon? "

"You're being ridiculous. Come inside, I want you to meet someone very important to me," she pulled his hand and walked him inside, leaving the bags of groceries in the truck. "Bennett, this is my Aunt Jean and Uncle Bob."

He happily stuck his hand out to greet her favorite aunt and uncle. "I have heard so much about you both, I feel like I know you already."

"I wish we could say the same," Aunt Jean said. "But from what we have heard so far it's been a rough few years for our Kaci. Now come give us a hug. Handshakes are for strangers."

Jean and Bob were staying at a nice hotel, neat the tourist part of Santa Fe. Nina made sure to invite them to the rehearsal dinner. She was grateful for the support. Her nerves were going crazy. She knew better than to worry about Bennett, but she wanted everything to be perfect.

Bennett had borrowed his dad's Cadillac Escalade to make sure they had room to haul everything to the ranch. They went and picked up Jean and Bob at the hotel about 5 o'clock to go to the rehearsal dinner. Julia had reserved the back room of the restaurant for Nina and Bennett.

The pastor who was marrying them had also married Beau and Charlotte. He stood up to give the wedding party a little instruction, then let them do a physical run through of what would happen. Uncle Bob walked up to Nina and asked her quietly, "I know Walter would love to be here, but since he can't, I hope you will let me give you away." Nina couldn't hold back the tears. She stood on her tip toes to give him a huge hug around the neck. "I'd love it."

They got the girls and Jay down the aisle without much effort, then the procession of the party. Once Nina arrived to meet Bennett in front of the pastor, everyone else took a seat. He announced, "this is where I will marry Nina and Bennett."

A loud wail came from the row of children. They all looked at Jay who was sobbing. "I don't want him to marry Nina, Uncle Benny is supposed to." The adults couldn't help but laugh at his comment. Becky went over to calm him down, and the pastor finished up.

It was nearly 10 o'clock when they got home that night. They were exhausted, and did not want to sleep apart that night, no matter what superstition said. Nothing was going to ruin their day. They did however plan to arrive at the ranch before noon with a truck load of decorations and wedding gear. Nina never let Bennett see her dress, she was waiting to surprise him.

"Do you how much I love you Nina Joan Smith?" he said into her ear as they snuggled close. She nodded with a big smile on her face as they drifted off.

# CHAPTER SIXTY-FIVE

The sun shone brightly in their bedroom window the next morning. It was so much easier to wake up to a beautiful day, she thought. However, nothing could make her stay in bed today, their wedding day. Bennett looked so peaceful, sleeping next to her, she didn't want to disturb him, yet. She quietly and gently shifted her body to be able to slip out from under his embrace. Nightly, while asleep, she would feel him turn over and hold her close. It was a feeling she would never tire of.

First on her list, after coffee, was to box up all the bags of bird seed that Becky, Daphne and Molly had made. The girls were so excited to be able to help with decorations in any way they could. Nina also had boxes of centerpieces for the tables that she and Lauren had assembled. The glass hurricane lamps, with red candles and red rose wreaths surrounding the base, were more delicate to transport and she was glad they had James' SUV.

She put on her sweatpants and hoodie before stepping outside to gauge the temperature. The forecast had predicted a little rain for later that evening, but at the moment, the skies were clear. and the temperature was around 40 degrees, with no wind. It was a perfect day to get married.

When she walked back inside, Bennett was standing in the kitchen with his cup of hot coffee, staring at her. "What? Why are you staring at me?" she asked. "It's my hair, isn't it? I haven't brushed it yet." She didn't mention to him that her nerves were going crazy, in a good, excited way.

"No reason, calm down," he laughed. "I was actually thinking this is the luckiest day of my life, because you look beautiful, and you are going to be my wife." Her face began to blush as she smiled. She never was good at accepting compliments.

They both agreed to drive separate cars out to the ranch to deliver all the wedding stuff they had. After that, she was coming home first to get her shower and gather up everything she needed to get ready. The dress was safely at Lauren's as she was doing final alterations up until two nights ago. She was going to pick her up in an hour to drive down to the ranch and use their suite to get dressed. The wedding wasn't until 5 p.m. so they had plenty of time to enjoy the day.

Beau had the suites with him, but the guys wouldn't arrive until about three o'clock. They probably could have been dressed and ready to go in 30 minutes, but Nina wouldn't risk it. Bennett would probably show up about two to make sure the band didn't have any trouble setting up their equipment.

When Lauren pulled into the parking spot in the back, closest to the Honeymoon Suite, they saw more than a dozen people milling around, unloading vans and carrying boxes in. She spotted Charlotte who had a few helpers bringing in buffet pans and dishes for the dinner.

Nina felt like she should offer to help, but realized that was the control freak in her, and she needed to let them do their job. She didn't want to be labeled a 'Bridezilla' and ruin the day. Lauren saw Sam in the dining area and waved him over.

"I didn't know you would be here this early/" She asked him after a quick kiss. "What are you guys doing?"

"Bennett asked us if we had time to come early to help with the tables," he answered. "I think he picked a task that even us cavemen couldn't mess up."

Nina and Lauren both laughed at that assessment, mostly because they knew he was right. Men and decorating usually don't mix. They were helpful though. Sam offered to drive into town to get them all something to eat. He insisted on paying for the food as part of his gift to the couple. He got back in under an hour with a back seat full of Subway hoagies. It was the least messy or spicy thing they could think of to eat on a day when their nerves were working overtime.

James was knocking on the suite's door in another hour, getting some behind-the-scenes photos of the bridal party getting hair and makeup done. The suite had high stucco ceilings and large windows to let in great sunlight.

"Have you seen Bennett?" she asked James anxiously. "How is he handling the pressure? I hope he's not as nervous as I am."

"Now, calm down," her future father-in-law said, comforting her, "he is fine. Us Moore men know how to handle a little pressure. Remember I was in the Air Force? And he was an Air Force brat." He laughed and gave her a big hug. "But yes, he is more nervous than I've seen him. He asked me to give you this." He handed her a box with a big ribbon on it. There was a card on top. She sat down to open it.

*'My Nina,*

*I hope you know how important this day is to me. I always knew I'd find you, before I knew you. You make me a better man just by your love and support.*

*I will never let you forget how much I love you and that I* need you.

*I plan to spend the rest of our lives making you happy.*
*With all my Love,*
*B'*

Her heart swelled with love for this man. She opened the gift box he sent to find a gorgeous pearl bracelet. The tag inside read, "Let this be your 'something new'."

All of a sudden, her hand flew up to her mouth as she gasped. "Lauren! I forgot my something old, new, borrowed and blue.! What do you have? Tonya? Do you have anything?"

"Hold on there, Sis," Lauren said calmly. She then handed her another small gift box. Tonya did the same. She sensed they had coordinated something special.

The first gift was a piece of dark blue ribbon with pearl-like beads attached. "This is for you to weave into the floral tiara you are wearing. The color matches their shirts, so it will look great," Lauren held it up in her hair and turned her to face the mirror.

Before she could say anything, Tonya prodded her to open her gift. Inside the box was a small, beaded coin purse. "This was my mother's and I carried it at my wedding. I am loaning it to you for yours. And since Lauren was smart enough to put pockets in your dress, nobody has to see it."

'You guys are the best friends I have ever had," she was crying now, but had to stop quickly before her makeup was ruined. "That just leaves something old. Any ideas?"

There was a soft knock on the road and Lauren went to see who it was. She opened the door to her Aunt Jean. Nina was about to start crying again, but Jean stopped her. "Don't you dare cry young lady." She gave her a hug and sat with her on the small loveseat. "I have something for you, from your mother." She was given another small box.

# CHAPTER SIXTY-SIX

Nina pulled out her mother's silver and diamond cross that she wore almost every day. "This cross, as you may know, was given to your mother by our mother, on her wedding day. She told me to make sure you got it." Jean pulled out a tissue just in time to gently wipe a few tears off Nina's face.

"I think you've got everything," Lauren announced. She was trying to lighten the mood and keep them all from crying. "Now, I think it's just about show time."

"Uncle Bob will be waiting for you outside this door in a few minutes. You come out when you're ready," Jean told her as she drew her close for another hug. "Your parents are so proud of you. You are a fighter and a beautiful woman, inside and out. Now, let's get you married!"

Lauren and Tonya had made their way to the hall behind the chapel where they stood in line behind Jay, Daphne, Molly and Amy. Nina had included Amy at the last minute, since she was good at following her cousins and she didn't want to leave her out.

The doors opened and the music processional played the bridal party down the aisle to the waiting groom and groomsmen. James was kneeling in front to capture the little ones on their eye level. It was hard to keep them from waving at their grandpa.

Uncle Bob walked Nina to the open door. She took a deep breather and exhaled. She felt like she had been waiting for this moment for ten years. He leaned over and whispered, "We love you and will be here whenever you need us."

Those little words meant the world to here. Last year she couldn't have imagined being free from Landon and the Mob. Now, she even had her family with her. It was amazing how things turn out, she thought.

Bennett was standing at the alter waiting for her. She had to watch the tempo of the song to be careful not to run down to be by his side. As she looked at his face, she saw a tear trickling down his cheek. He tried to wipe it away before anyone saw it, but she did. With each step her heartbeat grew faster and faster. She didn't know how she would be able to speak once she was by his side. Her stomach was in knots, swirling around, butterflies, she would so glad when they finally said, "I Do".

Many of her married co-workers and friends had warned her to take in the moment, because it will go by in an instant. She tried to capture the details of the ceremony, the children playing with the red rose petals they had scattered on the aisle, her Aunt and Uncle's smiles of happiness, James' and his camera.

They had decided to use traditional vows. She knew she wouldn't be able to put her feelings into words. As it was, he couldn't get through repeating the vows without choking up. Seeing him so emotional made Nina start to tear up also. They finally were doing it.

As soon as he put her custom-made ring on her hand, she felt like a princess who had found her prince. The kiss seemed different today, so much passion burning inside her, and yet she knew it could wait until that night.

The crowd was standing and cheering as they were announced as "Mr. and Mrs. Bennett Moore." Unbeknownst to the couple, they were showered with small streamers as the walked out of the chapel. She was sure it was Beth's idea. She was always the one pulling pranks at work.

They snuck out a side door to have a minute alone. "I can't believe this is real," Nina told him as she looked deeply into his eyes. "This ring is perfect, I'm not taking it off, ever. I feel bad that I didn't bring your wedding fit today. I must have left it under the bed at home."

"You know it's not that important. I got married to you today," he replied. "That is all the gift I need." She laid her head on his chest, careful not to leave a stain of makeup. "I am deeply madly in love with you." He grabbed her in a passionate kiss to make sure she knew he meant it. "Now let's go meet our adoring fans."

Bennett walked through the archway first to present his wife to their friends. And then, they were pelted with birdseed from all directions. Amy seemed confused and walked over to Nina and handed her the little bag of seed. Nina and Amy were a team, she thought. She held on to Amy's hand as everyone came on congratulated them personally.

"There you are, Amy," Charlotte had seen her with Nina and wasn't worried. "Are you bothering Aunt Nina and Uncle Benny?" She did make it sound like she had been looking everywhere for her though.

"Aunt Nia," Amy said as she pointed up to the bride. Nina felt so important in that moment to be recognized by the youngest Moore member.

"She is not bothering wither of us," Nina made sure Charlotte believed her. "Really, it's ok. She can stay with us, until she wants to leave. It will give Bennett some practice for the future." They all laughed at the idea of more babies.

"Wouldn't that be something," Charlotte answered. "More babies, that means Miss Amy won't be the youngest anymore."

His casino bandmates had played some soft live music as everyone was finding their table. The couple, and Amy, were just about finished greeting all their guests. It appeared as if almost everyone attended on their guest list. A few co-workers had told them in advance they wouldn't be able to come.

They both greeted Pat as he made his way to the shake Bennett's hand and kiss Nina on the cheek. "The one that got away," he joked. "You realize," he said looking at Bennett, "that you owe me one for introducing you two."

Bennett was quick to reply, "You mean after she turned you down?" They had always kidded each other, today was no different.

Everyone stood as they entered the room. The emcee, aka leader of the band, formally introduced the couple and directed them to their places at the head table. Nina felt a little uncomfortable sitting in front of everyone. That's the only thing that was similar to her other wedding.

Bennett took the microphone offered and announced, "I can't tell you how much we appreciate you joining us today. Each of you has played an important part in our lives, even the venue managers, Luis and Maggie. So, let's all have a great night. Dinner will be served in the room to your right in a few minutes." The crowd clapped and there were some whistles. "Oh, and the bar is behind you. Enjoy!"

"You said that perfectly honey," Nina beamed at him. "You are much better in front of people than me." She leaned in to give him a kiss. Everyone noticed and some started chanting, "kiss! kiss! kiss!" And they obliged.

If there was ever a night to drink champagne, this was it. They had promised each other to not get too drunk. They were spacing out their drinks by having a glass of water in between. Rebecca's husband, Ian, took their drink order and Jared delivered the two glasses of champagne. They asked him to work help out as a favor and he was in place to argue.

Beau had the microphone a few minutes later. "The buffet is now serving. We have made flank steak and grilled chicken. These are accompanied by roasted potatoes, glazed carrots, a side salad and your bread of choice. After Mr. and Mrs. Moore have gone through, please form a line, and Bon Appetit!"

At the mention of 'Mr. and Mrs. Moore', Bennett saw his parents stand up and pretend to walk to the buffet table. They acted like they didn't understand the confusion but laughed and sat back down. The room joined them in laughing at themselves.

Nina decided to eat both entrees; they both looked and smelled so good. She had only taken a few bites when she felt a cold sweat come over her and her stomach began turning. She politely excused herself and almost ran to the restroom. Lauren, being appointed her assistant to help with her dress, was right behind her.

"What's wrong Sis?" Lauren was calling after her. "What do you need? Do you want me to get Bennett?"

Bennett was already outside the door, calling to the women with concern. "Nina, what's wrong?" There was nothing he could do at the moment, except wait for one of them to answer.

Nina poked her head out of the bathroom stall and asked Lauren for some paper towels. "I feel so stupid, I just got sick. I don't even know why? I'll be okay in a few minutes. Please tell Bennett."

She gladly relayed the message, but he still waited for her to come out. Bennett wanted to see for his own eyes. Not to mention if he went back to the table without her, he would have to answer dozens of questions. He didn't have to wait long; she came out just a few minutes later.

"Are you okay? What happened honey?" Bennett's worried look made her feel a little silly for rushing out of her own reception. "Do you need a doctor?"

# CHAPTER SIXTY-SEVEN

"No, I'll be okay," Nina answered while holding his face in her hands. "I love you so much for worrying about me this way but I'm fine. It was probably nerves caused by of the stress of the day. I feel much better."

"Well, if you're sure," he said, kissing her forehead, "let's go back in and sit down. I wouldn't drink anything but water for a little while."

As soon as they walked into the reception the audience broke out into clapping and whispering. Nina was glad to finally sit down, next to her husband. Jared brought her ice water with lemon, which she drank quickly. She couldn't' figure out why she was so nauseous so quickly.

Beau stood up and raised his glass. "I think it's my turn to give a toast to the newly married couple." He paused for everyone to pick up their glasses and turn their attention to him. "Bennett, I know we don't spend a lot of time together, but I always know you have my back. Nina, I can see why Bennett is so in love with you, in fact I knew we'd be here eventually after meeting you the first time. Congratulations!"

Lauren took her cue to give her own toast. "Nina, we've been friends since the first day you moved to Santa Fe. We were mistaken for sisters early on. I consider it an honor to be your friend and sister. I am so happy for you both."

The dinner was a big hit, barely any leftovers, which made Nina a little sad. She could have eaten the entrees for days. She knew she would be asking Beau for the recipe or a special request dinner in the near future.

Chain Reaction took over for the casino band so they could eat and get a break. They started with some of the softer songs they knew, 'Wild Horses', 'Here, There and Everywhere' and 'Wonderful Tonight'.

The cake was sitting on a table in the corner, that was on casters so they could move it to the center of the room with ease. Charlotte had done a beautiful job of decorating it with blueish purple flowers cascading down one side.

Nina asked for water in her champagne flute for their toast together. Her stomach still wasn't feeling good. She was able to nibble at her dinner at least. Bennett handed her the cake knife so she could do the actually cutting. He gently placed his hands on top of hers for the pictures.

Then, they followed tradition and gently tried to feed each other the cake. Of course, the cake ended up on the floor more than in their mouths. It was good to have a reason to laugh. Nina was already feeling better.

As soon as everyone had been served cake, their choice being the strawberry wedding cake or the chocolate grooms' cake in the shape of a guitar, the table was moved to the side of the dance floor. It was time for the ceremonial dances.

Nina had been sad that she couldn't dance with her dad on her special day and didn't worry about picking a song. But, since Uncle Bob showed up, she knew he would take his place. She had talked to the band members who helped her pick out 'Have I Told You Lately That I Love You', by Van Morrison.

Nina walked over and asked Uncle Bob to join her on the dance floor. The confused look on his face told her he wasn't expecting to dance. "You get up there, Bob," Jean said, "Your niece is waiting." In a matter of seconds, tears were in almost everyone's eyes.

"I hope you know how much we love you," Bob whispered in her ear. "We are so honored to be here to celebrate this day. Now, what happened up there earlier? Are you pregnant?"

His words set off a series of questions in her mind. She couldn't believe her ears. Why would he say that? Her mind was thinking of everything she was experiencing the last few weeks. She had thought most of her stomach issues were her nerves acting up. If she was pregnant, then it was probably from about three weeks ago. She had to talk to Bennett soon, or should she surprise him with good news? There was no need to get his hopes up yet.

As soon as Nina left the floor, Bennett stood up and went to get Gwen for their dance. The band played 'God Only Knows' by the

Beach Boys. She knew her son wasn't the best of dancers, so she tried to lead a little, to make it look like he was doing all the work.

He kissed her cheek and said, "You and Dad have been great, even when I was in a rough place. I love you guys."

Those words were enough to make Gwen smile from ear-to-ear. The adoring look in her eye said she was so proud of her son. She tried to wipe away a little tear in her eye without smearing her makeup.

Before Bennett returned to the table, Nina asked Lauren to sit next to her. "I need a huge favor, a secret favor. Would you go buy a pregnancy test tonight?"

"Oh my God! Are you serious?" Lauren was trying to keep her voice down so as not to draw attention to their conversation. "Of course, I will. Do you really think you could be pregnant?"

Nina shrugged her shoulders with a humble look, "Maybe? I mean it would explain a few moments I've had this month. Most importantly, can you bring it back here tonight, so I can use it first thing in the morning? If I'm not, I want to enjoy some drinks on our honeymoon."

They planned for Lauren to get back there as soon as things wrapped up. She would have to make some excuse to Sam. He wasn't the type to ask a lot of questions anyway.

Chain Reaction played some of their most popular dance songs for guests for another hour before the casino band relieved them. Between the two of the bands, they played a good variety of rock and country, dance and slow songs.

The next big thing on the agenda was the tossing of the bouquet. "All single ladies please join me on the dance floor, and don't get in my way!" Lauren said laughing as Nina carried the fake bouquet. With a mighty toss over her head, the flowers went sailing. The little girls were squealing as they tried to catch it. Everyone's hands were up in the air. The flowers bounced off Renee's fingertips, then Lauren's before landing in Maggie's hands. Everyone cheered as the reluctant woman looked at Luis with a shy smile.

Bennett took off Nina's garter belt in order to fling it into the large crowd of single men. It wasn't easy to get most of them to participate. With his eyes closed, he shot it high in the air. It came down into the hands of Pat. The guys started laughing, everyone knew he was not the marrying type.

# CHAPTER SIXTY-EIGHT

Their honeymoon night was everything Nina could have imagined. Candles were lit to enhance the mood. An older turntable in the corner was playing some classics. Maggie had quite the collection of vinyl records, even though everyone else was buying CD's.

Nina had one small glass of champagne, but that was all. She still didn't great, and she didn't want to press her luck. She didn't really need any help feeling romantic anyway. The first thing she did was excuse herself to the bathroom.

"Let me slip into something more comfortable," she said and winked at her husband.

He couldn't help but laugh, "Really? I've never heard anyone say that in real life."

"If there was ever a time it was appropriate to say, it's after I have been in this dress all day," Nina replied.

"Oh, I understand, this tie is killing me," he said as he tugged at it to get it off.

She only took a few minutes to change into a beautiful white satin and lace negligee. When she saw his face, she knew she made the right choice.

"Come here, Mrs. Moore," he called from the bed. He was only wearing his boxers. She walked up to where he was sitting on the side of the bed and caressed his head, ruffled his hair and brought his face to her cleavage. His hands were moving up and down her back, which made her moan in delight.

He took her panties off and began kissing her stomach and thighs, making his way to her core. The feeling of his tongue between her legs made her cry with pleasure. She squirmed and felt her knees get weak. Her desire burned hot for him as she pushed him back on the bed. Instead of joining him on the bed, she knelt before him, pulled his shorts down and took him in her mouth. His groans told her he was wanting her as much as she wanted him.

He pulled her onto the bed beside him and softly touched her skin with his calloused hands. The sensation felt like electric jolts were running through her body. He suddenly turned over on top of her and began making love to her slowly and patiently. She begged for faster, harder, deeper, but he continued with his slow rhythm. She climaxed quickly and he followed.

The rest of the evening they spent in the jacuzzi tub and in bed making love again and again. Maggie had provided a tray of food, some from the reception, but mostly snacks and sandwiches to fill their empty stomachs. Even hours later, Nina could only nibble at the chips. The salty things tasted the best to her.

She opened the door the next morning to see Lauren had done what she asked. Nina went straight to the bathroom while Bennett was still sleeping. If she was pregnant, she guessed it was only two or three weeks along.

The next three minutes were the longest she thought she'd ever waited in her life. She fixed her hair, brushed her teeth, anything to pass the time. If Bennett awoke, he'd hear the sink running and know she was going through her morning routine.

After finishing counting to 180, she picked up the test stick and was stunned to see that Uncle Bob was right. She started crying softly. She wanted to rush out and tell Bennett immediately but decided to surprise him a little later, after all, she never gave him a wedding present.

"How did you sleep, Mrs. Moore?" he said as soon as she walked out of the bathroom. "I, for one, slept wonderfully. I think married life suits me."

She wasn't going to be able to keep her secret much longer she knew. "I slept like a baby. Should we go get some breakfast? Maggie said there was no rush to leave, just has to be in time for us to get to the airport."

"Sure. How about Denny's?" he grinned.

"Sounds perfect, Mr. Moore." They drove her car and she asked him to stop at the drug store on the corner. She was going to have to scour the aisles, to find for something suitable to present to him with the good news, quickly.

"I'll come in with you," he said, moving to open the door.

"No, stay here," Nina silently begged him, "I'll just be a minute. I need gum for the flight." She rushed in and went straight to the card aisle where she found a father-to-be card. She picked up a gift bag and a rattle, pair of baby socks and a pacifier.

"Did you get the gum?" he said as she got in the car.

"What? Oh yeah, they didn't have the kind I wanted," she answered, trying to hide the contents or the bag she carried.

"What's all that then?" Bennett asked her with increased curiosity.

"You'll see in a little bit," she was almost too excited to talk. She knew her wide smile gave her away.

They pulled into the parking lot and walked into the restaurant and got a booth. She usually sat on the inside and him on the outside. But she immediately jumped up. "Order me water please. I forgot something in the car."

She was back inside, holding something behind her back, before the waitress made it to the table. Without a word, she sat down close to him and gave him the small bag.

"This is officially your wedding present," she said. "I hope you like it." She was nervous to see his reaction.

He first pulled out the socks, then rattle and pacifier. He looked at the items again and then took out the card.

**'I hope you are as happy as I am right now!**
**Congratulations, you are going to be a father!'**

Bennett let out the loudest cheer she had ever heard. "Are you sure? When did you know? How long? I can't believe it." Tears were rolling down his face as he grabbed her in the tightest embrace. "I am over the moon, say something."

Nina finally got a word in, "Of course I'm thrilled. To answer your questions, 1. I'm pretty sure. 2. Found out this morning. 3. How long what?" She laughed as he was trying to calm down. "That explains why I haven't been feeling great for a couple of days."

"Are you sure you're feeling ok? Can you eat now? You should eat while you feel like it," he instructed her.

"I feel fine now, and yes, I'm going to get the same thing we got in Tucumcari."

They ate as the happiest couple on the face of the Earth. As soon as they got back to the ranch, they started packing. Before leaving they found Maggie and Luis and shared their good news.

"Oh my, Nina, that is just wonderful! You too Bennett," Maggie hugged them both and Luis shook Bennet's hand.

"Next stop, the airport," Bennett announced. "This baby is going to be a world traveler before she's born."

# EPILOGUE

By Labor Day, Nina was feeling the babies squirm and pushing for more room. They were told she was pregnant with twins in April. Since then, she had gained weight every week it seemed. Her doctor gave her a due date of September 30th. But she also advised that twins often come early, so be prepared for anything.

It had been a rough summer, the hot temperatures only made being pregnant with twins more exhausting. She couldn't remember the last time she saw her feet. Bennett had gone to every doctor's appointment with her.

His caring and excitement confirmed what she already suspected; he was going to be great dad. After the ultrasound, the doctor told them they were expecting two girls from the best view he could see. They had tried and tried to come up with two names for girls that they both liked. Nina didn't want to be too cutesy and have the names rhyme or have an obvious connection. Bennett thought any girl's name needed to have a 'Y' on the end.

The parents-to-be finally agreed to wait until they arrived to pick names. Nina was sure she'd know the right ones when she met her babies. His parents' thought he should carry on the 'B' tradition and go with Brianna, Brandy, Bella, Brooke, or Bernadette.

It was September 11th when her water broke. She had been asleep, taking a nap at the time. The contractions stated immediately. Bennett had been getting ready for work at the casino when he heard her cry out from the bedroom.

"Oh My God! What's wrong?" he asked as he ran into the room. One look and he knew it was time to get her to the hospital. He gently got her to her feet and grabbed her 'go' bag. She had packed it only last week, in anticipation of needing it quickly.

As soon as they took Nina up to Obstetrics, Bennett called their family and friends. He barely hung up the phone before one of the nurses came out to bring him into the room. He had gone to all the prenatal classes with her but still didn't feel like he knew anything.

Nina was in labor for several hours. Their first daughter finally arrived at 9:08 p.m. The staff got her cleaned up and the doctor looked her over. She had a healthy pair of lungs; they knew that much. She was making sure everyone knew she was in the room.

James and Gwen had been waiting for a few hours with Becky, Charlotte and Lauren. Lauren was put in charge of calling Evelyn and Walter and Aunt Jean. They were trying to be patient but that wasn't easy.

When Bennett rushed out after 9:30, they all jumped up. "We have a healthy, loud daughter so far. We are still waiting for her sister to arrive." Cheers went up in the room, even from the families of other moms.

He hurriedly went back to be by Nina's side. "What does she look like?" she asked her husband in a hoarse voice.

"She's perfect! Just perfect! She has a full head of blonde hair," he answered while kissing her forehead and wiping off the sweat trickling down her face. His face suddenly winced in pain as she squeezed his hand.

She was back in labor. This time she didn't have to push much, the second baby came rather quickly. The doctor paused for a minute, before calling Bennett over to cut the umbilical cord. "What's wrong?" the couple asked him in a panic.

"Nothing's wrong, unless you have a problem with having a son instead of another daughter." Bennett looked at Nina, then went to stand next to the doctor. He was handed the scissors to cut the cord and got a good look at his son.

"Honey, we have a son! A matched set." They both were crying tears of joy and laughing at the same time. "I better go break the news to the crowd."

Both babies weighed just under 5 pounds each at birth. They needed to stay in the NICU for at least a week. The doctor wanted to see them gain at least half a pound before he sent them home. The extra time gave Bennett, and Lauren and Becky and Gwen and Charlotte time to get everything a little boy would need.

The day after their birth, Nina and Bennett had to decide on their names. "This totally changes everything," she said. "Do you want to name him after you? What about 'Kaci' for her, or him?"

"I think we need to leave our past behind us and focus on our future. What about George and Lucy?" He asked, as the idea popped into his head.

Nina spent a few minutes thinking it over and sounding it out. "I like it. I love it I mean, LOVE it. How about Lucy Evelyn, after my mom and George Bennett, after you." He didn't need to explain that George and Lucy were named after the Beatles.

"It's perfect!" he said, "You're perfect! I love you so much!"

It was only three years ago that she fled New York. She wasn't the same nervous young woman she was back then. Now she had everything she ever wanted.

Made in the USA
Columbia, SC
01 November 2021